cheek

SPIKE EVANS

First published in 2015 by Up Yours! Publishing.

Copyright © 2015 Spike Evans.

ISBN-10: 1511628944
ISBN-13: 978-1511628945

Typeset in Garamond. Originated in OpenOffice.
No postgraduate qualifications in creative writing were harmed during the making of this novel.

Visit: www.spikeevans.com

prologue

If Wes had been half the reprobate that Gabrielle's father thought he was, he'd have never signed the prenup. He'd have told the old bastard to shove it up his arse. Or he'd have shoved it up there himself. He'd have run off to Vegas with Gabi – having enthusiastically impregnated her first – then left her weeping at the altar while he drove into the desert with her two teenage bridesmaids, never to be seen again.

Of course, if Gabi's dad *hadn't* mistaken Wes for a card-carrying libertine (largely thanks to his fondness for cashmere socks and the *Racing Post*), then marriage wouldn't have been on the cards at all. Gabi wouldn't have given him a second glance, let alone a blow job at the Freshers' Ball, if she hadn't spotted the long-term father-offending potential in his excitingly sallow complexion and archly cocked eyebrow.

It made no difference that the eyebrow in question had only been archly cocked at the state of the medical school's *vol-au-vents*, or that Wes's sallow complexion was largely the consequence of seven nicotine-deprived hours on the National Express down from Whitby – without them, the eighteen-year-old Yorkshireman wouldn't have stood a chance. And without them, a month before his twenty-fifth birthday, he wouldn't have found himself ineptly directing the garrulous Nigerian minicab driver towards his new home in Sefton Street, Putney, SW15.

'Which house, my friend?'

Wes manoeuvred himself into the gap between the front seats and pushed a tangle of matted hair from his eyes. The foppish quiff that Gabrielle had insisted he should cultivate for their wedding hadn't been treated kindly by the relentless winds of the Seychelles, and fell back across his face like the distended innards of a party popper. 'Sorry, Abiola?'

'Which house?' The minicab driver (who had introduced himself at Heathrow with the words 'Call me Abiola!', and repeated them until Wes began doing so) drummed his fingers lightly on the steering wheel. 'Where do you *live*, my friend?'

Wes glanced over his shoulder at the sleeping Gabrielle, curled cat-like on the back seat – a position she'd assumed having shrugged off her seatbelt at the Chiswick roundabout; a position she'd steadfastly refused to abandon, despite the Mondeo's shagged-out suspension and the agonised squealing of its fan belt. She stirred ominously as the car pulled into Sefton Street and a tiny frown flitted across her features – a frown that didn't invite further disturbance.

'My friend – hello? Hello? Which *house*, please?'

'I'm not a hundred per cent sure,' Wes admitted, his eyes flicking nervously left and right at the cars and houses gently rolling past, like some surreal version of the *Generation Game* conveyor belt. 'I don't really live there yet.' He leaned forwards conspiratorially and lowered his voice. 'The house is a wedding present, actually. I've only ever seen a photo of the place.'

The driver said nothing, but his anxious grin suggested

that a swift detour via the lunatic asylum might now be a serious possibility. Wes sighed inwardly – the kind of sigh he'd perfected over the previous six years – and glanced again at Gabi's sleeping form, which appeared to be exuding an indefinable grumpiness in all directions.

'Maybe the missus knows where you live, yes?'

Wes frowned. Abiola might just as well have recommended that Wes should consult his fairy godmother for all the sense he was making. *His missus? Who?* And then slowly, through a thick fug of jet lag and sleep deprivation, awareness dawned. *The honeymoon in the Seychelles. The church. The engagement. All that business with the cake and the speeches and the vicar.* 'Oh, yes. My wife.' Wes glanced once more at his sleeping bride – but still made no attempt to wake her. Waking her before arrival at their destination would, Wes knew, precipitate a mammoth sulk. Gabi was very much like Joni Mitchell or a late-night kebab in this respect – predictable, yet somehow utterly unfathomable. 'It's possible, isn't it?'

'I think you should ask her.'

Wes dropped back into his seat and rummaged deep in his trouser pocket. He was about to suggest tossing a five rupee coin to decide who should rouse the slumbering Gabrielle – himself or Abiola – when an all-too-familiar figure on the pavement caught his eye. He shivered in spite of the unforgiving midday sunshine and the Mondeo's risible attempt at air-conditioning. 'I don't think we'll need to.'

'No?'

'No.'

'Which house, then?'

The one with the certifiable nutter standing outside it, Wes thought, eyeing the slightly-built, Barbour-jacketed bloke peering down the street over half-moon spectacles. 'The one with the elderly gent standing outside it,' he said. 'Pull in behind the blue Merc.'

'S-Class. Nice, nice,' murmured Abiola approvingly, swerving to a halt three inches behind the pristine Mercedes. 'Five-and-a-half litre V12. Nought to sixty in under five seconds.'

Wes managed to restrain himself for a whole half second before speaking. 'V6, actually.'

'What?'

'That's only the V6.' Wes allowed a guilty eye to rest momentarily on the gleaming bodywork. It was a car he'd only seen in the brochure – but here, elegantly slumming it at the kerbside, it looked even more preposterously magisterial than on paper. He quietly cleared his throat, attempting to adopt an airy tone. For someone who'd spent most of his adult life trying not to sound like a prepubescent Alan Bennett, it wasn't an easy adjustment. 'I wanted Periclase green metallic, but Gabi simply *insisted* on Tansanite blue.'

Abiola swivelled in his seat and fixed his passenger with a keen eye. 'That's *your car*, my friend?'

'Uh-huh. Well, sort of.'

'Wedding present?'

'Mm.' Emboldened by steady rhythm of Gabi's gentle snoring, Wes leaned forwards conspiratorially. 'That guy over there's my father-in-law. Dr Claude Aloysius Wynstanley. Famous surgeon. Old money.'

Abiola's eyes narrowed on the famous surgeon. 'It is not easy, being married to a rich man's daughter,' he solemnly declared. 'She will have high expectations, my friend.'

'Actually, my wife's the breadwinner. Career girl. Dr Gabrielle Araminta Wynstanley. Doing rather well for herself in orthopaedics.'

Smirking wickedly, Abiola nodded first at the Mercedes and then at Gabrielle, his eye lingering a second longer than necessary on the soft curve of her upper thigh. Then he turned and winked at Wes. '*Nice package*,' he whispered.

'I know.'

'Are we there yet?'

The two men jumped guiltily at the sound of Gabi's voice, the genial African being the first to regain something of his former composure. 'Certainly, madam,' he purred, sliding out of the driver's seat and opening the passenger door with as much flourish as its rusting hinges would allow. '*Home sweet home.*'

Wes watched mutely as Abiola ferried the last of the suitcases into the hallway, horribly aware that the Nigerian's impending departure would leave him alone with Dr Claude Wynstanley. The fact that the minicab driver had openly letched over his wife's bottom (and charged an eye-watering fee for doing so) now seemed a trifling irrelevance. Wes couldn't believe his new friend intended leaving him in the clutches of his father-in-law, anyway.

Tête-à-têtes with the elder Dr Wynstanley were something Wes had come to dread. A sort of tweedy home counties Gurkha, Wynstanley possessed an intellect that seemed specifically designed to mentally debilitate its victims by simple dote of proximity. Two minutes' exposure was sufficient to have you scurrying up the nearest lamp post like an under-evolved simian, and at least five had elapsed before Wynstanley broke his silence.

'This place is Gabrielle's. Always will be,' the greying surgeon quietly intoned, his eye flicking from the departing Mondeo's exhaust fumes to the house behind him.

'Okay.'

Wynstanley seized Wes's unresisting hand and pressed a sizeable bunch of keys hard into the palm. 'So's the car. And the day Gabrielle tells me she's divorcing you – *and she will* – I'll be changing the locks faster than you can say 'daughter-defiling pervert'. Understand?'

Glancing from Wynstanley's gnarled visage to his own Liberty print shirt, Wes was tempted to ask which one of them the good doctor considered to be the 'daughter-

6

defiling pervert', but busied himself instead by fingering the thrillingly unfamiliar contours of his new car keys. He cleared his throat. 'Look, Dr Wynstanley. I know we haven't always seen eye to eye, over the years. But now Gabi and me are married, maybe it's time to make a fresh start.' Transferring the keys to the safety of his trouser pocket, he extended a hand to the elderly physician. 'And now we're family, I don't want you to be a stranger, eh?'

For a second, Wes's words hung in the torpid south London air. Then Wynstanley's face broke into a rictus of loathing. 'Fuck off, you smug little turd,' he snarled, turning on his heel. 'I'll be back when my daughter finally sees sense and throws your worthless carcass out. *And not a day before.*'

'Daddy's quite insane, you know,' Gabi observed later that evening, cutting herself a second line of post-honeymoon cocaine. 'He actually asked me if I planned abandoning my career to have babies as he was walking me up the aisle. I think he'd have had me sterilised if I'd said yes.'

Or had me castrated, Wes reflected, improvising a miniature sandwich with a fragment of discarded Roquefort and the last of the Waitrose blinis.

Old Wynstanley could have done it, too. He'd been deftly lopping off people's unwanted extremities for decades, up in his Harley Street consulting rooms – and there'd been a mad glint in his eye, the last time Wes had seen him dismembering the Christmas goose. 'I tried telling him – *you haven't lost a daughter but gained a son.* He said he was going to dissect my ignorant northern brain and find out what made me talk such cock.'

'He loathes the fact that you've got the balls to stand up to him.' Gabi smiled, fingering a tingling septum and nuzzling her way beneath her husband's unresisting arm. Wes breathed a silent sigh of relief, grateful that Gabi hadn't accompanied the word 'balls' with an affectionate squeeze of his testicles, as she usually did – apparently oblivious, in spite of her medical training, of quite how much it hurt. 'Anyway, *you'll* show him. When you're a brilliant surgeon.' She grunted contentedly to herself. 'Then he'll hate you even more.'

It was probably a good job that most of Gabi's aromatherapy candles had been extinguished, otherwise she'd have seen the expression of rank incredulity on her husband's face. No matter how many times she mentioned it, Gabi's 'brilliant surgeon' scenario had always seemed absurdly far-fetched to Wes.

Not that he didn't *look* the part. He'd possessed an unnerving aura of intelligence since childhood – lean and bookish, with piercing blue eyes and abundant blond hair. A rudderless meander through medical school had proved just how deceptive appearances could be, however, and now only Gabi still spoke of Wes's future surgical career with any real conviction.

Suddenly melancholy, Wes found himself reaching for the silver coke box. Cocaine wasn't his drug of choice, but Gabrielle could become tiresome company when she snorted alone, and a little nasal stimulation could usually be relied upon to fend off his bleaker moments. He deftly shaped a hillock of the white powder into a crude caricature of Gabi's father, hoovered up his handiwork and lay back on the floor cushion, his heart racing.

'Better?' asked Gabi, picking up the tub of Häagen Dazs and pulling herself up on to Wes's lap.

'Better.'

Somehow, though, Wes wasn't sure. In the thirty seconds since he'd flipped closed the lid of the coke box, familiar tremors of seismic activity had started emerging from the synaptic earthquake in his brain, but something – something he couldn't put his finger on – was wrong. His eyes darted around the darkened room, performing a lightning inventory of its contents – the Josef Hoffmann sofas, the Bang & Olufsen TV, the mountain of unopened wedding presents beneath the large bay window. *Was something missing?* Suddenly, Wes knew. 'We should have friends over. Phone everyone. Have a house-warming.'

'When?'

'Right now. Tonight.'

Gabi's spoon circled the rim of the Häagen Dazs tub, producing a delicate rosebud of ice cream that she admired for a moment before popping in her mouth. 'I don't think so, Wes. My friends actually have *lives*. They're not seventeen years old any more. They need more than five minutes' notice if you want to see them.'

'What about *my* friends, then?'

'You haven't *got* any friends, sweetheart.' Gabi smiled and leaned forward as if to kiss her husband, but drew away at the last moment and tapped him gently on the nose with the spoon. It was cold. 'Sorry to announce this, but you're a bit of a lone wolf. It's one of the reasons I like you.'

'I've got lots of friends. Loads.' *Friends from the pub. Friends from the bookies – the ones who call me 'Doc' and ask me to look at their ingrowing toenails. Friends like Abiola.*

'Not the kind of friends you could invite home.'

Wes's mind raced, desperate not to be so easily outmanoeuvred. 'Tim's housebroken.'

'Tim lives in Barcelona.'

'Lenny. Lenny Jones.'

'Lenny's doing two months' rep in Frinton. And he couldn't even be bothered to buy us anything off the wedding list.'

'Jeremy, then.'

For a moment Gabi's eyes scanned Wes's face, trying to work out whether he was deliberately trying to ruin her evening. Then she smiled. 'Perhaps not.'

Uncharacteristically voluble from the cocaine, Wes pressed on. 'He's calmed down a lot since he started living with Lisa. He doesn't call himself the Shagfinder General any more. He's stopped smoking. And he hasn't been arrested in over six months...'

Taking his face between her hands, Gabi silenced her husband with a kiss. 'No, Wes. Jeremy Sykes isn't welcome in our home.' She kissed him again, longer this time. 'Seriously. I feel the same way about Jeremy as my dad feels about you. Understand?'

Wes lay back on his floor cushion and tried not to enjoy the sensation of Gabi's tongue as it deftly sought out his own. It depressed him when she spoke to him like that. *Understand? Capish? Comprende?* She never used to talk that way – not when they'd been at medical school, occupying a damp maisonette in Dollis Hill, eating out of pizza boxes and making love on the sofa. And although Wes understood that the marriage register he'd signed a fortnight earlier had been a contract of incomprehensible complexity, he'd never thought that the 'forsaking all others' bit would include his old school friend Jeremy.

If only Jez had married Gabs instead, he mused. *Then I'd be able to see both of them.* But, given a toss-up between the two of them... well, there'd been no competition. He'd chosen Gabi. He'd chosen a deceptively spacious family home in Putney and an S-class Mercedes in Tansanite blue. He'd chosen several years of amply-funded prevarication on a Josef Hoffmann sofa, watching endless repeats of *Lovejoy* on an outsize Bang & Olufsen plasma. He'd chosen Waitrose blinis and fine wines and month-long holidays in Tuscany. And all he had to do in return was persuade his father-in-law that he was the bastard love child of Keith Richards and Che Guevara. *Nice package.*

Wes glanced down at the top of his wife's head, suddenly aware that her left hand had quietly begun unzipping his flies. 'Maybe your dad will grow to respect me, now I've married his only daughter,' he said. 'Maybe he'll come to cherish my company, to savour my finer qualities, that sort of thing.'

'I hope not,' Gabi snorted. 'It's not likely, anyway. He

thinks you're a mentally subnormal northern oik. And a socialist. And the ruination of all womankind.'

Wes rolled his eyes in the half-light. Perhaps, now they were married, the time had finally come to drop the tedious charade of rebelliousness that Gabi had so clearly enjoyed in the early stages of their relationship. Yes – maybe it was time to reveal his true colours. He squirmed against the floor cushion, scouring his brain for the best words with which to unveil The Real Wes. None, alas, sprang to mind. 'But I read the *Times*,' he eventually muttered. 'I've got shares in Glaxo. My granddad was a Rotarian.'

'You read the *Angling Times*, sweetie. And your grandfather was a Rotarian in *Whitby*.' Gabrielle finished removing Wes's trousers and flung them over her shoulder. 'Whitby doesn't count.'

It was true, Wes reflected. Whitby certainly hadn't counted at the wedding reception. All his friends from home – Jeremy, Daly-Boy, Jonesy, Tim – had been given a table so far from the rest of the party, they were virtually in the curry house next door. It might have been for the best, though. If they'd been any nearer the top table, they might have caught old Wynstanley's quip about being 'besieged by the fucking Vikings,' or his devastating remarks regarding Dave the barman's gift of an antique silver fish slice.

At the time, Gabi had sneered almost as much as her dad. Now, though, she was holding the fish slice lightly between her thumb and forefinger, allowing the soft-edged blade to pivot gently up and down. 'I've just worked out what we can use this for.'

'What?'

'*You're* a naughty boy.' Gabi bit her lip. 'Can't you guess?'

A moment later, Gabi's trembling fingers were wrestling with her own trousers.

'No, Gabs. Please. Not that. I've only just finished my

supper. I'm stuffed. Not now.'

Gabi pressed the handle of the fish slice into Wes's hand. '*Yes.*'

It was only the thought of Gabi's father that made him go through with it, though – specifically, the thought of him bursting through the door and catching them *in flagrante delicto* with Lancashire hotpot smeared up his daughter's forearms. *The old bastard would probably have a coronary*, Wes reflected. *Then drop dead, with any luck.*

Thoughts regarding Dr Wynstanley Snr had always troubled Wes during intimate moments with Gabi, of course. Any lass who insists on being vigorously spanked for the duration of coitus is bound to get you asking questions about unhealthy formative influences. *That's a girl with unresolved issues*, Wes ruminated, trying to disregard the crisp report of a sterling silver fish slice slapping a reddened buttock. *That's the girl I married. The girl I married – whose arse I'm now tenderising with Dave the barman's antique fish slice. Oh God.*

'Why've you stopped?' gasped Gabi, straining to catch Wes's eye over her shoulder.

'I can't do it.' Wes straightened up – as much as he could, anyway, given the tender nature of his conjunction with his new missus. He gently laid the fish slice across the top of the ice cream tub.

A note of panic entered Gabi's voice. '*Pick it up.*'

'I can't. It's daft. And anyway, it's got Häagen Dazs on it, now.'

'Just *do* it, Wes.'

'I feel ridiculous.' He leaned over Gabi spoonwise and brushed away some of the moist hair that had fallen in tangles around her face. What better time could there be to unburden himself than now, when he was ensconced so deeply inside his wife? Yes – *this* was the moment to reveal The Real Wes. The lazy, spineless, selfish Wes. The unambitious Wes. The Wes who had no real intention of getting a 'proper' job, anyway – and certainly not a job in medicine – and didn't want to play *Last Tango In Putney* with Gabi every Friday night for the next thirty years. He gave a little thrust from the hips, buying time while he thought about the best way to express his anxieties. *Sans* fish slice, Gabi didn't respond. 'Don't you feel a bit daft, getting your backside tanned every time we do it? You can barely sit down afterwards.'

'Don't *stop*, Wes, for Christ's sake.' She sounded almost hysterical, now.

'I'll carry on with this' – Wes gave Gabi's behind another encouraging nudge from the hips – 'but I'm not slapping anything while I'm doing it. Not now we're married. It'd make me a wife-beater.'

Gabi leant forwards on to her elbows, inadvertently raising her buttocks towards Wes. He could feel the heat rising off the two reddened patches. It didn't help. 'You won't do it?'

'Not like that, no.'

For a moment, they remained conjoined. Then Gabrielle eased herself forwards, causing Wes to slip out from behind her. 'Then there's no *point*, is there?'

Wes's next two thoughts weren't his most noble, he later reflected. Glancing down at his freshly exposed erection, unexpectedly cooled by the draught from under the door, he briefly lamented not having waited until he'd ejaculated before broaching the subject of Gabi's troubling sexual proclivities. *Another fifteen seconds would've done the trick.*

His second thought was more comforting. *I'll bung the fish slice on Ebay. Then I'll use the cash to take Gabi somewhere nice for dinner, a cocktail or two, then back here for a shag. A normal shag. We're married, now – we'll be doing it all the time.* He pulled on his underpants and wandered into the kitchen in search of a snack, only glancing upward at the sound of a bedroom door being slammed shut.

At least I hope we will.

six months later...

1

an uncomplicated, woman-free evening at the brick

Before embarking on the familiar trek over Putney Bridge, Jeremy paused to fire up a fresh Consulate. For such an evangelical non-smoker, he'd been getting through an embarrassing number of cigarettes recently – often lighting them, as he did now, from the smouldering tips of their predecessors. His Zippo would have been out of the question, of course – partly because of the stiff breeze that was flicking white horses across the surface of the gunmetal Thames, but mostly because his beloved lighter was currently residing in the People's Republic Of China.

Jeremy sighed and pressed on towards Putney. It was parky weather, even for an autumn evening – the sort of weather he normally despised. Any meteorological conditions that made lasses wrap themselves up like badly-lagged boilers could never be a good thing, he'd always reasoned – until he'd started seeing Lisa. Lisa, who'd positively encouraged a bit of recreational unwrapping when she got home from long days at Deutsche Bank.

Jeremy sighed again. Even though his relationship (he still thrilled at the word) with Lisa was less than a year old, they'd actually known each other since school. *We were different people back then, though*, he reflected, trying hard not to dwell on the wasted teenage years when – presumably through some inexplicable chemical imbalance of the brain – he had entirely failed to acknowledge Lisa Salt's incomparable beauty, intelligence and wit. *Aye, you're daft when you're young*, he ruminated. *And sometimes longer than that. Only interested in booze and fags and skirt. And it didn't really matter whose skirt it was.*

He'd known Wes since school too, of course. Which of the two scenarios was more surprising – that he'd ended up as Wes's mate or Lisa's bloke – was a head-scratcher he'd yet to fully figure out. After all, he'd never been hugely fond of young Byron Wesley, back home in Whitby – partly due to the lad's affected intellectual aloofness, he supposed, but mostly due to his unlikely sartorial innovations (kaftans with brogues, waistcoats with loon pants) – and their bizarre appeal to North Yorkshire's impressionable fairer sex. *But now they'd both found themselves living as exiles, down in London – now they'd both ended up attached to implausibly up-market womenfolk and laughably woeful job prospects – they'd somehow forged an uneasy alliance.*

Jeremy drew deeply on his cigarette, frowning behind drizzle-soaked curls. *Not that I'm really like Wes*, he reflected. *Particularly on the 'job' front. Better an underpaid furniture restorer than a dossing doctor.* He felt his fingertips, numb and calloused, pressing into the palms of his hands. Lisa had, early on, tried introducing him to the concept of moisturising, blithely recommending manicures and cuticle treatments and products costing half his weekly wage – before the grim truth of Jeremy's financial circumstances came to light. She'd moved him into her Docklands flat the same weekend. 'Doesn't matter that it's me paying the rent,' she'd said. 'We belong together. It's all that matters.'

Ah, Lisa. Such had been her profound influence on Jeremy's life, that even now – *even when she was on the other side of the planet* – a pang of guilt and a faint stirring of lust accompanied every illicit drag on his cigarette. His *menthol* cigarette. *Ugh.*

There were certain compensations to the inclement weather, of course. Summer – the endless, blistering summer – had been hell. It was the first time Jeremy could remember when he'd felt morally obliged to abstain from staring openly at girls' breasts. The first time he'd refrained from sidling up to them and attempting to procure a phone number. The first summer he could remember when he hadn't shagged, *oooh*, two or three different lasses a week.

He drew to a halt, suddenly short of breath. Two or three lasses... *a week.* Leaning against the stone wall, Jeremy flicked his half-smoked tab into the Thames, remembering the instant he did so that none of its colleagues remained in the packet. *Bollocks.* He hunched his shoulders against the wind and resumed his trek over Putney Bridge. *No smokes 'til the Bricklayer's, then.*

Of course, if Wes hadn't been such an idle git, they could have met at some mutually convenient 'halfway' pub. Somewhere north of the river. Somewhere noisy and beer-sodden in the West End, perhaps – or one of those City pubs where giggling office girls smoked Silk Cut and necked Bacardi Breezers after work. Jeremy didn't belong in pubs like that any more, though – gazing unapologetically at the tight skirts and black-stockinged legs, as the swelter of the bar caused jackets to be discarded and the top buttons of blouses to open... *No, no, no.* That was his life *before* Lisa. The bad old days. *The bad old Jeremy.*

Aye – maybe it was for the best that he'd given in to Wes's remorseless whingeing, and agreed to make the Bricklayer's Arms their regular fortnightly meet. *The Brick – a proper blokes' boozer.* Decent Yorkshire ale and a highly stimulating range of crisps and peanut options. That's all Jeremy craved, now he'd allowed Lisa to turn his life around; not meaningless sexual congress with an endless parade of willing, nubile young females. *Take those two lasses at the bus stop, for instance. The cheeky-looking ones with the naughty smiles and let's-fool-around hair-dos.* Even if they'd offered themselves to him *right then, right there,* he wouldn't be interested. Even if they dragged him back to their south London love cave for some manner of unspeakable shagathon – *girl/girl, Jez/girl, girl/Jez/girl, girl/girl/Jez/ landlady, girl/spliff/Jez/Hollyoaks/girl/landlady* – he'd politely but firmly turn them down. Eventually.

It's no picnic, this monogamy lark, he reflected, averting his eyes from the bus stop's forbidden fruit. Monogamy was okay for the likes of Tim and Wes, of course – but *they'd* never been known from Hartlepool to Scarborough as The Shagfinder General. *They'd* never juggled the attentions of bored shop girls, gap-year backpackers and sexually-frustrated cinema usherettes. Tim and Wes were one-woman men. Wes was even *married* – six months, now. Jeremy shivered again, fighting an urge to defensively cup his testicles. Dr Byron Wesley – *married.* And he hadn't even got Gabi up the duff.

Up the duff – oh, *God.* Jeremy's hand shot instinctively into his cigarette pocket. Finding nothing, it remained there, clenched into an empty, impotent fist. *Up the duff. In the family way. Pregnant.* Jeremy swallowed hard, trying to stop the thought unravelling in his mind like a badly-manhandled rubber johnny. *Well, there's no point dwelling on it now,* he thought. *Not if she's told me not to call. Not if she's gone all the way to Shanghai to avoid seeing me.* Jeremy blinked away the tiny fragment of grit that had somehow managed to inveigle its way beyond his fringe – the fringe that had grown increasingly Chewbacca-ish in Lisa's absence. *She needs time to think, that's all. Just like I did. Time to see I've changed.*

Clearly, an uncomplicated, woman-free evening at the

Brick with Wes was just what Jeremy's troubled psyche required. That was one of Wes's few redeeming qualities – his refusal to discuss the joys of married life while down the pub. Come to think of it, since he'd got hitched, Wes'd had a habit of neatly sidestepping pretty much *all* Gabi-related questions, and Jeremy couldn't remember clapping eyes on the lass since watching her chuck a glass of vintage Pommery in her dad's face at her wedding reception. *A good night.*

You couldn't deny that Wes had changed in the six months since he'd got spliced, though – and not necessarily for the better. He still pranced round like a cross between Top Cat and Gok Wan, of course, but with noticeably less spring in his step than before. And it was the same story with his clothes. When he'd been a penniless medical student, Wes had always made a point of emerging from his Dollis Hill bedsit looking like a latter-day Beau Brummel. And while he still wouldn't darken the bookie's doorstep in anything less than a Gieves & Hawkes two-piece, there was something indefinable about his appearance these days that was more *George At Asda* than Giorgio Armani.

Of course, Jeremy had initially applauded what appeared to be his friend's new chilled-out demeanour. He'd assumed it represented the subtle lowering of standards that generally accompanies the first few months of marriage – but now the signs were getting worrying. Last time they'd arranged to meet at the Brick, the once-fastidious Wes had forgotten to turn up at all.

Jeremy shivered at the memory, glad to have made it to the Bricklayer's twenty minutes earlier than planned – early enough, perhaps, to have a restorative pint before Wes arrived. Taking one last glorious breath of second hand smoke from the small clutch of tobacco addicts clustered on the pavement, he opened the door and stepped into the welcoming, softly lit bar of the Brick.

He enjoyed entering pubs. Being six foot three and fond

of Greek army boots and sunglasses, he understood the theatrical *frisson* that generally accompanied his entrance to a room. Of all the faces that rose to greet him, however, Wes's was notable by its absence. Jeremy peered over the top of his sunglasses, and was reassured a moment later by what he saw. There, on his friend's favourite table by the window, lay an open copy of the *Racing Post* and, behind it, a half-supped pint and the tell-tale detritus of several bags of crisps. Still no Wes, though. *Must be in the bog,* Jeremy reflected, ignoring the lure of the bar for a moment and sidling over to the vacant table.

He didn't quite know why, but Jeremy found himself glancing guiltily around the room as he picked up the *Post*. It was surprising that Wes hadn't taken it with him to the gents', as he usually did. After all, he'd always been weirdly protective of his racing selections. On the rare occasions Jeremy had managed to sneak a peek at Wes's newspaper, he'd found its pages to be heavily annotated with cryptic hieroglyphs and occult-looking symbols. This time, though, most of the paper was still in pristine condition – except for the back page where, in Wes's semi-legible doctor's scrawl, were a number of angular words hacked out in jagged strokes of black biro.

Intrigued, Jeremy peered closer, unconsciously reaching for Wes's abandoned pint glass as he did so. As far as he could tell (and it wasn't easy, given the state of Wes's handwriting), all of the lad's scribblings said the same thing. *Nikki. NIKKI. nikki. NikKi. Nikkkki.* Jeremy drained Wes's beer and dabbed absently at a few of the crisp crumbs on the table. *Who the hell was Nikki?* Not a horse, surely. It couldn't be a pet name for Gabi, could it? It seemed highly unlikely. Despite her striking similarity to the young Nicole Kidman, 'Nikki' was scarcely a name that sprang to mind when you thought of Dr Gabrielle Wynstanley. *'Snappy'* or *'Tetchy', perhaps –* but not *'Nikki'*.

Not that Wes would be likely to say. *He never really talks about anything*, Jeremy mused, closing the newspaper and placing it back on the table. *He banters. He jokes. He makes acid little comments about Game Of Thrones and tells you why Lucky Lad won't win the 3:15 at Lingfield. But he never talks.* There was a time, of course, when Jeremy would have seen this as an asset in a friend. But since he'd been seeing Lisa... well, his perspectives had shifted slightly. *You can learn a lot from lasses*, he mentally conceded, making his way over to the bar. *Even when they're on the other side of the world.*

Then, from behind the bar area, a commotion caught his attention. Someone – or something – was emerging from the gents' toilets, with some apparent difficulty. It stumbled dangerously between the tables, propping itself up from time to time against the bar's stout iron pillars, occasionally progressing towards the window table thanks to the assistance of sundry gentle, guiding hands. Frowning beneath his overgrown fringe, Jeremy peered between the milling groups of early evening drinkers. 'Alright, Wes?' he said.

For a second, his friend's eyes swivelled vacantly, and when they finally alighted upon Jeremy's face, it was clear that their owner was already pretty far gone. 'Ah. Jeremy. *Jez,'* Wes slurred, collapsing on to his chair and gently patting the seat next to him. 'Sit down, dear boy. I've been waiting for you.'

'Not late, am I?'

'No. No, Jeremy – I was early.'

'How early?'

'About five hours.'

Jeremy's brow creased in concern. For a moderate drinker who only lived fifteen minutes away, Wes's five-hour head start seemed excessive – particularly since he hadn't seen the lad drunk since the day they'd opened their A level results, back in Whitby, half a lifetime ago. Since then... well, Wes just didn't *get* drunk. Not 'drunk' drunk, anyway. He'd always avoided it for the same reason Jeremy had embraced it – the loss of self-control, the unguarded conversations, and the fact he could never *ever* remember what he'd done in the morning. *Aye – this was a queer one, no doubt. A monumentally drunk Wes, and a mysteriously unsupervised copy of the Racing Post.* 'Any particular reason for the early start?'

'Fancied a little drinkie, that's all. Thought a couple of light ales might clear my head.' Wes's hand reached unsteadily for the empty pint glass on the table, and presented it to Jeremy. 'Speaking of which...'

On instinct, Jeremy reached for the glass, but stopped short of taking it. Clearly, something significant and altogether unusual was occurring behind Wes's empty grin, and Jeremy needed to weigh up the situation carefully before deciding how to deal with it.

Stuff like this was easier when I smoked, he reflected bitterly. *You just took a drag on your Rothmans, closed your eyes and an answer would come. And if your ciggie didn't give you the answer, Phil Lynott would.* Jeremy sighed as a nicotine-scented cloud of nostalgia engulfed him. Phil Lynott had, of course, been telling him what to do for over a decade – ever since the late singer had taken up residence in his subconscious at the age of fifteen, on a school exchange trip to Mönchengladbach. Indeed, since his German pen friend Otto had first introduced him to Thin Lizzy's seminal *Jailbreak* album, Jeremy had more or less abdicated responsibility for all of his life's major decisions, preferring to address them on the basis of *What Would Phil Lynott Do?* Since that fateful evening, Phil had provided the soundtrack to his life; Phil had given him advice and companionship; Phil had given him a spiritual lodestar. But as Lisa had made abundantly clear, there was no room for a third party in their relationship – and certainly not a dead Irish rocker with a penchant for afros, heroin and group sex.

Jeremy smiled, trying to hide his anxiety from Wes. The time had finally come, he realised, to go it alone. *To take the*

22

initiative. He blinked hard, refocusing his attention on his ravaged-looking friend. 'So what's up with yourself, Wes?'

'Nothing.'

'Sure?'

'Of course. I'm absolutely dandy.'

'Nowt you want to talk about?'

'Not with you, no.'

Jeremy leaned back in his seat and gently rubbed his chin. 'I bet you'd spill your beans for Nikki.'

If Wes had looked green before, his face now took on pallor that was the wrong side of ghostly – and his voice, when it eventually emerged, was little more than a hoarse gasp of incredulity. '*How the fuck do you know about Nikki?*'

'You uncle Jeremy knows all sorts of things, mate.' He smiled benignly, hoping not to betray his surprise at Wes's gobsmacked expression. 'Fancy that pint, now? Get it all off your chest?'

'No.'

'What do you want, then?'

Wes closed his eyes, his hand reaching out to grasp the edge of the table in front of him. 'I want... I think I want to be sick.'

2

a porny old porn site, full of porn

It was hard to tell – particularly given the way he sprayed Gabi's muesli all over the sofa – whether Jeremy's words were intended to convey revulsion, incredulity or admiration. 'So you've been having an *affair* with this Nikki lass?'

'*Not* an affair. The whole point is that I *haven't* been having an affair.' Wes closed his eyes and gently massaged his forehead. It didn't help; not against the tsunami of caffeine and sugar coursing through his bloodstream. 'I'm a happily married man. I was very specifically *avoiding* having an affair. That was the whole bloody point.'

Jeremy stretched back on the sofa, propping the heels of his Greek army boots on the edge of the smoked glass coffee table. He'd done it a couple of times in the past hour, quietly enjoying Wes's wince of anxiety every time he heard the squeak of rubber on glass. Mentioning Gabi, Jeremy had noticed, elicited pretty much the same effect. *Aye – she might be spending the night at her sister's, but her spirit lingers on.* He was glad Gabi had littered every flat surface in the room with candles, though. After all, Wes had only really started opening up when Jeremy had created some shadows to skulk in – and if the lad's recent revelations were anything to go by, he was just about to reach his optimum confessional level. *Still drunk enough to let his guard down, but sober enough to make sense.* Jeremy's eyes narrowed as he regarded the curled-up form on the opposite sofa. 'Just imagine I'm Gabi, mate,' he urged softly, trying to keep the note of anticipation out of his voice. 'Try convincing me you've not been cheating.'

Imagining Gabi somehow inhabiting Jeremy's nicotine-addled cadaver was the last thing Wes wanted to do, of course. But the things they'd talked about in the hours since Jeremy had carried him home from the Brick... well, they'd been a real weight off his tired mind. *And if you can't talk to one of your oldest mates, who can you talk to? Abiola? That husky-sounding German lass who lives in the satnav? God?* Wes closed his eyes in the darkness and cleared his throat.

'Well, Jez – sorry, *Gabi* – you want to know about this friend of mine. Nikki. Well, I've never even clapped eyes on the lass,' he began, as gamely as he could. 'She lives on another continent. And I only ever met her in an internet chat room – text only – old school, no pictures or webcams or anything. And we never talked about anything filthy. So it was hardly an affair. Which means you don't have to divorce me or take away my access rights to the Merc or the PS4 or anything.' His performance over, Wes turned to face Jeremy again. 'Nikki was a friend, mate – a good friend. Someone I could really communicate with. But just as a friend. Just as... words on a screen.'

Jeremy frowned. Wes's latest version of events seemed to diverge significantly from his earlier, franker account of the relationship. *Maybe the bugger's sobering up.* Jeremy pointed the toe of his boot warningly in Wes's direction. 'Lies make baby Jesus cry, mate.'

'I'm not lying.'

'And that's the story you'd tell Gabi, is it?'

'Uh-huh. And she'd be totally cool about it.'

'And you don't think you've omitted any critical details in your account? The *juicier* details?' Jeremy's eyes sought out his friend in the darkness. 'Because baby Jesus also cries – pretty bloody bitterly – when you don't tell your uncle Jezzer all the juicy details.'

Wes frowned as a note of indignation entered his voice. 'Like *what*, exactly?'

'Like the fact that the chat room where you had your little heart-to-hearts with this lass just happened to be part of a porn site,' Jeremy said, not altogether unkindly. 'A *porn* site, kid. And that the lass herself just happened to be a porn actress. And that the chat room in question just happens to be a subscription service where lonely, deluded trouser-fumblers wank away their giros while some equally desperate tart tells them how deliciously plump her tits are.'

For a minute, the only sound that could be heard was Wes's laboured breathing from the far side of the room. Then he spoke. 'It wasn't like that, mate.'

'It wasn't like that, *Gabi*,' Jeremy corrected him. 'Get used to saying it. Because that's what you're going to be doing, when she's hoying your *Sopranos* DVD's into a skip.'

Wes turned and regarded Jeremy balefully from across the sitting room. If he'd known how Jeremy's post-pub 'man chat' was going to develop – or if he'd been even vaguely sober – he'd have handled it more circumspectly, glossing over a few details here and there. Things like the unfortunate 'porn' and 'actress' revelations. It was too late now, though. *Too late for the usual blokesy lies and evasions.* He closed his eyes. 'Actually, the fact that I met Nikki on an adult site...'

'...a *porn* site. A porny old porn site, full of porn.'

'...an *adult* site... well, it made it easier to be friends with her. So did the fact that I was paying to use the chat room. It meant that neither of us kidded ourselves about any emotional attachment. Although we actually got on really well, as it happens.'

'She was *paid* to get on with you, you daft prat,' Jeremy scoffed. 'It didn't matter whether she was gasping at the colossal magnitude of your willy or giving you advice on treating your ringworm. Becoming your extra-special new buddy was her *job*, kid. Just a job, that's all.'

'Maybe to start with. But in the end it was more than that.' Wes swung his legs off the sofa and sat up, fixing Jeremy with an ardent stare. 'Nikki's a person, Jez. A real person – real as you or me.' Suddenly Wes appeared to deflate, as with some effort he hauled his legs back on to the sofa. 'I felt closer to her than I've felt to anyone,' he added quietly.

Jeremy glanced across the room at Wes's tortured expression. The flickering light from Gabi's candles carved dark shadows across his forehead, and although his eyes were still hazy with drink, their meaning was unambiguous. It all seemed so... *unlikely*, though. After all, ever since school, Wes had been the cynical one. Jeremy eyed him intently, probing his friend's face for any sign that he might be taking the piss. Sincerity, he knew, was entirely alien to Wes's *modus operandi*, and coming across it in conversation with the lad was like finding nipple clamps in a geometry set. *Unexpected.* He peered closer. 'Seriously?'

'Afraid so.'

'So your whole life – everything about it – is just a sham. Blimey.'

Wes appeared to physically recoil from Jeremy's words. 'That was just a trifle blunt, mate.'

'Was it? Sorry, kid. It's just that it's all making more sense. You letting yourself go, these last six months. All the pieces have slotted into place, now I know about Nikki. Now I know you're living in a loveless marriage.'

Wes subjected Jeremy to a withering stare. 'You know nothing about Nikki. *Nothing.* And my marriage is hardly loveless.' He glanced momentarily around the room before curling up and tucking his knees beneath his chin. 'There are many things I love in this marriage. *Many* things. The telly – I love the telly. And the Merc. And the sofa you're sitting on, mate. Very, very expensive. Highly lovable.'

Had he been able to see it, Wes might have been surprised to witness Jeremy's left eyebrow shoot up a clear inch at this last statement. As a furniture restorer, Jeremy had been compiling a small mental dossier of observations regarding the sofa since the moment he'd first sat on it, some four or five hours earlier. *Iffy workmanship. Badly upholstered. Covered in muesli.* Now didn't seem the time to mention it, though, as he slid his boots off the coffee table and reached for his coat. He glanced down at Wes as he made his way to the door. The lad, it would have to be said, didn't look much happier for having aired his problems. In fact, he looked worse. Much worse. Jeremy zipped up his coat. 'So what happened with young Nikki, then?'

Wes gazed up at Jeremy, his face unreadable. 'She disappeared.'

'What do you mean, she disappeared?'

'One day I logged on and her name wasn't there. Her chat room had been deleted from the system. She'd just gone. No way to contact her. No email, nothing.'

Jeremy shrugged. 'Well, maybe it's for the best, mate. In the long run.'

'Not for her, it's not.'

'Why not?'

Wes sighed and glanced up at the clock above the mantelpiece. *Two o'clock in the morning.* He closed his eyes, held his hands over them, then slumped forwards with his elbows on his knees. 'Do you *really* want to know?'

'Aye.'

Wes nodded in resignation. 'I'm too knackered to explain. I'll have to show you.' He took unsteadily to his feet and tottered out of the room. 'Make us some more coffee. Pop outside and have a cigarette. You'll need one. I'll be back in five minutes.'

Jeremy's hand groped blindly over the surface of the coffee table until it found the mug. He dipped a finger inside. *Cold.* After a couple of seconds' consideration, he picked up the mug anyway and drained the contents. *Ugh.* He shivered. The central heating had gone off hours earlier, and even in his coat, the sitting room had become uncomfortably parky. *What time was it now?* Unable to see the clock – or indeed, anything at all – it was impossible to say.

'For heaven's sake, Jez *look* at her.'

'No can do, mate.'

'Just a passing glance.'

'It's not right – two blokes looking at porn together.' Jeremy turned his head away from the laptop screen. Even through tightly closed eyes, he could still make out its seductive glow in the darkened room. 'I've not looked at a naked lass – *not one, mind* – since me and Lisa got together. And I'm not starting now.'

'Just *look.*'

'Sorry, mate. I'm not the Shagfinder General any more, but he's only ever an inch or two under the surface. Could be very dangerous for me, a full-frontal porn injection. It's probably different for doctors. You're immune. You can look at what you like. But I'm like... I'm like a recovering alcoholic, mate. You can't just offer me a sweet sherry, then expect me to turn my nose up at the Special Brew. It's not on.'

For a moment, only the sound of the dawn chorus penetrated the room. Then Wes spoke, his voice shrill with excitement. 'Bloody hell. I've just flicked over to the BBC news page. Apparently they've discovered a whole album's worth of unreleased Thin Lizzy tracks at a recording studio in Chippenham...'

'Huh?' Jeremy's left eye flicked open. 'Oh, *shit.*'

There, juddering across Wes's laptop screen in a lurid low-res blur, were the scenes of unbridled debauchery Jeremy had spent the previous twenty minutes studiously attempting to avoid. Wes sighed with fleeting disappointment at how easily his friend had fallen for the ploy, and nodded at the screen. 'That one there – the blonde lass – that's Nikki. I downloaded this from the website, the day after they took down her chat room. This was the first time I found out what she looked like, actually. Her chat room had been text-only. For, you know… *shy* clients.'

Jeremy stared, transfixed, at the scenes of hardcore rogering that were currently dancing across his field of vision. *The rubbing. The licking. The grinding.* It wasn't difficult to imagine the kinds of things Lisa would say if she were there. Jeremy closed his eyes again, blanking out the image entirely, but to little avail. Squeals of simulated ecstasy filled his head. 'I can't look at it any more, kid. You're just going to have to give me a commentary. I got up to the bit where that bloke was just about to put his...'

'Jez, *look*.'

The tinny gasps and grunts from the laptop's tiny speaker stopped abruptly and Jeremy opened his eyes. There, on the screen, captured in a freeze frame close-up, was a vast expanse of pink... *something*. For a second, he struggled to work out exactly what it represented. 'Uh-huh?'

'What can you see?'

Jeremy peered at the image. Then he tilted his head to one side, wondering whether or not he'd missed something significant. Finally he returned his gaze to Wes. 'Well, that's a bum cheek, Wes. A lass's bum cheek. Not a shabby one, by the looks of things. Firm, but not too muscly.' His brow furrowed as he struggled to make sense of the situation. 'Are you trying to tell me you're an 'arse' man, mate? Because it's nowt to be ashamed of. Doesn't mean you're gay. Not these days.'

Wes sighed. He hadn't, he reflected, been an 'arse' man – either through choice or coercion – since the day he came back from his honeymoon, six months ago. He hadn't been an *anything* man, actually – not as far as relations with Gabrielle had been concerned. Not since the embarrassing *contretemps* over the fish slice. Not since he'd come home to find all his Calvin Klein boxer shorts and Kaiser Chiefs CD's moved into the spare room, and the fish slice lying provocatively on the spare bed. *The spare bed.* He glanced warily at Jeremy, momentarily fearful that some further stray, shameful secret had somehow leaked out of his head and into his friend's. Satisfied that it hadn't, he nodded at the screen. 'Look again, Jez. What *specifically* can you see?'

Jeremy shrugged. 'Well, there's a little bit of... you know...' – Jeremy mentally spooled through the extensive selection of words that could describe what he saw, and the tiny subset which Lisa generally let him use – '...*muff.* Aye, a smidgeon of muff. It's mostly cheek, though.'

Wes adjusted the zoom control on the toolbar, causing the distracting smidgeon of muff to disappear off the edge of the screen. 'What now?'

Jeremy nodded at the wide expanse of pink flesh. 'What, the scab thing on her bum? Is that what you're on about?'

'It's not a scab, Jez.'

'It *looks* like a scab. I had one down there, once. Itchy little bugger.'

'You've not had one like this.'

'No?'

'No.'

'Why? What is it, then?'

'Well, as far as I can tell – and I could be wrong, you understand – it's a malignant melanoma.' Wes glanced across at Jeremy's vacant expression. 'Nikki's got cancer, Jez. Skin cancer. Very, very nasty.'

'Do you reckon she knows she's got it?'

'I doubt it. She never mentioned it.'

Jeremy gently closed the lid of the laptop, noticing for the first time that the first blue glimmer of dawn was beginning to materialise around the edges of the curtains. He looked at Wes, searching his friend's face for any signs that might indicate exactly how serious the situation was. Even in the hushed half-light, the whites of Wes's eyes were visibly shot with jagged streaks of blood, his pupils dilated to fathomless pits, his expression grave. Jeremy slowly nodded in acknowledgement. 'Fuck.'

3

stockholm syndrome

Wes screwed his eyes shut and pulled the pillow tighter around his ears. *What time was it? And why couldn't someone turn off that bloody car alarm?* As if on autopilot, his free hand emerged from beneath the duvet and began scouting the periphery of the bed for further insulation. *Another pillow. A sack of cement. Anything.* A moment later it disappeared again. *Arse fanny bollocks.*

Opening one eye in the darkness of the bed-cave, Wes surveyed his subterranean realm. What he saw gave him comfort – six inches of dimly-lit duvet cover, bland but unthreatening. What he heard did not. *Didn't car alarms turn themselves off after a few minutes?* He closed his eye again and tried filtering it out. *La la la la la. I can't hear you.* It was no good, though. At this rate, he could expect to be fully awake in no more than ten minutes. *Time for drastic steps, then.* Summoning all his strength, Wes slid a leg down the bed and gently levered himself over on to his other side. And then – almost as if a tiny mercury switch had been tipped in his cerebral cortex – the pain began.

'*Fuck me sideways!*' he exclaimed. *What the hell did I drink last night?* More than the usual half dozen white Russians that generally characterised a Gabi-free evening, that was for sure – although the details remained horribly, evasively hazy. For a moment, despite knowing the folly of his quest, Wes twisted and contorted his body, trying to rediscover the position of pain-free tranquillity he'd occupied a minute earlier. It was no use, though – and now the wail of the car alarm had been joined by something else. *Knocking. Vigorous, angry knocking. Somewhere nearby.*

'Bugger off!' he volunteered, somewhat lamely. Telling the world to bugger off would not, he knew, make the knocking stop – and wrapping pillows around his agonised head would not block it out. 'Okay. You win,' he eventually conceded, throwing off the duvet and staggering to the top of the stairs. 'You can stop knocking. I'm coming. I'm coming.'

Twenty agonised seconds later, Wes arrived at the front door and flung it open. There, on the doorstep, was a woman he vaguely recognised. *One of the neighbours – a pretty young Putney mum.* Although he couldn't put a name to the face, it was certainly one he'd been introduced to at Gabi's recent coffee morning. He'd remembered rather fancying its owner at the time, although the face looked far less amenable now, flushed and clearly vexed, and glaring at him unblinkingly through the tortured wail of the alarm. 'Hello,' he shouted, trying to pitch his voice against the din while still sounding faintly alluring. 'Good to see you again.'

'Your bloody smoke alarm's been going off for the past quarter of an hour.'

Wes swivelled on his heel. Sure enough, the noise was noticeably louder behind him than in front. *And what in God's name was that smell?* Returning to the door, Wes was dismayed to discover that his attractive neighbour, having delivered her communiqué, was now striding purposefully around the gatepost. *Bollocks.*

Wes followed the wisps of acrid-smelling smoke like a semi-sedated *Bisto* kid, entering the kitchen at the precise moment that the alarm stopped. Standing in the midst of a scene reminiscent of wartime Dresden was… *Jeremy.*

Momentarily deprived of words, Wes surveyed the carnage. Most of Gabi's beloved granite worktops were slathered in some unidentifiable off-white glop that appeared to have emerged from her Kenwood Professional blender. The blender itself, Gabi's pride and joy, was lying on its side on the draining board, surrounded by a glop-encrusted selection of its attachments. Twin tributaries of coffee and orange juice had conjoined to form a river of unidentifiable hue on the floor, while a large bag of self-raising flour had seemingly upended itself into the sink. Meanwhile, the handle of Gabi's Le Creuset griddle pan could just be seen peeping out from below the grill, from which thick clouds of black smoke were billowing playfully.

Slowly, Wes's eyes returned to the motionless figure in the centre of the room. *Jeremy.* 'What the hell are *you* doing here? You know the rules,' he gasped. 'You don't come to the house. We meet in the *pub*, Jez – the *pub.*'

Jeremy frowned in concern. 'Don't you remember last night, mate?'

And then the memories – the unspeakable memories of the night before, the memories that his hungover brain had somehow contrived to suppress – burst through the front door of his mind. *The beer. The confessions. Nikki – Nikki, Nikki, Nikki.* Wes sank to his knees and buried his face in his hands. 'Oh God. Oh no.'

'I'm really sorry about the smoke alarm, mate.'

Wes glanced up at the spot on the wall that the device had silently occupied for the previous six months. The alarm was still there, but now with a large wooden spatula rammed through its centre. 'Don't worry about it, Jez.'

'It just wouldn't stop. It's not like the one in Lisa's kitchen. Yours is wired into the mains. I couldn't get it off its mountings.'

Despite a near-overwhelming urge to stagger back to the safety of his duvet, Wes found himself nodding understandingly. *What was that thing called, where hostages started sympathising with their captors? Stockholm syndrome. Ah, the Swedes – suicidal hardcore porn apologists. Just like me.* He smiled wanly and waved a hand in the general direction of Jeremy's culinary meltdown. 'What were you doing, anyway?'

'Making breakfast.' Jeremy took a tea towel, wrapped it round the handle of the griddle pan and gently lifted it out of the cooker. 'I was going to do pancakes but I couldn't work out the recipe. So we're having friend egg sandwiches instead.'

Suddenly the glint of something familiar made Wes catch his breath. Something sticking out of the back of the smoking grill pan. *Dave the barman's antique silver fish slice.* 'Is that what you've been using? To fry the eggs with?'

'Uh-huh. Just to scrape the burnt bits off the pan. I found it in your bedside drawer, actually, while I was looking for a little nightcap.'

Wes closed his eyes as the room swam around him. 'You slept in Gabi's... our... bedroom?'

'Aye.' Jeremy returned to the grill pan, half-heartedly hacking at its contents with the fish slice. 'You'd cleared off to the spare room, so I slept in yours. All set for a spot of brekky, then?'

Wes's stomach lurched. 'Can't eat, mate.' He closed his eyes. For a moment, the image of the devastated kitchen hung against the backdrop of his mind. 'Don't think I'll ever eat again, actually.' *Or drink,* he thought, as more memories of the previous night began stealing into his consciousness. *I'll never drink again. Or make friends with girls in internet chat rooms. Never, never again.*

From behind tightly closed eyes, the world looked no more comforting than it did in the technicolor glare of daylight – but it did have one appealing feature. *No Jeremy.*

Wes was absurdly tempted, in fact, to simply retreat out of the kitchen on his hands and knees, grope his way blindly back to bed, and never, ever have to look at Jeremy's ridiculous hangdog expression again. He sighed and opened his eyes. It was no good, he realised – he'd have to deal with the daft bugger. Get him out of the house as quickly and quietly as possible, and refuse to be drawn on any Nikki-related topics that might crop up.

I'll feign laryngitis, he thought. *Or amnesia. Or post-traumatic stress disorder. Anything that means we don't have to discuss Nikki. Anything that means we don't have to paw at her memory. Anything that stops us reducing her to a tumour on a buttock on the other side of the planet.* He eyed Jeremy warily as his friend obliviously picked fragments of cremated egg off the grill pan and popped them in his mouth, wracking his throbbing brain for the best way to sidestep the sticky 'Nikki' issue.

The thing about Jeremy, Wes knew, was that he'd want to help her. He'd want to get involved. Then he'd want to get other people involved. Then he'd get pissed and tell someone he shouldn't. He'd leave messages on the answerphone that Gabi would listen to, then turn up in the dead of night with some fresh ideas he'd just been airing in the pub. He'd probably bring his pub friends with him, actually – a wild-eyed subcommittee of well-meaning pissheads and dropouts who'd want to spend the early hours of the morning discussing *Debbie Does Dallas* and leaving roach burns on Gabi's Liz Claiborne rug.

And eventually, one way or another, Gabi would get to know about Nikki. *And if Gabi ever got to know about Nikki...* Wes shivered and absently hoisted his pyjama trousers a couple of inches higher, knowing very well what the consequences of such a revelation would be. *Divorce. Destitution. And – ultimately – the prospect of having to get a proper job.*

Trying to suppress his feelings of rising panic, Wes forced a smile to his lips. It was time, he knew, to confront the source of his fears – the shaggy-haired man-beast that was currently hacking a two-inch doorstop off Gabi's *pain d'Auvergne* and dipping it experimentally into the congealing glop on the worktop. Wes shivered again. Finding Jeremy in your house was like finding a horse's head in your bed – deeply, deeply sinister. Discovering him making breakfast in your kitchen was like finding the rest of the horse galloping around your garden with nextdoor's kids sitting on its back. *Terrifying.* It signalled the kind of impending apocalypse that you only generally saw in Charlton Heston movies, where the Nile has been turned into a river of blood and the death of the first-born is just around the corner. *Of course, I haven't got a first-born,* thought Wes. *But I have got a brand new Mercedes. And a Rolex. And some really lovely Hermès cufflinks. Oh God.*

Clearly, there was only one thing for it. Wes had to get Jeremy out of his house, out of Putney, north of the river and – for the foreseeable future – out of his life. He'd have to switch off his phone for a few weeks, or buy a new one and neglect to give Jeremy the number; he'd have to ignore the lad's inevitable avalanche of emails. *The issue of What To Do About Nikki would be something he'd have to handle solo.* He'd certainly never be able to mention Nikki in Jeremy's company again and, after six months or so had elapsed, he could quite reasonably pretend that he had no recollection of his drunken confessions.

He cleared his throat. 'Look, mate. I think we should get out of here. Get some fresh air. Get you back to Docklands, so you can get cleaned up before Lisa gets home. I'll walk you back to the Tube station.'

Jeremy appeared to weigh this suggestion for a moment. Then he nodded. 'Cool,' he said. 'We can talk about Nikki on the way.'

'I'll be haunted by that lass's arse 'til the day I die,' Jeremy declared, pulling his coat around him against the buffeting wind. '*Haunted.*'

'*Pas devant les enfants*, mate.' Wes inclined his head towards the small cluster of children who had, over the preceding ten minutes, slowly gravitated towards their park bench. *Nice children. Middle-class children. The kind of children he might someday want to produce with Gabrielle.*

'Yeah, yeah. Sorry.' Jeremy drew deeply on his cigarette, its glowing tip gently singeing a few strands of hair that had rashly strayed across his face. His eyes narrowed, focusing on some unseen object in the far distance – something far beyond his overgrown fringe, beyond the playground, beyond the treacherous Thames. The smoke from his Rothmans engulfed Wes and broke like a pestilent wave over the gaggle of young mothers sitting on the next bench along. 'Still. Cancer, eh? What bastard bad luck. That Nikki can't be any older than us, you know. Younger, probably, seeing as she's doing porn. *Porn.* Fuck.'

Wes lowered his voice, hoping that Jeremy would do likewise. 'She's twenty-two.'

Jeremy glanced apologetically at Wes. 'Of course. I'd forgotten you were friends with her, kid. Sorry.'

Wes cupped his hands and struggled to light his own cigarette. He'd regretted having spoken almost as soon as the words left his lips. *The sooner I get a ciggie between them, the better.* After all, the whole point of going for a walk had been to get Jeremy back to Putney Bridge Tube station – but Jeremy had insisted on taking a diversion via Leaders Gardens, and now seemed intent on embarking on a full-blown discussion on What To Do About Nikki.

Wes looked sidelong at his friend. Maybe Gabi had been right about him. If he hadn't known the lad since primary school, Wes reflected, there was no way they'd be mates now – and if he and Gabi were ever to have children, Jeremy would undoubtedly be the first friend he'd have to quietly cut adrift. *Then Lenny Jones. Then Tim Howden. Then Lakey-Boy and the Rosenthal brothers and Arthur and Dave the barman from the Fat Ox.* Wes looked away, flushed with guilt.

His friends – every last one of them – were loyal as barnacles. It would just be so much more convenient if they could all become television producers or barristers or aromatherapists, and move *en masse* to Putney. Then Gabi could invite them to her dinner parties, and Wes wouldn't have to systematically ostracise them through a decade of deleted emails, unsent Christmas cards and indifferent birthday presents. *Bollocks.*

Catching sight of his friend's haunted expression, Jeremy gently punched Wes on the upper arm. 'Chin up, kid. After all, we don't *know* it's cancer, do we?'

Wes shrugged half-heartedly. 'Well, it *could* be a mole or something. You just can't tell. Not without a proper poke around. A biopsy and such.'

'And even if it *is* cancer, she might get better.'

'Not really. Not if it's a malignant melanoma.' Wes beckoned Jeremy closer, anxious that none of the park's under-fives should overhear him. 'Just between the two of us, it's got a whiff of the slab. If you don't get it seen to, anyway. It all depends on whether it's spread.'

'Oh. I see.' Jeremy closed his eyes and allowed the fresh wave of nicotine to transport him back to the moment of grim revelation in Sefton Street. In the shadowy cavern of his mind, it wasn't difficult to recreate the images he'd seen on Wes's laptop – Nikki and her nameless, donkey-cocked beau, performing the kind of flicker-book sex that he fully expected to see on his deathbed when his life flashed before him. 'She looked lively enough though, didn't she – young Nikki? Highly energetic.' Jeremy opened his eyes and cast a pensive glance over the gang of children who were about to engulf the nearby climbing frame. 'Aye. Plenty of life in her,' he murmured, extinguishing his cigarette butt on the heel of his Greek army boot and groping in his coat pocket for another.

For a second, Wes fought the compulsion to shrug in tacit agreement. Shrugging in agreement would be the easy thing to do – the kind of cowardly, selfish reaction he'd based a highly rewarding lifestyle on. But his drunken self must have shown the video to Jeremy for a reason – possibly, he reflected, because Jeremy possessed something that Wes himself lacked. *A childlike desire to do the right thing? A long-standing debt to womankind? A spine?* He eyed his old school friend from behind his scarf. 'Thing is, Nikki probably doesn't even know she's got a tumour. What, with it being on her backside and everything.'

'And when do you reckon she'll find out?'

'Lots of people only find out when it's too late.'

'Ah.' Jeremy gazed out over the choppy water of the Thames. In his mind's eye, Nikki's face had now reappeared, frozen in an open-mouthed rictus. *Agony? Ecstasy?* It was impossible to say. 'It's lucky you noticed it, then. Because she needs telling, doesn't she?'

Wes sighed. 'I've already tried, mate. I've emailed the people who run the website a dozen times.'

Jeremy considered this for a moment, drawing deeply on his Rothmans. 'Tricky email to write, that. Not that I've ever had to tell someone they've got cancer.' He blinked away another cloud of cigarette smoke, reflecting on his own limited experience of dropping medical bombshells. 'I've had to tell a lass she had the clap, a couple of times. And unsightly facial hair once. But never cancer. What happened with your emails, anyway?'

'Not much. I just got stock replies saying that the company wasn't prepared to discuss its employees.'

'And there's no other way of getting hold of her?'

Wes shuffled uncomfortably and made a last half-hearted attempt to light his cigarette. 'Well, I've had a look at a few other... erm, *adult* websites, obviously. To see if she's working for anyone else.'

'No joy?'

'None so far.'

'So what do we do next?'

For a second, Wes fought for breath as though winded by an invisible blow. This was it; the moment he'd most feared. *The 'we' moment.* The moment when Jeremy quietly and unobtrusively hopped across the Venn diagram of Wes's life, out of the 'public' and into its 'private' bubble. *The bubble that housed Gabi and Nikki, Dave the barman's antique fish slice and the Mercedes.* Wes's vision swam sickeningly before him and he fleetingly felt he was about to faint until, not a moment too soon, he realised he'd been trying to draw an entire lungful of breath through the filter of his unlit cigarette. He opened his mouth and gulped down oxygen. 'We?' he eventually gasped. 'We? *We* don't do anything, mate. There *is* no 'we', okay? Not when it comes to Nikki.' He breathed deeply, trying hard to recompose himself. '*I* intend to try tracking her down on the internet. She's got to be out there – somewhere. But it's not a 'we' thing, Jez. It's just me – understand? *Just me.*'

For a moment Jeremy regarded his friend coolly. Then he quietly plucked Wes's cigarette from his lips and lit it with the smouldering stub of his own. He handed it back to his friend. 'Well, I could help,' he said. 'Get a few of the boys scouring the web. Put the word out to Lakey-Boy and Dave the barman. Get Big Rob on the case. Tim's a bit anti-porn, but Lenny Jones isn't averse to the occasional pert young nipple. He'd track down young Nikki in no time...'

'*Please*, Jez. Don't tell anyone about Nikki. No one at all. I'm going to sort out the whole 'Nikki' business by myself.'

Wes glanced at Jeremy's face, trying to read his friend's expression. *Equanimity? Resolution? Or simply the half-formed desire for a bacon sandwich?* You could never tell with Jeremy, and Wes was about to seek clarification from the lad when he suddenly spoke. 'Okay.'

'What?'

'I said okay.'

'You won't try to interfere?'

'It's your affair, mate.'

'It's not an affair. I haven't been having an affair.'

Jeremy sighed and began stretching out his legs in turn, as though limbering up for some taxing physical ordeal. 'That's not what I meant. But you're the doctor. You've got half a decade of medical training under your belt. I'm just a furniture restorer. You're the best person to deal with this, not me.'

'That's right. And you'll forget all about this 'Nikki' business, won't you?'

'Already have, mate.' Jeremy levered himself off the bench and pulled his coat tight around himself. He dropped his cigarette on the asphalt path and extinguished it. 'I shan't mention her to a soul.'

'Good lad. It's not that I don't appreciate what you're trying to do. And Nikki – well, she's really important to me. But just I don't want your help with this one. I can do this by myself.'

Jeremy smiled and extended his hand to Wes. 'Okay, mate. Anything you say.'

4

people should learn to face their responsibilities

'Wes wants me to help,' declared Jeremy as he reached the end of his story. 'He can't do this by himself.'

There was a tiny pause at the other end of the line – fractionally longer than the customary lag he experienced during his weekly phone calls to Barcelona. Then Claire spoke. 'Did Wes actually *say* he wanted help?'

If Jeremy detected the note of quiet warning in his friend's soft Glaswegian lilt, he chose to ignore it. After all, it was a momentary lapse of personal conviction that had caused the current (hopefully temporary) hiccup in his relationship with Lisa. *Not a mistake I'm going to make again.* Jeremy dismissed Claire's doubts with a tiny shake of the head. 'I've known the bugger since we were three years old. Almost as long as I've known young Timothy,' he added, smiling as he pictured Claire's boyfriend – his own closest mate – in the sailor suit he'd worn for the entire duration of his nursery education. It had occurred to Jeremy, of course,

44

to remind Claire that her relationship with Tim had wholly been due to a Jeremy-shaped intervention the previous year – but he thought better of it. There were some awkward, if not painful, memories there too. 'Wes is virtually family,' he said at length. 'And I know when my mates need me, kid.'

Another infinitesimal pause. 'If you say so, honey. So how have you helped him so far?'

'Well, I wrote some emails to the porn people, telling them I needed Nikki's contact details.'

'The same as Wes did?'

'Similar, aye.'

'Did you get any further than he did?'

'Not really.'

'I'm not surprised. You can't expect them to just give out the girls' email addresses. They must get loads of weirdoes and panty-sniffers trying to hunt them down. Not that *you're* a weirdo, sweetheart,' Claire added lightly. 'Just charmingly eccentric. And possibly insane.'

'Thanks, kid.'

'Any time.'

Jeremy wedged the phone beneath his chin and pulled Lisa's dressing gown cord tighter around his waist. Since the sun had disappeared behind Canary Wharf some hours earlier, it had grown bitterly cold out on the balcony – particularly since Lisa's dressing gown reached no lower than the tops of Jeremy's thighs. Tonight, though – like most of the nights he spent alone in Lisa's flat – he'd found himself unaccountably lured out on to his high-rise Docklands eyrie. Jeremy stared out over the lights of West India Quay and slid his hand back into the dressing gown pocket. Finding a crumpled packet of cigarettes there, he crouched momentarily behind the balcony wall to light one, then turned back to the glittering skyline. In spite of everything, Claire's voice – faint and tinny over the line from Barcelona – somehow seemed to warm him from within. 'You didn't write them... well, a *pervy* email, did you? Nothing specifically mentioning Nikki's bum?'

Jeremy frowned and shook his head, releasing a tiny swarm of tobacco fireflies into the starless sky. 'Nah. I was really sensible. First time I wrote, I just said I needed to get a message to her. The second time, I said it was urgent. And the third time, I said it was a life or death medical emergency. They just sent me back the same email.'

'Saying what, exactly?'

'That they appreciated my interest in their models, but that they weren't prepared to enter into correspondence regarding individual girls. *Blah, blah, blah.*'

'And there wasn't a phone number to try?'

'Nope.'

'Postal address?'

'Nah.' Jeremy took a final drag on his cigarette, extinguished it on the balcony wall and headed indoors. There, on the laptop, in various incriminatingly fleshy tones, was the web page where Wes had originally downloaded Nikki's video. Gently closing the screen, Jeremy collapsed into Lisa's outsize swivel chair, hoiked his bare knees beneath his chin and began rubbing them vigorously. 'There were no contact details at all. Just the email address of the porn company.'

'Hm.'

Jeremy extended a foot and gave himself a little push. The contents of Lisa's flat circled around him – the floor-to-ceiling Jaime Hernandez prints they'd been given by Callum, Jeremy's boss at the Brick Lane furniture workshop where he whiled away twenty or thirty hours a week; the threadbare Persian rug Lisa had brought from her parents' home in Whitby; the stout oak daybed that Jeremy had made for Lisa when he moved in. The *vacant* daybed – one of several venues around the flat where Jeremy often found himself waking up these days – invariably hungover, invariably clutching one of Lisa's coats, or a pillowcase, or a shoe. *Anything that still smelt of her.* He sighed and gave himself another spin. When Lisa was at home, there was never enough room to escape each other's arms or kisses. Without her, the flat was soulless – an echoing vault of memories and shadows, nine floors up in a cheerless edifice of glass and steel.

'I've got it.' Claire's triumphant tone jolted him out of his melancholy daydream. 'Definitely.'

Jeremy scrabbled for where the phone had fallen on to his shoulder. 'Huh?'

'I've got it. I know how you can get the address of the porn people.'

'How?'

'First, you set up another email account. And make sure it's got a really filthy name – *HotSlutVixen69* or something. Then send them an email with a few dirty photographs attached. Girly ones, obviously – not photos of *your* disgusting cadaver. Tell them you're the girl in the pictures, and that you're desperate to audition for them. Ask them what address to turn up at. Doddle.'

Jeremy processed the idea for a second. 'You are a *seriously* devious young woman, Claire Campbell.'

'Why, thank you, Jeremy,' Claire replied, her warm Glaswegian burr failing to conceal the merest hint of pride. 'All you have to do now is find some really depraved pictures. I'm sure that's not beyond the abilities of the Shagfinder General.'

Jeremy nodded modestly. 'The *ex*-Shagfinder, kid. You're right, though. Your uncle Jezzer *does* know a thing or two about the photographic arts. I'll crack on with it tonight.' He glanced at the photo of herself that Lisa had stuck to the window. She'd positioned it so that when you faced it from the giant swivel chair, you were looking directly towards Shanghai. *Clever lass, my Lisa.* 'It'll be good to think about you looking at me, back in London,' she'd said, breaking the awkward silence that had preceded the arrival of her taxi. She'd stuck a picture of Tim and Claire on the window, too (direction: Barcelona), and a blurry snap of Dave the barman standing in the snug of the Fat Ox (direction: Whitby), 'so you'll always know you've got your friends around you.' Then the taxi had arrived and she'd gone. Six weeks ago, now. *Six weeks without so much as a phone call.*

Jeremy swivelled a few degrees to the right, so that he was once more facing Barcelona. He sensed that his conversation with Claire had run its natural course, but didn't want to put the phone down yet. 'So what are you up to tonight, then?'

'Night in with young Timothy. Pizza, bottle of cheap Rioja and an episode of *House Of Cards*, dubbed into Catalan.'

Jeremy grunted approvingly. After all, he reminded himself, it was a picture of connubial harmony that he'd personally engineered, bringing Claire and his old school friend Tim together the previous winter. It was also a picture he'd recently witnessed first hand when he'd materialised uninvited on Tim and Claire's Barcelona doorstep, wild-eyed and incoherent, two months earlier. Claire had guessed that Jeremy's unexpected appearance had been Lisa-related, but not even Tim – who'd sat up all night with him, plying him with black coffee – had been able to extract any details. And when Lisa had left for Shanghai a few days later, Jeremy hadn't told his closest friends about *that*, either. Raising his can of Löwenbräu, Jeremy silently saluted the photograph of Tim and Claire on the window. 'And how's our extra special boy? Are you looking after him?'

'Well, he's missing you. Obviously. He pines sometimes at night.'

'Aw.'

'And how's Lisa? She okay?'

For a fleeting moment, Jeremy fought the urge to

confess everything. He gripped the handset, staring hard at his ingrowing toenail. 'Lisa's fine, kid. Absolutely grand.'

'And she doesn't mind you emailing porn stars in America, on Wes's behalf?'

'She's all for it,' he said airily and then, with more certainty, 'She thinks people should learn to face their responsibilities. She thinks *I* should, anyway.'

'Sounds like you two had a major discussion.'

'Mm. Something like that.'

For a second, the light hiss of the long distance phone line was all that Jeremy could hear. Then Claire spoke. 'Oh, I think Tim's back with the wine.' The sound of Claire's footsteps on the tiled apartment floor echoed in Jeremy's earpiece as she skipped over to the balcony. 'Yes, it's him. He's just coming up the stairs.'

Jeremy closed his eyes, recollecting the view from Claire and Tim's flat. His voice grew wistful. 'I bet there's a few pretty Spanish lasses out tonight, aren't there? Down in the square?'

'They are, actually.'

'Lots of them?'

'Few hundred, I'd say.' Claire's voice dropped half a register. 'Quite a few of them are naked, actually, Jez.'

'Seriously?'

'It's the festival of *Santa Desnudo*. It's traditional for the girls to go round naked. Google it if you don't believe me. I'd be out there myself, except for the fact that Tim gets really funny about it.' In the background, Jeremy could just hear the sound of a door closing. Claire's voice became faint as she held the receiver away from her mouth. 'You don't like me running around the streets naked, do you, sweetheart?'

Jeremy smiled at Tim's familiar grunt of assent from somewhere in the background. 'There are *seriously* naked girls in the streets?'

'Aye. Honestly. Look it up on Google. *Santa Desnudo.*'
'I will. I'll call you back.'

Claire's hand was already hovering over the receiver when the telephone rang some thirty seconds later.

'There *is* no festival of *Santa Desnudo*, is there?'

'*Sure* there is, Jez.'

'No one's running around naked, though, are they? Down in the square?'

'Thousands of people, Jez. Mostly eighteen year-old nymphomaniac blondes with a fetish for gullible Yorkshiremen.'

'Liar.'

'Pervert.'

'Goodnight, Claire.'

'Goodnight, Jeremy.'

5

a very pleasant little chat, actually

Later that night the phone rang in Sefton Street. Wes sat up in his bath and wiped the soap from his eyes, straining to make out who Gabi was talking to in the sitting room below. It was hard to tell; the lateness of the hour suggested family, but there wasn't enough savage invective or shouting for it to be Gabi's father. Suddenly, the temperature of the bathwater seemed to drop a degree. *Jeremy. It could only be Jeremy.*

Wes slipped out of the tub and tiptoed naked to the top of the stairs, momentarily torn between making a dash for his dressing gown in the spare bedroom and lingering in the chilly breeze on the landing. Then Gabi's voice made the decision for him. 'Byron! Come down. Jeremy's on the phone.'

'There in a tick.'

When Wes entered the sitting room a minute later, Gabrielle's body language was impossible to read. She didn't look up from her book as he crossed to the telephone table and picked up the receiver, although Wes knew that his

51

wife's apparently languid posture – serenely feline, feet tucked neatly beneath her bottom – was nothing more than flimsy camouflage for her real purpose. *Earwigging. Analysing. Archiving.* From her neutral expression, however, it was clear that Jeremy hadn't been asking Dr Wynstanley any questions about cancer or how frequently most women self-examined their buttocks. Wes had actually half expected to find the word 'Nikki' hanging in foot-high speech bubbles in the air... but no, no, there was nothing. He smiled, hoping that an unaccustomed stretching of his mouth muscles might somehow disguise the note of dread in his voice. 'Hey. Jez.'

'Evening, Wes. Sorry for dragging you out of the bath. I wouldn't have called on the landline, but your mobile's been switched off for days.'

'Has it?'

'Aye. Anyway, I've got some good news about Nikki.'

'Wonderful, wonderful.' Wes's smile became an icy rictus. *So you decided to ignore my very simple request, did you? You bastard. You utter, utter bastard.* 'That's really great. Good stuff.'

At the other end of the line, Jeremy's voice darkened in confusion. 'Is Gabi still in the room, mate?'

'Yes, yes!' Wes laughed. 'You're quite right.'

'Ah. Got you. Enough said. We had a very pleasant little chat, actually.'

'So I heard.'

'Nice lass, your missus. Witty. Intelligent.'

'Very much so.'

'Aye, well. It doesn't matter that she's listening. I'll need to see you face-to-face, anyway. It's time for an emergency summit, kid.'

'Right, right.'

'How about tomorrow afternoon? Three o'clock at the Brick?'

Wes tucked the receiver beneath his chin and turned

with a reassuring smile towards Gabi. While he'd been talking to Jeremy, she'd silently put her book down, and now she returned his glance with an unblinking, enquiring stare. Unable to hold her gaze for more than second, Wes turned back to the wall. 'Tomorrow? Splendid, Jeremy. Splendid.'

'Good lad. Don't be late.'

The line went dead.

6

no one gets left behind

Wes had guessed, even before he arrived at the Bricklayer's Arms, that Jeremy's 'emergency summit' would be an awkward encounter. The morning after Jeremy's phone call, Wes had rung his friend back but he'd been more irritated than reassured by the lad's insouciant tone, and how evasive he'd sounded when questioned regarding progress on the 'Nikki' front. 'Can't really talk on the blower, kid,' Jeremy had declared, breezily sidestepping the issue. 'Proper 'man' talk needs to take place in the pub. And anyway, I never had my pint on Tuesday. I've got some catching up to do.'

Since arriving at the Brick, though, they'd already 'caught up' three pints each, and despite Wes's pointed requests for information and repeated reminders that Nikki's welfare was meant to be his exclusive concern, it had been impossible to lure Jeremy into revealing any details regarding his 'good news'. It was an ominous sign; Jeremy had a history of exploiting his tolerance for alcohol to soften up the unwary.

Bracing himself against the toilet wall, Wes splashed a

handful of water over his face, rubbed his eyes and attempted to recompose his features in the mirror. It was no good, though – after three pints of strong beer, the edges of his mind were starting to feel squidgy and suggestible, and for the past half hour he'd found himself fighting a near-overwhelming urge to disappear back to Sefton Street for a Peperami Wideboy and his daily dose of *The Chase*. It didn't bode well. *No more beer*, he resolved, closing his eyes and positioning his face beneath the hand dryer. The scream of its motor rang in his ears as hot air scorched his eyelids. *No more beer or evasion or pork scratchings. Not until the bastard tells me what he's been up to.*

'I got you another pint,' Jeremy announced, the moment Wes emerged from the toilet. 'That's proper beer, fresh from Yorkshire. Comes down a big pipe from Keighley. Unlike these double Jack Daniel's' – he reached behind him and retrieved a further pair of glasses – 'which come courtesy of the good folks of Lynchburg, Tennessee. Get it down you, mate.'

Wes regarded the brimming pints with apprehension. 'I can't, Jez. I don't feel so good. I'm full.'

'Nonsense. You've just had a wee-wee.' Jeremy delved into his coat pocket and withdrew a fistful of small, gaudily-coloured bags, which he tossed on to the already-crowded table. 'And you'll need your beer to wash down your pork scratchings. Drink up, kid – while it's nice and frothy.'

'I don't think so.' Wes slid the beer to one side, composing his features into his best impression of uncompromising rectitude – a look he'd picked up from the more repressed ex-public schoolboys at medical school. After a second or two, he began wishing he'd practised the look in the pub toilet first, since he suspected it might faintly resemble the 'smouldering' one Gabi had been so absurdly keen on during the earlier, more sexually exhausting years of their courtship. 'Not until you tell me what's happened with Nikki.'

He felt Jeremy's eyes boring into him, searching him out, scanning his features for any signs of weakness. Finally, his friend nodded and slid his own beer to the side of the table. Now, at last, the two men could talk. 'Okay. Well, I've made some headway, kid. I've found out the address of the porn people. It's in California.'

Wes chewed this over for some moments before nodding warily. Nodding to Jeremy could have the same status as a legally binding contract with anyone else – you didn't do it lightly. 'Nice one. Cool. That's progress,' he eventually conceded. 'I'll write them a letter tomorrow morning. Tell them about Nikki. Tell them how important it is that she gets to a doctor as soon as possible.'

It was a huge relief, actually. Wes's own furtive trawls of the internet hadn't revealed any new sightings of Nikki and, alone in the darkness of the spare room, he'd spent a fretful night considering the terrible consequences of failure. After all, while Nikki had in one respect only been a name on his laptop screen, she'd also been his sole companion through countless insomniac nights, his only human contact during the endless empty evenings when Gabi had been forced to work late. *The only one he could talk to. The only one he'd felt truly close to.* Wes reached for his fresh pint of beer and downed a mouthful. It tasted good.

'Mm. Well, you *could* write to them, yes.' Jeremy regarded his friend over the top of his own pint glass. 'But I don't reckon it's such a fantastic idea, mate.'

Wes frowned. 'You don't?'

'No.'

'How so?'

Jeremy lowered his glass and shrugged. 'It's just that when we emailed them, they didn't seem particularly bothered. Didn't send us replies. Didn't say they'd pass on the message to Nikki.'

'So?'

'So why should they pass on a letter? It's easy to ignore a

letter, kid. Think about all the bills you've never opened. All the junk mail. And even if the porn people *did* open your letter, who's to say they'd take it seriously?'

Fleetingly, Wes was tempted to point out that the bills for Sefton Street tended to be addressed to (and very efficiently paid by) Dr G A Wynstanley. Then he thought better of it. Jeremy's face, after all, was quite serious, and his observation had some merit. 'What do you think I should do, then?'

'I think we should go over there and tell them about Nikki. Try to see her ourselves, if we can.'

'Go where?'

'California.'

For a moment, Wes held Jeremy's gaze. Then, for reasons he couldn't quite explain, he suddenly found his eyes swivelling around the half-empty pub, a manic grin on his face. Had anyone else heard what Jeremy had just said? Not by the look of things. In fact, everything in the Brick looked entirely untouched by the tiny hand grenade that had just fallen from his friend's lips. The middle-aged bloke with the dog who'd just settled down with half a mild? *Oblivious.* The two old boys quietly putting the world to rights at the corner table? *Indifferent.* Wes's eyes slowly began returning to Jeremy's face, hoping that the face in question would have broken into a sarcastic leer by the time they got there. It hadn't. Wes cleared his throat. 'Beg pardon, mate?'

'We should go to California. It's the right thing to do.'

'I can't go to California, Jez.'

'Why not? It's not like you're madly busy, is it?'

Wes shrugged. It was, he supposed, a fair point – but not one he was prepared to concede to his clearly insane companion. He already felt, only two minutes into their discussion about Nikki, that things were getting out of hand. And experience had taught him that letting Jeremy gain the advantage in situations like this could have disastrous, potentially life-changing consequences. *Time to get unreasonable, then.* 'I'm not going to California. I don't go anywhere without a 'W' in the post code – you know that, mate. That's why I can never come and visit you in Docklands, or go back to Yorkshire to visit my mum.'

'You're coming to California.'

'Like hell I am. Do you have any idea how expensive it'd be to fly there?'

'About five hundred quid, give or take.'

Wes eyebrows arched in surprise. 'Is that all?'

'Aye. Bugger all to a man of your means.'

'Ah, well, you're forgetting that I'm like the Queen, Jez. I've no money of my own.' Wes leaned back in his chair and took another sip of beer. 'And young Gabi keeps a very tight hold on the purse strings.'

Jeremy smiled and edged forwards across the table. 'I think she'll cough up the readies.'

'Why?'

'Because you're going to tell her you want to attend... *this.*' Jeremy reached into his coat pocket and pulled out a dog-eared computer print-off. He wiped the puddles of beer off the table with his sleeve and placed the paper in front of Wes. 'It's an international conference on *New Paths In Surgery*. It's in San Francisco, it's in just over a week's time, and they're still accepting registrations. I phoned them up.' Like clouds parting, Jeremy's mouth broke into a sloppy grin. He raised his pint glass, drained it in a single mammoth gulp and pointed the opening at his friend. Wes stared into the foamy orifice with a gnawing feeling of apprehension. 'It's bloody amazing what you can find on the internet, isn't it? And Gabi's always on at you to get a proper job. So she can't object to you going to a surgery conference, can she?'

'So – let me get this straight – you expect me to go to this conference in San Francisco, and while I'm out there, you expect me to pay Nikki a little visit and tell her she's got cancer?'

'Precisely. The porn place is only about an inch-and-a-half away from San Francisco on the map. Place called Chatsworth. Sounds quite nice.'

Horror-struck, Wes surveyed his friend's expression of blank intransigence. Whichever way he looked at it, he seemed to have the case sewn up. The only thing Jeremy hadn't considered was the extent to which this further involvement with Nikki would inevitably seep into other areas of his life. The bits of his life he really, *really* liked. The bits that were currently being very generously funded by members of the Wynstanley family. Wes closed his eyes, trying to buy a moment's relief from Jeremy's laser vision, but it was no good. There, in the dark cavern of his mind, was an equally vexing image of Nikki's bottom. 'I still can't go,' he eventually muttered. 'I just can't.'

'Why not?'

In desperation, Wes scoured his mind for an argument Jeremy would identify with; a position he'd instinctively understand. And then an idea occurred to him. It was a risky strategy, certainly, to take the battle to the enemy's gate. *To confront Jeremy with his own specialist subject – the films of Dan Aykroyd.* 'Remember *Ghostbusters*?' he said.

Jeremy's eyes narrowed. 'With almost uncanny clarity. What of it?'

'Well, in *Ghostbusters*, they weren't allowed to cross the streams from the proton packs, right? Because it would cause the destruction of all life in the cosmos.'

Jeremy nodded slowly. 'Uh-huh.'

'Well, that's why I can't go to California, mate. It'd be crossing the streams. I'd be bringing the 'Nikki' stream of my life into contact with the 'Gabi' stream.' Wes slammed his fist into his palm to illustrate the point. 'Nikki's been a real friend to me. She's funny, she's clever, she's kind. But she's only ever been *virtual* to me,' he continued, possibly trying to convince himself as much as Jeremy. 'A name in a chat room. Not part of real life. I never wanted to *meet* her.

I'm a happily married man. I don't want to cross the streams. It'd end badly, Jez. Very badly.'

Jeremy's eyes narrowed further. 'Aye, aye,' he breathed. 'Crossing the streams *would* be bad. But not as bad as leaving someone behind.'

'Leaving someone behind? Who? Where?'

'Nikki, kid.' Jeremy reached across the table and poured half of Wes's beer into his own empty glass. 'She's got cancer, in case you'd forgotten. Not virtual cancer. Not computer cancer. 'Cancer' cancer – which, we have to assume, she hasn't got a clue about. And you know the rules – no one gets left behind. *Black Hawk Down.*'

'*Black Hawk Down?*'

'Aye, I've been watching a lot of Ridley Scott films, recently. There's more depth to his work than Dan Aykroyd's.'

Wes's stomach sank. *How could he have possibly known that Jeremy had abandoned Dan Aykroyd for Ridley Scott?* He leaned back in his chair and sighed. 'Well, if you don't want to leave Nikki behind, maybe you should go visit her by yourself.'

Jeremy drained his glass, refilled it from the remainder of Wes's beer and drained it again. 'I would. Gladly. Nikki might be your friend, but any friend of yours is also a friend of mine. And I'm not leaving my friend to snuff it. But at the end of the day, I'm just a grunt – GI Jeremy. You're a bloody medic. This is what you trained for six years to do. This is your gig. So you've got to go.'

'And if I don't?'

'Don't make me answer that, mate.' Jeremy shook his head sadly. 'Your uncle Jezzer's a reasonable bloke, but he's only got so much patience.'

It was true, Wes reflected – there was definitely a limit to how far you could push Jeremy. And although it had been a while since he'd put the Wednesday night kickboxing on hold, his friend still possessed the commanding physique of a freshly-shaved baboon. Regardless, Wes had to know where he stood. 'Seriously, though. What'll you do if I don't go?' he said.

Jeremy sighed. 'If you won't come to California with me, then I'm going to tell Gabi all about Nikki. All about the porn site. About everything.'

'You'd be shooting yourself in the foot, I'm afraid.'

'Can't see why.'

'Because I'd tell Lisa exactly the same thing, you bloody idiot.' Wes smiled sadly. It was exactly the kind of Mexican standoff he'd spent the last five minutes hoping for – exactly the kind of comfortable stalemate that had, thus far, characterised his brief marriage to Gabi. Wes regarded Jeremy narrowly from beneath the brim of his imaginary sombrero. 'It's just not going to happen, *gringo*.' He reached for the pork scratchings and tore open the bag. 'Not unless you want me telling Lisa that I got the address of Nikki's website from the personal recommendation of my good mate Jeremy.'

'Doesn't bother me, pal,' said Jeremy. He tossed a pork scratching high in the air and cocked his head backwards. Two seconds later, it dropped noiselessly into his gaping maw. 'Tell her. Tell Lisa whatever lies you like. I'll give you her number if it'll help.'

Wes's smile never wavered, but something about Jeremy's expression had started making him feel uneasy. 'I don't think you mean that.'

'Certainly do. Seriously. I might tell her myself, actually.'

'You'd have to be off your noddle. She hates porn. She'd be livid.'

'Probably, yes. But I reckon she'll get over it, given time.' For a moment, Jeremy was silent. Then he reached once again into the pork scratchings bag and withdrew the largest he could find. Leaning back in his chair, he placed the scratching on the very tip of his nose so that it balanced there like a tiny, salty ballerina. He closed one eye and addressed Wes over his left cheekbone. 'What you've got to remember about me and Lisa, mate, is that we go back a long, long time. Right back to nursery school. So she *knows* me. She knows that the first girl I showed my willy to was Abigail Pollard in Miss Peck's class, aged six. She knows that the first girl I snogged was Debbie Miller, aged eight, under the tarpaulin in Tim's dad's allotment. She knows what you and me got up to on that geography field trip to Nidderdale in the fourth year of secondary school. I shagged her cousin Erica in her bed on the night of her eighteenth birthday party, and three of her closest friends in the two months that followed. She knows what happened to the rear suspension on Thick Brian's Datsun.' Suddenly, Jeremy jerked his head backwards. The pork scratching flew six inches into the air, before landing squarely in Jeremy's mouth. His grin seemed to loom towards Wes over the table as he rearranged his gangling limbs. 'What I'm trying to say is that Lisa *knows* I've been a bad, bad boy. Bad as bad can be. And she *still* wants to be with me. So, yes – while there's no doubt that she'd be mightily pissed off if she thought I'd been hanging round in porny chat rooms, I hardly think it'd be a dumping offence.' He turned the pork scratchings packet around so it now faced Wes. 'How do you think Gabi's going to take it when I tell her about you and Nikki?'

'I don't think you *are* going to tell her.'

'I hope I won't have to, Wes.'

Wes took a pork scratching, attempting to imbue the gesture with a bravado he now no longer felt. 'How, exactly? Are you going to yell it through the letterbox? Send her anonymous notes? Track her down at work?' He popped the pork scratching in his mouth. *Ugh one of the squidgy ones.* 'I don't think you know which hospital she works at, do you, Jez?'

'Don't need to. I'm going to call her mobile.'

'You don't know her number.'

'Don't need it.'

'No?'

'No, kid. Because I'm psychic. I'm going to read your mind.'

Jeremy's eyes narrowed and his face assumed an expression of eerie calm. Then his hand extended across the table until his forefinger hovered an inch from the bridge of Wes's nose. 'It's coming through, mate. Here it comes. Gabi's phone number... is... 0... 7... 7... 0...'

Wes stared back at Jeremy's flickering eyelids, horror-struck. Although he didn't believe for a moment that Jeremy had somehow acquired the third eye, the way he was reeling off the digits made him feel increasingly uneasy. 'Sod off, Jez.'

'0... 9... 0... 0...'

'For Christ's sake, Jez.'

'9... 2... 4.'

Wes felt the remaining colour drain from his face. 'How the hell do you know that?'

'I *told* you, infidel,' Jeremy sighed. 'I'm psychic.' He grinned and reached into his coat pocket. 'And I borrowed your phone while you were in the khazi.' Jeremy held up the iPhone and waggled it playfully. 'That helped, too. Which symbol do you press to make a call? Is it this one at the bottom?'

'*Bastard.*' Wes launched himself across the table. Even as he did so, however, he knew it was little more than a gesture – and he felt nothing but a predictable wave of resignation when Jeremy caught his wrist with his free hand and clamped it to the table's edge, locking him in an ungainly sprawl across the beer mats and the pork scratchings packets. 'Bastard.'

'*Shhh.* I'm on the phone.' Jeremy smiled at his friend's face and gave his wrist a companionable twist. 'Oh, it's ringing. Oh, hi. Gabrielle? Hello. Hello, yes. No, it's Jeremy, actually. That's right. Jeremy. Lisa? Oh, she's very well, thank you. Ah, well, it's not Wes I wanted to talk to – although I did want to talk to you *about* Wes. Uh-huh.' Jeremy tucked the phone under his chin and groped beneath Wes's sleeve for a pork scratching. He popped it in his mouth and winked at Wes. 'Uh-huh. Well, it's something I think you should know about. Difficult to put into words. Mm. No, nothing's happened to the Mercedes. Well, it's porn, actually. Pornography, yes. Not gay, no. Not as far as I know, anyway. Apparently, yes. A chat room. Aye, there *was* one particular girl. Uh-huh. Uh-huh. Well, I don't blame you. Yeah. That's perfectly understandable. Men *are* all bastards, aren't they? Mm. Aye, he is, actually.' Jeremy released Wes's wrist and passed him the phone. 'It's Gabi on the line, mate. She wants a word.' He lowered his voice to a hoarse whisper. '*Just between the two of us, she sounds a bit pissed off.*'

Wes snatched the phone, standing up so abruptly that his chair tumbled backwards on to the floor. 'Gabs? It's all complete bollocks. Whatever Jeremy's just told you, he's just been fooling... *Dave?* Dave – is that you?' He retreated a few steps, suddenly aware of the rapt attention of the pub's afternoon drinkers. Brushing himself down, Wes cast a baleful eye in Jeremy's direction. 'How's tricks at the Fat Ox, mate? Good, good. Excellent. Me? No, no. Still not working, *per se*. Gabi? Oh, you know. Feisty as ever. Yes. Uh-huh. Loving the fish slice, yes. Thanks again.'

Jeremy picked up the packet of pork scratchings and tipped its remaining contents into his mouth before retrieving Wes's chair from the floor and gently guiding his friend back to the table. 'So you're going to ask Gabi to stump up the cash for the San Francisco conference?'

'It's totally hypothetical, anyway. She'll say no.'

'But you'll come with me to find Nikki, if she says yes?'

'I've got no choice, have I?' he sighed. 'Although I'd like to have it put on the record, here and now, that I have a profound sense of foreboding about the whole venture.

Not just my normal, day-to-day sense of foreboding.' Wes reached into his pocket and withdrew a rumpled cigarette packet. 'I feel like I've just made a pact with the devil.'

Grinning, Jeremy waved away his friend's pained expression. 'I'm only doing this for you, kid. For your spiritual wellbeing. For your karmic stability and to keep you on the right side of the big guy upstairs. It'll be fine. It'll be more than fine, actually – it'll be fun. Remember fun? Trust me.'

7

all work and no play makes jez a dull boy

I'm only doing this for you, kid. What on earth had possessed him to say that? Jeremy flicked unseeingly through the TV channels, guiltily weighing the words in his mind. He despised lies, but whichever way he added them up, the things he'd said in the Bricklayer's Arms hadn't amounted to the truth. Not even close. He sighed, pausing mid-channel-surf on a flickering image of two leathery-looking blokes having a set-to in a pub. *Eastenders.* For a second he peered into the screen, trying to make sense of it, but their words seemed over-rehearsed and full of implausible Cockney bluster, like they'd just stepped out of some nightmarish Chas & Dave sing-along. Jeremy had never been much of a one for TV, mind. Even when he was a kid – even before he'd discovered Thin Lizzy, and the Fat Ox, and lasses – he'd always instinctively sensed that television represented captivity. That it was an insidious drug, lacking the intensity of mucking about in the street, of the school playground, of moonlit cliff-top rambles, of a bag of chips from the Magpie Cafe and – when he was a few years older – the slim possibility of a bunk-up afterwards.

There'd been more telly than bunk-ups in his life recently, mind – *Eastenders* especially. When Lisa had left six weeks earlier, Jeremy had silently pledged to watch every episode of the bloody thing in her absence, so he could bring her back up to speed when she got home. So they could pick up seamlessly from where they'd left off. So that, looking back, it would seem like the unfortunate incident that drove Lisa away had never happened. But the momentum of their life together had only taken one empty weekend to peter out, and the chaotic vacuum that had been left in its wake seemed to grow silently wider every day. Maybe that was why he'd been so heavy on Wes to get a collaborator on board with Project Nikki, to help him fill the void? Or maybe he'd seen a similar void in Wes that the lad hadn't seen himself? Or maybe – quite possibly – it really *was* all about belting round the globe to save a young lass's life?

Whatever the explanation, the Nikki situation had clearly come to light just in time. Jeremy flicked off the TV and wandered over to the large pile of Lisa's CD's that he'd spread out on the sitting room rug. *Just in time to stop me going a bit peculiar. Just in time to wedge a sponge in my mental plughole.* He'd always needed to prevent himself getting bored or introspective, though. He'd known it since he'd first watched *The Shining* on video with Tim, back when they were twelve or thirteen. Tim's terror had been immediate and fleeting, arriving in a flurry of axes and snow-covered mazes, and departing just as quickly. But Jeremy's fear had grown on him in the days and weeks that had followed, as he'd come to recognise the qualities he shared with the young Jack Nicholson. *All work and no play makes Jez a dull boy.* And six weeks holed up in Lisa's Docklands flat was enough to make anyone go a bit mental.

There were clearly more benefits to Project Nikki than a complimentary dose of therapy, though. It was a situation from which everyone emerged a winner – not least young Nikki herself. *Aye*, thought Jeremy, picking out a Belle & Sebastian CD and slipping it into the hi-fi. *Going to California's definitely the sensible thing to do.* After all, doing something so unequivocally good was bound to level things up in the grand cosmic scheme, surely? That was just plain karma, wasn't it? *Jeremy does a bad thing – Lisa goes away. Jeremy does a good thing...* well, would it really be too much to ask for the universe to do him a little Lisa-shaped favour? Such golden opportunities for redemption didn't just fall into your lap – or, he mused, your laptop – every day.

Jeremy gently turned up the volume on Belle & Sebastian and took a sip of bourbon. He usually found Lisa's taste in bands (mostly fey indie boys with crap hair) to be quite depressing, but tonight he could almost see the appeal. He looked at the CD sleeve. Aye – clearly this Stuart Murdoch bloke could do with getting a square meal inside him, but he certainly knew how to hold a tune. He'd mention it to Lisa when she got home; show her he was prepared to widen his horizons. To change. To grow.

He closed his eyes and imagined the conversation they'd have, when she got back from Shanghai. *What did you do while I was away?* she'd ask. *Oh, nothing much*, he'd reply. *Listened to a bit of Belle & Sebastian, actually. Saw Wes a couple of times. Oh, and I saved someone's life.*

It was all so very different from the conversation they'd had before she left, he reflected. Even now, six weeks down the line, he could still recall it with sickening clarity – word for word, blow for blow. He remembered creeping back to the flat after his weekend in Barcelona; padding barefoot across the floor towards the kitchen; then seeing Lisa's sleeping face, pressed against the arm of the sofa, still streaked with the tears she'd cried during the night.

You've never had to think about anyone but yourself, she'd said later, passing him a second cup of coffee. *Never had to be an adult. Never had to take responsibility for anything or anyone. You've never even had to apply for a job, or lived away from your mother's.* Jeremy winced, as he always did, as he recalled the look of quiet resignation on Lisa's face. *I love you, Jeremy*, she'd said. *But I need to be with another grown-up. Someone who can take responsibility for their life without pegging it to Barcelona at the first hint of grief.*

If Jeremy'd had a few more girlfriends – as opposed to quickies, or knee-tremblers, or leg-overs – he might have been more certain about whether or not this constituted being dumped. He'd avoided thinking about it at the time, and had managed to force the thought from his mind every time it had raised its ugly head since. After all, if she'd *really* wanted him out of her life, why would Lisa have let him stay in the flat while she was in Shanghai? Why would she have said she needed to 'think about things'? But these last couple of weeks... well, it'd been getting harder and harder to stay optimistic. Maybe she'd only come back after he'd left? And if she *did* still want him, then why hadn't she called?

Jeremy downed the last of his bourbon and poured another, and turned up the Belle & Sebastian again, flicking the tracks backwards towards *The Model*, Lisa's favourite song. It was now so loud that it could only be moments before the neighbours started banging on the ceiling, but nothing could have been further from his thoughts. He closed his eyes and let Lisa's music wash over him, let himself go with it, felt his feet begin to move across the softly vibrating floor. In fact, he wouldn't have even noticed that the telephone was ringing if, dancing blindly across the room, he hadn't fallen headlong over the coffee table and crashed unceremoniously into the bookcase. Heart racing, he staggered back to the hi-fi, killed the music and breathlessly pulled out the antenna on the phone. 'Lise?'

'Er... no.'

Jeremy blinked away the sadness that suddenly threatened to overwhelm him. 'Ah. Wes. Sorry, mate. How's tricks?'

'Fine. I asked Gabrielle about paying for the San Francisco conference.'

'Yeah? And what happened?'

'She said yes. She said I should go, Jez. She's paying for everything. First class.'

8

it's not a self-indulgence thing; it's a legroom thing

Sefton Street, Putney SW15. 15.54 GMT.

'Let me just get this straight.' Jeremy's eyes flicked from Wes to the minicab driver and back again. 'You two lads *know* each other?'

If Wes had been able to speak – if his mouth hadn't contained quite so much of the minicab driver's outsize puffa jacket – then an outright denial would have seemed like a certainty. He'd undoubtedly looked startled when Abiola had leapt from the wheezing Mondeo and engulfed him in an unyielding bear hug. '*Sure* we know each other,' the driver finally declared, releasing Wes and turning his attention to the Mondeo's misshapen boot. 'Dr Wesley is my good friend. I know his lovely wife and his father-in-law too. How *is* Dr Wynstanley?'

Wes eyed him sceptically. 'Which one?'

Abiola's mouth split into a leer that even Jeremy couldn't help but admire. 'Your *wife*, man. Your charming wife.'

'She's very well. Thank you.'

'And your father-in-law?'

'He's a borderline psychopath with a God complex.'

'Wonderful. And are you enjoying married life?'

'Every minute.'

'Good, good. And the Mercedes?'

'...is enjoying married life, too, yes.'

'Splendid!' Abiola finished loading the boot and turned conspiratorially to Jeremy. 'Nice package, eh? *Nice package!*'

Jeremy said nothing, but allowed a tiny smile to play around the edges of his mouth. He'd been doing a lot of that today, Wes noticed – that 'tiny smile' thing – and it unnerved him. In fact, everything about Jeremy had unnerved him today, from his freshly-shaven countenance and crisp linen shirt to the apparent loss of his broad Yorkshire accent. Wes would be much relieved, he reflected, when he could dump Jeremy at the Economy check-in queue at Heathrow – although the striking visual image of his friend would take several large gins in the First Class Lounge to fully obliterate.

'What the hell's going on?' he'd demanded when Jeremy turned up at Sefton Street, seemingly dressed as a leisurewear model from a 1980's golfing catalogue. 'Where are your Greek army boots? Who helped you put the tie on? You haven't got religion, have you?'

'I'm getting into character,' Jeremy had replied, carrying a brown leather holdall across the threshold. 'I need to feel... *doctoral.*' That's when he'd done his first tiny smile, and he'd continued doing them, seemingly at random, while Wes had finished secreting miniature tins of snuff into his hand luggage.

'What are these, then? It's customary to shove any druggy contraband up your arse, mate,' Jeremy observed helpfully, removing one of the tins from the pocket of Wes's bag and holding it up to the light.

'They're snuff,' Wes replied. 'Powdered tobacco. Perfectly legal,' he'd added, noticing Jeremy's expression of bewilderment. 'You can have a tin if you want. It's the only civilised form of tobacco you can use on a plane.'

Jeremy had done another of his tiny smiles, shaken his head sadly and returned the tin to the bag. 'It's very bad for your health, the baccy, mate. I've given up smoking, myself. Filthy habit.'

And then the agonised moan of Abiola's approaching Mondeo had drawn the two friends out on to the pavement, and the first steps of their six thousand mile mercy mission.

The atmosphere during the ride to the airport was, however, somewhat strained, with even Abiola abstaining from talking until shortly after joining the M4. Then, clearly buoyed by the Mondeo's triumph at having negotiated the motorway slip road (and detecting only a light smattering of traffic on the road ahead), he turned round to address his passengers. 'So. Are you going on holiday, Dr Wesley?'

'No. Medical conference. California.'

'And we're looking for a porn actress called Nikki. *Fuck!*' Jeremy stared incredulously at the spot on his upper thigh where Wes had just punched him. 'What the hell was that for?' He lowered his voice a fraction, just below the level of the minicab's agonised exhaust note. 'You can tell taxi drivers anything, mate. They're not allowed to repeat a word. They're like psychiatrists, or lawyers, or barmen.'

'Just don't do or say anything that's going to bump up the fare. Last time I saw him, he charged me a tenner just for offering his opinion of my wife's arse.'

Wes glanced up fearfully. Sure enough, there was Abiola's face, beaming in the rear view mirror. It winked chummily at the pair in the back seat and spoke. 'And why would Dr Wesley be looking for a porn actress?'

'Because she's got cancer, poor lass, and Dr Wesley wants to make her better.'

The Mondeo's gentle drift towards the central reservation indicated that this was truly a 'hands off the wheel' revelation for Abiola. He twisted round in his seat to better marvel at the saintly figure in the back of his minicab. 'Dr Wesley is a wonderful man! A brilliant physician and a truly wonderful man.' He turned to face Jeremy. 'And a very *generous* man. When I found out that Dr Wesley needed a cab to the airport, I jumped at the chance. Last time I gave Dr Wesley a ride, he gave me a fifty pound tip. *Fifty pounds!*' Abiola momentarily redirected his attention to the road, dabbing the brakes just in time to prevent the Mondeo ploughing into the rear of a Belgian motor home. The he returned his attention to Jeremy. 'And you, sir. Are you a doctor too?'

'I'm a colleague of Dr Wesley.'

Wes looked at him accusingly. Then his jaw slowly dropped. 'Oh, God,' said Wes. 'I've just worked it out. The shirt and tie. The new haircut. Those horrible little smiles you keep doing. You're trying to be *me*, aren't you? Why are you trying to be me?'

'Just trying to look the part, mate. Just trying to look the part.'

United Airlines Check-In Desk, Heathrow Airport. 17.54 GMT.

It's not a self-indulgence thing; it's a legroom thing. It's an arriving-in-the-morning-and-still-being-able-to-function thing. Jeremy straightened his tie and approached the check-in desk. *Lisa would understand.*

The check-in attendant took his passport, and Jeremy watched as her eyes skimmed down the back page. She was a pretty lass, he reflected – the sort of lass who, in his pre-Lisa days, he'd have definitely made a move on. *But not today.* No – today was about business, not pleasure. The

74

attendant swiped the passport, handed it back to Jeremy and smiled.

It was, even by Jeremy's standards, a seriously inviting smile. At its epicentre was a mouth that was on the naughty side of generous – but beyond its delicately lip-glossed borders, the smile radiated up over flawless skin towards the kind of eyes that Belle & Sebastian could have written whole albums about. Jeremy smiled back. Not the wry, nervous smile he'd stolen from Wes's repertoire, either, but his old Friday night special – the smile that was half in the eyes, half in the mouth, and half in the recipient's underwear. *Cue the Shagfinder.* 'Hi.'

'Hi.'

Jeremy allowed a moment to pass before speaking again, and when he did, he managed to imbue his words with just the slightest hint of enquiry – the suspicion that he'd half-recognised the girl behind the check-in desk from somewhere. *A recurring dream that had haunted him since adolescence? The front page of Vogue? Lovers in a former life?* 'Just the one bag today.'

Gently flexing his shoulders to lift it on to the scales, Jeremy was delighted to observe the tiniest hint of surprised delight in the girl's eye. He smiled again – and this time he really meant it. *I love it when they go all melty.*

The check-in assistant reached across for his documents. 'So, are you flying alone this evening, Mr Sykes?'

'I'm afraid so. And it's Dr Sykes, actually.' Jeremy lowered his voice and leaned forwards an inch, thrilled when – after a moment's agonised hesitation – the girl did likewise. 'I once met a Estonian girl who thought it was pronounced Dr Sex.' The gap between them closed by another half-inch. 'Imagine.'

The check-in girl inclined her head a millimetre to the side, arching her eyebrow as she did so. 'And what sort of doctor are you, Dr Sykes?'

'I'm a cardiologist. A heart surgeon. Best in the

business.'
    'Gosh.'

First class cabin, United Airlines flight 142, Heathrow Airport. 19.42 GMT.

The main thing about flying First Class, the way Wes saw it, wasn't so much the luxury. After all, most of the First Class perks – the gratis booze, the goodie bag, the lie-flat seats – were also available in Business. And a First Class ticket made no difference when it came to turbulence, or the recycled air, or the ridiculous plane-wide smoking ban.

No. The main thing about First Class was what it excluded. And at the moment, the most significant thing it excluded was Jeremy. Wes prised off his shoes and flexed his toes into the thick carpet. *No Jeremy, poncing around the place like a latter-day Dr Kildare, with his ridiculous new haircut and Oxfam suit. As if.* Closing his eyes, Wes spent a moment mentally listing the additional benefits of his First Class environment. It was the third time he'd played this game in the past five minutes, but he was a nervous flyer at the best of times and found the routine comforting. And there were, after all, many very pleasant things to account for. *The sublimely proportioned cabin crew; the six tins of Poschl snuff secreted in his hand luggage; the refined tones of his fellow flyers; the abundant champagne; the tastefully understated menu cards promising 'a dining experience to remember.'*

Wes opened his eyes and stared at the menu in his right hand. Somehow, in the past twenty seconds, it had become a screwed-up relic of its former self. Unclenching his fist, he flattened the menu out and tried to re-engage his enthusiasm for its lavishly-worded descriptions of the culinary delights to come, but to little avail. In fact, what had previously promised to be the gastronomic equivalent of a trolley-dash round Kim Kardashian's underwear drawer now sounded more like the last meal of a condemned man.

Gently cradling his stomach, Wes emitted a low moan that had little to do with his impending flight and even less to do with food. It was a sensation he'd become alarmingly familiar with over the past week – not quite the twitching cramps he experienced nightly when Gabi's key turned in the front door, but more like the uncontrollable butterflies that accompanied a first-race win on a twenty-pound accumulator. The last time he could remember a similar sensation was when... *oh God. When he'd first stumbled across Nikki's chat room on the internet. When he'd gasped at her bold, uninhibited questions; when he'd guiltily admitted how disastrously his marriage was going; when she'd sympathised, and said the kinds of things he'd always wished Gabi was capable of saying; when he'd first laughed at her wry observations and unhinged anecdotes...*

Wes fought the urge to squirm in embarrassment – not for the daft personal things he'd carelessly divulged during his six-month online dalliance, but for what he knew the next couple of days would undoubtedly hold in store. Materialising unannounced on Nikki's doorstep had never been part of their arrangement. Materialising with Whitby's Shagfinder General, even less so. *And as for telling the poor lass that she had cancer...*

Shaking his head clear of such thoughts, Wes seized his champagne glass and took a hearty swig. Whatever horrors tomorrow might bring, there was no point fretting about them now – not on a flight that had cost Gabi something in excess of three thousand quid. *I should be enjoying my last misery-free evening,* thought Wes, forcing a smile of acknowledgement as a passing member of the cabin crew topped up his wine. *The food; the champagne; the absence of Jeremy.* Ah yes – the absence of Jeremy.

Not that he wouldn't be pleased to see Jeremy when they got off the place in San Francisco, of course. He was actually rather looking forward to that part of the journey – catching sight of his ravaged-looking friend at Baggage

Reclaim, sleep-deprived and half dead from eleven hours in Economy. *Not looking as chipper as you did in the taxi, are you, mate?* Yes – whichever way you looked at it, Jeremy deserved to be severely punished. His scam in the Bricklayer's Arms had crossed a line, and a six thousand mile journey with his knees wedged beneath his chin should just about settle the bugger's hash.

Wes sipped his champagne and tried expunging the unpleasant *contretemps* in the Brick from his mind. It wasn't easy, though. There had been something about Jeremy's eyes – the unholy *fervour* in them – that had been profoundly unsettling. Wes had seen that look of fierce resolution before, of course, and suspected he knew what it meant – that Jeremy wouldn't rest until he'd installed himself as Nikki's personal fairy-godfather-cum-fuck-buddy. *Look at the lad's unseemly haste in organising the San Francisco trip; how effortlessly he'd ditched the ciggies, how alarmingly he'd smartened himself up.* Aye – Jeremy was a man on a mission; a mission upon which Wes feared he was little more than a passenger. He smiled to himself. *A first-class passenger.*

Suddenly, he sat bolt upright in his seat – so suddenly, in fact, that the ankle of his left foot slammed painfully into one of the seat's steel legs. Within a moment, one of the cabin crew – a slender, blonde girl he'd failed to flirt with when she brought him his champagne – materialised at his side. 'Are you all right, sir?'

Wes nodded, beckoning her closer with his non-drink hand. He swallowed hard, trying to suppress the inevitable note of anxiety in his voice. 'I don't want you to panic or anything...'

'Yes, sir?'

He motioned her concerned face even closer and lowered his voice. 'But you see that man over there?'

'Yes, sir?'

'Well, I think he's up to something. Something bad.'

Raising himself an inch from his seat, Wes surreptitiously observed the figure chatting with an even prettier flight attendant by the entrance to the First Class cabin. He tried making sense of what his eyes were telling him. *Airlines don't play practical jokes, do they? Surely not. Not even airlines owned by Richard Branson.* 'I think that man's trying to sneak into First Class.'

'Really?'

'Uh-huh. He should be in Economy. He certainly hasn't got a first-class ticket.'

'How can you be sure? Do you know him?'

Wes fought the urge to wring his hands. 'We're very vaguely acquainted. He's a semi-employed furniture restorer.' He discreetly covered his champagne. 'He drinks like a fish. You'll get complaints from the other passengers. You've got to get rid of him.'

'I'll pop over and have a quiet word.'

A second later, Wes's flight attendant had joined her colleague at the interloper's side – and while Wes was initially reassured by the way she scrutinised his boarding card, his heart sank when she began gazing affectionately at his ridiculous, impish grin, and smiling at whatever desperate quips he was inflicting upon her. And then – horribly – she leaned forward, whispered something in his ear, and with a tiny gesture pointed at Wes's seat. And then laughed. *Betrayer! Harpy! Judas!*

Wes's agitation escalated as his eyes panned left and right in search of vacancies in the cabin. It took approximately a heartbeat to realise that the only unoccupied space was in the seat next to his. *The one he'd mentally reserved as his spare, if he fancied a change of scenery somewhere over the Atlantic.* The next moment, Jeremy was upon him. 'Wes! Kiddo! Good to see you.'

'Wow. Jeremy. What a nice surprise. Paying me a little visit?'

'Not really. I got an upgrade.'

'To *First Class?* How did you wangle that?'

'Couldn't say. It was a complete shocker. Maybe the lass on the check-in desk took a shine to me. And they always like having a doctor in First Class, don't they? Just in case a captain of industry chokes on his melon balls.' For a moment Jeremy was silent, his smile ossifying dangerously beneath narrowed eyes. Then, seemingly on impulse, he seized Wes's glass – and drained it in a single, swift gulp. 'Look, you're not going to be hacked off, are you? Not resentful or anything – that I'm in First Class?'

Wes felt suddenly queasy as his friend's eyes bored into him. Jeremy, he knew, took issues of personal loyalty very seriously, and would often wax lyrical about the 'social club' aspects of mafia families while drunk. Forcing a smile to his dry lips, Wes steadied his voice. 'Resentful? *God*, no. Not at all. It's good to have you here, mate.'

'And you didn't say anything to that air hostess, did you? About my ticket?'

'They prefer to be called cabin crew, these days.'

'But you didn't try to get me shunted back down to Economy?'

'Certainly not. No way. *No way.*'

'Good.' Jeremy stretched out in his seat and looked sidelong at his friend. 'I'm glad we're sitting together, actually. Because if I'm going to pass myself off as a doctor in the States, I might need to swot up on some of the basics. You can teach me.'

Wes regarded Jeremy warily. Jeremy 'passing himself off' as a doctor had never been part of the deal, but it didn't seem like the best time to mention it. 'You're not going to keep me awake all night with banal questions, are you?'

'Life and death questions are never banal, mate. And the only reason I'm here at all is to prevent a young woman from dying needlessly. A man of your training should have some respect for that.'

Wes scanned his friend's face for any hint of an agenda.

Nothing. He sighed. Jeremy was, of course, quite right. 'I'm sorry. Just don't keep me up all night, right?'

'God, no. No way.'

First class cabin, United Airlines flight 142. Somewhere over Newfoundland. 05.13 GMT.

'Wes? Wes? You still awake, mate?'

'*No.*'

Curled into a foetal ball, Wes screwed his eyes even tighter shut. In spite of the muted roar of the engines – and the fact that he'd wedged half a paper napkin into his non-pillow ear – Jeremy's low whisper sought him out remorselessly in the dimly-lit cabin. 'I've got another one.'

'*Go to sleep.*'

For a few moments, Wes tried retreating from the chaos in his brain, allowing the jumble of proto-dreams and half-thunk thoughts to recover from their unceremonious interruption. In the fifteen minutes before Jeremy had spoken, he'd almost – *almost* – fallen asleep. Lying in his First Class sarcophagus, Wes had opened his mind to the phantoms of oblivion, invited in the insubstantial wraiths of slumber and – like timid woodland creatures into an enchanted clearing – they had come. *And now the fickle bastards had legged it forever.*

'Wes, mate. I said I've got another one,' Jeremy continued. 'Another medical question. It's really been disturbing my kip, this one.'

'*Bugger. Off. And. Go. To. Sleep.*'

'In a minute, kid. In a minute.' From the other side of the cubicle's dividing wall, Jeremy could be heard rearranging his limbs. 'I just wanted to know why the Vulcan nerve pinch can only be given by Vulcans. That's all.'

In the blue half-light, Wes found himself scrabbling

feverishly for his discarded napkin. Failing to find it, he pulled the free half of his pillow around his head and clamped it there with his forearm. 'I know *nothing* about it.'

'Seriously?' A new clarity in Jeremy's voice indicated that he'd hoisted himself up above the cubicle wall and was now gazing down at his prey. 'I'd have thought it'd be one of the first things they'd teach you at medical school.'

'*About the Vulcan nerve pinch?*

'Well, no, not specifically that. But about nerve pinches in general. Medicine in popular culture, the difference between medical fact and fiction, that sort of thing.' For a moment Jeremy's words hung in the stale cabin air. 'Well, what about that thing in *Kill Bill*, then? The five-finger death punch? Does it really exist?'

'How the hell should I know?'

'No reason in particular. I just thought this would be a good opportunity to ask.'

For a moment Wes considered his options. The way he saw it, only one of them didn't involve a lengthy residency in a padded cell. Swinging his legs off the mattress, Wes scrabbled around the foot of his seat for the slippers he'd popped in his hand luggage a lifetime earlier. 'Right. That's it. I'm going to the toilet.'

'What again?'

'Yes, again.'

'Are you all right? Down there?' Jeremy's index finger made a beeline for Wes's midriff. Despite the protection afforded by the cushioned partition, Wes found himself instinctively drawing away from the uninvited digit. 'An abnormal need to pass urine is often symptomatic of dicky kidneys, mate,' Jeremy continued, a palpable note of pride in his voice. 'You said so yourself, when we were flying over Greenland.'

'My kidneys are fine.' Wes hurriedly gathered together a handful of essentials and got to his feet, ignoring the pins and needles in his legs as he tottered along the aisle towards the toilets. 'My kidneys are absolutely dandy.'

Two minutes later, facing the toilet mirror for the fourteenth time, Wes was forced to confront the fact that regardless of the state of his kidneys, very few other parts of his person could be described as 'dandy'. *'Jesus,'* he breathed, gently pressing down the skin below his cadaverous eye sockets. In the mirror, two pairs of eyelids – eyelids he scarcely recognised – parted a fraction of an inch, revealing two unnaturally dilated pupils that returned his mortified gaze with an expression of bloodshot accusation. 'Fuck me sideways.'

Wes reached into his trouser pocket and withdrew the tiny tin of Poschl's Gletscherprise snuff that he'd dipped into at hourly intervals since shortly after dinner. *The only means of getting a half-decent tobacco fix on a long-haul flight.* He smiled to himself beneath the flickering florescent light, only regretting having done so when he was forced to lick his own front teeth in order to free them from the desiccated insides of his lips. *Secret snuff.* Pouring a generous pile of the chocolate-coloured powder on to the back of his hand, Wes leaned low over the toilet bowl, closed one nostril and snorted. For a second, his head span with an intoxicating rush of fatigue, tobacco, nausea and the gathering thunderclouds of a migraine. Then he sneezed.

When, after some moments, Wes felt able to open his eyes, he immediately wished he hadn't. There, eight inches in front of him, rendered on the mirror in an obscene *gouache* of powered tobacco and drying phlegm, was the clear image of a face. A smiling face. *Jeremy.*

US Customs And Immigration Hall, San Francisco International Airport. 00.39 PST.

I'm hallucinating. It's the only rational explanation. Wes grunted to himself, relieved at last to have worked it out. *No one naturally looks that fresh. Not after a transatlantic flight. Not without snuff.* He glanced across at Jeremy who, having given his bag a cheerful punt across the tiled floor of the Immigration hall, had just begun whistling to himself. *He's not whistling, either. That's another illusion. Only a looney whistles within five yards of a customs officer. He's just as knackered as me. I'm just imagining that he looks human.*

Jeremy gave his bag another gentle kick forwards as the couple in front moved to the head of the Immigration queue. Then, noticing that Wes appeared to have become strangely fixated with his own shoes, he reached for the lad's shoulder. 'You all right, kid?'

'Very, very relaxed, Jeremy. What makes you ask?'

'You just look a bit peaky, that's all. Tired. Did you sleep okay on the plane?'

Wes's brow furrowed with apparent concentration. Then his eyes closed and a beatific grin spread across his face. 'Not much, now you come to mention it.'

'Nervous flyer?'

His friend shook his head in exaggerated denial, almost as if he was trying to prevent the misguided suggestion from lodging in his brain. 'Nah,' he finally declared. 'Actually, I had some wanker asking me cretinous questions about penile elephantiasis and rectal prolapses all night.' He reached out and gently took Jeremy's cheek between his thumb and forefinger, looking for one dizzying moment as though his fragile grasp was the only thing standing between him and complete collapse. 'Mustn't grumble, though. *Mustn't grumble.* Because I think I *might* have passed out on the toilet at one point. So I think, in total, I must've had perhaps... ooh, maybe fifteen minutes' sleep last night.'

For a second, Jeremy appeared stunned at his friend's revelation. Then he silently made the 'wanker' gesture with his right hand and pointed towards himself with his left, while his face assumed an expression of pained enquiry.

'Yes, Jeremy,' answered Wes. 'You, Jeremy Sykes – *you*

are the wanker of whom I speak.'

'Shit, kid. I'm sorry about that. I thought we were just having a nice little chat. I didn't realise I was keeping you awake.'

Wes waved aside his apology with another good-natured bout of head-shaking. 'It's not a problem. After all, we're here now. America. You don't need full command of your mental faculties in America. Not once you're through Customs, anyway.' He beckoned Jeremy closer, dropping his voice to a hoarse pantomime whisper. 'They're very fussy, American immigration people. Not very friendly *at all*.'

'Well, personally I reckon you'll be fine.' Jeremy put a hand on Wes's shoulder and gently steered him towards the head of the queue. 'They'll probably overlook your little bit of contraband, anyway.'

Through the dreadful fug of sleeplessness, Wes's eyes narrowed on his friend. 'What... *contraband?*'

'The porn, mate.'

'Porn? What porn?'

'Nothing serious. Really, don't worry about it. Chill.' Jeremy crossed his arms and stared into the middle distance, over the heads of the gently milling crowd and the Immigration officials, clearly aggrieved at Wes's sceptical attitude. 'I wish I hadn't mentioned it now.'

'What porn are you talking about?'

'Just some pictures of Nikki. From the video. I printed them off so we'd have something to recognise her with.' Jeremy inclined his head in the direction of Wes's bag. 'I popped them in your luggage, back in Putney. While you were doing all your bets on the Ladbrokes website.' Catching sight of his friend's aghast expression, he shook his head dismissively. 'I don't think they'll even look.'

For a second, Wes's face managed to hide his inner turmoil. Then, without warning, he seized Jeremy and addressed him in an anguished whisper. 'Why the *hell* did you put *porn* in *my* bag? Why, Jez? *Why?*

'Well, I thought it'd help with your quest, kid. Looking for Nikki.'

'And you didn't think to mention it before now?'

'I didn't want to worry you. I didn't want you panicking.' He gently unpicked Wes's fingers from his jacket and nodded at the expectant face behind the Immigration desk. 'It's your turn to go, mate. You're up.'

Wes turned his horrified eyes in the direction of the Immigration officer. Sure enough, he was beckoning. 'Come with me,' Wes whispered urgently, glancing sidelong at Jeremy. 'Explain everything to them.'

'I can't go with you. Unless we're married, I have to stand behind the yellow line.'

'*Please*, Jez. I can't think straight. I'll say something stupid, I know I will.'

'Just relax. You'll be great. Just don't think any porny thoughts, and you'll sail through.'

Sensing that it was time to bring out the big guns, Wes fixed Jeremy with an accusing stare. 'We are no longer friends,' he hissed. 'We *used* to be friends, but *no more*.'

'You're *dumping* me? That's cold, man.' Jeremy shook his head, his eyes narrowing on his former friend. 'Almost as cold as trying to get me thrown out of First Class.' And then, correctly guessing that Wes's guard was down, Jeremy placed a hand squarely between his shoulder blades and propelled the trembling doctor firmly towards the Immigration desk.

Wes's numb legs conveyed him across the tiled floor. And then, like a drowning man chancing upon a piece of driftwood, he collided with the desk and clung on to it. The face of the Immigration officer loomed ominously into his line of vision. *A nice face*, Wes reflected, surveying it from his half-crouched position. *Stern but kind.* The nice face regarded him solemnly. 'Please stand up straight, sir.'

'I'm sorry,' said Wes, levering himself fully upright. 'This is my first time in America.' He scoured his sleep-deprived brain for further small talk, but nothing was forthcoming.

'You appear to be nervous, sir.'

'Just a little tired. Long flight.'

The Immigration officer picked up his passport, his eyes flitting over the visa waiver before coming to rest on Wes's photograph. 'You're Dr Wesley?'

'Yes.'

'Dr Byron Wesley, just arrived from London, England?'

'Yes. What's wrong?'

The officer looked up to meet Wes's eye. 'Would you step this way, please, sir?'

'Why?'

'Just step this way.'

'I don't think I want to.' Wes felt suddenly sick. Looking over his shoulder towards Jeremy, he noticed for the first time that his ex-friend's eyes were filled with as much apprehension as his own.

'*Step this way.*'

From behind the yellow line, Jeremy's stomach was also being afflicted by an unfamiliar churning sensation. *This wasn't supposed to happen. I was only winding you up, mate — because you were such a knobhead about my upgrade.* He watched with mounting anxiety as Wes was led away by two officers. Standing on tiptoes, he was just able to catch Wes's eye as he was escorted out of the Immigration hall through a small, grey door. *There's no porn in your bag. I was just kidding,* he mouthed. But it was too late. Wes had gone.

9

hertz don't do cars like this

It's good that I'm being punished, thought Jeremy, shifting his weight from one foot to the other. *If anyone deserves a ruptured kidney, it's me.* He gasped at the apparent sensation of hot needles being driven into his bladder. It had been some time since he'd last wet himself – six months at least – but at least he'd been drunk and lying on a park bench at the time. *No one to witness my shame. Unlike here…*

Jeremy allowed his gaze to drift from the Arrivals gate to the toilet, some fifty yards distant. Was it just his imagination, or did the doorway seem to be shimmering invitingly, as though submerged in a limpid pool of water? He blinked and shook his head, holding his breath to prevent any stray vibrations reaching his agonised groin. Jeremy knew that without Lisa's stabilising influence, he generally possessed all the self-control of a randy macaque monkey after half a gallon of semi-fermented prune juice – but standing here, waiting for Wes to emerge from his ordeal with US Customs, was something he simply had to do. *No one gets left behind. Even if it means irreversible crotch damage to the finest pair of strides I've ever possessed.*

He shifted his weight back to his other foot, winced again, and fixed his eyes on the steady *drip drip drip* of humanity making its way through the automatic Arrivals door. *Pepperpot grandma. Kurt Cobain wannabe. Tattooed lovegod.* None of them looked liked they'd been intimately probed by US Customs. None of them looked like they were about to irrigate their own undies, either. Bastards. *Preppy sports-casual couple. Lusty hausfrau. Asian Über-nerds. Wes.*

'Wes. *Wes.*' Jeremy waved at his stunned friend, astonished by the hoarseness of his own voice. He'd barely spoken to anyone since he'd picked up the rental car nine hours earlier, cowed into silence by fatigue, anxiety and guilt. 'Wes, mate. How the hell are you?'

At a hobble, Wes made his way over to the elasticated barrier and peered myopically at the source of the disturbance. His eyes finally focused upon Jeremy's contrite face and an uncertain smile formed on his pale lips. 'Ah. Jez. Good to see you.'

Jeremy returned the smile, relieved beyond words to detect no hint of malice in either Wes's expression or voice. 'You too, kid.' He reached over the barrier and clamped a bear-sized hand around the back of his friend's head, and pulled him close. 'I was scared shitless when they hauled you off.'

'Hairy moment, mate. Very hairy.'

Gently unhanding the lad, Jeremy began edging sidewise with crablike fairy steps. 'Come to the bog and tell your uncle Jezzer all about it.'

'There were never any pictures of Nikki, you know,' Jeremy confessed some five minutes later, guiding the still-dazed Wes through the sliding doors and out into the San Francisco afternoon. 'I made it all up. I'm really sorry.'

For a second the two men paused, adjusting to the bread-oven warmth of the air and the unblinking gaze of the California sun. Although it was hours since Jeremy had first emerged on to the broad sidewalk, he still found its constantly-shifting tableau of alien life just as arresting as it had been in the first light of morning. The lithe concrete curve of the approach road, snaking like an outsize Scalextric past the taxi ranks and shuttle buses, indifferent to the shell-shocked travellers stumbling on to the sidewalk with their guidebooks and trapped wind and over-stuffed suitcases... Jeremy smiled in wonder and shook his head. Despite the evidence of his own bloodshot eyes, it was still hard for him to believe that Americans truly *existed* – that they weren't just something made up by the rest of the world to keep itself entertained. And yet here they were – hundreds of the buggers, swarming everywhere, with their leathery skin and day-glo leisurewear, their klaxon voices and voluptuous backsides, mountainous cars and prairie-wide roads, their factories, fields and houses, far as the eye could see. *Absolutely bloody amazing.*

Peering around Jeremy's shoulder, Wes also scanned the horizon, his eyes narrowing upon its diminishing palate of dusty blues and browns, peppered with the glittering reflections of car windscreens, blanched to a fizzing haze of static where land met sky. *Like watching TV with the brightness turned up too high,* he thought. Then, noticing that Jeremy had already begun meandering down the sidewalk towards the shuttle buses, Wes sighed, drawing in a lungful of the dry, ozone-y Californian air and trotting after his friend.

'I didn't put anything iffy in your bag,' Jeremy announced as Wes fell into step beside him. 'I wouldn't. Not to a mate. I only invented the 'Nikki' pictures to put the willies up you, because you tried getting me chucked out of First Class.'

Wes's face reddened. 'Ah, yes,' he said. 'Sorry about that.'

'I never wanted you to start giving off a 'porn mule' vibe or anything,' Jeremy continued, making his way towards the open door of the nearest bus. 'Or have one of your panic attacks at Immigration. I just wanted to give you a swift kick in the knackers, metaphorically speaking. Get your heart racing a bit. For being such a wanker.'

'Fair enough.'

'I never thought they'd haul you off, anyway.' Jeremy clambered up the steps, deposited Wes's suitcase on a vacant seat and dropped heavily into the one in front. 'Not just for coming over all nervous and dribbling down your shirt.'

'They didn't.'

'What?'

'They didn't haul me away for looking shifty.'

'Didn't they?'

'No.' Wes glanced warily back towards the terminal building as the bus pulled away from the kerb. He'd be glad, he reflected, when the airport was well behind him. 'They actually detained me because they'd been tipped off by the flight attendants on the plane.'

'What for? Why?'

'Because I kept on scuttling off to the toilet during the flight, then coming back to my seat with a runny nose and the sniffles.' Wes leaned closer to his friend, anxious that his words shouldn't be overheard. 'They thought I'd been snorting cocaine. I told them it was snuff, but by that point I'd already been jabbering for half an hour about porn. It took six hours of questioning and a blood test before they'd stamp my visa.'

Jeremy frowned, replaying the previous night's events in his mind. 'So it wasn't my fault you got hauled off at all?'

'It's your bloody fault that I haven't slept for thirty-six hours.'

In his pre-Lisa days, Jeremy reflected, he might have taken Wes's last comment as a cue to administer a gentle slap to the back of the lad's head. After all, *he* hadn't complained that Wes's incarceration had resulted in nine guilt-addled hours of fretting and pacing up and down in front of the Arrivals gate – three hours of which had involved suppressing an eye-watering urge to urinate. 'Well, no hard feelings, eh, kid? Not now we're here.' He held out his hand to Wes. 'Let's put it all behind us. Start off again with a clean slate. No grudges. Mates again.'

Wes eyed the hand for some moments before taking it. 'Just as long as we're totally honest with each other from now on,' he eventually conceded. 'No more of your little jokes. No more 'Jeremy' bombshells.'

'Fine.'

'Fine.'

'Good.'

'Right, then. Let's go pick up the car.'

It took Wes three complete circumnavigations of the rental car before he was fully able to marshal his thoughts – three open-mouthed examinations of its extravagant chrome work; three incredulous investigations of its cavernous interior; three slack-jawed inspections of its demonic radiator grille. Eventually, he had to reach out and run two fingers along its ludicrous bonnet and down the wing before he could fully convince himself of its existence and then – only then – could he find the words to express his feelings. He looked at Jeremy in numb incomprehension. 'Hertz don't do cars like this, mate.'

Jeremy nodded slowly. 'Ah, well, that's the thing. This particular vehicle didn't actually come from Hertz.'

'No?'

'No.' Jeremy broke Wes's enquiring gaze and stared off beyond the compound's wire fence and dusty, flyblown asphalt. 'It came from a place that does classic rentals. It's a sort of treat. To cheer you up.'

Wes's brow furrowed in confusion. He raised his hand against the glare of the sun and peered again at the gleaming black paintwork and long, sculpted rear wings, the hint of a vestigial tail fin. 'I booked a car from Hertz,' he declared at length. 'An E-series Mercedes.'

'Yes, well, that booking was actually cancelled,' Jeremy said airily. 'I went round there just after you were taken away by the Customs people.'

'You went to the rental office and they told you they'd cancelled my booking?'

'They confirmed that it'd been cancelled, yes.'

Wes frowned as he mentally wrestled with Jeremy's slippery combination of linguistics and logic. Slowly realisation dawned. 'Did *you* cancel my booking, Jez?'

'Maybe. I wasn't wholly uninvolved.'

'But they already had my credit card number. They'll still charge me.'

'They won't.'

'They bloody well will.'

'They *won't*.'

'Why not?'

Jeremy smiled reassuringly. 'Because they seemed to have acquired the impression that you'd snuffed it on the plane. Suspected heart attack. Congenital weakness, apparently. You never knew what happened to you. One minute, fine. The next...' Jeremy's hands shot to his throat, his face twisting into a rictus of pantomime agony. 'Fair play to the Hertz lads, though – they've already returned your deposit. Very understanding.'

'You told them I'd died, and they *believed* you?'

'Certainly. People believe anyone wearing a suit. Suits are great, aren't they? I never realised before, but you can do whatever you want in a suit. You just drift under the radar, don't you?' Jeremy gazed down at his ensemble. It still looked the business, despite the ravages of the past couple of days. 'I just have to keep it decent until after we've seen Nikki. Then we can head back to San Francisco and hit the fleshpots for the rest of the week, eh?'

Refusing to be drawn by Jeremy's 'fleshpots' scenario,

Wes pointed once again at the steel leviathan that stood between them. 'So what the hell's this, then?'

'The car? That's a 1967 Dodge Charger, mate. Detroit's finest.'

'And *why* have we got a 1967 Dodge Charger?'

'Well, partly to cheer you up. Partly because it's the closest thing I could get to the baddies' car in *Bullitt*. And partly because when we turn up at the porn place, we're going to want them to take us seriously.'

'As *doctors*.'

'As men, Wes. As men.'

'It's got a flame motif coming from the edges of the wheel arches.'

'It does, doesn't it?' observed Jeremy, as though noticing the car's spectacular paint job for the first time. 'I bet you wish you'd had that done on your Merc, now, don't you?'

Wes looked at his friend levelly. 'Oh yes, Jeremy. I can't imagine why it never occurred to me. It'd look lovely against the Tansanite blue.'

For a moment the two men glared at each other across the Charger's bonnet. Jeremy was the first to crack, striding around the front of the car and opening the passenger door. 'Look, if you don't like the flames, get inside. Then you won't see them.'

'Has it got air conditioning?' Wes lowered his head and peered sceptically at the four space-age portholes on the dashboard. 'An immobiliser? Airbags? An assisted braking system? Impact protection?'

'Who cares?' Jeremy opened his own door and dropped into the driver's seat. 'It's got an engine, though. Listen.' He turned the key in the ignition. Under Wes's hand, the door handle began vibrating as the engine spluttered into life, although he couldn't be sure *quite* how much of the rich, delighted gurgling was coming from under the bonnet and how much was coming from Jeremy. 'Get in, kid. Let's go. Please.'

Realising that further resistance was futile, Wes dropped into the passenger seat and closed the door. While he'd been locked in the holding cell behind the Immigration hall, he'd come to the comforting conclusion that his tortured psyche could only cope with life's stresses and tribulations in manageable, bite-size chunks. During his three hours of interviews, this had meant focusing all his attention on when the next cup of coffee might appear, or mentally correcting the dodgy grammar in the signs behind the Immigration officer's head. As a survival strategy, it had worked. *Complete and utter denial of the bigger picture, that's the answer.* Wes smiled to himself, relaxing into the Charger's vast leather bucket seat, allowing his attention to be absorbed by the blur of parched verges and dusty scrub as the car began racing up the Bayshore freeway slip road. *There's nothing else he can throw at me now. Nothing that could possibly stress me out.*

Suddenly Wes sat up straight in his seat. 'Why are we heading south, Jez? We're going the wrong way. We should be heading towards San Francisco. Turn the car round.'

Jeremy gently squeezed the accelerator and eased the Charger into the middle lane. 'There's no point, kid.'

Wes twisted in his seat. Through the elongated letterbox of the rear window, he could just make out an urban skyline of skyscrapers and apartment blocks receding in the distance. 'I need to get to the hotel,' he wailed. 'I need to get my hair sorted. I need a shower and some fresh clothes. I need to register at the conference centre. I'm a day late already. Turn the car round, Jez. Let's just go to the hotel, eh?'

'Actually, there's a problem with your hotel booking.'

'What problem?'

'The problem of it not existing. It's okay, though. We're going to head south and find a motel instead. Hole up there for the night.'

'What happened to my hotel booking?'

'It was cancelled.'

'By whom?'

Jeremy said nothing.

'Oh, God. They think I'm dead, too, don't they?'

'They may be labouring under that morbid misapprehension, yes.' Jeremy turned and grinned at his friend. 'Just relax. We're going to find Nikki, mate.'

10
drifting psychopaths, lowlife depravity and cheap sex

Wes took another drag on his cigarette and exhaled an extravagant lungful of smoke into the crisp morning air. It was, he had to admit, a heck of a good spot for your first ciggie of the day. The two hundred miles that Jeremy had driven the previous evening had brought them down Route 101 to just beyond Santa Maria and – at the very moment their eyelids threatened to close in ill-suppressed exhaustion – the glowing oasis of the Harbor Inn Motel had silently materialised in the Charger's headlights.

In the first light of morning, the Harbor Inn's vast neon sign looked no less enchanting, a sixty-foot bloom of pink and purple against the vast, inky heavens, a quarter-mile distant at the edge of the deserted highway. In the ten minutes before he'd fallen asleep, Wes fancied that he'd heard the far-off buzz of ancient neon mingling with the call of crickets in the scrubland beyond the silent carriageway. Now, as the last stars were being extinguished overhead, Wes stared out to where its twin lanes converged in blackness at an unseen point on the southern horizon. Somewhere out there – somewhere beyond the highway, still asleep and oblivious to what the day would bring – was Nikki.

Nikki's intrusion upon his thoughts suddenly made Wes feel slightly seasick, as she had every time he'd thought about her since... well, since the day he'd first glimpsed the horror story on her backside. For a long time, he'd assumed the feeling was a symptom of his guilt, a dash of 'Nikki' guilt, hurled into the familiar cocktail of shame and self-reproach that accompanied most of his thoughts and deeds. But now he wasn't so sure. Since Wes had been in America, the sensations that accompanied his 'Nikki' thoughts had somehow become more defined until they'd eventually coalesced into a tangible feeling of inner emptiness, an absence he couldn't name. *Maybe it was just being here, alone in the middle of nowhere, staring into nothingness.* The parched plain was certainly the kind of landscape that could stir up unspoken longings. *But what am I pining for?* thought Wes. *Not Gabi,* he reflected with a shiver. *No. I'm pining for something I really shouldn't – a girl in a chatroom who loves Allen Ginsberg and spending Sunday afternoons in junk shops, who couldn't live without the White Stripes or Camper Van Beethoven or her 1950's letterman jacket.*

Wes blinked away the smoke from his cigarette, locked the Charger's trunk and made his way back across the car park to the Harbor Inn's office, where he'd left Jeremy settling the bill with Claudia, the yawning receptionist – the very pretty receptionist who had uncomplainingly risen before dawn to make coffee and scrambled eggs for the two English doctors who had appeared only hours earlier, seeking a room for what little remained of the night. *You wouldn't get service like that in Britain,* Wes thought. *You don't get too many motels in Britain either, mind. Not proper motels with the thrilling subtext of drifting psychopaths, lowlife depravity and cheap sex.*

Actually, Wes had wished there'd been a bit less cheap sex in the atmosphere the previous night, as Jeremy had undressed for bed. Why had the lad so coyly insisted on disrobing with the lights out? And why had the process been accompanied by quite so much panting and groaning? It wasn't as though Jeremy was generally particularly modest when it came to exposing his manly assets. Only the day before, he'd insisted on hearing about Wes's misadventures with US Immigration while performing his one-man impression of the Trevi Fountain in the airport toilets. Wes shivered in the chill morning breeze, extinguished his cigarette and stepped back into the inviting glow of the motel office.

If he'd been able to predict the sight that greeted him, however, he'd have stayed outside in the car park. There, bent forwards over the Reception desk, was Claudia. Behind her, his hands only visible as meandering bulges beneath her blouse, was Jeremy. Clearly absorbed by his task, the tall furniture restorer jumped guiltily as the door clattered shut behind him, yet still managed to maintain a level voice as he caught his startled friend's eye. 'Ah, Dr Wesley. All packed and ready to go? I've sorted the bill, mate...'

'*Uh?*' Wes replied, momentarily lost for words.

Jeremy gently extracted his hands from inside the rear of Claudia's blouse and rubbed them absently on the lapels of his jacket. The young receptionist, meanwhile, straightened herself up from the position she'd been occupying, brushed herself down and skipped back behind the desk. 'I was just telling young Claudia, here, that she should always bend from the knees when she's lifting heavy objects. Isn't that right, Dr Wesley – bend from the knees?'

'Right, right,' Wes muttered, unable to look either of them in the eye.

'She's been getting terrible back pain, poor lass. And she

asked me if I'd give her a quick examination. Seeing as I'm a *doctor*, and all.'

'I see,' said Wes through gritted teeth. 'And did you find anything, Dr Sykes?'

'Nothing to worry about, no.'

'Right. Okay. Then perhaps we should be on our way. We've a long day ahead.'

His face reddening despite the morning chill, Wes turned on his heel and headed for the car – and he was still quietly seething in the passenger seat when Jeremy finally emerged from the office some minutes later and installed himself behind the steering wheel.

'I know what you're thinking,' said Jeremy quietly.

'You reckon?'

'You think I was groping that lass.'

'There's no 'think' about it.'

Jeremy shook his head sadly and turned the ignition key. The Charger's engine coughed into life. 'Actually, there was no 'groping' about it. I was examining her, mate. *Medically*. Brushing up my bedside manner. Practising for when we see Nikki, later today.'

'*If* we see Nikki, all that'll be required will be a highly cursory look at her arse.' Wes stared accusingly at his friend's face, silhouetted in the faint blue light from the dashboard. 'And the poor lass'll have enough to worry about without having to fend off *your* bloody great paws.'

'I was *examining* her as best I could, given my very limited medical expertise.' Jeremy shrugged, slipped the car into drive and dabbed the accelerator. Behind them, the Harbor Inn motel receded into the darkness until only the pink glow of its neon sign could be seen in the rear view mirror.

Sensing that conversation might be in short supply, Jeremy reached for the radio. A moment later, the car was filled with the same brash country and western they'd both endured for four long hours the previous evening – but even the shrill piping of the Dixie Chicks couldn't alleviate the laser beams of silent condemnation emanating from the Charger's passenger seat. After five strained minutes, Jeremy turned to his friend in exasperation. 'I don't why you're being so judgemental. At least I'm trying to put people's minds at ease with my smattering of medical know-how. When was the last time *you* examined anyone?'

Wes tried staring out of the passenger window, but all he could make out in the darkness was the dim reflection of his own shifty expression. He closed his eyes, resenting the fact that Jeremy had waited until they were cocooned in the car before broaching this particular topic of conversation. 'You *know* why I haven't examined anyone recently,' he said at length. 'It's because I haven't got a job yet.'

'I don't know why. You finished medical school. Unlike me.'

'Never having *set foot* inside a medical school, mate, you'd hardly understand. It's impossible to describe my current situation to someone lacking even the faintest conception of how the National Health Service operates.'

'Try.'

'I can't. It's too complex. It's about getting a training position in the field you really want. It's all to do with specialisms and quotas and things.' Wes glanced across at his friend's uncomprehending expression. 'I'll give you an analogy to describe my situation. Imagine Lisa wasn't around.'

Jeremy fought the urge to take his eyes from the road, to search Wes's face for any sign that he might know about the delicate 'Lisa' situation. Despite appearances to the contrary, Wes wasn't *completely* insensitive to unguarded comments and offhand remarks. 'Uh-huh. Right,' he eventually muttered.

'And now imagine that you were the Shagfinder General again – footloose and fancy-free.'

'Okay.'

'And imagine that Mila Kunis was desperate to be your girlfriend. *Desperate*.'

Jeremy shrugged in the darkness. This bit of Wes's scenario, at the very least, sounded faintly plausible. 'Go on.'

'Now imagine that you'd heard Keira Knightley was going to be moving in next door.' Wes's voice became silky. 'Well, you'd wait to see how things worked out with Keira before you jumped in the sack with Mila, wouldn't you? Even if it meant being single for a few months.'

'Possibly, possibly.'

'Well that's like me, mate. Except it's not lasses we're talking about, it's jobs. I'm just biding my time, waiting for the perfect job to come along.'

Jeremy's brow furrowed. 'And this job's going to involve shagging Keira Knightley, is it?'

'No, Jez. It'll probably involve cutting holes in people, taking the bad bits out and sewing them back up again. But it hasn't come along yet, and I'm letting Gabi offer me a little financial support until it does.'

'And this analogy describes your life, does it?'

'Uh-huh.'

Happy that the road ahead was traffic-free for the next half a mile, Jeremy turned to face his friend. 'I've actually got a simpler analogy to describe your current situation. The way I'd describe it would be as... a *train*. A train that's carrying a very specific cargo. And that cargo appears to be... brown. And warm. And savoury. What can it be? Oh yes. It's a gravy train, mate.'

'Piss off.'

Jeremy returned his attention to the road, grinning. 'Admit it. You leech off that poor lass. Always have.'

'No more than you leech off Lisa.'

'At least I do some *work* every now and then.'

'Helping an Irish alcoholic tart up second hand furniture and flogging it on Spitalfields Market – that pays half the mortgage on Lisa's flat, does it?'

'Not quite. But at least I don't love Lisa *for* her money, do I?' Jeremy turned to face Wes once more. Framed by the glowering red of the rising sun in the driver's window, his silhouette looked eerily demonic. 'You'd have never married Gabi if her folks hadn't been loaded. *Never.*'

For a moment Wes was speechless. Jeremy had voiced a truth which he'd never, even in his most reflective moments, honestly admitted to himself. When he eventually managed to string a sentence together – far too late to represent a serious attempt at self-defence – his voice was tinged with hysteria. 'Well if *that's* how you feel, Jez, I can't imagine why you didn't mention your concerns during the wedding ceremony. There's a bit where you're allowed to, you know. The vicar asks everyone...'

'I *wanted* to saying something,' Jeremy interrupted. Wes turned to look at him, aghast. 'Seriously. I was going to stand up and tell everyone that you were a money-grabbing parasite. It was Tim and Claire who stopped me. I had one sitting either side of me in the church. Tim kept threatening to tell Lisa about my Drew Barrymore phase if I did anything. And Claire kept whispering that it didn't matter how morally iffy something was, you didn't ruin a lass's wedding day.'

'So you weren't worried that it might ruin *my* wedding day too?'

'You were generally seen as the exploiting party, mate.'

'You only know the half of it,' Wes snapped.

Jeremy waited a beat before pitching in. 'Uh-huh?'

For an agonised second, Wes debated the merits of a full and frank confession. Then he sank into his seat and stared pointedly at the horizon, now starkly visible against the glowing skyline. 'Country and western's shit,' he eventually muttered.

Jeremy looked affronted. 'This is only on for your benefit, mate.'

In a momentary fit of pique, Wes made a half-hearted lunge for the radio, but Jeremy intercepted him halfway and placed his hand firmly back in his lap. 'Play nicely,' he advised, 'and listen. The thing about country and western – however crap it might be – is that it's the only genre of music dealing exclusively with adult issues. You could pick up a lot of good advice from this. Marriage guidance tips and such.' Jeremy nodded fondly at the softly glowing fascia of the radio. 'Aye – that radio's going to be doing my 'spiritual advisor' job for me while I'm concentrating on the road. Or if I need a little nap.'

Wes sighed. 'And what's this particular gem called, then?'

'This? *Redneck Woman*, mate. Gretchen Wilson. Huge hit, a few years back.'

'And I'm supposed to picked up marriage guidance tips from this, am I?'

'Not specifically this, no. But there'll probably be some Handsome Family or Waco Brothers along in a minute. A nice bit of cowpunk. You could learn a lot from the Waco Brothers.'

Suddenly overcome with weariness, Wes unbuckled his seatbelt and, having established that the Charger's front seats would only recline to a forty-five degree angle, wormed his way over the wide leather armrest and into the car's cavernous rear. Tucking his knees up towards his chin, he closed his eyes to the world. 'Wake me up when we get to Nikki's place,' he said. 'Not a moment before.'

And thirty seconds later, despite Gretchen Wilson's entreaties to join her in a 'hey, y'all' and 'yee-haw', he was snoring.

11

it's not exactly the playboy mansion

'You're absolutely certain this is the place? They all look the same.'

Jeremy inclined his head and squinted through the Charger's nearside window. Wes was right – all the houses *did* look the same. Not actually identical, but all long and low, with gently sloping roofs and wide, corrugated garage doors – featureless to the point of looking sullen, all rendered in the same dusty pastels and laid out on a remorseless grid pattern of wide, deserted streets. *Suburbia in widescreen.* 'It's not exactly the Playboy mansion, is it?' he finally conceded, unbuckling his seatbelt and straightening his tie.

'Mm.'

Since turning off the ignition a minute earlier – and with it, the cooling fan – the atmosphere inside the car had grown unpleasantly stale. Jeremy wiped a bead of sweat from his beneath his shades and turned to Wes, trying to imbue his voice with a cheer he didn't feel. 'Best get it over with, then, eh?'

Wes didn't speak but continued to stare, transfixed, at the house. In the previous half hour – ever since he'd woken up in the Charger's back seat with a cricked neck and a headache – he'd said almost nothing. With every passing mile, he'd experienced an almost tangible sensation of the insulation around his life being quietly stripped away. Now he visualised himself as an exposed nerve, painfully sensitive to the slightest tremor or vibration. He turned his hunted eyes to Jeremy. 'Can't you go by yourself? I don't feel good.'

'I don't mind doing most of the talking, kid. But you'll have to do the heavyweight medical bits.' Jeremy reached across and gently ruffled Wes's hair. 'It'll be fine. Honest. We'll be in and out in five minutes. Then we can drive back to San Francisco and start having some fun, right?'

Wes swallowed hard. 'Right.'

It still took the two men three minutes to leave the car, though – and a further three, prevaricating by the kerbside, before they'd both composed themselves sufficiently to approach the front door.

'I still don't think it's the right place,' Wes hissed, hanging back at the end of the drive as Jeremy mounted the steps. 'It feels weird. It feels wrong.'

Glancing over his sunglasses at the peeling paintwork on the doorway's overhanging canopy, Jeremy fought the compulsion to agree. Whoever lived inside, it certainly wasn't Hugh Hefner, and it was with unusual apprehension that he extended a finger towards the doorbell. It was only some moments later, when the final echo of the chime had faded into silence, that Jeremy realised he'd been holding his breath all along. Taking another deep lungful of air, he strained to detect any signs of life within the house. Eventually, satisfied that he could discern nothing over the distant rush of traffic from the freeway, he stepped back from the door and addressed his friend in a low voice. 'You can't hear anything inside, can you?'

Wes shook his head.

'Me neither.' Jeremy glanced at the street. Were his eyes playing tricks on him, or did the Charger seem to be looking even more conspicuously like a getaway car, hunkered low over its haunches by the kerbside? 'Maybe no one's in. Maybe they're all out, stocking up on lube or something.'

'Or getting their carpet burns seen to.'

'Or getting measured up for butt-plugs.'

Wes appeared to weigh Jeremy's words heavily. 'Could be, mate. Could be.'

Jeremy looked longingly at the Charger. 'We could always drive around the block a few times and come back. Or go grab a burger or something.'

Wes, who'd unshouldered his holdall some moments before, looked up. In his hand was the dog-eared package of medical literature he'd assembled back in Sefton Street two days earlier. 'Or we could just shove the information through the letterbox and go. We've tried our best.'

'Aye,' said Jeremy, taking the sheaf of paper from Wes and returning to the door. 'Maybe that's the way to handle things.'

And then – at the very moment Jeremy was about to discharge his debt to humanity – the door opened. Taking half a step backwards, he found himself confronting the kind of pectoral muscles that brought to mind an over-inflated bouncy castle. No less impressive were the walnut-coloured biceps dangling either side, or the leathery veneer of the man's stomach, visible between the bottom of an exercise vest and the waistband of a pair of electric blue cycling shorts. Unblinking eyes stared down from beneath a low hairline, close-cropped and bleached to an alarming shade of yellow. For a second Jeremy searched his memory, trying to recall where he'd seen him before – and then he realised. *The guy in Nikki's porn film.* Unconsciously taking a further step backwards, Jeremy performed a swift mental calculation, subtracting the height of the doorstep from that of the man-beast standing on top of it. *You're a big lad,* he thought, coaxing a half-smile to his lips. *I'm going to watch you like a hawk.*

The man-beast's eyes narrowed on Jeremy, then Wes, then the Charger. He didn't seem particularly pleased to see any of them. 'Yeah?'

Jeremy fought the urge to clear his throat, aware that an unfamiliar sensation had taken up residence there. His smile widened. 'Is this where the films are made, mate?'

'Films?'

'Films. Movies. Pornos. The ones with teenage nymphomaniacs in them.'

The man-beast's eyes narrowed still further. 'Who wants to know?'

Jeremy notched up his smile to a millimetre below 'idiot'. 'We do. Me and him.' He turned to Wes, half expecting to find him gone – and much relieved to find his reluctant lieutenant still standing there, a look of suicidal resolution in his eyes. *Good boy.* 'My name's Dr Sykes, and this is my colleague, Dr Wesley.'

'What do you want?'

'We need to see one of the girls who works here.'

The man-beast's voice dropped to a threatening growl. '*No one meets the girls.*' Stepping back inside the house, he began to close the door.

Without thinking, Jeremy drove his foot into the narrowing gap between the door and the doorframe. Deprived of his Greek army boots, it only took a fraction of a second before he could feel the bones inside his foot begin to compress in an eye-watering sandwich. He threw his shoulder at the door, buying himself a moment's relief. 'This is important, pal. We've come all the way from England,' he grunted, wrapping his fingers around the doorframe and flexing his forearms. For a second he contemplated the fingerless, one-footed lifestyle he'd be forced to endure if the man-beast succeeded in closing the door – and then Wes was there, negotiating his way awkwardly beneath Jeremy's arms and lending his insubstantial weight to the struggle.

'We need to see Nikki,' he panted. 'We're British.'

The man-beast's next words were accompanied by a further assault on his side of the door. 'I don't care who the fuck you are. *No one meets the girls.*'

'We need to see Nikki, and we're not going until we have.' Jeremy caught Wes's eye and the two men redoubled their efforts with the door. The hinges began to creak ominously, and then the pressure on the other side suddenly subsided a fraction. Braced against the door in tense stalemate, Jeremy and Wes caught their breath.

When the voice from other side of the door spoke again, a new tension was evident in its quavering note. 'Why do you want to see Nikki?'

'That's private, pal.' Jeremy pounded the door with his shoulder once more, for emphasis. 'That's between us and her.'

'Are you friends of Nikki?'

'Right now, we might just be the best friends she's got.'

For a moment there was silence. Then a second voice, deeper than the first, could be heard from somewhere inside the house, in muted discussion with the man-beast. While the words themselves were indistinct, Jeremy could hear the second man's voice thicken with apparent excitement as their discussion continued. An edge of nervous expectation still coloured his words when his face suddenly appeared at the six-inch opening that Wes and Jeremy had managed to create between the door and its frame. Older than the man-beast, he eyed Wes and Jeremy appraisingly from below greying eyebrows. 'I'm Danny. Karl says you're friends of Nikki.'

'Uh-huh.' Jeremy glanced down at Wes, who appeared to have frozen in a rictus of fear. 'We're doctors. From England.'

'Well, any friend of Nikki is a friend of mine.' The eyes - quick, furtive - flicked momentarily between Wes and Jeremy before disappearing once more into the shadowy darkness of the house. 'Let 'em in, Karl. Come through, guys. I'll go find Nikki for you. Come in.'

And then the door swung open.

Jeremy slowly straightened up, at first reluctant to take his agonised foot from its beachhead inside the house – and then, suddenly realising that his goal had been achieved, and that a workable truce had been reached, he stepped through the doorway. Nodding to Wes to do likewise, he hobbled past Karl – who returned his gaze with the ill-suppressed loathing of a muzzled pit bull – and into the ill-lit, sparsely-furnished room beyond. Danny closed the door behind the two pallid Englishmen. Suddenly deprived of sunlight, Jeremy reached for his sunglasses – which was the moment he was hit squarely across the bridge of his nose by a foot-long rubber cock.

Although it had been a while since Jeremy's last saloon-bar brawl, he still knew a thing or two about how to administer a shoeing. He knew, for instance, that having failed to land the first blow, his chances of coming off best in this particular altercation were vastly reduced – and he acknowledged, as he lay on the threadbare carpet, that the 'rubber cock' manoeuvre had been a masterly stroke.

He also knew, however, that the little guy – the one calling himself Danny – really should have been dealing with Wes, not himself. And the fact that Danny was failing to capitalise on his initial success with the latex cosh (by, perhaps, planting a few decent kicks in Jeremy's kidneys) was an error he'd probably live to regret. 'Where the fuck's Nikki?' Danny snarled, spittle raining from his mouth as he bent low over Jeremy's prone form. Dropping to a squat, he waggled the dildo in Jeremy's face. 'Tell me where Nikki is – unless you want to get better acquainted with my little friend. Where the fuck's Nikki?'

Bantering before the job's done, thought Jeremy, using the precious seconds to gather his wits and appraise his opponent. *A pretty fundamental error.* Raising his hands as if in defence, Jeremy made a lightning grab for Danny's ankle and pulled hard. Caught off-balance, Danny gently tipped backwards, extending his non-dildo hand too late to save the back of his head from a satisfyingly loud collision with the wall. In an instant, Jeremy was upon him, seizing a handful of his polo shirt and pulling him six inches off the floor. He drew his fist back on impulse, his eyes narrowing on Danny's nose – but despite every compulsion to the contrary, he didn't strike. 'You're a lucky lad, Danny. Violence is the last resort of the morally enfeebled. My girlfriend, Lisa, says so.' He unclenched his fist, took Danny's cheek between his thumb and forefinger, and gave it a sharp squeeze. 'That's why you've still got a nose, okay?'

Leaving the whimpering Danny lying by the wall, Jeremy took to his feet in search of Wes. It wasn't hard to track him down. Drawn to the clamour of voices at the rear of the house, Jeremy emerged into a well-lit kitchen where Wes – clearly more nimble than the muscle-bound Karl – had evidently spent the previous two minutes darting between chairs, tables and an upturned butcher's trolley in order to evade his pursuer. Both men turned to face Jeremy as he entered the room and, for a second, no one spoke or moved.

Re-appraising Karl's ludicrous dimensions in relation to the ruined kitchen, Jeremy slowly raised his hands and attempted to catch his breath. 'Karl? Your name's Karl, isn't it?' Karl's eyes narrowed, his comic-book face revealing some confusion at Jeremy's 'softly-softly' approach. 'You're the guy from the films, aren't you? Well, Karl,' Jeremy continued, 'me and Dr Wesley love your work, but we're leaving now. We made a big mistake coming here. We don't want any more trouble, okay?' *Violence is the last resort of the morally enfeebled, Karl!* 'Is that cool?'

Jeremy licked his lips, aware for the first time of the blood pouring from his nose. He momentarily considered wiping it away on his jacket sleeve, but decided against it. If it came to a hands-on dust-up with the man-beast, any stray bodily fluids – blood, piss, puke – could end up being valuable assets. *No one likes getting covered in someone else's gunk.* Jeremy grinned and edged forwards into the kitchen, pleased to see Karl recoil at the leering horrorshow of his face. 'We'll just be on our way, now, Karl. You'll never see us again.'

And then, without warning, Wes bolted for the door. In an instant the fragile truce was shattered as Karl lunged after his prey and seized the sleeve of Wes's jacket. Wes spun on his heel and flailed ineffectually at Karl's outsize fist, but the man-beast simply grabbed his other wrist and began slowly bending it backwards over the edge of the kitchen unit. '*Shit!*' Wes yelled, his face contorting at the searing pain from his wrist – a wrist that would have been seconds from snapping if Jeremy hadn't vaulted the worktop and flung his muscular, furniture restorer's arms around the top of Karl's skull.

A moment later, a barrage of sledgehammer blows began raining down on his stomach and chest, and the two men collapsed unceremoniously on to the tiled floor. For some seconds, the only sounds that could be heard were the strained grunts as the two fighters sought to renegotiate their position between the cupboards and the overturned butcher's trolley – and then Jeremy cried out in pain as the heavier man's fist rammed into the gap between his ribs and his kidneys. '*Jesus Christ!*'

From somewhere behind Karl's head, Jeremy could just make out Wes's slim figure, pounding vigorously at the man-beast's back. With his right arm pinioned below Karl's knee, however, he knew that his friend's efforts would be too little, too late. The blow beneath his ribs had made breathing an agonising ordeal, and experience had taught him that a similar assault on his face or stomach could easily spell disaster. *Another one of them, and I'm done.* Jeremy glanced feverishly left and right for a weapon, for anything – but to no avail. Then he glanced up at Karl, now twisted around to face Wes, whose blows continued to rebound harmlessly off the man-beast's shoulders. *You're not going to stop, are you? You don't know how, do you? Not 'til you've delivered the money shot.* Jeremy braced himself against the floor, his decision made. *Only one thing for it, then.* Arching his back, Jeremy raised his head an extra two or three inches off the tiles and took aim at Karl's lurid blue cycling shorts. Then he struck. For a moment, Jeremy's teeth sought purchase on the slippery fabric and its unfamiliar contents – then he closed his eyes and, satisfied that he could cram no more of the man-beast's lycra-clad undercarriage into his mouth, bit down as hard as he could.

In a split second, Jeremy felt the pressure of Karl's thighs relax around his ribcage as the man-beast sought to tear himself free from this unexpected assault. Then one of Karl's enormous hands seized a handful of his hair. Fighting the urge to retch, Jeremy teeth closed even harder on their prize – and a moment later, his hair was released.

'*Fuck! Fuck!*' Karl's screams filled the kitchen as he flailed impotently against the kitchen units, his fists now clenched in agony rather than anger.

It was only when Wes's voice joined the cacophonous racket that Jeremy allowed Karl's blood-drenched cycling shorts to slip from between his teeth, and their owner to crawl away across the floor like a wounded beast. 'For God's sake, Jez, leave it,' Wes implored, now backing away from the kitchen door and installing himself like a protective barrier between Karl and Jeremy. 'Leave it, Jez.

It's over.'

With some effort, Jeremy raised himself on to his elbows and looked over towards the doorway where Wes's gaze was fixed in undisguised terror. There, holding a small pistol in two shaking hands, was Danny.

12

no one's going to kill anyone

'They're going to kill us.'

'I wish you'd stop saying that.'

'They will, though. They'll bloody kill us, Jez. Soon as they get back from the hospital.'

Jeremy twisted his head painfully in Wes's direction. In the half hour since they'd been chained to the dungeon wall, his eyes had started to acclimatise to the darkness, and he could just make out the sorry profile of his friend's face, five yards to his left. 'No one's going to kill anyone, kid. Not when everything's calmed down.' He closed his eyes and let his head hang forward, ready to be sick again if necessary. He'd already thrown up twice – the first time, shortly after the lights had gone out, in an unexpected spasm of agony, fury and adrenaline; the second time, some minutes later, in a silent, hollow retch of dread. Now, the same feelings of blind terror gathered once more at a point an inch above his bowels, making his knees buckle and his stomach lurch. *No one's going to kill anyone.* Jeremy didn't believe it for a moment. He'd known precisely what was happening as soon as Danny had shoved the two of them down the basement steps and flicked on the lights. *A fully-equipped torture dungeon. But of course.* What more could the forward-thinking suburban pornographer wish for? Manacles, chains and a highly professional-looking lighting rig – the full studio set-up. *Convenient. Discreet. Soundproof.*

Soundproof. Either that, or the neighbours were stone deaf. They'd have to be, not to respond to the ten minutes of throat-shredding yells and shouts that had issued from Wes's mouth as soon as the lights went out. Jeremy looked across at his friend, straining once more against the manacles that held both wrists fast to the wall. Somehow, flexing his shoulders hard against the brickwork alleviated the feelings of sick terror for a moment. 'It'll be okay, mate,' he grunted. 'I promise it will.'

'That bloke had a fucking *gun*, Jez.'

'That doesn't mean he's going to do anything daft.'

'That's why people *buy* guns.' A familiar note of shrill hysteria had entered Wes's voice. 'In order to do wacky, tripped-out, *seriously fucking daft things.*'

'Not necessarily. My granddad's still got his old service revolver from the war. Keeps it in a drawer next to his bed. He's never shot anyone.'

'You said he once shot a bloke in the Fat Ox. Over a game of dominoes.'

'He didn't kill him, though. He just took off a bit of his ear.'

For a moment neither of the men spoke, and when Wes next broke their silence, Jeremy initially mistook his ill-suppressed laughter for quaking sobs of terror. 'You...' Wes began, struggling to catch his breath against the tide of deranged hysterics that threatened to overwhelm him. 'You bit that bloke's...' – he struggled to form the word – '...penis.'

'That's not something I'd appreciate being widely known, mate.'

'My lips are sealed.'

'Good lad.' Jeremy closed his eyes in the darkness. He wasn't given to over-analysing things, but he wasn't so insensitive to the symbolism of the encounter to pretend that something a pretty primal hadn't taken place in the kitchen. 'I'd have given it a kick instead, but my foot was really sore from being stuck in the door.'

'Of course, Jez.' In the lightless dungeon, it wasn't difficult for Wes to mentally conjure up the cross-section diagrams of the male genitalia from his medical school anatomy lectures – the tubes and glands and veins. *Lots of human calamari.* 'There's a huge blood supply to the penis, mind. Potential for serious nerve damage, too, if you got the testes. He's probably going to be out of action for quite a while.'

Jeremy's eyes narrowed. '*Good.*'

Suddenly, both men's heads twisted in the darkness. From behind the door at the top of the basement steps, a sound could clearly be heard – the frantic scratching of several keys being tried in a lock – and, after some moments, the soft metallic scrape of a bolt being drawn back. For what seemed like an eternity, Wes could only hear the sound of his heart pounding in his ears. Then the door opened, casting a long triangular shaft of light into the dungeon's gloom.

A second later, silhouetted against the wall, a figure descended the stairs and flicked on the light. Wes winced and turned away, withdrawing instinctively from the harsh illumination. Jeremy, however, squinted at the figure in the corner of the room until its features took on form and definition. *A lass. Twenty-something. Scared shitless, by the look of her.* Glancing fearfully back up the stairs, the figure hesitated for a moment before skipping over to the two manacled prisoners. Her eyes searched Jeremy's face urgently. 'Are you guys looking for Nikki?' she stammered.

'That's right,' said Jeremy, as calmly as he could. 'We're

doctors. We need to see her. It's urgent.'

For some moments the girl didn't move, clearly paralysed by fear and anxiety. 'Are you Nikki's friend?' pressed Jeremy, trying to keep the creeping terror from his own voice.

The girl nodded.

'If you help us, we can help Nikki,' said Wes gently. 'What's your name?'

'Faye.'

'Well, Faye,' said Jeremy. 'We'd be really, *really* grateful if you could lend us a hand getting out of this dungeon. You wouldn't mind trying a couple of your keys in these handcuffs, would you?'

13

two years in hardcore doesn't look so good on your résumé

It didn't matter that Danny's dungeon was now over fifty miles behind them, lost in the glittering hinterland of neon and streetlight on the outskirts of LA – Faye still refused to be coaxed from her prone position on the Charger's back seat, except for occasional meerkat-like glances snatched through the rear window.

'They won't be following us, kid,' Jeremy murmured, more to himself than Faye. '*No way.*' Earlier, he'd tried adjusting the mirror so that he could address her directly, but to no avail. Whichever way he'd turned it, Faye had shifted position to avoid Jeremy's gaze, and now his remarks had grown increasingly mechanical and repetitive, almost as if he was simply avoiding falling into the shell-shocked torpor that had afflicted his two passengers. If Wes had been capable of coherent speech, he'd have pointed out that the lack of breezy chit-chat in the car might have something to do with the liberal spattering of dried blood on Jeremy's face and shirt – but since he'd slammed the car door behind him an hour earlier, he'd offered little more than the occasional hyperventilated whimper.

For some moments, Jeremy's words hung in the air – as had most of the seemingly random observations he'd made since pulling on to Interstate 15. Then the car's three pairs of eyes resumed their individual lookouts on the encroaching night. If they could have been seen behind Jeremy's shades, Faye's eyes – now narrowed upon the sinking sun – would have been hardest to read, alternating between docility and blind panic. Wes's eyes, trained unseeingly on the southern horizon, relayed little more than blurred static to his bruised mind, while Jeremy saw only a dizzying star-field of approaching tail lights on the road ahead, as the Charger weaved in wide, slo-mo arcs between thundering trucks and indifferent automobiles.

Then, as if waking from a dream, Wes blinked and cast his eyes around the car's darkening interior. He leaned across the armrest and gently tapped the speedo, already bathed in the refrigerated blue of the dashboard light. When, at length, Jeremy showed no sign of response, he spoke. 'You're aware that there's a speed limit, Jez?'

'What?'

'Speed limit. Fifty-five miles per hour.'

Jeremy glanced at the rear view mirror, possibly seeking an ally in Faye. 'For the locals, mate. For the locals.'

'For *everyone.*'

Jeremy shook his head tersely. 'We're Brits. It's seventy for us. Plus or minus a discretionary ten. So, eighty.'

'We're doing over ninety. And I think you'd be unwise to attract the attention of California's law enforcement community. Particularly since you look like you're going to a fancy dress party as a youthful Hannibal Lector.' Wes slumped back into his seat, his piece spoken.

Glancing down at his shirt front, Jeremy felt forced to

concede the point – but it still took some moments, and a considerable effort of will, before he was able to gently draw his foot away from the accelerator. The Charger's engine note dropped to a semitone below 'agonised' and Jeremy slid the car into the nearside lane.

'There's a service station coming up.' Wes pointed out a low building lying some half a mile distant, where the cadavers of a million desiccated shrubs cast long, ochre shadows across the Mojave desert. 'Next right. I think we could all do with a break. Get cleaned up. Work out how we're going to help young Faye, here.'

Jeremy said nothing but flicked the indicator stalk. Illuminated by the intermittent green light from the dashboard, his motionless face looked even more unsettling than before – and it was only after some moments, with the slip road just yards ahead, that Wes's eyes fell once more upon the Charger's speedo. 'Slow down, mate. Slow down.'

'What?' As if emerging from a trance of his own, Jeremy glanced first at Wes, and then at the approaching bend in the road where his friend's eyes were fixed. '*Oh shit.*' The Charger's protesting tyres wailed as Jeremy tried to compensate, too late, for the tightening radius of the slip road's curve. '*Oh shit oh shit oh shit oh shit oh shit.*'

Pressing himself hard into his seat, Wes surveyed the deadly parabola of the carriageway, estimated the camber, did the maths, worked out the odds. It was going to be close. *Very close.* He closed his eyes, forcing himself to confront the g-force of the curve as Jeremy wrestled the unwilling Charger into an insane slingshot against the lethal centrifuge of the road. And then, miraculously, the Charger slowly righted itself, its engine note died, and it rolled to a gentle halt beneath the wide, illuminated awning of the roadside gas station. Wes opened his eyes and stared at Jeremy, whose face at last betrayed his unspoken terror at the horrors of the day. 'I can't let go of the steering wheel, mate,' he said. 'My fingers are locked.'

'Danny's a bad man,' said Faye, staring out over the desert towards the twinkling lights of the Interstate. 'Very bad. But Nikki should never have taken his money and cameras. He's still real mad. Keeps hollering and screaming about what he's going to do when he finds her.'

Jeremy shivered, pulled his jacket close and dropped to his haunches next to Faye. Then he leant back against the front wing of the Charger, glad when the heat from its engine begin seeping into his shoulder blades. Only in the last five minutes had the stress from the fight, the dungeon and the getaway started to ebb away, but his muscles were still sore with hair-trigger tension. 'Would he really have killed us?'

Faye shrugged and took a deep drag on her cigarette. 'Maybe. Maybe not. He knows people who do. He'd have killed *me* if he knew I'd helped you escape. And Nikki's dead if she ever shows up in LA again.'

'And what about you? We've cocked up everything. You can't go back because of us.'

'Are you kidding?' Faye laughed and slipped her free arm through Jeremy's. 'You guys are my knights in shining armour.'

'Aye?'

'Oh yeah. I've been meaning to get out for months.' Faye looked away, suddenly wistful. 'Things got worse after Nikki left.'

'I don't understand why did you didn't leave before.'

'Danny's very controlling. And getting out of the industry can be hard.'

'Uh-huh?'

'Well, it can be tough making a start in anything else. People recognise you. Family don't want to know. Word gets around. Then you have to move on. And two years in hardcore doesn't look so good on your résumé, does it?'

Jeremy, whose own CV would easily fit on the back of a Rothmans packet – and who, pre-Lisa, would have considered 'two years in hardcore' only slightly less appealing than a major lottery win – shrugged diplomatically. 'Probably not for a nice lass like you, no.'

'It's time to get out now, though. Time to go home. Make things up with my folks.' Faye turned to Jeremy, suddenly serious. 'I'm twenty-six, Jeremy. The parts you're offered don't get better as you get older.'

Acutely conscious of Faye's eye upon him, Jeremy stared resolutely into the darkness beyond the Interstate. He was a man, he'd have to admit, who'd been a bit of a connoisseur of porny treats in the past – but he'd never given much consideration to the career trajectory of its foot soldiers. *The Fayes. The Nikkis.* And this scarcely seemed like the moment to tell Faye that, in his layman's opinion, she still had plenty of years left in her slim figure, straight dark hair and wide, expressive eyes. *No, no, no, no, no.* 'I s'pose you're right, kid,' he eventually conceded, taking a last drag on his cigarette and flicking the smouldering butt into the dusty scrub where the parking lot became desert. 'No game to grow old in, is it?'

He stood up, stretched his legs and flexed his fingers. At the far end of the parking lot, silhouetted in the light from the service station awning, Wes's gangling figure could clearly be seen, his head swathed in cigarette smoke. He approached the Charger, set down his bags of groceries on the bonnet and handed sandwiches to Jeremy and Faye. 'There's a Greyhound out of Barstow in less than an hour,' he finally announced when he'd caught his breath. He turned to Faye. 'I called the ticket office. If we leave now, you'll catch it. You'll be back home in Topeka by Friday lunchtime.'

'Or you could come with us, if you wanted,' Jeremy said. 'See Nikki again.'

Faye looked from Wes to Jeremy and back again, her brow furrowed with indecision. Then she shook her head. 'No. I just want to get out of California. Get back to Kansas. Dye my hair, change my name. Try starting again. But give Nikki my love when you see her. Tell her I miss her.'

Jeremy nodded solemnly, put his hand in his trouser pocket and withdrew a bundle of notes. He put down his sandwich, peeled off a large sheaf of bills and offered them to Faye. Her face clouded with doubt as she regarded the money. 'Take it, kid,' Jeremy urged her. 'You've five hundred dollars, there. It'll pay for the Greyhound, and you'll have a few bob to spend on your folks when you get back to Topeka.'

'Are you sure?'

'Aye, go on. It's the least we owe you. You saved our bacon back there. And you spent twenty minutes massaging my fingers away from that steering wheel. I'd still be stuck behind the bloody thing if it wasn't for you.'

Then Wes delved into his own pocket, withdrew a handful of tiny tins and handed them to Faye. 'That's Poschl's Gletscherprise snuff. Finest money can buy. It'll keep you going on the bus when you're gasping for a cigarette.' And then, fearing that his feelings of gratitude might overwhelm him, he smartly opened the Charger's door and began ushering his companions inside.

'You okay to drive, Jez? No more of your little blackouts?' he asked as Jeremy installed himself behind the wheel, regarding it with obvious apprehension.

'Aye, aye. No worries,' he declared dismissively. 'I just lost it for a minute back there. Stress. Near-death situations. Not something your uncle Jezzer's used to dealing with. But I'm fine now. Raring to go.'

Wes slammed the passenger door behind him. Then, as though submitting to a desire he'd tried hard to suppress, he turned to Faye. 'I'm just curious about one thing. When you came and unlocked the dungeon, had you already decided to help us escape?'

Faye nodded. 'When I'd heard you were looking for Nikki, I knew I had to help. She wouldn't have given me her new address if she didn't think someone was going to use it. It was one of the last things she said before she left – that someone might come looking for her.' Faye smiled in the dark cavern of the Charger's rear set, her next words lost beneath the guttural roar of the engine. '*A friend*.'

When Wes strode into their Barstow motel room shortly after midnight, Jeremy only just had time to jump beneath the bedclothes before being seen. He pulled the sheets up to his chin and regarded his friend warily. Both of them had expected Wes's phone call to take at least ten minutes, but he'd barely been out of the room for two. Jeremy cleared his throat and smiled wanly. 'Did you get through to Gabi?'

'Uh-huh. She'd just woken up. It's already tomorrow morning over there.'

'And how did she sound?'

Wes went over to his bed and started taking off his shoes. 'Surprised. Distracted. Like she was watching telly or something.'

'What did you tell her you'd been up to?'

'That I'd just come back from a gripping seminar on diagnostic developments in proctology.'

Jeremy nodded, impressed. 'Sounds pretty sexy. And did she buy it?'

'She didn't seem particularly interested, actually.' Wes turned and regarded Jeremy through narrowed eyes. 'Have you still got your shoes on?'

'Aaaah... yes.'

'Why?'

'Haven't quite finished getting undressed.'

'But you're in bed.'

'I was cold. Just got out of the shower. Turn the light

off, mate.'

'Why?'

'Just turn the light off, will you?'

'Why?'

'So I can finish getting my kit off.'

'In the dark?'

'In the dark, aye.'

'Why?'

Jeremy growled in exasperation – so much so, that Wes almost felt like edging back towards the door. 'Call it girlish modesty,' he eventually muttered. 'Turn the light off, get into bed and shut your eyes.'

Wes pulled off his trousers, folded them over the back of the room's sole chair and dropped his socks into the side pocket of his holdall. Then, with a final sceptical glance at Jeremy, he slipped between the sheets and flicked off the light. 'You're getting weird, you know. Distinctly peculiar.'

'I've had a bloody stressful day. I almost died. Twice.'

'It's not just today, though, is it? You actually started panting when you got undressed last night. I heard you.'

'Shut up.'

'It frightened me a bit, I must say.'

'Shut up and go to sleep.'

Wes heard the bedclothes being thrown back on the adjacent bed and the sound of Jeremy struggling with his shoes and trousers. 'It was a bit like *The Blair Witch Project*.'

'Are you going to *shit! Bollocks! Ow!*'

Squirming around on to his side, Wes flicked on the table lamp. When both men's eyes had adjusted to the light, Jeremy was still clutching his stubbed toe. He glared accusingly at Wes, who could only stare back at his friend, open-mouthed. Eventually, he summoned the power of speech. 'Wow. Is that one of Lisa's nighties you're wearing, mate?' he said. 'Because it looks a bit tight round the arse.'

14

how late is late?

'I'm not a transvestite.'

Wes – generally not a fan of big breakfasts – wiped the last smear of fried egg from his plate, popped the final morsel of bread into his mouth and cupped a hand behind his ear. 'Pardon?'

'I said I'm not...' – Jeremy glanced warily around the diner. In the booth opposite, a young couple in baseball caps were already starting to take an abnormal interest in their conversation. Jeremy lowered his voice. 'I'm not one of those people I just mentioned.'

Wes frowned and leaned back expansively. 'What, a transvestite? A big old tranny?'

'Piss off.'

'All I'm saying is that you wear women's clothes in bed,' Wes declared, seemingly to the diner's entire clientele. 'And 'transvestite' is the term applied to a bloke who wears women's clothes. You know – one of those chaps who's just never lost their taste for the dressing-up box. Nothing to be ashamed of, mind. Even if society at large might deem it *just a bit weird.*'

For a moment, the pair glared at each other in silent enmity while the waitress topped up their coffees. Jeremy poured his customary three sugars into his cup and fixed Wes with an uncompromising stare. 'There's nothing weird about me. *Nothing.*'

'It's less than twenty-four hours since you had another man's penis in your mouth.'

'In self-defence, Wes. And in the defence of *your* worthless arse. It doesn't mean I'm gay or anything.'

Wes's eyebrow shot heavenward. 'That sounded just a trifle homophobic.'

'And *that* sounded a bit bloody harsh, mate,' said Jeremy, genuinely stung. 'I'm highly pro-gay, as you're fully aware.'

'Are you?'

'Certainly. I supported you during *your* gay phase, didn't I?'

'Doing GCSE French doesn't make someone gay, Jez.'

'If you say so, mate. You were crap at being gay, anyway. You were the least fun gay person I ever met. *Normal* gay people enjoy a pint or two and the odd late night. A bit of friendly banter. And I'd never oppress anyone on account of their sexual preferences. *Never.*' Jeremy leaned back and gazed out of the window at Barstow's half-hearted attempt at a rush hour, affording Wes the optimum view of his 'martyr' pose – the once that looked like a dyspeptic spaniel. 'Your Uncle Jezzer knows what it's like,' he said quietly. 'I've suffered discrimination myself, you know – I've been vilified because of where I've wanted to put my willy.'

'Was it into another man's bottom?'

'Nah.' Jeremy's eyes clouded with nostalgia. 'It was into twins, actually. Lovely twins. Sally and Justine. They both worked at B&Q in Middlesbrough. I used to run into them sometimes when I was picking up chipboard for dad.'

'And who did the vilifying?'

'Sally's boyfriend and Justine's husband. Big lads.'

Wes nodded philosophically and sipped his coffee. If Jeremy had thought his diversionary tactic would throw his friend off the 'cross-dressing' scent, though, he was sorely mistaken. Wes put down his cup and addressed his friend with quiet malice. 'None of which explains your recent transvestism, does it?'

Jeremy sighed and cupped his face in his hands. He'd spent a good deal of the previous night listening to Wes's contented snoring and the bluebottle buzz of the motel room's air conditioning, and didn't have the mental energy for this kind of early morning gamesmanship. 'Look, if you must know, I just wear one of Lisa's old nightshirts in bed when we're away from each other. That's all. It helps me sleep – particularly when I've had one of those stressful, getting-locked-in-a-dungeon kind of days.'

Wes weighed Jeremy's words carefully. 'You've only been apart for three nights, mate,' he eventually said, trying to reposition himself so he could catch his friend's eye. When at last Jeremy looked up, his expression told a truth that his voice never would. And, suddenly, everything made sense. 'Except it's not just been three nights, has it? Has it, Jez?'

Jeremy drained his coffee and lowered his eyes. 'I suppose it's been a little bit longer than that.' He took a cigarette from the packet on the table and wedged it behind his ear – a habit he'd been affecting since they first arrived in California – and took the bill over to the counter.

Outside, despite the earliness of the hour, a dry breeze was already beginning to hint at the heat to come. Jeremy unlocked the Charger's doors, retrieved the cigarette from behind his ear and lit it. Then he took a scrap of paper from his trouser pocket – the one with Nikki's address on it, pressed into his hand by Faye the previous night on the steps of the Greyhound. 'How long until we get to Santa Ana?'

Wes shrugged. 'Hour and a half. Two, tops.'

For a moment, Jeremy appeared to be paralysed by indecision. Then he strode round to the other side of the car. 'You drive,' he said, tossing the keys to Wes. 'I'll tell you about Lisa on the way.'

Even though it had all happened nearly two months ago, Jeremy could remember every last detail. He remembered explaining the concept of Poet's Day to Callum and managing to bunk off work at a record four o'clock. He remembered bounding off the DLR at Canary Wharf and rushing straight to Davy's Wine Bar without changing out of his work boots. He remembered the way they'd eyed him up when he'd ordered a thirty-five quid bottle of Chablis and paid for it in pound coins and shrapnel. And he remembered the way Lisa had looked as she weaved between the tables of half-cut salarymen and braying suits. *Still the prettiest lass in the room,* he'd thought. *Prettiest lass in London. Prettiest lass I've ever seen.*

He remembered wondering, as he leaned down and brushed his lips with hers, whether he preferred her public or private kisses. And then he remembered taking the wine out of its bucket, pouring two brimming glasses, and Lisa not touching a drop of it. 'Did I get the wrong one?' he'd asked, peering at the unfamiliar wording on the label. 'Isn't this the one you like?'

'No, no. It's exactly right.'

'It's not corked, is it?' Jeremy raised his own glass and took a hefty sip. He'd only learned what 'corked' meant a week earlier, and had been secretly longing for his first opportunity to upbraid an arsy sommelier for palming him off with a bottle of vintage turps.

Lisa had raised her glass, sniffed it, and replaced it on the table. 'It's not corked.'

'Then why aren't you drinking it?'

For a moment Lisa said nothing. From experience, Jeremy knew that by this point he was expected to have read her mind – Lisa led an all-male team at the bank, and liked 'her boys' to be 'intuitive' and 'assertive'. Jeremy also knew, however, that it took at least an hour – and half a bottle of wine – before Lisa slipped out of 'corporate battle-axe' mode into her 'weekend' persona. *Not a good moment to aggravate the situation with unfounded guesswork.* He shrugged, leaned over and – very helpfully, he thought – gently kissed their mutually-agreed favourite spot at the top of her neck. And that's when Lisa had whispered in his ear, her voice faltering as her self-control fractured. 'I think I'm pregnant.'

Halting mid-kiss, Jeremy weighed Lisa's words in his mind and – for a split second, in the reassuring noise and chaos of the bar – he felt a sensation of complete and utter calm. Then his stomach lurched and his throat contracted to the width of a cheese wire. Valuable seconds passed as he tried recalibrating his larynx so that when words eventually emerged, they'd come out sounding friendly, off-hand and unfazed. 'What makes you think that?' he rasped.

'The horrific cramps. Peeing all the time. Late period. And I keep getting these overwhelming urges to eat soil and pop into Mothercare for a pram.'

'Seriously?'

Lisa's eyebrows rose imploringly, and when she spoke Jeremy could detect quiet desperation hiding behind her apparent lack of emotion. 'Everything but the last bit.'

'And how late is late?'

'Late enough to be worried.'

'Shit.' Jeremy clutched the arms of his chair in the forlorn hope that this might stop the room spinning quite so enthusiastically. *Had there been a period-sized hiatus in their shagging recently?* He couldn't remember one. *What about a drunken, condom-free episode beneath the bedclothes?* He swallowed hard and cast his mind back. *Condom, condom, two condoms (one after the other), condom, condom, no condom...* Shit. *Just the once.* 'I think I need to go to the toilet.'

And although it was Jeremy's honest intention to go

straight to the gents', something strange happened as he took unsteadily to his feet. For as his lungs fought for air, his legs somehow took over his higher functions and before he knew where he was going, Jeremy found himself standing outside the bar. His left hand gripped the steel railings as he struggled to marshal his thoughts, and some moments had passed before he realised that his other hand was wrapped firmly around the neck of the Chablis bottle. He raised it to his lips and drained it in one. And as the bottle slipped from Jeremy's fingers into the greasy waters of West India Quay – as it slowly filled with fluid and disappeared from view – he knew with simple and complete conviction that wherever else in life his feet might take him, there was *no way on earth* that he could go back inside the bar.

Turning briskly, with no clear thought of a destination in mind, Jeremy took his heels and ran blind towards the DLR station, slipped his ticket into the barrier and was gone.

'That doesn't sound so bad,' said Wes, glancing across at his friend as the Charger squealed to a halt at an intersection. He'd managed quite a few unorthodox little tricks and manoeuvres *en route* from Barstow – stalling, skidding, wheel-spinning – but Jeremy didn't seem to have noticed. Now, having just pulled off Interstate 5 into the broad, suburban Santa Ana streets, Jeremy appeared suddenly aware of his surroundings again, reaching out of the window and giving the car a reassuring pat on its front wing. Then the lights changed and Wes tapped the accelerator, causing the Charger to lurch suicidally into the sluggish lunchtime traffic. 'People screw up. Lisa can't hold it against you. I mean – you were just a bit freaked out. It might have scuppered your chances of winning Boyfriend Of The Year, but it's perfectly understandable. Needing a few minutes alone to think about things. Clear your head.'

Jeremy shook his head mournfully. 'That was the

problem. I took longer than a few minutes.'

'Half an hour?'

'A long weekend. In Barcelona.'

Wes's eyes panned left and right in search of something – anything – that might tell him which street he was now drifting along. The houses – all exuding an indefinable, bland menace from behind their railings and palm tree borders – looked eerily similar to Danny's. 'You took Lisa to Barcelona?' he eventually replied, when he'd found sufficient mental space to process Jeremy's pronouncement. Gliding to a gentle halt about a yard from the sidewalk, he turned to face his friend. 'That was a *nice* thing to do, Jez. Top marks. Proper 'boyfriend' behaviour.'

'No, mate,' Jeremy sighed. 'It was proper 'moron' behaviour. *I* went to Barcelona. Alone. Without telling Lisa I was going.' He reached behind him and set about retrieving the street map from beneath the mound of discarded burger wrappers and soda cans on the back seat. 'I went straight back to the flat from the bar, picked up my passport and got the Tube to Heathrow.' Flicking a fragment of popcorn off the map, he opened the door and made his way over to the sidewalk, peering left and right in search of a landmark. Eventually satisfied, he got back in the car and slammed the door. 'I got to Tim and Claire's apartment around midnight. Holed up there 'til Monday. Thought things over. Then I went home.'

For a moment Wes stared at his friend in horrified fascination. Seeing Jeremy replay the events in his mind had the same morbid attraction as watching a slow-motion car crash, and nine tenths of his moral faculties recoiled instinctively from it. Still, somewhere in the darker recesses of his mind, Wes couldn't suppress a sneaking admiration for the lad's behaviour. *The sheer fuck-off selfishness of it. Its deranged disregard for consequences. The way it neatly bypassed all considerations of introspection, forethought or basic decency. Wow.* In the pit of his stomach, Wes felt a tiny flicker of warmth as he imagined the outrage on Gabi's face that would accompany a similar flit from their Putney love nest. Then he felt a deep, churning chill as he contemplated how she'd react if she ever, *ever* found out about Project Nikki. Wes shivered and turned his attention to the point that Jeremy had just marked on the map with a large 'N'. 'Why did you go to Barcelona, then?'

'Because I'm an unreconstructed hedonist with narcissistic tendencies who's living in a state of protracted childhood, insulated from the realities of everyday life through the construction of a fantasy existence, and artificially buoyed by the complete absence of a restraining superego,' said Jeremy, gazing unseeingly out of the window at the parched lawns and broad driveways drifting by. 'That's what Lisa thinks, anyway.'

'And what do *you* think?'

'Same as Lisa. I *can* be a bit of a cock, sometimes.' Jeremy turned and faced Wes again, his expression unnervingly sincere. 'The thing is, I just wanted some time to make the mental adjustment. I thought my life was over when I got on the plane. But when I got home, I realised it was just beginning. That I loved Lisa, and that I'd stick with her no matter what. You must've felt like that when you married Gabi.'

Wes pulled up to another intersection, glad that the steady flow of cars and trucks ahead meant he didn't have to meet his friend's eye. 'Definitely. Is this South Euclid Street?'

'Aye. Turn here, hack along for a couple of hundred yards, and it'll be on your right.'

'Cool.' Wes eased out into the traffic, hugging the nearside sidewalk. 'So Lisa threw you out when you got back from Barcelona?'

'She didn't throw me out, mate. She *left* me. I know there's only a minor distinction, but it's an important one. She said that I'd had some time to think, and that's what she was going to do too.'

'Think?'

'Aye. Think about whether she wanted to be with a feckless dick-brain who pegs it to Spain at the first sign of grief.' Jeremy took a deep breath. 'And she's gone to Shanghai to do it.'

'*Shanghai?*

'Uh-huh. A secondment had come up at the bank. She was going to tell me about it in the wine bar. By the time I came back from Barcelona, she'd already rushed it through. Booked her flight, packed her bags. She was gone by the next weekend and I haven't heard from her since.' Jeremy glanced down at the scrap of paper in his hand, then at the shabby-looking signpost at the roadside. 'I think this is it. The mobile home park. Stop here.'

Wes pulled the Charger into the park's wide driveway and drew to a halt in the shade of a broad-leafed palm. He switched off the engine and turned to his friend, grey-faced in spite of the noonday California sun. 'So is Lisa actually pregnant?'

'Don't know.'

'And when's she coming back?'

Jeremy got out of the car, stretched, and peered at the insalubrious dwellings clustered around the park's entrance. 'I don't know, kid,' he finally muttered. 'The secondment's for at least six months. After that... I just don't know.'

15

say hello to my little friend

'You're not nervous, are you, mate?'

Wes lit his cigarette, discarded the match with a testy flick of the wrist and hurried to catch up with Jeremy. 'Not nervous, no,' he lied, falling into step with his friend and hunching his shoulders against an imaginary gale. 'There just seem to be quite a lot of eyes on us.'

It was true. In the five minutes since they'd left the Charger's protective force field, an alarming number of people had come to their doors and windows to stare impassively at the two pale Yorkshiremen. And now that they'd wandered deep into the mobile home park's complex of lanes and driveways – now the car was out of sight – Wes couldn't suppress a creeping sense of dread. 'There's no need to worry, kid,' Jeremy said, drawing to a halt in front of a patched-up clapboard trailer and retrieving his own cigarettes. 'It's just a friendly, twenty-minute house call. And it won't be like yesterday.'

Wes immediately wished he hadn't said it. *Yesterday*. That single word brought everything hurtling back into focus. He realised now that since putting Faye on the Greyhound, he'd probably gone a bit demob-happy. After all, he'd escaped from a torture dungeon, cheated death and – fantastically – discovered Jeremy's penchant for nocturnal cross-dressing. Best of all, he'd been reprieved from having to tell someone they'd got cancer. In fact, in his quiet euphoria, Wes had almost contrived to forget that Nikki existed at all – but now she was back, hovering in the forefront of his mind, accompanied by a recently-acquired aura of menace. He shivered and took a drag on his cigarette.

As if sensing his apprehension, Jeremy put an arm around his friend's shoulders. 'In the highly unlikely event that any of Danny's mates are here, we've got insurance.'

'What insurance?'

Jeremy grinned and turned to Wes, pulling back his jacket to reveal an abnormally bulging waistband. 'Danny's pistol. I nicked it yesterday. He left it on the kitchen table in the house.' Ignoring Wes's horrified expression, Jeremy gazed wistfully into the middle distance. 'I've always fancied having a gun.' He thrust his tooled-up pelvis in Wes's direction, adopting his best Al Pacino voice. '*Say hello to my little friend.*'

'You want me to talk to your crotch?'

Jeremy appeared to consider this for a moment. 'If you want to.'

Wes regarded his grinning friend with an expression of undisguised contempt. '*You're a fucking lunatic,*' he hissed.

'Chill, Wes.' Jeremy stepped on to the tiny veranda and rapped smartly on the door. 'Everyone's got a gun in America. I'm only doing my best to integrate. And it's just taken your mind off worrying about Nikki, hasn't it?'

Shaking his head in disbelief, Wes joined his insane companion on the doorstep. Jeremy had a point, he reluctantly conceded. Even since he'd been hauled away by US Immigration, he'd scarcely had the time or energy to catch his breath, let alone dwell on what he was going to say to Nikki – the only person he'd ever really opened up with, the only girl he'd really felt close to. And now he was about to actually *meet* her. He thrust his hands into his trouser pockets, suddenly aware of how badly they were shaking.

It wasn't surprising though. After all, so much had changed in his life so incredibly quickly. A fortnight earlier, he'd have probably described Nikki as a friend – a mental lifeline in the churning whirlpool of his marriage. But now, on the verge of his first real conversation with her, it suddenly occurred to him that he might not know her at all. He tried desperately to list all the things he could remember about her. *She likes Depeche Mode, but thinks their recent stuff is too rock,* he thought. *She thinks David Lynch is a better film director than Fellini. She can't eat anything, no matter how good it tastes, once she knows it's got coconut in it.* Wes closed his eyes, trying to ignore the fact that Jeremy had dropped to one knee and was now squinting through the keyhole. *Her first crush was Big Bird from Sesame Street, aged five. If she ever goes to Europe, the first place she wants to visit is Jim Morrison's grave in Paris. She doesn't believe in reincarnation, but if it existed she'd want to come back as an armadillo. If Mark Chapman had read The Maltese Falcon instead of The Catcher In The Rye, he'd have shot a different Beatle. Nothing is more refreshing than a cool Mai Tai on a hot day. You can't get a good night's sleep unless your bed is correctly aligned to the North Pole...*

'I think I can hear something.'

Wes opened one eye. 'What?'

'Dunno. Could be movement.' Jeremy knocked on the door again, harder this time. 'Someone moving round inside. I think it's her. Nikki.'

Nikki. Closing his eyes again, Wes tried recreating his mental shrine to their friendship. *What else do I remember about Nikki?* he thought. *She'd prefer to be stuck in an elevator with Steve Buscemi than Brad Pitt. If she could bring one person back from the dead, it'd be George Elliot. She gets paid for having sex on*

CHEEK

camera. She might be dying. She might be dying. She might be dying...

'I can see her.'

Wes swallowed hard and knelt down next to Jeremy, extinguishing his cigarette on the peeling paint of the door jamb. 'Are you sure?'

'Pretty sure.' Jeremy subjected the door to a further fusillade of knocks and put his mouth to the woodwork. '*Hello! Hello! Anyone home?*' He stood up and gave the wall a couple of gentle kicks. '*Hello! Is Nikki there? We need to see Nikki.*'

For a second, the only sound that could be heard was the tinny buzz of a television in a neighbouring dwelling and the hum of invisible insects, secreted in the bushes below the veranda. Then, from behind the door, a small voice could clearly be heard. 'Go away.'

Jeremy lowered his mouth to the keyhole again. 'We need to see Nikki. It's very important.'

'She's not here. Go away.'

'Can you open the door, please? We need to know where Nikki is.'

'What do you want her for?'

'We've got something very important to tell her. We're friends of Faye. She gave us the address. We're doctors. Hello?' Jeremy moved his eye to the keyhole. At the end of the gloomy junk-strewn hallway, peering around a saloon-style louvre door, a face had appeared. Jeremy beckoned Wes closer and lowered his voice to a whisper. 'She's there, but I don't think she's going to let us in. She's scared shitless, probably thanks to Danny and Karl. Maybe we should just write a note instead and leave it under a plant pot.'

Suddenly, both men's attention returned to the door. From the other side, the sound of bolts being withdrawn could be heard. A moment later, it opened a couple of inches. Four slim, elfin fingers appeared around the edge, followed by a small, heart-shaped face beneath an untidy

139

mop of dirty-blonde hair. The girl's eyes darted from Wes to Jeremy and back again. Then she spoke. 'Did you guys say you were... *doctors?*'

'That's right.' For a moment, Jeremy toyed with the idea of giving the girl one of his tiny 'medical' smiles. Having abandoned his blood-spattered suit in a dumpster behind the Barstow motel, he felt sorely underdressed for the part he was now required to play – but the expectant face at the door didn't seem remotely troubled by his Thin Lizzy t-shirt and three-day stubble. He cleared his throat. 'This is Dr Wesley. And I'm Dr Sykes. You're Nikki, right? We've come a long way to see you, kid.'

Nikki's eyes darted back and forth between the unlikely pair standing on her doorstep. Then they narrowed in amused disbelief on Jeremy's lopsided grin. 'Your name's *Dr Sex?*'

Wes turned away from the grimy bay window and allowed the Venetian blinds to snap back into place. He'd been peering along the driveway at intervals for the previous ten minutes, ever since Nikki had gone into the bedroom to make a phone call, and his nervousness was beginning to rub off on his friend.

Jeremy watched as Wes crept over to the bedroom door and put a cupped hand to his ear, then crept back to the window. Eventually, draining his lemon tea, he levered himself off the sagging sofa and made his way to his friend's side. 'What?'

Wes cast an apprehensive glance at the bedroom door. 'I'm just not one hundred percent sure that it's her, that's all,' he hissed.

'You're not sure it's who?'
'I'm not sure she's Nikki.'
'Why not?'
'Gut feeling.' Wes lowered his voice still further and beckoned Jeremy close. 'She *looks* like the girl from the

video, I'll grant you. But I spent a long time talking to Nikki online. A *long* time. And I'm just not getting... you know... the same *vibe*.'

Jeremy shook his head dismissively. 'It's obviously Nikki, mate. I mean – I know she looks a bit different with her clothes on, and when she's not, you know...'

'When she's not shagging Karl?'

'Aye, aye – when she's not shagging Karl... but it's still her. Definitely. It's in the eyes.' Jeremy rubbed his chin wistfully. 'It's a sort of vulnerability. It just makes you want to, you know... *protect* her.'

'If you say so,' said Wes, shrugging disdainfully. 'All I'm saying is that *I* didn't feel that spark you get when you recognise someone. And I don't think she got it when she saw me. And *if* she's not the real Nikki, then she might be a friend of Danny and Karl. And if she's friends with Danny – who's probably not particularly thrilled that you've nicked his Saturday night special – who's to say she's not phoning him now? Who's to say that they're not heading over here *as we speak?*'

Jeremy weighed his friend's words for a moment. 'I think she's nice. She made us lemon tea. I've always been a bit wary of lemon tea, but it's not too bad.' He stared at the sticky, magazine-covered coffee table, where Wes's cup sat untouched. 'Danny and Karl didn't make us tea. Danny tried breaking my nose with a rubber cock. I trust her.'

'You trust her because you *fancy* her.' Wes's eyes narrowed accusingly on his friend, whose reputation for becoming a dribbling halfwit around pretty girls was legendary. 'It was obvious before you even stepped through the door. When she called you 'Dr Sex' and did that thing with her eyelashes.'

Jeremy turned to the window and pulled open a peep hole in the blinds. 'Now you're talking bollocks.'

'Am I? And if she's so trustworthy, why wouldn't she let us in until she'd found out we were doctors?'

'What's *that* got to do with anything?'

'Danny and Karl think we're both doctors.'

'So?'

'So they could have called her. Told her two doctors were on their way. Told her to keep us here until they arrived.'

'But they're looking for her, too.'

'They're looking for Nikki, mate. *Nikki*. But what if our girl's not Nikki? What if she's someone else?'

For the first time, a note of doubt crept into Jeremy's voice. 'How can we tell?'

'We're going to have to examine her. The minute she comes off the phone.'

Jeremy puffed out his cheeks, his brow furrowing in anxiety. He cast a final glance through the window at the empty driveway and rubbed his chin. 'I don't know, mate. I mean, it's asking a lot, isn't it?'

'She knows why we've come here,' Wes urged. 'She knows about the video. And, frankly, she was a bit bloody cagey when it came to discussing unidentified lumps on her *derrière*. Wouldn't the real Nikki *want* us to check it out?'

'She's in a state of shock. All that talk about tumours and suchlike. Bound to throw you a bit off-kilter, that.'

Wes shook his head emphatically. 'I don't care. Either she lets us examine her, or I'm off.'

From behind the bedroom door, sounds of movement indicated that a decision would have to be reached quickly. Shooting his friend a glance that was wracked with anxiety, Jeremy sighed heavily. 'Okay,' he said. 'We'll ask her now.'

A second later, the door opened and Nikki came back into the room. For a moment nobody spoke, and when Nikki finally broke the uncomfortable silence, it took every ounce of Wes's self-control not to flinch in embarrassment and guilt. 'How are you boys doing?' she said, affecting a forced cheer as she breezed into the small kitchenette at the far end of the room. 'Would you like some more tea?'

'I think we're fine for tea,' said Jeremy, exchanging significant glances with Wes. 'Actually, we were wondering whether this might be a good moment to have a gander at...' he waved a hand airily in the direction of Nikki's pale grey sweatpants '...the problem zone.'

'You're sure you wouldn't like another cup of tea first?'

'Not really, no,' said Jeremy, hoping the resolve in his voice wouldn't dispel the friendly bedside manner he'd been trying to cultivate. 'What we'd really like to do is take a quick squint at your bottom.'

Nikki's eyebrow arched mockingly. 'I'm sorry, Dr Sex – you'd like a quick squint at my...' – her lips pursed into an aristocratic pout as she struggled with the correct enunciation – '...*bottom?*'

'It's Sykes. *Sykes*. And yes, we'd like a look at your...' Jeremy's eyes pleaded with Wes's for assistance. When none was forthcoming, he beckoned his friend closer and lowered his voice. 'What's American for 'arse', kid?'

'*Fanny*,' Wes muttered, staring pointedly at the floor.

Jeremy glanced back towards Nikki in horrified disbelief. That word – the one Wes had just used – was near the top of Lisa's list of taboo phrases and expressions. Suddenly, and entirely unbidden, Lisa's face materialised in Jeremy's imagination, her brow furrowed in disapproval. Jeremy swallowed hard and turned to Nikki in desperation. 'Please, kid. Just show us your bottom.' He thrust two cupped hands towards her, hoping she'd understand the international sign language for 'buttocks'. 'You know – your backside. Your bum cheek. *Please*.'

'Can it wait a few minutes?' Nikki's upturned eyes flitted momentarily towards the door before alighting once again on Jeremy's angst-torn face. 'Ten minutes really won't make any difference, will it?'

Knowing very well how quickly Jeremy's resolution could be derailed by a pretty face, Wes gently pushed his friend aside. 'We *are* in a bit of a hurry, Nikki. We were hoping to get back to San Francisco tonight.'

'And you actually have to see it?'

'It'd very awkward trying to give you a diagnosis if we can't,' said Wes as delicately as he could. 'I mean, if you wanted to visit your own doctor, that'd be fine. But you've really nothing to be embarrassed about. After all, it wouldn't be the first time we'd be seeing your... private area.' He cocked a wry eyebrow at Jeremy. 'Dr Sykes has seen more girls' private areas than you've had hot dinners.'

For a moment Nikki said nothing. Then, with a final glance at the door, she sighed and turned to Jeremy. 'Well, maybe you'd better examine me, then, Dr *Sykes*.'

'Me?'

'Uh-huh. You're a doctor, aren't you?' Nikki crossed her arms as the slightest note of challenge entered her voice. 'And *you've* seen more girls' private areas than I've had hot dinners.'

'Oh yes. But I'm a cardiologist. Dr Wesley's more of an expert in the specific field of... bottom medicine.'

'I'd prefer *you* to look.' Nikki's eyebrow rose a flippant quarter-inch as she took a step back, almost as though she was squaring up for a fight. Then she bit her lip and cocked her head to one side. 'How do you want to do this?'

Jeremy's eyes swivelled madly around the room, almost as if they were looking for an escape route. It was a feeling Wes clearly remembered from medical school and, in an unaccustomed flash of empathy, he considered confessing how, since the unfortunate incident with Gabi and the fish slice, the mere thought of examining another person's backside had made him faintly nauseous. Then he pulled himself together and quietly made his way over to the window. Outside, beyond the driveway, a pretty, dark-haired girl with a brown paper shopping bag was meandering along the roadway. *I wish I was out there with you*, he thought, allowing her quiet self-possession and sad, faraway eyes to distract him from the fretful head-scratching behind him.

'Perhaps you'd best lean forwards over the table, here,' Wes eventually heard Jeremy declare. 'And lower your pants.'

Wes closed his eyes. In the comforting darkness, all he could detect of the physical world was the sound of outer garments being obligingly lowered and the rapid-fire beating of his own heart. By concentrating on the in-out-in-out of his breathing, he almost felt as though he was personally nudging time forward, second by agonising second, towards the moment when he and Jeremy could leave – but it was difficult, even in the darkness, to ignore the electric, ozone-y scent of expectation that appeared to be emanating from just a few yards behind him. It was something he remembered from long ago – from the night he'd first met Gabi, in fact – but despite the fact that many years had passed, he recognised it instantly. *The hot, prickly static charge of sex.* Only now it wasn't being generated by, or for, him. No – it was being generated by the surreal encounter taking place between the Shagfinder General and the porn star, just over his left shoulder. *The porn star. Nikki. A girl with whom I thought I might be falling in...*

'How's that?' Nikki's voice cut through Wes's unhappy reverie like a fish slice. 'Is that okay?'

'Well, it's a start. Except that by 'pants' I really meant 'underpants'.' Jeremy lowered his voice. 'Your knickers.'

'I see.' A second passed. 'Better?'

'Oh yes,' Jeremy breathed. 'Better.'

For some seconds, Wes tried not to imagine whatever it was that Jeremy was now looking at. It was difficult to rid his mind of the recurring image from Nikki's video, caught in Technicolor close-up in his mind's eye. The tumour, of textbook appearance, staring unblinkingly back at him. In fact, he was so absorbed by *not* thinking about it that he almost jumped when he suddenly felt a gentle tap on his shoulder. Turning, he found Jeremy's anxious eyes boring into him. 'Wes, mate? Dr Wesley?' Jeremy nodded in Nikki's direction. 'I think you should have a look at this.'

'I don't want to.'

'I think you should.' Jeremy's voiced hardened as he placed a firm hand in the small of his friend's back. 'In fact, it's imperative that you do. I've come across something most unusual about the patient's condition, and I'd value a second opinion. *Right now.*'

As if on autopilot – and assisted all the way by Jeremy's hand – Wes made his way over to the table and glanced downward. There, between the bottom of Nikki's t-shirt and the top of her sweatpants were two small, perfectly formed buttocks, still lightly imprinted with the elastic marks from her underwear. For a moment, Wes considered extending a hand to gently touch the exposed patch of skin, to confirm the information that his eyes had already given him, but he knew it was pointless.

The tumour, it was perfectly clear to see, had disappeared without trace.

Nikki looked over her shoulder and bit her lip, adopting an expression chillingly similar to the one Gabrielle had given him during their final moment of marital intimacy. Wes swallowed hard.

And then, without warning, the door flew open. Standing in the doorway, her eyes burning with fear and fury, was the young woman who Wes had seen a minute earlier through the window. She abandoned her shopping on the floor and extended both hands sideways, effectively barring the exit despite her diminutive size. She glared at Wes accusingly. 'And what the *fuck* are you doing to my sister's ass?' she demanded.

16

it's a good fucking job we didn't fucking go

When Jeremy eventually emerged from the bathroom, the altercation in the sitting room was just reaching its peak. He sidestepped the abandoned shopping bag and, seemingly invisible to the two combatants, joined a wretched-looking Wes on the dilapidated sofa. From this angle, it appeared that Caitlyn was gaining an upper hand in the frank exchange of views, although Nikki's look of righteous indignation didn't suggest that she was about to throw in the towel quite yet. 'For God's sake, Cait, I did it for *you*,' she thundered, her eyes narrowing on her sister. 'You don't think I did it for *fun*, do you?'

'You stuck a replica carcinoma on your ass for *my* benefit?'

'Faye put it there. And it was a melanoma, if you must know. But yes, it *was* for your benefit.'

'And then you made another porno with Karl? *Jesus*, Nikki.' Caitlyn shook her head in disgust. 'After everything we talked about.'

Nikki turned on her sister in exasperation, no longer pretending to maintain any façade of politeness. 'We needed a doctor. I got us a doctor,' she roared, flinging an arm extravagantly towards the sofa.

'Two doctors,' Jeremy piped up gamely. 'My name's Dr Sykes and this is...'

'Shut *up*,' barked Caitlyn, turning on the sofa's spectators for the first time, 'and get the fuck out of this trailer. Both of you. This fucking minute.'

'No, no, no,' countered Nikki, manoeuvring her way between Caitlyn and the two stunned Yorkshiremen. 'They're not going anywhere.' She turned to Wes and Jeremy, her ferocious expression brooking no disagreement. 'You're going nowhere. *Nowhere*.'

Wes and Jeremy said nothing and Nikki, interpreting their silence as agreement, turned back to her sister, clearly expecting a retaliatory salvo of invective. When none was forthcoming, however, even Wes felt compelled to stop staring at the carpet and glance up at the quarrelling sisters. What he saw made him leap from the sofa in alarm. Caitlyn, recently so animated, had taken on a ghostly pallor and was staring unseeingly at the wall. *Beyond the wall*. Wes caught her a split second after her knees gave way, cushioning her head against his shoulder and lowering her limp form gently to the floor.

'*Cait!*' cried Nikki, dropping to her knees at her sister's side.

'Give her space,' Wes grunted, raising a commanding hand to Nikki's shoulder. 'Jez – get her ankles up. Eighteen inches should do.' Then he slipped his index finger beneath Caitlyn's jaw line and leaned lower over her mouth. 'Zip,' he commanded, glancing sidelong at Nikki, who'd seemingly frozen in terror. 'Undo her zip. Her zipper. *Now*.'

For a split second Nikki remained rigid before reaching for Caitlyn's jacket in a flurry of fingers and thumbs. 'What happened?'

'She's fainted.' Wes glanced at his wristwatch, removed his fingers from Caitlyn's neck and performed a swift mental calculation. 'But she'll be just fine. Not diabetic, is she?'

Nikki shook her head.

'Pregnant?'

'No.'

'Having her period?'

'I don't think so.'

'Has she fainted before?'

Nikki bit her lip and shrugged. 'She gets tired easily.'

'When did she last eat?'

'She hasn't been eating much recently.'

'Today?'

Nikki shook her head. 'She's been kind of depressed.'

Wes glanced down at Caitlyn's face as her head stirred against his knees. A few seconds later, her eyes opened sleepily, unseeingly. 'What happened?' she moaned, half-heartedly trying to lift her head from Wes's lap. Then, noticing the trio of faces clustered over her, she frowned first at her sister, and then at the two strange men peering down at her. 'You two,' she said, her eyes passing from Jeremy to Wes with mild disapproval. 'I thought I told you to get the fuck out of here?'

'You did,' said Wes, gently. 'But that was before you fucking fainted.'

'So it's a good fucking job we didn't fucking go, isn't it?' said Jeremy, relieved that the crisis appeared to have passed. 'In fact, you should be fucking grateful we were here. I'm Jeremy, incidentally,' he said, reaching for Caitlyn's hand and pumping it enthusiastically. 'And that lanky bloke who's just given you the kiss of life is Dr Byron Wesley. Wes.'

Caitlyn's brow furrowed again. 'Your name's Wes?'

'Uh-huh.'

She seemed to process this for a second. 'Did you just

give me the kiss of life?'

'Er, no.'

Caitlyn frowned again, but with less conviction than before. 'Good,' she said softly, allowing Wes's knees to take the weight of her head again. 'And why precisely are you here?'

'Long story,' Wes replied, his eyes seeking out Nikki's. 'We'd somehow got it into our silly heads that your sister might be suffering from a particularly lethal form of skin cancer.'

'On her arse cheek,' added Jeremy, neatly circumventing any possible language barriers by waving a helpful hand in the region of Nikki's behind. Her face reddened a touch and she stared at the floor, but she didn't move away.

'In the region of her bottom, yes,' Wes continued, 'Except it seems we were misled. And that, in fact, Nikki just gets a kick out of occasionally wearing prosthetic tumours under her knickers.' He glanced from Nikki to Caitlyn and back again. When, after some moments, no explanation was forthcoming from either sister, he turned once again to Nikki. 'Earlier you happened to mention that you needed a doctor,' he said matter-of-factly.

'My sister says lots of things,' Caitlyn replied, sitting up awkwardly. 'You shouldn't believe them all.'

For a moment Wes said nothing, hoping that the silence might embarrass one of the sisters into casting some light on the situation. When neither spoke, he carefully propped Caitlyn against the sofa and turned to Nikki. 'Right. Fine. Where's your nearest chemist, then?'

'Chemist?'

'Erm... drugstore? Pharmacy?'

'Why?' said Caitlyn, struggling to pull herself up on to the sofa.

'There's one a few blocks away,' said Nikki, disregarding her sister's attempts to squirm her way upright. 'Right on the intersection across from the Sands Estate. You can't miss it.'

'I don't need anything,' Caitlyn insisted.

'I'll be the judge of that,' said Wes airily, leaning low over his patient and peering into her eyes. 'How old are you?'

'Twenty-two.'

'Well, normal twenty-two year olds don't go passing out every five minutes.' Wes gently placed his fingers against the glands on Caitlyn's neck and pressed. For a moment she returned his concerned expression with a baleful glare before dropping her eyes and swallowing hard. 'I wouldn't be remotely surprised if you were a touch anaemic,' Wes continued. 'Maybe slightly low blood pressure. Have you been sleeping properly?'

'No, she hasn't,' said Nikki.

'Any abnormal stresses?' Wes glanced from Nikki to Caitlyn. Neither would meet his eye. 'I'll take that as a yes. Right. You – Nikki. Go find a nice thick blanket for your sister. Then make her a drink. Anything hot and sweet. We'll be back in half an hour.' Wes stood up and started for the door. 'Come on, Jez. We're going shopping.'

'I've never seen you so assertive,' said Jeremy, unlocking the Charger and stowing the shopping bags in the trunk. 'Really *doctoral*. You're quite sexy, actually, when you're shoving people around. It's a bloody shame you're not still gay. I think you'd be a real hit on the scene – firm but caring. Very attractive combination, that, mate. *Very* attractive.'

Wes cast a weary glance in his friend's direction. Following a series of half-baked speculations regarding What Really Happened To Nikki's Arse, Jeremy had begun an equally riveting account of How Wes Got His Groove Back. There'd been an embarrassing quantity of the lad's blather while they'd been in Pharmacy 9, and while some of it had been quite flattering, the effect was now beginning to wane. Wes tried ignoring the inane country and western drifting from the car's stereo and closed his eyes, replaying the afternoon's events in his mind. Few of them seemed to make much sense – although the fear on Caitlyn's face had been real enough, even before she'd fainted.

It hadn't taken a medical genius to work out that there was more to her blackout than anaemia, anyway – and Wes was still weighing up the possibilities in his mind as Jeremy guided the Charger's nose back through the entrance of the mobile home park and into the maze of tracks and driveways beyond. Drawing up on the parched grass outside the girls' veranda, he turned off the ignition and nodded over his shoulder at the rear of the car. 'So what exactly have we just bought, then?'

'Thinking time.'

Jeremy nodded, impressed. 'You see? Firm, caring and *deep*. That's you. So you reckon Nikki's sister's got... what was it, again?'

'Anaemia?'

'Aye, that's the lad. You reckon that's what's wrong with her?'

'Possibly. It's certainly not her main worry, though.'

'No?'

'I don't think so, Jez.'

Jeremy unloaded the car while Wes knocked at the front door – and, when no one came to answer it, let himself inside. 'We're back,' he called, making his way around the dusty packing crates and discarded clothes into the sitting room. In the kitchenette, Nikki was washing up with manic ferocity, the sound of clattering plates and splashing water only punctuated by her intermittent sobs.

'You all right?' said Wes softly, maintaining a diplomatic distance halfway across the room. 'Where's your sister?'

'Caitlyn's in the bedroom,' Nikki replied without turning around. 'We argued again after you left.'

'What about?'

Nikki sighed and resumed washing up, a shade less vigorously than before. 'She didn't want me to tell you why

I... did what I did. In the video. With the fake tumour.'

'But you're going to tell me anyway, aren't you?' Wes pressed, motioning to Jeremy to be quiet as he bustled into the room.

Finally Nikki turned round, revealing a face lined with tear tracks and fatigue. 'I just needed to find a doctor. For Caitlyn. She's real sick.'

'Can't she just go to a clinic, kid?' said Jeremy, clearing the coffee table and putting down his bags and boxes. 'You know, the local one?'

For a second it appeared that Nikki was about to speak. Then she swallowed, turned back to the sink and began scrubbing furiously at a plate.

'You can't afford a doctor, can you?' said Wes quietly.

'No.'

'And Caitlyn hasn't got medical insurance, has she?'

In the window's reflection, Jeremy thought he saw a tight little smile on Nikki's face as she inclined her head and put down the plate. Then she gulped, squeezed her eyes closed and wiped her brow on her forearm, clearly struggling to keep the bitterness out of her voice. 'We haven't even got money to pay for food, honey. And Caitlyn's been sick before. She uninsurable. Officially. Medicaid won't touch her. Nobody'll touch her.'

Wes nodded, quietly bracing himself for the Big One. 'And what's wrong with Caitlyn, Nikki?'

'Have you ever heard of soft tissue sarcoma?' Nikki raised her eyes as though consulting her mental Rolodex, and when she spoke it sounded like the recitation of an all-too-familiar mantra. 'Soft tissue sarcoma – rare, painful, and a complete fucking bitch to treat.'

Jeremy's eyes searched Wes's face for a reaction. A prognosis. Anything. 'And is it..?' he eventually began, his voice trailing off as Wes returned his gaze.

'Oh, I'd imagine so. If it's left unchecked,' he said, nodding gravely.

'Ah. I see.'

For some moments no one spoke, all three of them lost in their thoughts.

Nikki's thoughts, wordless and formless, broke across her face in a series of tiny, painful spasms. Wes's thoughts, clearly visualised, were a headrush of diagnoses and half-remembered treatments, spiked with a terror of the words he instinctively sensed Jeremy was about to speak. And Jeremy's thoughts, plucked half-formed from the chaos of his subconscious, harried into shape by optimism and principles and a wilful disregard of the facts, met with no resistance whatsoever between brain and mouth. 'Well, we're going to help Caitlyn,' he quietly announced, glancing from Nikki to Wes and back again. 'We've already been out shopping. We've got loads of good stuff here.' Jeremy cleared his throat and pressed on, drawing Nikki's eyes away from Wes's expression of slack-jawed incredulity. 'It's not all, you know, specific to Caitlyn's condition, but it'll all help.'

Nikki stared at Jeremy, the first nervous flicker of a smile beginning to play at the corner of her mouth. 'You think so?'

'Aye, kid, I do. Me and Dr Wesley are going to do everything we can for Caitlyn. Everything we possibly can.'

As Nikki stumbled into his open arms, Jeremy's eyes locked with his friend's in a furious battle of wills. *We can't do it, Jez,* Wes seemed to be saying, his head shaking almost imperceptibly from side to side. *We can't help her. Not with this.* And then Jeremy's eyes broke free from the deadlock and turned to the bedroom door where Caitlyn now stood, her face drenched with tears and anxiety.

'Everything's going to be okay,' Jeremy persisted, nodding Caitlyn into the room and enfolding Nikki in a bear hug. 'You've nothing to fret about now.'

'Thank you. Thank you,' Nikki sniffed, taking Jeremy's hand and leading him over to the coffee table. 'So what is it you've bought?'

The unfamiliar packets and boxes stared up at Jeremy's uncomprehending face from where he'd deposited them some moments earlier.

'Why don't you tell them, Jeremy?' asked Wes dryly.

'I think *you* should, Dr Wesley,' Jeremy eventually replied. 'In fact, I insist you do. After all, it's all your... stuff.'

Wes shook his head, sat down on the edge of the sofa and began passing the motley collection of items to his friend. Now he knew what Caitlyn was suffering from, it almost seemed like an insult to palm her off with such a hopeless array of oddments and geegaws, but Nikki and Jeremy seemed to gain comfort from the stark clinical appearance of the bottles and cartons. 'That's vitamin B. This is a home screening test for diabetes. These are iron tablets. And that's a blood pressure monitor. It's probably useless, but it was only fifty dollars...'

Nikki pushed the empty bag aside, revealing the two wide flat boxes underneath. 'And what are these?'

'Eighteen inch double pepperoni pizza, and a fourteen inch vegetarian.' Wes sighed, casting a wan smile from Nikki to Caitlyn, whose own expression remained unfathomable. 'No one makes a miracle recovery on an empty stomach, do they?'

17

all girls can read minds: 1

'Faster. *Faster*,' screamed Nikki. 'Come on, Jez. *Please*.'

'You want me to go faster?'

'Oh, God, *yeah*.'

'You're sure?'

'*Sure* I'm sure. Please, Jez. For me.'

Tearing his eyes from the road, Jeremy glanced sideways at where Nikki's head had been a moment earlier. Unexpectedly, the space was now occupied by Nikki's bottom, while her face – the bit of her he'd just been addressing – had somehow made its way out of the Charger's passenger window, along with most of her upper torso. Either side, Nikki's tanned arms braced her above the door while her bare shoulders kept her precariously wedged beneath the car's roof.

Jeremy shook his head and returned his attention to the road, but now he'd registered Nikki's bottom – now that he'd taken a mental snapshot of its curves and contours, the low-rise waistband of her jeans and the gentle crease in the denim at the tops of her thighs – well, it was difficult to blank it from his peripheral vision. He closed his right eye and dabbed the accelerator as lightly as he could. It was madness, he knew, to restrict his field of vision in the midst of the thundering trucks and cars of the Corona Del Mar freeway – but it was infinitely more sensible than allowing himself to be distracted by the illicit temptations of Nikki's miraculous self-curing backside.

Sighing inwardly, Jeremy eased the Charger into a long, slow arc around a rumbling oil tanker in the middle lane, and flipped down the sun visor. They'd been on the freeway for a good ten minutes, now, but there was still no sign of the promised shopping mall. Scanning the fast-approaching horizon, all Jeremy could see was same blank vista of parched asphalt, dusty verges and featureless concrete and, of course, the startled expressions of the freeway's other drivers, gaping open-mouthed at the laughing blonde lass leaning out of the 1960's muscle car, her eyes narrowed against the oncoming typhoon, her hair a blur of yellow and gold in the afternoon sun. Jeremy slid into the nearside lane and tapped Nikki very diplomatically on the side of her thigh. 'It's allowed round here, then, is it?' he yelled. 'Climbing out of the car while it's moving?'

Nikki dropped back into the passenger seat, rubbed her eyes and smiled. 'Since when were we the kind of people who cared?'

Since I started seeing Lisa, thought Jeremy ruefully, glancing at the rear-view mirror for any signs of possible pursuit. 'I thought you were trying to keep a low profile,' he eventually said, struggling to keep a note of levity in his voice. 'Trying not to be recognised. Danny's got friends everywhere – that's what Caitlyn said last night.'

Nikki pouted theatrically then smiled again, seizing the rear-view mirror and adjusting it in order to assess the toll that her *al fresco* exploits had taken on her hair. A moment later she twisted the mirror back in Jeremy's direction and slid down in her seat, perching her slender ankles lightly on the dashboard. 'I don't think anyone'll recognise me now,' she finally declared.

Not unless you're famous for your Eddie Van Halen impersonations, Jeremy reflected, glancing down at the windswept vision beside him, relieved beyond words that Nikki's bottom was now concealed from view. 'Maybe we should just find this shopping mall of yours and get back to Wes and Caitlyn,' he said, fixing his eyes resolutely back upon the horizon.

'Okay, Jez. You're the boss,' said Nikki sweetly, doffing an imaginary cap to the frowning Yorkshireman.

'That's right,' said Jeremy, after a moment's consideration. 'I *am* the boss. I'm responsible for your welfare, me.'

From the corner of his eye, Jeremy watched as Nikki quietly repositioned herself in order to catch the bright rectangle of sunlight now slowly creeping across the Charger's interior. It was exactly what she'd done on the veranda the evening before, he reflected – shifting position like a cat, trying to catch every last warming ray, moving from Caitlyn's side to between Wes's knees, and eventually ending up lying unselfconsciously asleep across his own lap. It'd been difficult enough keeping track of Wes's quiet explanation of primary and secondary cancers, but it became harder still when Nikki had begun gently snoring against his inner thigh – and she wasn't proving much less distracting now, with her hair glowing like golden filaments in the low Californian sunshine.

Clearing his throat loudly, Jeremy turned off the radio and gently nudged his semi-recumbent passenger. 'So where's this shopping mall, then?'

Nikki opened one eye and smiled at Jeremy. 'No idea. I'm just enjoying the ride.'

'But I thought you knew where we were going?'

'Nuh-huh. We're just driving along until we see a mall we like. Didn't I say?'

'Not as such, no.' Jeremy cast a sidelong glance to his right, first at Nikki's face and then at the approaching slip road. Thirty seconds later, the freeway was receding behind them as the Charger pulled to a gentle halt at an anonymous suburban intersection. *Thinking time.*

Spending so long with Lisa, Jeremy realised, had eroded his tolerance for the daft scattiness that certain girls tended to specialise in. There was a period of his life, of course, when he'd have regarded a whiff of feminine giddiness as a positive omen – the whims of flighty lasses being easier to pander to than those of their more serious sisters – but he'd changed since then. And, Jeremy reminded himself, he wasn't here to jump in the sack with Nikki – no matter how memorable it would undoubtedly be. *No. We're here to help Caitlyn*, he thought. *Even if it's just getting Nikki out of Wes and Caitlyn's way for a couple of hours and picking up a few essential odds and ends.*

Jeremy blinked in the low afternoon sun, trying to dislodge the carnival of mental images that had leapt into his mind's eye alongside the words 'jump in the sack with Nikki'. No matter how he tried, however, a few refused to budge – even when he tried ousting them with a pictorial version of their shopping list. *Shampoo. A change of clothes. Fruit and veg. Some TV dinners, for when Wes gets the electric stove working.* Jeremy gently squeezed the accelerator as the lights turned green, his eyes scanning the approaching cluster of low-rise buildings before falling once again on his passenger. 'Do you actually know where *any* of the local malls are?' he said.

Nikki shrugged, not unhelpfully. 'I'm from Texas, honey. Southern gal.'

'I'm not driving all the way to Dallas, kid. Not just for groceries and fresh underpants.' Jeremy frowned, immediately regretting having mentioned underwear. 'Anyway, I thought you were Californian.'

'No way,' said Nikki, shaking her head emphatically and

finally sitting up in her seat. For some moments she gazed through the open window at the passing cars and houses, and when she next spoke, her voice had acquired a strange, faraway quality. 'California's the dung heap, sweetheart. Nikki's just one of the flies.'

Jeremy cast an eye fleetingly over the sun-baked sidewalks and sheltering palms, struggling to equate his limited experience of California with his equally limited experience of dung. He shrugged inwardly. Apart from its torture dungeons and the gun-toting maniacs and its liberal abundance of near-death experiences, there'd been something about California he'd grown unaccountably fond of. 'So why did you come here?'

'Economic necessity.'

'How so?'

'We can't all be heart surgeons, can we? And a girl's got to earn a buck.' Nikki sighed, registering Jeremy's uncomprehending expression, then turned back to the window. 'Adult entertainment. Porn. The dung heap.'

'Ah.'

'Were you doing it long?'

'Little over a year. Ever since I got thrown out of college.'

Jeremy tried hard to prevent his eyebrows shooting upwards in surprise. *Porn college? Surely not. Some other kind of college, then.* Well, Nikki *did* seem sharp enough – frighteningly so at times – but they'd hardly spent the previous twenty-four hours debating Jacques Derrida or quantum mechanics. 'You were at college?' he eventually asked.

'University of Texas, Austin. Sophomore year. I was going to major in psychology.' Nikki treated Jeremy's upper arm to an affectionate punch, mistakenly assuming that his respectful expression had been put on purely to flatter her. 'Come on, Dr Sykes. Don't pretend to look impressed.'

Jeremy shook his head. 'I *am* impressed, though. Fair

play to you. Psychology, eh? Wow.' For a second, Jeremy wondered whether two years of undergraduate psychology had equipped Nikki with rudimentary mind-reading skills – and, if so, whether she'd registered quite how intimately he'd pictured the two of them five minutes earlier. Then he remembered – *all girls can read minds anyway*. He coughed nervously. 'So why did they chuck you out?'

'Because my ex-boyfriend sent some photos he'd taken of me to a website.'

'Photos?'

'Candid photographs. Of me. Drunk. No clothes. No inhibitions. Plenty of everything else,' said Nikki, indicating with two flicks of the wrist the kind of 'everything else' she was referring to.

For a moment, Jeremy rather hoped that Nikki could mind-read his mental image of slapping the offending ex-boyfriend vigorously around the chops – an ex-boyfriend who looked remarkably similar to the man-beast, Karl. 'And your college found out?'

'*Everyone* found out,' Nikki laughed, not without a note of sadness. 'Friends, other students, my mom, my tutors, everyone.'

'Couldn't you get the photos taken down?'

'I did. The very next day. But it was too late. Other websites copy things, Jez. Stuff moves around.' Nikki turned to Jeremy, her face suddenly serious. 'Once you're out there, on the web... well, you're just *out* there. Forever. It doesn't go away. You can't get rid of it. It changes everything.'

'And what happened to the original site?'

'Oh, they apologised,' Nikki said. 'Told me it'd never happened before, told me it'd never happen again. Then they offered me five hundred bucks and a one-way ticket to Chatsworth. They said I had a big future in the movies, if I wanted one.'

'So that's how you got into the whole... porn... thing.'

'Uh-huh. I met Danny two months after I arrived, and I've been working for the bastard ever since.'

'So was Caitlyn already living out here?'

Nikki shook her head. 'We were both living at home in Austin. Cait was an intern on the local newspaper. She was involved with SXSW – photography, promotions, that kind of thing. Played bass in a couple of bands. But then Mom threw me out after the pictures appeared. I came out here, and Cait came with me. To look after me.' She turned to stare out of the window again, although it was unclear whether her eyes were registering the passing houses and gardens. 'Cait's always looked after me,' she said quietly. 'Now it's my turn to look after her.'

Jeremy nodded. 'So that's why you stole Danny's money and cameras? To pay for Caitlyn's medicine?'

'Let's get one thing straight, Jeremy,' said Nikki, her voice suddenly flint-hard. 'I didn't steal a *fucking thing* from Danny. I earned *every fucking cent* of that money. I did shit you wouldn't fucking believe. I just took what the fucker owed me.' Then, as quickly as they'd gathered, the storm clouds dissipated. 'It wasn't enough, anyway. Whatever I do, it's never going to be enough. I got money, I got doctors. I got us out of Chatsworth and found us a new place to stay. I tried Medicaid. I tried every fucking thing I could.' Nikki turned to Jeremy, her passion suddenly spent. 'And Caitlyn's still going to die, isn't she?'

Jeremy blinked hard as the road swam sickeningly before him, scarcely able to register the mindless scenery passing by on either side of the car – the trees and shops and street signs, all rendered eerily featureless and two-dimensional by the frozen hand that had just seized hold of his insides. It was a feeling he'd been trying to forget ever since he'd first experienced it, the moment Lisa had told him she was leaving – a sickening sensation from which the only respite had been the distractions of work and alcohol and Project Nikki.

Project Nikki. Jeremy glanced sideways at his mute companion, resisting an urge to reach out and take her hand. She had no idea how much he had to thank her for – for giving him some faith in the possibility of setting matters straight with the universe, if nothing else. *Except it isn't Project Nikki any more*, he reflected. *It's Project Caitlyn. And I'll be buggered if I'm going to let that lass die on my watch.*

Jeremy turned once more to Nikki. 'Caitlyn's not going to snuff it, kid,' he said. 'I promise you. She's got me and Wes looking out for her now, hasn't she?'

Nikki smiled wanly. 'No offence, but I don't really see what you can do. You've both been real nice, helping out in the trailer and buying stuff for us. And dinner last night, and taking me out today.' From the driver's seat, Jeremy could sense Nikki's eyes searching him out. 'You're the nicest thing that's happened to me in months. And I know you're both doctors. But you're not, you know, *American* doctors.'

Jeremy puffed out his cheeks contemptuously, feigning outrage at Nikki's professional slight. 'You cheeky little moo,' he declared. 'Me and Wes are a million times better than American doctors. We're British doctors. Best in the world, us two.' He pulled the Charger round at an intersection signposted towards Santa Ana and glanced across at Nikki, serious again. 'What's happened to Caitlyn could never happen in Britain, you know.'

'No?'

'No. In Britain, if you're sick, doesn't matter who you are, you just go to hospital. Simple as that. Everything's free. It's called the NHS.'

'That's well and good,' said Nikki, exasperated, 'but Caitlyn doesn't happen to *be* in Britain, Jez.'

For a second Jeremy said nothing – and when he did, his voice was almost too soft beneath the engine's rumble for Nikki to make out his words. 'Aye, she isn't, is she?' Then, ignoring his earlier apprehension, he reached across and gave Nikki's hand a firm squeeze. She placed her other hand over his, pulled it into her lap and held on tight. 'Never lose faith, kid. Never. You don't know what might happen. Hey, look there's a Wal-Mart.'

One handed, Jeremy manoeuvred the Charger down the Wal-Mart slip road and into the busy parking lot, deftly directing the car's outsize bonnet into a narrow gap between two looming vans and turning off the ignition. In the quiet shade of the stationary vehicle, Nikki was the first to speak, gazing straight into Jeremy's eyes and addressing him matter-of-factly. 'Okay, give me your t-shirt.'

'What? Why?'

'You know what Caitlyn said last night. I'm hiding from Danny. I'm not supposed to be seen. Therefore I need to be in disguise if I'm out of the trailer park.' Nikki finally let go of Jeremy's hand and folded her arms expectantly. 'I'm trying to be the responsible one, Jeremy. Now give me your t-shirt.'

Speechless with indecision, Jeremy held his breath for what seemed like an eternity and then, still not fully understanding his own reasoning, he reached down and began yanking his t-shirt up over his stomach and chest. It was over his eyes before Nikki's shaking hand on his forearm restrained him. 'Stop, stop! I'm kidding! *Jesus*, Jez,' she laughed. 'I was kidding.' She leaned over the broad leather armrest and began pulling Jeremy's t-shirt down over his stomach, holding the hem firmly down over the waistband of his jeans. 'I don't want to wear your t-shirt. Honest, I don't. I'd have your 'guy' smell all over me.'

Nikki mimed the 'vomit' gesture and laughed again, harder this time, until her quaking exhalations sounded like sobs or sighs, then little more than soft, aching gasps – the same noises Jeremy had heard her make when he'd first seen her on Wes's laptop. Back in Sefton Street, he hadn't been able to look at Nikki – but here, with her hand resting on his, he could scarcely draw his gaze away from hers. He blinked hard, hoping his eyes hadn't betrayed the thoughts that were racing through his head. Then he remembered. *All girls can read minds. All girls can read minds.*

With a superhuman effort of will, Jeremy removed his hands from beneath Nikki's and opened the car door. 'We'd best get the groceries, then, eh?' he said with forced levity. 'And I promise we'll find some way of helping Caitlyn.'

For some moments they walked in silence towards the shadowy awning over the supermarket entrance. Then Nikki spoke. 'So if Cait was in England, she'd really qualify for healthcare?' she said.

Jeremy frowned, unsure of the technicalities. 'Well, it'd certainly be easier for us to sort something out, wouldn't it?'

Nikki's eyes narrowed slightly as she considered the prospect. Then she shook her head. 'She'd never go.'

'Why?'

Nikki sighed. 'Because she's started believing it's hopeless. And she's getting sick of fighting the disease alone. She's tired of being let down, Jez. Tired of having her hopes raised and then torn to pieces.' She stopped and faced Jeremy, squinting in the bright sunshine. 'Half the time, she says she's prepared to let the cancer just *happen*. The rest of the time, she just pretends it doesn't exist. Staying here – just waiting – well, I think it's the only way she feels like she's got any control over her life.' Nikki shook her head as the pair entered the cavernous, air-conditioned interior of the supermarket. 'She'd take a hell of a lot of persuading before she'd even *think* about going to England for treatment, anyway.'

'Well, I *do* have something of a reputation when it comes to persuasion,' said Jeremy, trying to imbue his voice with as much modesty as possible. 'The lasses, in particular.'

'I can believe that, Jeremy,' Nikki laughed, pretending to appraise him afresh. 'In fact, I believe a sweet-talking boy like you could persuade a girl to do pretty much anything. But maybe I should talk to Cait first. Prepare the groundwork. You might want to start with Wes.'

'Aye, aye.' Jeremy sucked his breath over his teeth, acknowledging the potential magnitude of the challenge. 'I'll have to use different superpowers, there,' he admitted. 'With blokes like Wes, you've really got to appeal to their sense of logic. Their intellect. Their higher moral sensibilities.' He smiled, striding out purposefully along the fruit and veg aisle. *And if that doesn't work, you've got to threaten to pull their tripes out*, he thought.

18

you can't fall in love with someone on the internet, can you?

Trying to ignore the smell of burnt fat, Wes squinted at the grease-encrusted junction box and tried positioning the screwdriver at something approaching a right angle to the electric stove. For a second, the blade appeared to connect with the head of the offending screw before slipping out again, sending a small cascade of rusty flakes directly into his eye. He cursed under his breath. The forty minutes since Wes had started 'mending' the girls' stove had already ruined a particularly treasured shirt – a floral Versace one that Gabi had bought him for his birthday – and the fetid carpet behind his head had imparted a number of further horrors into the matted mass that had once been his hair.

Still, there was something cheeringly tangible about Wes's current task that had kept him engaged in a way that only the *Racing Post* could usually manage, and it was with an unfamiliar feeling of job satisfaction that he gave the troublesome screw a final twist and extended a hand beneath the low oven door. Unseen on the other side, Caitlyn took the screwdriver from him and set it aside.

'Nurse – ceramic cover,' commanded Wes.

'Ceramic cover,' Caitlyn replied, a hint of good-humoured indulgence in her languid Southern drawl.

Wes took the cover and snapped it back into place. *Mending knackered stoves really was a doddle compared to mending people – it really was.* 'Oily rag, nurse.'

'Oily rag, *doctor*,' said Caitlyn pointedly, pressing it firmly into Wes's hand.

Behind the stove, Wes made a few half-hearted swipes at the larger clots of filth on the rusty enamel and began edging his way back into the room, wiggling his shoulders gamely against the unspeakable carpet. In some ways he was disappointed that his task was over. After the awkwardness of his 'consultation' with Caitlyn – which had involved lots of vague healthcare tips and dietary advice, but told her no more about soft tissue sarcoma than she already knew – there'd been an air of unbearable melancholy in the room. But as soon as Wes had offered to try fixing the stove, as soon as Caitlyn's face was out of view behind the oven door, something had lifted in the atmosphere and they'd both opened up.

What's more, fixing the girls' stove had been a practical thing to do. *A pretty manly thing, actually*, thought Wes, sitting upright on the floor and accepting the glass of lemonade that Caitlyn passed him. When burly tradesmen came to fix Gabi's kitchen appliances, Wes reflected, it was always his job to meekly make them cups of tea while they effed and jeffed and smirked at his requests for them to smoke their cigarettes in the back garden. *Here, in Nikki and Caitlyn's semi-derelict mobile home, he was Mr Fixit. A can-do kind of guy.* Wes sipped his lemonade and glanced at the clock. 'What do you reckon's keeping Jeremy and Nikki?' he said.

'I guess she's busy molesting him in a parking lot,' Caitlyn replied, with apparent seriousness.

'Really?'

'She likes him. She said so after you left last night.' Caitlyn shrugged resignedly. 'And he's single, isn't he?'

Wes shrugged. Following Jeremy's revelations during the drive down from Barstow, there didn't seem much doubt regarding the lad's singleton status. 'Well, he did have quite a serious girlfriend, but she left him about six weeks ago,' he said. 'She's in Shanghai now. Why?'

'Nikki can sniff out single men. She can detect their pheromones.'

'And if they're single, she molests them?'

Caitlyn appeared to consider the matter deeply then smiled, nodding. 'Uh-huh. Pretty much.'

Wes absorbed this information for a moment. He somehow doubted whether Jeremy, still so evidently hung up about Lisa, would permit himself to be molested by Nikki – although everything Caitlyn had said about her sister in the past hour *did* suggest that Jeremy might have his hands full. It was a slightly disturbing thought, actually. After all, only a matter of weeks ago Wes would have described Nikki as a friend. More than a friend, if he was being honest – someone he'd grown deeply, almost scarily fond of. And while he'd known what she did for a living – what she did *professionally* – it still made him feel queasy to think of her doing the same things recreationally with the Shagfinder General. Wes drained his lemonade, stood up and shoved the stove back against the wall, only speaking when his face was once again hidden from Caitlyn's. 'Nikki's different from how I expected her to be,' he said quietly.

'How so?'

Wes bent low over the stove, feigning a sudden interest in the wall socket above the kitchenette worktop. 'Well, when I met her in the chat room... we used to talk. For hours, sometimes. I really felt we had, you know, a bond.'

'And you don't feel that now?'

'I hardly feel I know her at all,' Wes replied, struggling to keep the note of hurt out of his voice.

When, after some moments' consideration, Caitlyn next spoke, her voice was kind but reproving. 'You don't think you were, you know, projecting your fantasies on to her a little bit?'

'Why do you say that?'

Caitlyn sighed in quiet exasperation. 'Well, because she worked in *porn*, maybe? Just in case you missed the memo, that's the whole *point* of porn, Wes. It gives you unrealistic images to project your fantasies on to.'

As a connoisseur of daytime television, this type of analysis was highly familiar to Wes, although he'd never envisaged applying it to his own rather rarefied lifestyle. Something in Caitlyn's words had struck a guilty chord, though – while still utterly missing the point about his friendship with Nikki. He shook his head, trying hard to make his face convey quite how un-porny his feelings for her had been. 'I know what you mean,' he eventually said. 'But with your sister, it really wasn't about the – you know – *images*. I felt the way I did because of what she *said*, not what she looked like.' He turned back to the stove and began groping on the floor for its power cable. 'I almost felt I was – you know... I felt I was really making a *connection* with her. I've never known anything like it. Not even with Gabi, my wife.' Wes felt his face flush as he fumbled with the plug. '*Especially* with Gabi, actually. But you're right. It's all bollocks. You can't really fall for someone on the internet, can you?'

'Maybe. Maybe not. I don't know.' Caitlyn cleared her throat and walked over to the window. 'You're sure you don't feel that way about Nikki now, though?'

Wes shook his head slowly, anxious not to cause offence. 'No. She's really lovely, obviously. But she's really not who I thought she was.'

Caitlyn smiled. 'I'm glad.'

'You're glad?'

'Glad you're not madly besotted with her. For both your sakes. I mean, I love my sister – I love her to bits. But she's actually completely fucking deranged.'

'Uh-huh?'

'Oh yeah. And she's got worse since she started doing porn. All the normal inhibitions – gone.'

'I suppose they would be.'

'Take the guy who got her into porn in the first place. Martin.'

'The boyfriend from university?'

'Him, yes. She wrecked his car, you know, half an hour after she found out what he'd done. Totalled it.'

Wes weighed this up for a second. It didn't seem a particularly extreme reaction in the circumstances. 'Well, fair enough,' he shrugged.

'Then she torched his house.'

'You're kidding.' Wes's eyes sought Caitlyn's for confirmation. 'Seriously?'

'Totally. She got two five-gallon cans of gasoline and burned it right down to the ground.'

'Was he inside it at the time?'

'Not for long. That's why we had to leave Texas. Nikki tells people it was because of the pictures, but it wasn't, not really.' Caitlyn turned to Wes with a rueful half-smile. 'And look at the luxurious life we're leading here. This place belongs to another one of Nikki's exes, Moises. He's in prison. Gets paroled in three months. Then we'll have to move on again.'

Wes's eyes reappraised the room afresh, scanning the walls and floor for any telltale signs of dried blood or bodily organs. 'So what's he inside for, this bloke?'

'Grand theft auto. Crack dealing. Little pimping on the side. Nikki just thinks he's misunderstood.'

'Misunderstood... but essentially guilty?'

'Oh God, yes,' laughed Caitlyn. 'Totally guilty.'

For a while neither of them spoke, although it wasn't

until Caitlyn quietly stretched backwards on the sofa that Wes realised over five minutes had passed since he'd had an urge to wedge his head behind the stove – and he was still marvelling at his own lack of anxiety when Caitlyn turned to him with her slow, easy smile. 'I'm glad we've had a chance to talk, anyway. Just you and me.'

'Uh-huh?'

'Yeah. So I could, you know, fill you in about Nikki. Now you can warn Jeremy not to get too involved.' Caitlyn bit her lip and looked away, her voice suddenly brittle – as though she were struggling to recall a prepared speech. 'And I also wanted a chance to talk without Jeremy and Nikki around. Because I think we're the adults here, aren't we? The realists. I mean, Nikki probably thinks that somehow you'll be able to help me. With my sickness. The cancer. But I think we both know that you can't. Not really. And I wanted you to know that it's okay, and that it doesn't matter. And that you coming over here was a really kind thing to do. And I know it was for Nikki, not me, but I think it was a real nice gesture. And I'm really, really glad I got to meet you.'

For a moment Wes was speechless. He was, he knew, generally the kind of bloke who'd prefer to undergo a scrotal wax than deal with another human being's emotions – but something about Caitlyn's frankness caught him off guard, and before he really knew what was happening he'd enfolded her in his arms and was resting his chin gently on top of her head. 'Where there's life there's hope, kid,' he eventually muttered – although even as he spoke, he couldn't be sure whether he was trying to convince himself or Caitlyn.

Against his shoulder, he felt Caitlyn smile. 'Thanks, Wes,' she said, gently pulling away and straightening herself out. 'So, are you going to stay for supper tonight? Now you've fixed the stove?'

'I don't know. I think I might need to talk to Jeremy

alone, back at the motel.'

'Tomorrow, then? Your last night before you fly home. We'll have a barbecue out in the yard. Our way of saying thank you. You can sleep over, if you want. Then you can have a drink and not worry about driving.'

'Okay. That'd be cool. I'll look forward to it.'

19

I'd let you choose which arse cheek, obviously

Wes watched mutely as Jeremy drew the curtains and turned to face him again. If they'd chosen a swankier motel, Wes reflected, there'd have been complaints from the other customers by now – but Motel 6's clientele were evidently used to raised voices in the wee small hours, and clearly content to allow the two Yorkshiremen's altercation to run its course. Wes glanced up at Jeremy, whose narrowed eyes indicated that their owner had just summoned up a fresh line of attack. 'But Yorkshire is the Texas of England,' he declared. 'You know that, mate.'

'So?'

'So these two lasses are *Texan*. They're our spiritual cousins. Our homegirls. They're family.'

'And that's why you want to take them back to London?'

'Aye. Obviously. Well partly, anyway.'

'But *why*, Jez? What can you possibly hope to achieve?'

Jeremy stopped mid-stride at the foot of Wes's bed and

peered down at his friend, regarding him for a few incredulous moments before slapping his own forehead with the flat of his hand. 'I don't *hope* anything,' he fumed. 'I *intend* to save a young lass's life by taking her, and her sister, back to England.'

Shaking his head, Wes got out of bed and went to the bathroom, splashing cold water in his face and towelling himself dry. Behind him, clearly visible in the mirror, Jeremy continued pacing back and forth in front of the flickering TV. It was a worrying sign. The lad normally only entered 'barrister' mode after several pints of strong beer. Tonight he'd only managed half a dozen lukewarm Budweisers and a couple of tacos at Reyna's Mexican Grill over the road, but was still fighting his corner with an unholy passion, refusing to be sidetracked by Wes's many spirited attempts at distraction and evasion.

More worrying still, Jeremy had seemingly dispensed with the formality of changing into Lisa's pyjamas under cover of darkness – and, indeed, tonight he'd actually augmented her *Forever Friends* t-shirt with one of her old plastic bangles and the ridiculous spangly purple scarf she'd worn in the sixth form, both of which now hung at his side like occult talismans.

'I like Caitlyn too, Jez,' Wes finally conceded, when Jeremy had switched off the TV and curled up on top of his own bed. 'I really like her a lot.'

I really like her a lot. Wes had only said it to mollify his friend, but even as the words emerged from his mouth, he could almost visualise them squirming with embarrassment at their own inadequacy. Because although Wes had yet to come up with a more articulate description than 'like', it scarcely conveyed the eerily familiar feeling that threatened to engulf him every time he thought about Caitlyn. *But the feeling didn't last with Nikki*, he reasoned. *It disappeared as soon as I met her. So why should I trust it? Best to try staying completely detached from the situation.* 'But if we take her home with us then she'll just die in England, same as she's going to die here,' he eventually said, hoping the motel room's darkness would absorb some of his words' crassness. 'Except she'll be an illegal immigrant in a foreign country in a city she doesn't know, surrounded by people she's never met. Is that what you really want?'

'If we take her home with us, we can make her better again,' Jeremy pressed.

'No we *can't*. She knows we can't. And the NHS won't touch her. It's only free for us, not for anyone who just happens to drop in.'

'I know that. I'm not completely retarded.' Jeremy reached across and flicked on the bedside light. 'But we're not just a pair of civilians, are we? You're a bloody doctor, for Christ's sake.'

'Yes, but...'

'I mean, you've just finished a bloody medical degree. You're a great doctor. The best – you said so. And apart from me and Lenny and Tim and Dave the barman, the only people you *know* are doctors. Dozens and dozens of bloody doctors. You're connected, Wes. You're on the inside. Your wife's a doctor. All your in-laws are doctors. Are you trying to tell me that between the lot of you, if you really put your minds to it, *none* of you could help Caitlyn? That you couldn't pull some strings somewhere?'

Wes sighed, reluctant to admit quite how swiftly his medical school friends had dropped him after graduation, or to what extent relations with the Wynstanley clan had soured following the wedding. And as for his own practical skills – well, treating someone's cancer wasn't the same as chiselling out their ingrowing toenail or singeing off a wart. Wes raised his eyes to his friend's simmering stare. 'I just don't think I can help, Jez. It's my final word.'

And for a second – *just a second* – Wes actually thought the subject might be closed. Then, Jeremy exploded. 'If you leave her here, *Caitlyn's going to die*. To die. To *die*.'

'But what can I *do?*'

'Your fucking job.'

'Which is?'

'Cut a hole in her, take out the bad bits and sew her back up again. That's what doctors *do*, isn't it?'

'There's a little bit more to it than...'

Jeremy's outstretched hand cut his friend off at a stroke. 'Look, Wes,' he said, his voice suddenly horribly calm. 'I don't want to twist your arm or anything...'

'*Then don't,*' Wes snapped, sensing instinctively where Jeremy might be heading. *His weak spots – Gabi. The house. The car.* Suddenly he felt a sharp pang of something he hadn't experienced for nearly a week – a profound longing to throw himself on one of the Josef Hoffmann sofas in front of the Bang & Olufsen TV, to flick through the *Racing Post*, to gaze out at his Tansanite blue Mercedes, and maybe have Ocado ferry him over a few *vol-au-vents* from Waitrose. 'Don't threaten me, Jez.'

'Well, I'm afraid I'm going to have to.' Jeremy reached underneath his pillow and pulled out Danny's pistol, levelling the sights at a spot directly between Wes's incredulous eyebrows.

Wes stared at the angular metal object in his friend's hand, unable at first to fully register what it represented. Then, with a suddenness that jarred him, the cold, banal actuality of the unsheathed firearm struck home. Gripped by a hitherto unknown fear, Wes found himself manically attempting to outstare the pistol, which appeared to be silently growing as it sucked heat and light from the motel bedroom like a tiny, lethal black hole. Eventually, after a seeming eternity, he found something resembling his voice. 'For fuck's sake, Jez,' he croaked. 'You should never point guns at people. It could be loaded.'

'It *is* loaded, you pillock,' Jeremy replied, still squinting along the sight. 'One in the chamber and six in the clip.'

'And you're actually threatening to *kill* me?'

'Don't be daft,' Jeremy chided. 'Of course I'm not going to kill you. I love you like a brother. You're one of my very, very best mates – in spite of our little disagreements.' He lowered the pistol to waist level. 'But I'd have no qualms whatsoever about putting a bullet through one of your arse cheeks, if that's what it took to make you see sense.' He waggled the gun playfully at Wes's lower portions. 'I'd let you choose which cheek, obviously.'

Wes swallowed hard, desperate to introduce a note of gravity into his voice. 'If you shot me in the arse, you could shatter my pelvis,' he said. 'Rip my bowel and colon to shreds. You could totally destroy my lower spine. The blood loss alone could easily be fatal.'

'See?' Jeremy smiled chillingly. 'You've remembered you're a doctor at last. So now you've remembered what you are, I won't have to pop a cap in your ass, will I?'

Jeremy lowered the gun, hitched up Lisa's t-shirt and tucked the weapon into the waistband of his pants. *His pink pants*, Wes observed. *With little love hearts on them. A pair of Lisa's panties, in fact.* Suddenly buoyed by the absurdity of the situation, Wes's eyes narrowed on his cross-dressing friend. 'You'd never shoot me, anyway,' he said.

Jeremy turned to Wes with his most chilling 'try me' expression. 'I never make idle promises, kid,' he declared, removing the gun from his panties and levelling it once again at Wes's midriff. 'Especially where arses are concerned. And let's be honest, I'm not asking much from you.'

'Aren't you?'

'Not really, mate, no.' Jeremy sighed, putting the gun down again and collapsing back against his pillows. 'I just want an honest commitment that you'll try your best to help Caitlyn once we're all back in London. Talk to some friends who are cancer specialists. Network with your old medical school buddies. Find out what sort of operations are available. Get hold of some drugs, call in a few favours, that kind of thing.'

'So it's all down to me, is it?'

Jeremy glanced sidelong at his friend. 'Hardly, kid. I mean, Nikki and Caitlyn will both stay with me in Lisa's flat while you're sorting out the medical side. And I'll pay for their flights. And I've already shelled out nearly three grand. Money for my flight. Money for Faye. Money for the Charger, and petrol and motel rooms. And I've had to stick my knob on the chopping block to get it.' He reached across for the TV remote. 'Your uncle Jezzer's not a well-heeled bloke, you know.'

'So where'd you get all the money from?'

Jeremy flicked unseeingly through a few TV channels, his face visibly touched with anxiety. 'Well, you know the van I borrowed from my dad?' he said. 'The one I sometimes use for work?'

'The Transit?'

'Aye. Well, I flogged it.'

'You *sold* your dad's van?'

'To a feller in a pub in Barking, the day before we flew out.'

'And what did your dad say?'

'Not much. Not yet, anyway. He doesn't really know.'

'So what did you do about the log book?'

'Didn't need it.'

'You'd have needed the log book to sell it.'

Jeremy shook his head impatiently. 'I told the bloke in the pub that I'd nicked the van. It's not a problem, though. Dad'll get the insurance.'

For a second Wes said nothing, and when he did speak it was with both fear and awe in his voice. 'That's fraud, Jez.'

'I suppose it is, aye.'

'People go to prison for fraud.'

'Sometimes. But it's all for a good cause, isn't it?'

Wes glanced across at his deranged friend. Despite the

glittery purple scarf and girl's nightie, it wasn't difficult to picture Jeremy standing in the dock, trying out the same pitch on the judge and jurors. Wes shook his head. 'Doing this won't bring Lisa back, you know,' he said softly.

In the other bed, unseen by Wes, Jeremy silently reeled as though winded. 'I know, mate,' he replied some moments later. 'But it's still worth doing. For Caitlyn's sake. And if it doesn't work, then at least we'll both know we tried everything we could. You can live out the rest of your horrible parasitic existence knowing that you really tried to do one truly decent and honourable thing in your life.'

'And if I said I didn't want to help, you'd still shoot me in the arse?'

'In the arse, up the arse – yes.' Jeremy shrugged. 'So you're in?'

Wes closed his eyes, and there, in the darkness, was Caitlyn's face. 'She won't come, you know,' he said quietly. 'She resigned herself to... well, you know.'

'She *will* come, mate. Nikki's talking to her tonight. Persuading her.'

Wes sighed. 'And why's Nikki so keen?' he said. 'Because she thinks she'll be getting you, into the bargain?'

'Does it really matter?' shrugged Jeremy. 'And anyway, Nikki's got to want to come too. Caitlyn won't come by herself. And if she doesn't, she'll snuff it.'

Wes's eyes sought out Jeremy's. 'You're not leaving me a lot of choice, are you?'

'None at all, kid. But taking Caitlyn home is the right thing to do.' He reached over to turn off the bedside light. 'We'll sort out the nitty-gritty at the barbecue, tomorrow night.'

20

are you sure you can't smell something burning?

Even before Jeremy and Wes had stepped out of the Charger, Nikki was upon them. 'Don't be mad,' she said, wiping her fingers nervously on her apron, 'but Caitlyn doesn't know yet.'

'Doesn't know what?'

'That we're flying her to England tomorrow morning.'

Both men's eyes narrowed on Nikki's contrite face. 'Didn't you discuss it last night? After we'd left?' said Jeremy quietly. Caitlyn, he knew, would be harder to persuade than Wes, and it'd be very poor form to pull Danny's pistol on the lass – even for her own eventual benefit.

'Caitlyn's been acting real weird, Jez. She was up before dawn doing housework. She's been making food on that gross stove all afternoon. Putting up decorations. I keep on telling her to chill out, but she won't.'

'And you haven't talked about going to London at all?'

'We've talked about you guys flying back tomorrow –

but whenever I tried mentioning the two of us moving on, she just started making more potato salad.' Nikki shrugged. 'She seems to think all English guys are obsessed with root vegetables.'

Jeremy nodded solemnly and slammed the car door before striding purposefully around the side of the mobile home. Behind him, reluctant to leave the Charger's invisible force field, Wes and Nikki lingered awkwardly, avoiding each other's gaze. 'Maybe you should speak with Caitlyn,' Nikki eventually muttered. 'She's always listened to you. Apart from potato salad, you're all she's been talking about.'

Wes sighed inwardly as a hot flush of embarrassment passed over his features. Ever since they'd checked out of the motel that morning – ever since they'd stepped out into the torpid Santa Ana heat – he'd been harbouring dark premonitions about the barbecue. All afternoon – while Jeremy had pored over NHS websites in a downtown internet caff – he'd watched the clouds gathering and toppling overhead, felt the heat breaking over the city in shimmering waves from the desert. Now, perspiring freely despite the lengthening evening shadows, his sense of foreboding was growing palpable. He closed the Charger's passenger door and smiled wanly at Nikki. 'I'll see what I can do.'

Rounding the corner of the veranda, Wes was surprised to find the entire yard criss-crossed with strings of tiny Chinese lanterns and a stunned-looking Jeremy, freshly installed behind a glowing barbecue with a pair of stainless steel tongs in his hand. Wes approached his friend with a glance towards the open double doors of the kitchenette. 'You haven't *actually* spoken to Caitlyn, then?' he whispered.

'Er, no. Only about whether potato salad should have chives in it. I tried getting her outside but she won't leave the bloody cooker. And you can barely breathe in there. I tried mentioning tomorrow, too, but she just told me to put the steaks on the barbie.'

Wes sighed outwardly this time and headed inside, leaving Jeremy alone by the barbecue. A moment later, Nikki joined him in front of the sizzling meat. 'Is Wes going to talk to Caitlyn?' she said.

'Hopefully.'

'Good. She'll listen to him.' Nikki reached over and took the tongs from Jeremy and began gently nudging the steaks around the blackened wire mesh. 'And she'll feel so much better when she's in England. We both will.'

'Mm,' grunted Jeremy, trying to look as absorbed in the cooking process as a tong-less man can. Wherever his gaze fell, however – and he was trying desperately not to let it fall on Nikki – he couldn't help but be aware of the proximity of the small blonde lass by his side, or be conscious of the heat emanating from her, despite the warmth of the evening and the orange glow of the hot coals. He blinked hard. Flip-flops aside, Nikki was only wearing two items of clothing – three, if you gave her the benefit of the doubt on the 'knickers' front – a backless halter-neck top, seemingly constructed entirely from beads, and the briefest denim hot pants he'd ever seen.

She moved an inch closer – close enough for Jeremy to feel her breath on his upper arm when she spoke. 'When this is all over, maybe I'll stay on in England,' she said. 'Make a new start. Maybe I could stay with you, huh? In your apartment? What do you think?'

'Oh, I don't know. Would that be wise? You'd want your independence, wouldn't you? Get a job or something. Maybe finish your degree.'

'It's tough for a girl trying to make it on her own.'

'Aye, I know,' countered Jeremy, 'but there must be loads of stuff you can do. You're obviously a bright lass.'

'Oh, you're sweet, Jeremy. But only one thing ever really come natural to me. Only one thing I've ever been *real* good at.' Nikki lowered her voice to a whisper. 'Didn't you think so, first time you saw my little movie?'

If Nikki noticed Jeremy's jaw drop or his eyes bulge outward in panic, she declined to say so – and the two companions maintained a breathless silence for the next thirty seconds as Jeremy sought desperately to fill his mind with images of algebra homework, suet pudding and bulldog-faced maiden aunts. *That was just a bald statement of fact*, he said to himself. *A candid observation – hardly a come-on – even though she said 'come natural' in exactly the same way Nigella Lawson would say 'warm chocolate sauce'.* After half a minute had passed without breathing, Jeremy couldn't be sure whether the Chinese lanterns were stirring in the humid breeze, or the tremors of his own heartbeat were causing them to throb gently in the periphery of his vision. He gulped hot air into his lungs and cleared his throat. 'Couldn't you do something in, you know, the media or IT or something?' he eventually gasped. 'You must've used computers when you did that chat room thing.'

Nikki edged closer, dropping her voice to a conspiratorial whisper as she shook her head. 'You've got to promise not to tell Wes, but – well, that wasn't me at all.'

'It wasn't?'

'No.' Nikki bit her lip. 'I can barely type. That was Caitlyn. She used to pretend to be me in the chat room. It was an easy way to make a little extra money. She could log into the system from home, do a few hours here and there…'

For a second, the cogs whirred in Jeremy's overheated brain. 'Caitlyn? It was *Caitlyn* who Wes was chatting with, all those months? Not you?' *Caitlyn, who Wes was falling in love with. Confiding in. Obsessing about.*

'Uh-huh. She used to talk about him all the time – her neurotic MD.'

'Did she?'

'Sure. She didn't mean to, but she was starting to really like him.'

Jeremy frowned. There must be, he reasoned, a small

proportion of the world's women who might conceivably find Wes engaging company. Not having to share a continent with him might help. 'So why doesn't she want him to know that it was her in the chat room?'

'Because while he was talking to *her*, he was jerking off over pictures of *me*. That's a pretty big deal for a girl like my sister to get her head round.' Nikki's voice grew playful, provocative. 'Did you look at me too, Jez? Online?'

'God, no,' Jeremy blurted. 'And even if I *had* looked – well, top-flight cardiologists are trained not to get all hot and bothered by that sort of shenanigans. And Wes – well, to be honest, kid, *he* never looked at you, either.'

'*Sure* he didn't.'

'No, really – he only signed up for the chat room because he wanted someone to talk to. And I reckon he only went for a chat room on a porn site because he wanted it to be – well, *professional*. A service he was paying for. Wes likes spending money on stuff. It makes him think he's getting something better than everybody else. Does that make sense?'

Nikki shrugged, unconvinced.

'He only went looking for pictures of you when you – sorry, *Caitlyn* – disappeared from the chat room. The first time he clapped eyes on you was the day he spotted the tumour on your bum.'

'He said that? And you believe him?'

'Aye, I do actually. He can be a slippery sod, young Wes, but there's no reason he'd lie. And he's not, you know, massively *stimulated* by the visual stuff. His missus likes to think he's a rampaging viking, but he's a bit of a softie, deep down.' Jeremy lowered his voice. 'He had a gay phase, you know, when he was at school. I was all for it, at the time.'

'So he really wasn't jerking off over me at all?'

'I doubt whether he even had a cheeky one.'

'Well, it explains a lot of things. I mean, Caitlyn was amazed at how fast he could type one-handed, and how long he stayed online,' Nikki reflected, clearly performing an unspeakably lewd act of mental arithmetic. 'It's good that he eventually looked for my picture, though. Otherwise he'd never have seen my tumour. I only got Faye to put it there so he'd come looking for me. I got the idea when Caitlyn told me that she'd made friends with a doctor. I just never thought he'd live so far away...'

Jeremy nodded, silencing Nikki with a gentle nudge as Wes emerged from the sweltering mobile home bearing an armful of beer bottles. It was obvious from his expression that he'd made little progress with Caitlyn, and he passed drinks to the others without comment.

'You still haven't told her that we're taking her to London, then?' Jeremy asked, wiping the bottle's condensation across his forehead.

For a moment Wes appeared lost in thought, his eyes vacant as the rising wind caught a shower of incandescent fireflies from the barbecue and sent them swirling off over the low, sloping roof and into the darkening sky. Then he shook his head. 'I couldn't talk to her. Not about anything serious.' He cast his mind back to his fleeting brush with psychiatry at medical school, then his year's post-graduate study of *The Jeremy Kyle Show*. 'She must be at breaking point. What with her sickness, and being borderline homeless, and penniless – and then us, turning up out of the blue.' Wes turned his troubled eyes on Nikki, and then Jeremy. 'I still don't know if taking her back to London is the best thing we can do for her, mate.'

'I'll go check she's okay,' said Nikki, passing the barbecue tongs back to Jeremy and heading inside.

In the awkward hiatus that followed, all that could be heard was the sound of sizzling fat falling on to hot coals and the rustling of a stiffening breeze in the low palms that lined the approach road to the mobile home park. Eventually Jeremy spoke. 'There's something I think you should know, kid,' he said, taking a hearty slug of cold beer.

'Something I've just found out from Nikki.'

'What?'

'When you were in the chat room, all those months ago – well, it wasn't actually Nikki you were rabbiting to.'

'Of course it was.'

'No, no. It wasn't. It was Caitlyn – Caitlyn who had all those deep conversations with you.' Jeremy nodded solemnly at Wes's disbelieving expression. 'Caitlyn who you confided all your secrets to. Caitlyn who you shared all those tender late-night non-wanking moments with...' He downed the remainder of his beer and, noticing that Wes hadn't started his own, removed the fresh bottle from his friend's unresisting hand. 'Nikki can't even type. The only thing she's ever been good at is...' – he struggled to find the kindest form of words – '...her pioneering work on behalf of the Kleenex Corporation.'

'Nikki told you this?'

'Aye. She also said that... well, that when you were having all your late-night chats, Caitlyn had felt the same way about you as you'd felt about her. God knows why.'

Wes's forehead furrowed in confusion. 'Why didn't she say anything to me when we turned up here, then?'

'Embarrassment, mostly.'

'Embarrassment?'

'Aye. She was embarrassed that she was falling for someone who was wanking themselves silly over mucky videos of her kid sister.'

'But I wasn't,' Wes exclaimed indignantly.

'I know.' Jeremy peered beyond the smoky veil that had been blown across the veranda at the animated conversation taking place in the kitchenette. 'And I think Caitlyn probably knows now, too.'

For a moment Wes didn't move, pinned to the spot by indecision. Then, without warning, he started towards the open double doors – but not fast enough to evade the large furniture restorer's hand that seized hold of his wrist in a companionable – but unyielding – grasp. '*I need to talk to her,*' Wes said hoarsely, frantically flailing against the big man's grip.

'*Whoa, whoa, whoa...*'

'I need to tell her how I *feel*, Jez...'

'Just get off your mustang, there, Sally.' Jeremy tightened his grip with one hand, expertly flipping the steaks with the other. 'What you *need* to do is get Caitlyn out here so that we can talk about taking her to England. She's got enough on her plate without you mooning all over her, mate.'

'But...'

'No buts, Wesley. Tell her we've brought champagne and we're opening a bottle in the yard. Tell her we're celebrating some good news and that she needs to come out.' He regarded his friend's agonised expression sternly, then nodded towards the open door. 'Go tell her now.'

Shaking his wrist free of Jeremy's hand, Wes made his way back into the sweltering living room, his eyes dodging Nikki's as they passed in the doorway. There, in the far corner of the kitchenette, occupying the same spot where she'd been two minutes earlier, stood Caitlyn. But when she turned to look at him – when she registered his presence with a tiny, expectant smile and unconsciously flicked the hair out of her eyes – it felt like he was gazing at an entirely different girl. For a moment, Wes struggled to work out what had changed. There was nothing in the soft contours of Caitlyn's face that he hadn't seen before; nothing about the intensity of her expression that he hadn't committed to memory the moment his eyes first fell on her. Caitlyn's small, defined figure was familiar too, and the way her pale skin caught the eye at the base of her throat, where the dark curtains of hair closed over the top of her blue cotton sweater. And even the way he felt when he saw her – his desire to take her in his arms, to reassure her that everything would be okay – hadn't changed one iota. Only now, Wes realised with a sudden and sickening jolt, he just wouldn't be able to let her go.

And when, after a moment's silence, Caitlyn's eyebrow bent into an enquiring circumflex, Wes had no recollection of why he'd come into the kitchen in the first place. *Must be something to do with kissing*, he thought, his gaze panning around the room and eventually coming back to rest on its sole occupant. *That, or potato salad.* He nodded at the bowls of food crammed on to the low coffee table. 'Have you been cooking all afternoon?'

'I just wanted to say thank you. For everything. How are the steaks?'

'Cooked the Yorkshire way. Cremated.'

'Cool.'

'Cool.' Wes cleared his throat, aware once again of the room's greasy, metallic smell. 'You should come outside. Jeremy's getting champagne from the car. He wants to propose a toast.'

'What to?'

'I'm not really sure. It's just what we do in Britain. Toasting this, toasting that.' *Oh, and going to California and falling head over heels for lasses who aren't our wives.* 'It's how we relax. Come outside and see.'

'I'm just finishing off...'

'Come outside. Please. Doctor's orders.'

Caitlyn put down her wooden spoon, regarding Wes sidelong.

'Friend's request, then.'

Wes held out his hand, failing to suppress a tiny smile of schoolboy elation when Caitlyn took it, allowing herself to be led out into the yard, beneath the strings of Chinese lanterns and along the side of the trailer. And for one glorious instant, rounding the rough verge where Jeremy and Nikki were removing bottles from the Charger's trunk, Wes was filled with an optimism so unfamiliar that he felt like probing his own stomach for a butterfly infestation. *I can really do this*, he caught himself thinking. *I can do anything.*

I can take you to England and make you well again. Then Caitlyn squeezed his hand so tight that he gasped, pointing with her free hand at the low-slung profile of the Charger. '*Is this your car?*' she gasped.

Looking up, Jeremy grinned broadly. 'Well, it's a rental actually...'

'But this is the car you've been bringing here for the past three days?'

'Aye. It's a 1967 Dodge Charger...'

'I don't give a shit what it is,' Caitlyn declared quietly, shaking off Wes's hand and advancing slowly upon Jeremy. 'You've been driving around in a one-of-a-kind custom car with flame motifs coming off the wheel arches and my little sister – my sister who's supposed to be hiding from her psychopathic ex-employer – riding shotgun. And this self-same vehicle – the most distinctive set of wheels I think I've *ever seen* – has been sitting outside our safe house for three consecutive days, advertising our presence to anyone in Orange County might be even distantly acquainted with one of the most dangerous, notorious and well-connected pornographers in southern California.' Caitlyn turned on Nikki, her eyes blazing. 'And just in case you've forgotten, Danny Giordano is a man who has very publicly made known his plans to tear you limb from fucking limb, should he ever enjoy the pleasure of your company again.' She shot an accusing glance at Jeremy (who had, by this point, begun edging diplomatically away from the Charger) and then – to his horror – at Wes. 'So, Doctor Wesley – do you think that bringing this car to our home was a smart thing to do?'

'Well possibly not, but...'

'*But what, exactly?*' Caitlyn shouted, drawing breath in the silence that followed and trying to wave away the thin smoke now breaking over the low roof of the mobile home. She glanced around, momentarily distracted by the acid tang in the air. 'Can you smell burning?'

'It's just the steaks on the barbecue.'

'It's not the barbecue,' Caitlyn said quietly, remembering her train of thought and shaking her head in renewed exasperation. 'The point is that this place is no longer fucking safe. Our home is no longer a safe place to be.'

'It doesn't matter,' said Nikki, trying to keep her voice calm in the face of Caitlyn's anger.

'Of *course* it fucking matters.'

'No, no. It doesn't.' Nikki glanced from Wes to Jeremy for support, then turned back to her sister. 'We're not staying here.'

'Well, we *can't* stay here, can we?' said Caitlyn in desperation, a note of shrill hysteria creeping into her voice.

'No because...'

'Why don't we all have a drink?' asked Jeremy brightly, reaching into the Charger's open trunk and withdrawing a bottle of something that might, or might not have been, champagne. He wiped the condensation from the glass and peered at the label. 'Mexico's finest, this.'

'I don't *want* anything to drink,' Caitlyn cried, now advancing on her beaming sister. 'I *want* to know what the fuck you're talking about.'

'We're going to London, Cait. We're going to England.'

'*What?*' said Caitlyn, her eyes swivelling back to Wes for explanation. 'What do you mean, we're going to London?'

'We're going to London. Tomorrow morning,' said Nikki with barely suppressed excitement. 'With Jeremy and Wes. They're going to make you well again. Get you the treatment you need. We were going to tell you about it tonight. That's why Jeremy brought champagne.'

Caitlyn's face twisted in confusion and anxiety. 'What? What are you talking about? We're not going anywhere.' She turned to Wes in desperation. 'I'm not going anywhere. Are you sure you can't smell something burning?'

'It's the steaks,' began Jeremy. 'We like them a bit crozzled in Yorkshire...'

'It's not the fucking steaks,' snapped Caitlyn, turning

once more to Wes. Her eyes narrowed inexorably upon his, and when she next spoke he could only just make out her words over the rising whine of wind between the mobile homes. '*It's the stove.*'

For a second, all four of them stood transfixed by the now-audible crack of splintering woodwork. Then, as one, they rushed back around the side of the trailer. The wave of dry heat hit them like an oven door opening. Jeremy was the first to speak. '*Fuck me!*' he declared, raising an arm above his eyes and slowly advancing towards the double doors. At ten yards' distance he was forced to raise a second arm against the urgent barrage of heat, and at five he could only squint through half-closed eyes as a tsunami of black and orange flame rolled languorously across the ceiling before emerging from beneath the smoking lintel. A moment later, he felt Nikki's hands seize his arm and pull him away from the veranda. 'Bloody hell. The whole place is going up,' he rasped, his throat already painfully parched. He turned to the horror-struck Nikki. 'You've nowt valuable in there, have you?'

'Oh *shit.*'

'You can't go back in.'

'*Oh shit, oh shit, oh shit...*'

Suddenly, Jeremy felt another hand on his arm. Wes, who'd been frantically tapping away at his mobile phone for the previous ten seconds, caught his eye and shook his head at his friend. 'Fire department,' he hollered into the mouthpiece. 'Santa Ana. South Euclid. The mobile home park. No. No one's inside... *Nikki!*'

'*Nikki!*' yelled Caitlyn, covering her face as another incandescent tongue of flame broke free of the veranda and spiralled into the darkening sky. '*Nikki, no!*'

But Nikki, unheeding, was now edging towards the trailer, flexed at the knees like a fencer, her eyes scanning the low wooden building for a point of entry. And then, without warning, she was gone, bolting for the half-open bedroom window and slithering into the smoke-filled room beyond.

A moment later Jeremy was at the window too, his shoulder wedged beneath the ancient sash, trying to drive it upward. '*What the fuck are you doing?*' he shouted, his eyes searching for Nikki in the lightless room.

For a second there was no reply – and then Nikki's voice emerged from beyond the wraiths of smoke streaming through the open doorway. '*Passports.* Get Caitlyn in the car, Jeremy. Get Caitlyn into the car *now*.'

Momentarily paralysed with indecision, Jeremy blinked into the darkness. Then he felt a familiar hand on his shoulder. Unthinkingly, he turned and roughly shoved his friend away. 'Get Caitlyn into the car, Wes. Start the engine. We'll be there in a sec.' And then he, too, was gone, wrestling his way beneath the half-open window into the choking gloom of the bedroom, half-stumbling, half-crawling towards the hall doorway and the dim silhouette beyond.

Jeremy caught Nikki at the moment she fell, more by accident than design, hooking a forearm beneath her ribcage as he groped blindly for his quarry. Then he pulled against the limp, rag-doll weight of her body, back towards the window and breathable air. And there, finally, were other hands, four of them, frantically seizing his own arms and legs, pulling the pair of them out into the yard, into the night, and into safety.

21

you're a full-blown arsonist now, kid

'I actually thought you were in there, mate.'

Wes swivelled round in his seat, anxious to see whether Jeremy's murmured remark had been overheard by Caitlyn or Nikki. It seemed unlikely. In the two long hours since midnight, he'd trained his ears to follow their soft, syncopated breathing beneath the steady drone of the Charger's engine, and the fifteen seconds following Jeremy's quiet observation hadn't seen any alteration in the reassuring rhythm of grunts and exhalations from the back seat. Wes allowed his eye to linger guiltily on the dim outlines of the sleeping girls for a further moment, then turned once more to the softly illuminated profile of his friend. '*What?*'

'I said, I thought you were in. With Caitlyn. When you came round the corner of the caravan, hand in hand.' Jeremy glanced sidelong at his friend, a half-leer compensating for an inability to perform his customary 'shagging' gesture. 'You looked very cosy, you two. Consequently, I thought you were – you know – *in*.'

Wes sighed inwardly. Years of underage drinking with Jeremy in Whitby's Fat Ox had given him a fair idea of where the conversation was likely to be heading. 'You did, did you?'

'Oh, aye. Definitely in.'

In the darkness of the Charger's cabin, Wes shuddered. He'd always felt faintly queasy around the whole 'in' expression, and now was no exception. Was Jeremy using it as a metaphor to be 'in' Caitlyn's affections? Or did he have an altogether more graphic meaning in mind? Wes had been trying not to think about the latter possibility for some time – failing miserably on most occasions. There was something rather unwholesome, he sensed, about a doctor with such a non-medical agenda in mind for his patient. He shook his head, trying to rid his mind of the image that had lodged there, and stared out into the pitch blackness beyond the Charger's headlights. 'Cheers.'

'I reckon you might've blown it now, though,' added Jeremy conspiratorially. 'She looked pretty freaked out by all the fire engines and police cars. And she's probably right about you turning her into a fugitive from justice. And making her homeless probably didn't help much, either.'

'Oh, you think so, do you?'

Jeremy shrugged. 'She's a sensitive lass, mate. You can't go round making lasses homeless and not expecting them to feel aggrieved about it.'

He was quite right, of course. And the fact that the mobile home hadn't technically belonged to the girls – and that they would have had to abandon it when carjacker Moises was paroled from Chuckawalla Valley anyway – had scarcely softened the emotional blow of the evening's events. Everything but the clothes they stood up in (and, thanks to Nikki, their passports) had gone up in smoke, seemingly due to Wes's wildly misplaced faith in his skills as an electrician. He shuddered again, vividly reminded of the similar confidence he'd felt only hours earlier when he'd reconsidered the prospect of treating Caitlyn's cancer. For all his swagger and bravado in front of Jeremy and his betting shop cronies, he couldn't think of one life he'd actually helped save as a consequence of his medical training. And tonight, thanks to his own stupidity, he'd almost been responsible for Nikki losing *her* life.

Wes twisted round in his seat again, his eye now resting upon Nikki's slumbering form. Apart from minor smoke inhalation and a few cuts and bruises, she'd emerged from the burning building remarkably unscathed. She'd seemed to revel in the attention, actually – Jeremy's spirited attempts at mouth-to-mouth, in particular – although she'd sounded pretty rough in the car afterwards, retching out of the open window, tears streaming down her smoke-mottled cheeks. Her breathing had settled now, though, and in sleep her face had somehow opened, like a child's.

The same, he reflected, could scarcely be said of Caitlyn. She'd barely uttered a dozen words since the car pulled out of Bakersfield on Route 99, and none of them to Wes. It had initially been unclear whether she'd been rendered incapable of speech, or was merely unwilling to attempt it, but the silent barrage of baleful glares in the rear-view mirror had given Wes a clue. He'd carried on glancing around at her, however, ostensibly on medical grounds, although actually because he wanted to detect some hint in her countenance that she'd begun to forgive him for burning down her home. Even in sleep, however, her brow remained furrowed into a tiny, perfectly-formed frown.

'I'm sorry, kid,' Wes whispered, turning back to the road.

A moment later, he sensed the approach of Jeremy's hand across the cabin. It groped blindly in the darkness for a second or two before finding its mark and scratching him companionably on the back of the neck. 'Chin up, mate,' its owner grunted reassuringly. 'She'll forgive you for burning her caravan down when you've got her cancer sorted. Then you'll probably be 'in' again. And if it doesn't work out with Caitlyn, you could always try your luck with Nikki,' he added helpfully. 'You're a full-blown arsonist now, kid – just like her. Young Nikki's very fond of rebellious types. Same as your wife is.'

22

it all got a bit emotional, to be honest

The hour it took Jeremy to return the Charger to the rental firm was among the longest of Wes's life. He'd tried offering to buy the two girls some fresh clothes, but Caitlyn had mutely declined to budge from the spot on the airport sidewalk where Jeremy had dropped them, and Nikki (despite several longing glances towards the terminal's brightly-lit boutiques) had refused to leave her sister's side. And so they huddled like three shell-shocked POW's in their smoke-blackened fatigues, their silent incongruity ignored by the waves of oblivious travellers breaking blindly around them.

Wes tried telling himself he was relieved. The last thing he wanted was an inexplicable assortment of female apparel materialising on his credit card statement – and besides, he had some serious thinking to do. Allowing his gaze to dissipate over the now-familiar Californian horizon (and feeling no regret that this would be his final glimpse of its sun-blanched trees and buildings), he tried picking up the threads of the story he'd begun concocting at four o'clock that morning – the story that would hopefully convince Gabi that he had, in fact, spent the week holed up with surgery's *crème de la crème* and not, say, in a Santa Ana mobile home park with an ex-porn actress and her distressingly fetching sister.

It wasn't going well. He'd cooked up a handful of incidents and characters to relate to Gabi – a hilariously officious concierge at the hotel, a few worthy-sounding lectures and seminars he'd attended – but little that would, in his current mental state, bear much scrutiny. And scrutiny, Wes knew, was what Gabi *did*. He groaned beneath the roar of approaching taxicabs and the multilingual hubbub of their disembarking passengers, thinking how ill-defined and cartoonish his fabricated tales would sound under Gabrielle's withering stare. Her reaction would be *nothing* compared to what she'd do if she ever learned the bizarre truth of his Californian odyssey, of course – but that simply didn't bear thinking about. And if he *had* been capable of constructive thought, Wes knew exactly where he'd be directing his mental powers. He allowed his gaze to linger momentarily upon his two silent companions, passing over Nikki's watchful expression before alighting guiltily upon Caitlyn's unblinking, unfocused eyes. *Caitlyn, Caitlyn, Caitlyn.*

Every time he looked at her – an indulgence he'd been covertly allowing himself every forty or fifty seconds since Jeremy's departure – Wes experienced the same intoxicating cocktail of emotions. First came something resembling relief – a profound sense of gratitude that Caitlyn was still there, by his side, regardless of the circumstances. Then came something more primal – an unholy, unscratchable itch in the deepest recesses of his imagination, undeterred and unmoved by her state of emotional shutdown, furtively feeling her out in the privacy of her own unspoken thoughts. And finally, darkly eclipsing both lesser feelings behind a billowing smoke-cloud of despair, came wave upon wave of shame, fear and guilt. Wes looked down at Caitlyn's slight form, fighting a near-overwhelming urge to enfold her in his arms – to apologise, to beg for forgiveness for everything he'd done, and everything he knew with sickening certainty that he'd fail to do for her in England.

Oh, Christ. I've bloody well fallen in love, haven't I? he suddenly thought, his eyes swivelling wildly around to see whether his seismic revelation had been registered by anyone else. *This is love. The real deal. Shit!* A momentary appraisal of the sidewalk's other occupants was enough to convince Wes that no one else had been floored by the shockwaves from his epiphany, although he was startled by his own doe-eyed reflection in the airport's plate glass window. It was an expression he'd remembered pulling when he'd first set eyes on the Mercedes from the back seat of Abiola's cab; it was the same way, Wes suddenly realised, he'd recently caught Nikki glancing at Jeremy. *The same way that Jeremy sometimes eyes up the Charger. The same way that Caitlyn looks at...*

'You all right, mate?'

Wes wheeled guiltily around, surprised to have been caught off-guard by his returning friend. 'Cool, Jez. Cool. No problems with the car?' he said.

'It all got a bit emotional, to be honest.' Jeremy shook his head and drew reflectively on his cigarette, seemingly oblivious to the fact that Nikki had just wrapped a sympathetic arm around his waist. 'I didn't want to hand over the keys. I don't like to think of anyone else tooling round in her.' He transferred his cigarette to his other hand and draped his free arm absently over Nikki's bare shoulder. 'She didn't half shift when you put your clog down.'

'You've got to learn to let go, mate.'

'The guy offered to sell her to me, actually. But once you've added on your import duties and shipping costs...'

Jeremy shrugged and swallowed hard, dropping his smouldering cigarette butt on to the asphalt and extinguishing it with a twist of his heel. 'It's just hopeless, really, isn't it?'

He reached down and hoisted the two biggest bags effortlessly on to his shoulder, then gently nudged Caitlyn with his free elbow. She looked up as though woken from a deep sleep and smiled wanly at him. Jeremy beamed back, shrugging off his moment of melancholy, and looked at his watch. 'Right, then. Reckon it's time we bought you two lasses some airline tickets, isn't it?'

Jeremy leaned forwards over the check-in desk and lowered his voice conspiratorially. '*Technically* we're booked into Economy, yes,' he said, glancing back towards Caitlyn and Nikki. '*Technically*. But I don't really feel we're 'Economy' passengers, if you get my drift.'

'You don't?'

'Not really, no.'

The check-in girl released a tiny, exasperated sigh and returned her attention to the three sets of travel papers. When she looked up at Jeremy, her expression of fractious incomprehension wasn't quite the one he'd been hoping for. 'I'm still not quite following you, sir,' she said.

Jeremy sighed inwardly, regretting having given Nikki and Caitlyn quite such lavish descriptions of the First Class travel experience. Images of Wes, quaffing champagne in the First Class lounge, flooded his mind. He smiled in spite of his bitterness. 'Well, on my outward flight, your airline's representative was kind enough to offer me a complimentary upgrade. She said they liked having doctors in First Class.'

'You're a *doctor?*'

Disregarding the note of amazed incredulity in the check-in girl's voice, Jeremy mentally prepared the Friday Night Special. 'I'm a cardiologist,' he purred. '*A heart surgeon.*' His smile lingered desperately around his sleep-deprived face, but he could tell by her look of bafflement that it had failed to negotiate its way into the check-in girl's underwear. 'I've just been at a conference exploring new directions in surgery.'

'We've had a number of your colleagues through this morning,' said the check-in girl. 'I've checked in several doctors myself.' *Real doctors*, her eyes seemed to say.

'First class passengers?'

'Some of them.'

Jeremy smiled again, even more desperately than before. 'I don't suppose there's any chance I might join them, is there? Me and my two colleagues? Please?'

For a moment the check-in girl's eyes panned left and right, clearly unable to locate the two mystery physicians Jeremy was referring to. 'Your colleagues?' she eventually said, her gaze coming to rest on Nikki and Caitlyn. Somehow, the airport's strip-lighting seemed to make their slept-in clothes and faces radiate even more bewildered desperation than before. 'The two young ladies?' *The hooker and the mental patient?*

'They're the ones. Both experts in their respective fields.'

The check-in girl smiled icily. 'I'm sure they are, Doctor...'

'Sykes. It's Dr Sykes.'

'...but I'm afraid that...'

'Some people think it sounds a bit like Dr Sex.'

'...under the circumstances...'

'*Dr Sex! Dr Sex!*' Jeremy's urgent whisper echoed around the check-in area.

For some moments, nothing could be heard except the almost imperceptible sound of breath being held and a dozen heads gently swivelling in Jeremy's direction. The check-in girl was the first to regain her composure. 'I don't feel able to offer you or your colleagues an upgrade on this occasion, sir. But I'd like to thank you for choosing to fly United Airlines, and I wish you a very, very pleasant flight.'

23

the usual bittersweet cocktail of hope and desperation

In the week following Wes's return from California, nothing Gabi did or said suggested that she harboured any suspicions whatsoever regarding his trip. In fact, her feelings for her husband (which had, prior to his departure, seemed decidedly frosty) appeared to have thawed a little during his absence. The fact that she'd sent Abiola to pick Wes up from the airport, for instance – and readily stumped up an additional fee for allowing her husband to chain smoke duty-free Marlboros in the loquacious Nigerian's minicab – hinted at a warming of relations that promised to be as confusing as it was unsettling.

'I blame that bloody conference,' Wes confided to Jeremy three days after his return. 'I wish I'd never gone. Gabi keeps banging on about 'finally maxing my potential' and 'shifting my career into overdrive'. I caught her polishing my stethoscope yesterday.'

'Bollocks to your stethoscope, and bollocks to your

career,' Jeremy had growled, shielding his phone from the noise of the crowded market. 'You've got a *vocation*, now, cowboy – getting Caitlyn a hot date with a friendly radiotherapist.'

The implication that he'd been neglecting his doctorly duties was an unfair one, Wes reflected, grunting his farewells a couple of minutes later. After all, he'd resumed work on Project Caitlyn the day after his return to Sefton Street, and devoted every Gabi-free moment to it since. There'd been no point telling Jeremy about that, though. The ex-Shagfinder simply wasn't the kind of person who'd understand the silent torment that Wes had suffered in the back of Abiola's minicab, watching Caitlyn disappear from view in a blue haze of exhaust fumes – or the fleeting moments of respite he'd achieved, jotting particularly significant discoveries into the margins of Gabi's textbooks.

He hadn't told Jeremy about his insomnia or his lack of appetite, either. In spite of Lisa's feminising influence, Jeremy was still more likely to attribute such symptoms to 'a lack of decent Yorkshire ale' than being forcibly parted from the girl he loved. *The girl I love.* Wes shook his head, trying to dislodge the unhelpful thought and the mental image that accompanied it, and turned back to the sheets of handwritten notes he'd scattered across the sitting room floor. It was no good, though. Despite his best efforts to focus on his erratic, sleep-deprived scribblings, Caitlyn lingered in his mind's eye – beautiful despite her frown, breathtaking regardless of the lengthening shadows that seemed increasingly to surround her.

Wes yawned and drained his coffee, grateful to the lukewarm liquid for dragging him back to the task in hand. Every time he thought about Caitlyn – every time since she'd thrown her arms round his neck at the door of Abiola's wheezing Mondeo – it had felt like a bereavement, a chilling premonition of the one that would surely follow if he couldn't find some way to help her. *I used to be the kind of bloke who could ignore everything,* Wes thought. *All I'd need was the Racing Post and a relaxing afternoon at the bookies. But I'm a different person now – a totally different person.*

It was a realisation that had first struck him somewhere in the skies above Montana, when he'd tried persuading the unyielding cabin crew to let him swap seats with Jeremy. 'Dr Sykes has the worst haemorrhoids I've ever seen,' he'd declared, puffing out his cheeks for added emphasis. 'Let him have my seat, and I'll have his. Fourteen hours in Economy could give him a rupture. He puts a brave face on it, but he'll be in agony by now. *Agony.*'

Wes hadn't made any mention of wanting to sit next to Caitlyn in his account of Jeremy's phantom piles, of course – and although the cabin crew hadn't let him exchange places with the self-styled heart surgeon, the fact remained that Wes's former self wouldn't even have bothered trying. In fact, the more he thought about it – the more he allowed his feelings and perceptions to be filtered through the Caitlyn-coloured contact lenses he'd recently acquired – the more obvious it became that the old Wes had been... well, a bit of an arsehole, really.

Stirring boiling water into three heaped spoonfuls of Gold Blend, Wes was chillingly reminded of the first conversation he'd ever had with Gabi, all those years earlier at their Freshers' Ball. *I can't resist a guy who takes what he wants,* she'd said, laughing into the glass of champagne he'd just liberated from an adjacent table. *You know – a Heathcliff. A James Bond. A bit of a bastard.* At the time, the teenage Wes had felt strangely thrilled by the way she'd said it – intoxicated by the way the first syllable of 'bastard' had come out rhyming with 'far' instead of 'gas'. Now, though, reflecting on how such an offhand remark had subtly governed his behaviour over the past half-dozen years, he couldn't help feeling that 'a bastard' was remarkably similar to 'a knobhead' or 'a wanker' in the broader scheme of things. *And I don't want to be a wanker,* he thought. *Not any more.*

For a second, Wes toyed with the thought of picking up the phone again and announcing his ex-wanker status to Jeremy. But Jeremy was 'up to his eyeballs in patchwork pouffes' at Spitalfields, and had made it abundantly clear that his next phone call from Wes should demonstrate some concrete progress on the Project Caitlyn front. Retrieving the cigarette he'd been using as a bookmark in *Cancer For Dummies*, Wes sipped his turbocharged coffee and settled back into the crater of notes and diagrams he'd recently vacated on the sitting room floor. The view was no more promising than it had been before his coffee break, however, with all his findings pointing towards one inescapable truth – that however well-informed about soft tissue sarcoma he managed to make himself, he'd still need some seriously generous collaborators to put his new-found knowledge to good effect. *People with access to drugs, equipment, expertise.*

Setting Gabi's textbooks reluctantly aside, Wes began fishing out a second set of notes from the pile on the floor. From the persecuted look in his eyes, it was obvious that the lists of names and contact details now scattered at his feet were causing him considerably more grief than joy. Working out which of his medical school friends to approach was always going to be bloody tricky, though, given the need to keep Gabi safely out of the picture. Restricting knowledge of Project Caitlyn to people outside his wife's extensive social and professional circles was going to be a virtual impossibility, however – like trying to avoid diarrhoea on a Turkish holiday – and it didn't help that Gabi had been closest to the highest fliers and brightest minds on their course.

Julian Gilmore, oncologist at the Royal Free – married to Gabi's squash partner, thought Wes, striking a thick red line through the name at the top of his list. *Georgia Fiddes, radiologist at Bart's – takes the same yoga class as Gabi's sister. Celina Patel, anaesthetist at the Whittington – buys her coke from the same paramedic as Gabi's best friend Colleen.* Wes stared down at his lopsided spider's web of names and job titles, mostly obliterated by red marker pen, his face flushing a deep crimson as he imagined the embarrassment of phoning any one of the people remaining on the list. And even if they spoke to him – even if they were in a position to help – what could he possibly offer them in return for their time and expertise? Guided tours of the Putney area in the Wynstanley Merc? A lifetime supply of racing tips?

Wes groaned under his breath. Even his prowess in the latter area was looking distinctly shaky following his return from California. During the seemingly endless Caitlyn-free days that had elapsed in Sefton Street, Wes had only ventured to the bookies on one occasion (more to clear his head than for his own amusement), and he'd only placed one bet while he was there – a deranged, hundred quid punt on a 6-race accumulator, leaving before the even the first horse had come in. It didn't take a medical genius to see that he was getting depressed, he reflected – seriously depressed, in love, and with his eerily friendly wife due home within the hour. *Oh God. I wish I was Jeremy*, he thought, shuffling his papers together and stowing them safely under the sofa. *Life would be so easy.*

If only I was Wes, thought Jeremy, subjecting Callum to a half-hearted scowl. *Wes doesn't get the third degree every time he goes to work. Wes doesn't go to work at all,* he reflected, switching off his scowl and returning his attention to the leather-topped desk in front of him. *The lucky git.*

Not that Callum was generally a bad boss. Normally Jeremy appreciated Callum's 'light touch' approach to management – his refusal to succumb to modern fads like income tax or National Insurance contributions; the way he habitually adjourned to the Ten Bells shortly before lunchtime, leaving Jeremy in a happy cloud of Rothmans smoke and wood shavings in the Brick Lane workshop. But whichever way you looked at it – and there appeared to be several – Callum possessed a highly developed interest in Jeremy's love life.

'So there's actually *two* of them,' said Callum, his soft Irish brogue stealing its way insidiously around the gentle tapping of Jeremy's chisel.

'Uh-huh.'

'And they're sisters.'

'Yup.'

'*American* sisters.'

Jeremy looked up, scanning his employer's rheumy eyes for some clue as to where the conversation might be heading – and why he'd said the word 'American' the way most men of his age said 'Britt Ekland'. 'Texans, Cal,' he eventually conceded. 'Decent, well brought-up God-fearing Southern lasses. Churchgoers, probably.'

'But one of them's...' – Callum swallowed hard and leaned low over the desk – '...a *porn* star?'

Jeremy sighed. It was the fourth time they'd discussed Caitlyn and Nikki since their mid-morning ciggie break. The day before, his boss had postponed his visit to the Ten Bells by two hours to hear about them; today, it looked as though he was prepared to forego his liquid lunch altogether. 'An *ex* adult entertainer,' said Jeremy pointedly. 'She's a civilian, now. Just a mate.'

'But Lisa doesn't know she's staying with you?'

'No.' Jeremy's eyes narrowed on his employer, fixing him with the kind of stare that brooked no disagreement. 'And she's not going to find out, either.'

'And you swear you're not – you know – having it away with either of them?' Callum pressed.

'No,' Jeremy growled. 'Caitlyn's really very poorly, Cal.'

'But Caitlyn's not the porn one, is she? The sex sister?'

'No, Cal.'

'And the other one – Nikki – the sex one. She's perfectly

fit?'

'Oh yes.'

'And you're not giving her one? On the quiet, like?'

'Certainly not. I'm devoted to Lisa.'

For a moment it seemed that Jeremy's interrogation was over. Then Callum's face creased in triumph. 'She won't let you!' he cawed. 'You want your oats, but you can't get 'em!'

Jeremy fought the urge to subject his employer to a glare of cold contempt, rightly assuming that Callum would interpret it as an admission of guilt. *It's not an oat-related problem*, he wanted to say. *I've had more oats than the Ready Brek kid.* In fact, he thought, picturing Nikki's wide, expectant eyes, it was more like a problem of *surplus* oats – a high-fibre landslide that threatened to engulf him every evening. That was something Callum would never understand, though – Callum who, like most of the blokes Jeremy knew, seemed to regard women with a bizarre mixture of awe, fear and incomprehension, usually through the bottom of a pint glass. He shook his head sadly, picking up his chisel again and resuming work on the desk, aware in that precise moment that he knew something fundamental about human relations which Callum never would. *Sex is like credit*, he wanted to tell the wheezing Irishman. *A doddle to get if you look like you don't need it.*

Still, there was a niggling aspect of Callum's assumption that rang true. Jeremy had, he'd have to admit, devoted a fairly large chunk of the previous decade to pleasures of the flesh, and couldn't pretend he regretted it. Maybe he'd feel differently if he'd been like Wes, or Tim, or Jonesy, or Dave the barman – if it had taken him more than fifteen minutes of teenage introspection to work out how to get lasses into bed. But it'd always been embarrassingly easy – easy, he supposed, because he'd never treated girls as a different species. Easy, because he'd always been funny and respectful and kind to them. Easy, because he'd honestly liked pretty much everything about them. He'd liked the way they looked in their underwear, and they way they looked when they took it off. He'd liked the way they felt, their tastes and smells, and the special sounds they sometimes made in the warm folds of his duvet. He'd liked the look in their eyes as desire overwhelmed their guilt, when curiosity turned into anticipation. And then he'd liked sleeping with them. *All of them.*

And if having Nikki staying at the Docklands flat had taught him anything, it was that recalibrating his libido was like trying to turn round an oil tanker in the middle of the North Sea – *a bloody long process.* He'd given the orders somewhere off Dogger Bank, but he was about to hit Grimsby and the ship still hadn't stopped. It hadn't even slowed down much, he reflected – because every time he looked at Nikki, he had the same feeling he'd had a thousand times before. *The sort of feeling that made him want to turn the oil tanker right back round again.*

For a moment, Jeremy considered sharing his 'oil tanker' analogy with Callum, but quickly decided not to. There was, after all, something alarmingly Freudian about comparing your sex drive to an unsteerable 250,000-tonne sea vessel. Still, Jeremy reasoned, Callum was the kind of bloke who'd persist in seeing him as a 'randy old goat', even if he ditched furniture restoring for the life of a Benedictine monk. He forced an apologetic smile to his face and cleared his throat. 'You're absolutely correct, Cal,' he murmured. 'I desperately want to shag them both, but they just won't let me. I'm being driven out of my mind with repressed sexual desire.'

'I *knew* it.'

'And for this reason, I'd like the rest of the afternoon off.'

Callum's face clouded with incomprehension. 'What? Why?'

'So I can go home and continue my quest to give them both a bloody good seeing-to. The little teases.'

'And if I let you go home early – and if you get them

both into bed – would you tell me about it tomorrow?'

'Certainly.'

'*All* about it?'

'Every last gynaecological detail. I swear.'

For a second, Callum contemplated the offer. Then he grinned. 'Off you go, then.'

'Hey, Jez.'

'Nikki.'

'How was your day, doc?'

Jeremy smiled ruefully and edged past his houseguest into the sitting room. He'd decided at the start of the week that 'rueful' was the kind of smile doctors ought to come home from hospital wearing, and it had served him well on the previous two evenings. *Saved a few, lost a few*, his smile seemed to say. *But let's not talk about it now.* 'Oh, you know,' he said, slipping off his jacket and taking the stethoscope and thermometer out of the breast pocket. 'You've seen *House* – the usual bittersweet cocktail of hope and desperation. How was yours?'

Nikki shrugged and skipped back to the outsize sofa, launching herself upon the soft leather with a playful back flip. 'Okay. I went shopping again.'

Jeremy fought a near-overwhelming urge to wince. On Monday he'd volunteered his Barclaycard to Nikki so she could buy new clothes for herself and Caitlyn – but despite the fact that she'd strayed no further than Marks & Spencer in the Canary Wharf shopping centre, Nikki had still contrived to find a dozen outfits that made both sisters look like downmarket strip-o-grams. 'No more swimwear, though?' said Jeremy.

Shaking her head, Nikki stretched back on the sofa. 'I went on the Tube, like you said I should. Right into the city centre.' She indicated a cluster of bags in front of the glass balcony doors. Most of them had the kind of worrying 'boxy' look and loop handles that signified alarmingly pricey contents. 'I found Harvey Nichols eventually. They have fabulous shoes, Jez. *Fabulous.*'

'Do they?'

'Oh yeah.' From her recumbent position on the sofa, Nikki inclined her head in the direction of her feet. There, wrapped sinuously over her toes and around her ankles, were two implausibly narrow thongs of peach-coloured suede. Nikki stretched her toes towards Jeremy and bit her lip enquiringly. 'Like them?'

Gazing at her from beyond the end of the sofa, Jeremy couldn't help noticing that Nikki's body seemed alarmingly foreshortened, with all her most distracting features clustered unhealthily together – *feet, calves, knees... then all the other bits.* 'They're certainly very... strappy,' he eventually said, diplomatically making his way over to the balcony window. 'And how's your sister been?'

'Caitlyn's doing real good. She's starting to feel more at home here. We both are. We walked around St Katherine's Dock this afternoon.' Nikki lowered her voice conspiratorially. 'She's having a little nap.'

'Is she?'

'Uh-huh. Fast asleep.' Nikki twisted around, seeking Jeremy out. By the time her eyes had eventually found his, her limbs had somehow contrived to arrange themselves into an even more intriguing tangle of sheer knitwear and exposed flesh. 'If we're real quiet, I don't think she'll wake up,' she whispered.

'That's great. Cool.' Jeremy looked furtively around the room, wondering what sort of loud noise he could accidentally make that might bring Caitlyn padding drowsily from the guest bedroom. To his alarm, a cursory glance at the tables and shelves revealed that since the morning, several familiar objects had disappeared, while many others had shuffled around the room into entirely new positions.

If only I'd mentioned Lisa, he thought, mentally noting how many of her pictures and books and DVDs had gone mysteriously AWOL. *If only I'd mentioned Lisa, like Wes mentioned Gabi to Cait. If only, at some point last week, I'd happened to mention that I live in my girlfriend's flat, and that she was currently residing in the People's Republic of China, but that I love her, and miss her, and don't want to rearrange her flat into some hideous minimalist porno shag pad.* It was an entirely pointless train of thought, though, Jeremy knew. If Nikki hadn't thought he was single, and living alone, and was a highly-regarded cardiologist at the Royal Free Hospital... well, she'd never have agreed to bring her sister over here. And while Jeremy didn't doubt that she'd acted with the best of intentions towards Caitlyn, he couldn't help feeling that he'd gravely underestimated the extent to which Nikki would seek out his doctoral attention for herself. He'd gravely underestimated how quickly and completely she'd make the flat her own, too; in fact, there was something faintly sinister about the way Nikki had begun treating the place as though it was hers.

'I bought a book on *feng shui*,' she said. 'You'll find the apartment a whole lot more relaxing, now – I promise.'

'You think so?'

'I *know* so, honey. Come sit down here. This is the spiritual centre of the room. The womb. This is where all the energies converge. It's a very intense spot.'

Jeremy stared at the tiny space at the end of the sofa that Nikki was now pointing towards, reflecting that a herd of bull elephants – if they should, at the moment, stampede through the flat – wouldn't be sufficient to drag him to her side. *If she'd been like this in California*, he thought, *then who knows what might have happened.* But while airbrushing Lisa from his mind had been a pragmatic necessity on the other side of the planet, it was impossible – and even less palatable – here in her own flat, surrounded by the furniture she'd chosen, the CD's she loved, the books she'd adored. Jeremy turned back to the window (now devoid of the photos that Lisa had stuck there, he noticed), suddenly struggling to withstand the tidal wave of loneliness and emotional exhaustion that threatened at any moment to engulf him.

In the breathless moment that followed, the only sound that could be heard was the opening of the guest bedroom door and two soft footfalls on the polished wood flooring. Summoning the remainder of his mental energy, Jeremy gulped back the lump that seemed to have formed in his throat and tried forcing an optimistic smile to his face. Then he turned around. 'Hey, Cait,' he said.

'Hey, Jez.'

'Good day, kid?'

'Cool. We went for a walk around the docks. You live in a city of many ducks.'

'Aye, good stuff.' Jeremy turned back to the darkening Docklands skyline and stared out over the water. 'I spoke to Wes again this afternoon.'

'How is he?'

The tremor and urgency in Caitlyn's voice, so different from Nikki's, unsettled Jeremy slightly. It wasn't really the sort of question that boys asked other boys, and for a moment he struggled to find an answer that didn't involve the words *slightly hopeless* or *an indolent slob who has the good fortune not be chased round his own home by your ex-porn star sister.* Eventually he shrugged diplomatically. 'I don't know. He's just Wes, really, isn't he?'

A moment later, Nikki was by his side. 'Did he have any news? About treatment for Caitlyn?'

Jeremy shrugged again. He'd given the lad a hard enough time on the phone, but little had been forthcoming on the 'progress' front. 'He's been swotting up on his oncology, working out who to approach, that sort of thing.'

'But it's all going to be okay?' Nikki pressed.

'Oh aye. Sure, sure.' Jeremy turned back to the window, suddenly desperate to be out of the flat. Empty since the previous evening, his stomach seemed to be tying itself in knots beneath the waistband of his trousers. He turned back to the two anxious faces of the girls, wondering whether they'd fancy an evening in one of the smarter Docklands pubs. It seemed doubtful. 'Wes is working his socks off, actually,' he eventually muttered, kicking off his shoes and picking up the TV remote control from the top of a tiny onyx pyramid that had mysteriously appeared on Lisa's coffee table. 'He's spending all day tomorrow phoning up his contacts. He's bound to have some positive news soon. No question.'

24

you never know when you might need to pop a cap in someone's ass

It was at times like these, Wes reflected, that he wished he possessed a little more of Jeremy's impetuousness. A little more of his blather. Perhaps even a little of his sheer goat-brained idiocy. If he *had* been a little more like Jeremy, for instance, then he, too, might have inadvertently wandered through both US and UK customs with a fully-loaded semi-automatic pistol in his the bottom of his suitcase.

'Aye, mate – it's Danny's,' Jeremy had told him on the phone. 'I meant to chuck it in a river or something, before we got to San Francisco airport. But then, what with the excitement of you burning the lasses' trailer down, it totally slipped my mind. I might hang on to it, actually. I've got it stashed in the bedside drawer. 'Cos you never know when you might need to pop a cap in someone's ass, do you?'

At the time, Wes had done what any right-thinking person would have done – informed his friend what an utter fucking mentalist he was being, and how he should chuck the offending weapon into the Thames without a moment's delay. Now, though, after a morning of being left on hold, of unreturned phone calls and blunt, uncooperative secretaries, he could almost appreciate the confidence-enhancing feel-good factor of having a murderous tool of bloody violence sitting on his lap.

So badly was Wes's day going, in fact, that he could scarcely believe his good fortune when, shortly after lunch, he was told that Giles Crozier was happy to take his call – and even more astonished at the enthusiasm with which he was greeted. After all, they'd hardly been close friends, and hadn't spoken for at least two years. Still, the warmth in Giles's voice was undeniable. 'You're through to Dr Crozier,' it drawled companionably. 'Talk to me.'

'Giles? Is that you, mate?'

'Guilty as charged,' said Giles, a hint of confusion creeping into his tone. 'Who is this?'

'Byron Wesley. Wes.'

'From Range Rover? About the new wheels for my Freelander, right?'

'Er, no. Not quite.'

'Oh,' said Giles, his disappointment swiftly turning to irritation. 'Then who the hell are you?'

'It's Wes. Wes. From medical school.' He sighed inwardly, realising he'd have to resort, for the umpteenth time that morning, to his university nickname – the one he'd tried painfully hard to forget. 'Dewhurst,' he said quietly. 'Dewhurst the butcher.'

In the pause that followed it was almost possible for Wes to discern the distant chime of the penny dropping. A sharp intake of breath confirmed the situation. 'Ah, *Dewhurst!* Giles exclaimed. 'How the fuck *are* you? Slaughtered anything recently? *Ha ha!*

'Not recently, no.'

'No lawsuits pending, eh? Gross negligence? Pulled the wrong bollock off? Catheter up the wrong hole?'

'Nothing like that, no.'

'Good show, good show.' An empty clucking in Giles's throat told Wes that his friend's supply of small talk was running dangerously low. 'So. Dewhurst,' he eventually continued, his voice frostier now. 'Who the hell gave you my number?'

'Simon Cumming-Brown.'

'Spunker Brown?'

'Spunker, yes.'

'And how the hell's he doing?'

'Very well. He's gone into obstetrics at the Whittington.' Wes tried introducing a note of honey into his voice – the way Jeremy used to, back in his 'Shagfinder' days. 'Spunker said you'd been making inroads into oncology at Bart's. Flying start to a promising career, according to Spunker.'

'Well, I don't like to blow my own horn – *although I would if I could reach, ha ha!* – but it's not going too shabbily. The head man here's fond of the sauce. Monumental drinker. The smart money in-house says it's only a matter of months before he majorly screws up. Then it'll be early retirement for him, and a fast pass to the big money for yours truly.'

Fighting the urge to mime the 'wanker' gesture, Wes composed himself in the hall mirror, turning back to the phone only when he'd twisted his features into an approximation of Giles's own self-satisfied leer. 'Bloody good for you, mate. That's really excellent. Actually, I was hoping to pick your esteemed brains about something. Take advantage of your undoubted expertise.'

'Pick away, dear Dewhurst. Pick away.'

'Right. Well, I've got this... private patient. American girl, no health insurance, living over here. And she's got soft tissue sarcoma...'

'*Bummer!*' roared Giles, cupping the mouthpiece and wheezing a few breathless bars of the funeral march down the line.

'...and I just wondered whether there's any way we could

help her out?' Hooking the receiver beneath his chin, Wes found himself nervously crossing both sets of fingers. *I'm a doctor*, he told himself. *All my friends are doctors. I can pull strings. I'm connected.* He swallowed hard, praying that Giles's silence was his cue to continue. 'Some meds going missing, maybe? Perhaps an hour or two with a friendly specialist every now and then – or a few hours' lab time, maybe the odd chemo session when the shop's shut. Off the books, obviously. As a favour. To an old friend.'

For some moments Giles was silent – and when he finally spoke, his former mirth had all but evaporated. 'As a *favour?* he said. 'You're out of line, Dewhurst. Way out of line. You know that isn't how it works.'

'I know that officially...'

'If I was heading my own department, then maybe,' Giles continued, an echo of his former pomp returning to his voice. '*Maybe*. But I'm not going to shit on my own doorstep for the sake of some Yank bint I've never met, am I? Am I, Dewhurst? Some of us have got careers to think about.'

'Well, what about drugs trials or something?' said Wes, now not bothering to hide the desperation in his voice. 'Is there anything she could be put up for, on the quiet? You read the journals, mate. You know what's going on.'

'You're right,' Giles snorted. 'I *do* know what's going on – and it's sweet Fanny Adams at the moment. Don't you know there's a recession?'

'And there's nothing else you can think of? Anything that might help?'

The pause at the end of the line seemed to indicate that Giles was at least considering the question seriously. Then he delivered his verdict. 'Get her to sign the organ donor register!' he roared. '*The organ donor register!* No, seriously, though – don't. All her bits'll be totally fucked by the time she snuffs it. No good for anything. Not even fit for stew, Dewhurst. Not even stew!'

At length, when the echoes of his laughter had finished reverberating down the line, Giles spoke again. 'Anyway, who was that red-headed bit of stuff you used to be knocking off? Tabitha something, was it?'

'Gabi. Gabi Wynstanley.'

'Still porking her?'

'We got married six months ago.'

'You're a lucky fucker, Dewhurst. Give her one from me, eh? *Give her one from me!*'

And with that, the line went dead.

In the empty moments following the conversation, Wes's pen hovered above his notepad before eventually marking the words 'Giles Crozier – World Class Tosser' with a couple of semi-optimistic question marks. It had, after all, been the longest, most Caitlyn-focused phone call he'd managed all day. After that, still numb from the encounter, he'd made a cup of tea and slipped into the back garden for a cigarette, returning to the telephone only when the empty packet lay discarded in one of the ornamental plant pots by the door.

For quite some time, staring at the list of names by the telephone table, Wes wrestled with the urge to call Jeremy on his mobile and ask for two hours' rental of Danny's pistol. A flying visit to Giles Crozier's office – enquiring about his own position on the organ donor resister, perhaps – would certainly be a head-clearer. It wouldn't get him any closer to helping Caitlyn, though. Only the list of names, now heavily scored with crossings-out and scribbled annotations, could help him do that. He stared at the next number – Annabel Ives, now doing something absurdly high-powered at a research lab in Cambridge – and picked up the telephone. But as he began tapping the keypad, it was another number entirely that he found himself dialling.

'Hi,' said the familiar voice at the other end of the line, taut with expectation. 'Jeremy?'

'Erm, no. It's Wes, actually.'

'Oh, hi Wes,' said Nikki. 'Do you want to leave a message for Jeremy? Because he isn't back from the hospital yet.'

'No, no. Actually, it's Caitlyn I want. If she's there.'

'Sure.'

In the hiss of static that followed, Wes found himself glancing furtively around the hall. Between the churning emptiness in his stomach and the peppery prickle of guilt across his shoulder blades, he couldn't work out whether he was more likely to be suffering from acute IBS or the menopause, and the eventual arrival of Caitlyn's voice at the other end of the line did nothing to relieve his symptoms. 'Wes?' it said, its soft neutrality revealing nothing of its owner's feelings.

'Hi, Cait,' said Wes, struggling to keep control of his own quavering vocal cords. 'How are you feeling?'

'Okay. Tired, but basically fine.'

'Cool. Good.'

'Actually, I'm really glad you...'

'...I was just phoning to...'

'You first.'

Wes took a deep breath and swallowed hard. 'Well, I was actually calling to see if you wanted to come out tonight. For dinner. In town. Chinese or Italian, maybe. Tex-Mex, if we can find it. Tapas if we can't. Whatever you like.'

'Is there anything you need to tell me?' said Caitlyn, the strain of not being able to read Wes's expression clearly audible in her voice. 'Anything, you know, medical?'

'No, no. Well, not specifically. I've been phoning people all day, but I haven't really had any major breakthroughs. Not yet, anyway. The main reason I wanted to see you was just... well, I just wanted to see you.' Wes leaned back against the stairs and closed his eyes. 'Because to be honest, I've been missing you like hell. And I really wanted to apologise, face to face, for burning your home down.'

'Go on.'

'I'm still getting these, you know, occasional twinges of guilt about it. And I think that seeing you – and buying you dinner, somewhere really nice – might make me feel a little less... you know, twinge-y.'

For several heart-stopping moments, Wes could only hear the faintest sounds of breathing at the other end of the line. Then Caitlyn spoke. 'Well, I wouldn't want you feeling twinge-y,' she said. 'Not on my account.'

'So you'll come?'

'Uh-huh. I'd love to. Tapas sounds good.'

Wes closed his eyes again, already anticipating the electric shock of pleasure he'd feel when he saw Caitlyn later that evening. 'Great,' he said. 'I'll book at table at Navarro's. Do you know how to use the Tube?'

'Nikki does. She'll explain it.'

'I'll see you in the ticket hall of Tottenham Court Road station at seven, then. I'll be right by the barrier. You won't be able to miss me.'

'I wouldn't want to.'

'Cool,' said Wes, putting down the phone. 'Cool.'

25

the trained eye misses nothing, mr sykes

Casting an anxious glance over his shoulder, Jeremy picked up half of the clean plates and cups from where they were draining and lowered them back into the washing up bowl. If Nikki were to inspect his handiwork, she'd detect his ruse in an instant – but she'd shown scant interest in the kitchen during her stay in Lisa's flat, and it seemed unlikely that she'd choose this precise moment to reveal a new-found fascination for Fairy liquid and scouring pads. Jeremy strained his ears for a moment, trying to detect Nikki's whereabouts. Since she'd kicked off her pumps, it had become almost impossible to discern her movements around the flat, and Jeremy's emotional state was already heading beyond 'anxiety' on its now-habitual journey towards 'outright panic'.

It had all started over an hour ago, of course, when he'd come back from Callum's workshop to find Nikki alone in the flat. 'Cait's gone to meet Wes in town,' she'd said,

223

relieving Jeremy of his stethoscope and pressing a cold beer into his hand. 'They're having dinner together. Some Spanish place called Navarro's.'

'Weren't we invited?' he'd replied, trying to suppress an all-too-familiar feeling of foreboding.

'I think they wanted to be alone,' Nikki had said, turning on her heel and heading for the stereo. A moment later, the sound of Lisa's Cinerama CD began permeating the flat. 'Or maybe they just wanted to give us some privacy.'

'*You* don't fancy heading out, do you?' Jeremy had said, hoping that Nikki wouldn't detect the note of desperation in his voice. 'Grab something to eat? My treat. We can go wherever you like – West End, anywhere.'

Nikki had shaken her head slowly. 'I wanna stay right here,' she'd said.

For a moment, Jeremy had considered his options. Then he'd smiled brightly. 'Okay,' he'd said. 'I'll cook.'

Before he'd put the plates on the table, Jeremy would have said it was impossible to eat a supper of bacon, black pudding and tinned tomatoes with any overt erotic subtext. But Nikki had proved him wrong, lifting each morsel of food to her mouth as though she was an extra in a Fanny Craddock sex tape. 'You might be able to give someone a heart bypass, but you really can't cook at all, can you?' she'd eventually sighed, pushing away her plate. 'I'll light candles. Get rid of the burnt smell.'

Jeremy had shrugged as noncommittally as he could, glancing at the clock on the wall. *Not even half past seven.* Picturing the evening stretching out before him – and with it, Nikki – a terrifying premonition entered his mind, a weirdly compelling flesh-tone slideshow of bodies, candles and rugs. *How are we going to fill the time without shagging at least a couple of times?* he thought. *Is it physically possible?* He'd looked up as Nikki dimmed the lighting to a soft umber glow, hurriedly taking to his feet as she made her way back across the room. 'I'll wash the pots,' he'd said, and scurried for the kitchen.

Twenty minutes later, he was still at it. Jeremy stared down at his hands, raw and wrinkled as two newborn puppies, wondering whether he dared drop the clean plates back into the dirty water one more time. The barely discernible sound of Nikki's approach clinched it. 'Aren't you done yet?' she said, glancing at the bowlful of newly-immersed crockery and pulling herself lightly on to the granite worktop.

'Reckon I'll be a while yet, kid,' Jeremy shrugged, trying not to stare at the pair of bare feet now swinging freely a couple of inches away from his left thigh.

'I'm bored.'

'You can watch TV.'

'I don't want to watch TV.'

'You might just catch the end of *Emerdale*. It's about Yorkshire. They're your spiritual cousins, Yorkshiremen. You could learn to speak Yorkshire. Add another string to your bow.'

'I don't wanna watch TV, Jez.'

'No?'

'No.'

'What do you want to do, then?'

'I wanna take a bath.' Nikki leaned in close to Jeremy's ear – so close, in fact, that he had to grip Lisa's *Bagpuss* mug with both hands beneath the water to stop himself being drawn into her gravitational field. 'Do you wanna take a bath?'

'No,' he lied.

Nikki smiled, so close now that Jeremy could feel her hair falling on the bare skin at the nape of his neck. 'Well I'll keep the door open,' she whispered. 'Just in case you change your mind.'

I hope you didn't hear any of that, thought Jeremy, retrieving Lisa's *Bagpuss* mug from the washing up water and placing it upside down on the draining board. He stared at the picture of the pink and white striped cat as the soap suds gently rolled down its wise, ancient face. In circumstances like these, it was difficult not to feel slightly envious of Bagpuss, Jeremy reflected. *No emotions. No desires. No fending off the advances of amorous lady cats.* He sighed, listening to the distant sound of rushing water and allowing his gaze to stray towards the guest bedroom door, slightly ajar where Nikki had left it a moment earlier. *I don't think she meant it, anyway, kid*, thought Jeremy, turning and starting resolutely out of the kitchen window. Outside, the Docklands skyline was already in darkness, with only the crossword puzzle of office lights punctuating the deep nocturnal blue. *Lasses are always saying stuff they don't mean.*

Jeremy shook his hands free of the washing-up water and dried them on his trousers, casting his eyes around the kitchen for other jobs to do. Flipping open the kettle lid (and idly wondering whether Lisa had fulfilled her promise of buying de-scaler before decamping for Shanghai), he suddenly stopped short, eyes widening silently as he sought to retain his grip in the wet handle. There, reflected in the kitchen window, was Nikki, padding softly back across the candlelit sitting room. Her hair, which had previously hung loosely about her shoulders, was now held aloft in the loose folds of a diaphanous purple scarf. The rest of her – every last inch of her – was naked.

It was wrong, Jeremy knew, to stare. Wrong to allow his gaze to secretly wander over the curves and crevices of Nikki's flawless skin. Wrong to let it linger on her snub, upturned breasts and perfect cupcake buttocks. And wrong to imagine himself naked next to her, allowing his hands to roam freely up her muscular legs and into the soft, trimmed furze of pubic hair beyond. *Wrong, wrong, wrong.* But when she turned her head to the window – when she caught his eye and steadfastly held it – it didn't feel so very bad at all.

Oh God, he thought, gently turning Bagpuss towards the kitchen wall. *I want to take a bath with Nikki.* And while

226

Jeremy knew with one hundred per cent conviction that it would *only* be a bath – a companionable way for two close friends to relax, to throw off the stresses of the day – well, experience had taught him that accidental slip-ups could very easily occur in an overcrowded tub... slip-ups which, despite appearances, wouldn't *technically* constitute having sex and certainly wouldn't constitute cheating on Lisa. *Hell, no*. Almost unconsciously, Jeremy found himself fingering his shirt buttons and then, a moment later, when his brain finally received notification of the decision reached forty minutes earlier in his underpants, he found himself staggering sideways like a drunk escapologist, madly wrestling with his belt buckle.

He was at the bathroom door, and down to his pants and socks, when he heard the sharp, resolute knocking at the front door.

If Detective Constable Paul Sanders had even remotely suspected that he'd just saved Jeremy from an unforgivable moral lapse, nothing about his demeanour said so. 'Do you know who I am?' he asked, making his way briskly into the sitting room and flicking on the lights.

For a moment, Jeremy was stumped. *Some long-lost English boyfriend who Nikki somehow neglected to mention? A wandering amnesiac?* He stared at the piercing eyes hovering just beneath his line of vision, wondering where he'd seen them before. *Oh God – you're not my conscience, are you?* Now he came to think of it, there *was* something weirdly familiar about the square jaw line and close-cropped hair – a hint of something he almost recognised. There didn't seem much point dwelling on it, though. From the look on the policeman's face, it didn't seem likely that Jeremy would have long to wait before discovering the identity of his mystery visitor. 'Well, you're a copper, aren't you?' he eventually said. 'Paul something. You just said so, when you showed me your warrant card.'

'But you don't remember meeting me before?' pressed the policeman, inching towards Jeremy.

'Not that I can think of. Sorry.'

For a moment, DC Sanders's eyes probed Jeremy's, seeking out any sign of deception. Then he smiled. 'You were involved in a fight in a pub in Leicester Square. Last October.'

'Really?'

'Yes you were. A drunken altercation. I was one of the arresting officers. It was before I transferred to CID.'

'Afraid I don't recall it,' Jeremy lied. He tried another smile – the one he'd used two minutes earlier, urgently imploring Nikki to stay silent behind the bathroom door – but sounds and images from the night in question were already flooding his head. In his mind's eye, DC Sanders's face loomed towards him across the broken glasses and shattered furniture, his muscular hand outstretched. *Aye I remember you*, thought Jeremy. *You're a tenacious sod, you are.* His smiled widened. 'Nope. Still nothing.'

'Really?' said the policeman, appearing to appraise Jeremy afresh. 'You made me look a proper charlie in front of that magistrate.'

Strangely warming to his visitor – and cheered by the memory of his hapless performance in court – Jeremy found himself shaking his head sympathetically. 'I didn't reckon so,' he said. 'You came across very professionally. I almost thought about applying to join the force myself afterwards, actually.'

'So you remember now, do you?'

'Well, just the haziest of details,' Jeremy admitted. 'But we should let bygones be bygones. What can I do for you tonight, anyway?' Suddenly, the candlelit room seemed to grow uncomfortably cold. 'It's nothing to do with a lass called Lisa Salt, is it? Nothing bad?'

'I'm here regarding a van, Mr Sykes.'

Jeremy shook his head in apparent confusion, still

unable to shake the room's recent chill. 'A van?'

'Yes, Mr Sykes. A van. They're like cars, only roomier in the back. We locked you in one after the fight in Leicester Square, if you remember. The one I'm interested in is a brown Ford Transit, registered to your father, one Richard Archibold Sykes of St Hilda's Terrace, Whitby. You reported it stolen to your father's insurance company a fortnight ago.'

'Oh, *that* van.'

'Yes, *that* van.'

'You haven't found it, have you?'

'Alas not, Mr Sykes.' DC Sanders slowly advanced on Jeremy, his voice growing icy. 'But the case has raised a couple of questions at the station.'

'Has it?'

'Yes, Mr Sykes. Like why you didn't report the theft to the police.'

Jeremy fought the urge to scratch his head, pantomime-style. 'Didn't I?' he said.

'No, Mr Sykes. You didn't.'

'Ah.'

'You didn't actually mention it to your father, either. Not until a week after the theft.'

'Ah, well, I was in California.'

'Odd time of year for a holiday, Mr Sykes.'

'I was there for a medical conference, actually.'

'A *medical* conference?'

'Aye, well,' said Jeremy, raising his voice so that he would be clearly heard by Nikki on the other side of the bathroom door. 'I *am* a doctor, you know. Fastest stethoscope this side of Holby.'

For some moments, Jeremy's words hung in the air. He imagined them gently wafting past the policeman's head, drifting out of the sitting room and through the bathroom door. He imagined Nikki on the other side, wrapped in one of Lisa's thick cotton towels, her shoulders visibly relaxing at the sound of the word 'doctor'. He smiled inwardly, allowing his mind's eye to linger on Nikki's still-damp arms, the gentle rise and fall of her bosom. 'A medical man through and through, me.'

'No need to shout, Mr Sykes,' said DC Sanders, following Jeremy's gaze towards the bathroom door. 'But I seemed to recall from our last meeting that you were working as a furniture restorer. Yes – *definitely a furniture restorer.*' His eyes rounded once more upon Jeremy, who flinched beneath their gaze. 'When you were in court, you said your family had been in the business for generations. You even offered to strip some paint off the magistrate's Welsh dresser.'

'Did I?'

'Yes, you did. Do you know what reminded me?'

Jeremy shook his head mutely.

'The van. The van you had stolen.' The policeman's voice dropped to a soft purr. 'The van with *Sykes and Son, Furniture Restorers* painted on the side.'

Jeremy glanced over DC Sanders's shoulder at the bathroom door. Although no sound had emerged from it since the policeman's arrival some minutes earlier, it now seemed to be exuding a particularly belligerent silence. *Accusing, almost.* Suddenly it opened and Nikki – fully clothed but barefoot – crept noiselessly across the narrow hallway and into the master bedroom. Jeremy's eyes followed her until the bedroom door – *his* bedroom door – the one he'd *very specifically* asked Caitlyn and Nikki not to venture beyond – swung gently closed behind her. Then he returned his attention to DC Sanders. 'Beg your pardon?' he said.

'I was enquiring about the furniture restoration business, Mr Sykes.'

'What about it?'

'Pays well, does it?'

'Mustn't grumble,' Jeremy shrugged.

DC Sanders allowed himself a leisurely look around the sitting room. '*I* wouldn't grumble if I could afford to live here,' he said.

'Mm.'

'You can provide proof of your income, of course.'

Jeremy frowned, unsure whether this constituted a statement or a question. 'Can I?' he said.

'Certainly you can, Mr Sykes,' smiled DC Sanders. 'Payslips and suchlike.'

'Ah, well. Not as such, no.' Jeremy lowered his voice, anxious that his words shouldn't be overheard by Nikki. 'Actually, my girlfriend pays most of the mortgage on this place.'

'The young lady who was in the bathroom?'

Jeremy's face now began twitching with panicked incredulity. 'Did you see her?'

'I saw her reflection in the window. Pretty girl. She didn't look very happy,' said the policeman, allowing a conspiratorial leer to play across his features. 'The trained eye misses nothing, Mr Sykes.'

'Nikki's just a friend, actually. Her plumbing's on the fritz so she popped over for a quick dip.'

'And your *girlfriend* doesn't object?'

'She hasn't *said* she does,' Jeremy winced, praying that DC Sanders might deliver his next observation at something less than 'megaphone' level. 'She's in Shanghai.'

The policeman's face grew radiant with delight. 'Of course she is, Mr Sykes. Of *course* she is.'

Realising he now had nothing to lose in acknowledging Nikki's presence in the bedroom, Jeremy glanced round at the firmly-closed door. Sounds suggesting frenzied activity were emerging from within. He turned back to the smiling policeman. 'Do we really have to discuss all this now?' he hissed.

For a moment, DC Sanders feigned a look of utter astonishment. 'Heavens, no,' he said. He leaned in close towards Jeremy, lowering his voice to a hoarse stage whisper. 'But it's been fun, hasn't it? Your zip's undone, by the way. So's your belt. Has been since I came in.' He grinned broadly and began making his way back towards the front door. 'Enjoy the rest of your evening. Let's hope your father's van turns up soon, eh?'

Tiptoeing back down the hallway, Jeremy had expected at least a minute or two to gather his wits before the onslaught began. Even before DC Sanders's steps had died away in the corridor outside, however, Nikki had launched herself upon him, forcing the bedroom door so far back that it strained at its hinges. '*Fucker!*' she yelled, landing half a dozen blows on his upper arm before retreating back towards the bedroom. '*You piece-of-shit motherfucker.*'

Reeling from the ferocity of Nikki's assault, Jeremy raised his hands appeasingly. 'So you overheard our conversation, then?' he said. 'Me and that copper?'

'Every last fucking word.'

'And you're angry, aren't you? I can tell.'

For some moments Nikki was speechless, and when words eventually came they were choked with tears and rage. 'I'm fucking *scared*, Jeremy.'

'There's no need to be scared...' he said, ignoring the guilty churning in his stomach and edging towards her.

'Stay where you are, cowboy.'

'Just try to chill out, and I'll explain...'

'*Stay right where you are.*'

He wasn't sure what it was about Nikki's voice that compelled him, but Jeremy found himself pinned to the spot. 'Okay.'

'So you're not a doctor.'

'Not a fully qualified doctor, no.'

'You're not *fully qualified?*' said Nikki, clearly fighting her body's desire to begin hyperventilating. 'You're a fucking *furniture restorer.*'

'Yes.'

'And this isn't really your apartment.'

'Not technically, no.'

'And you've got a girlfriend.'

'Yes.'

'Fucking great.' For a moment, Nikki's anger threatened to eclipse the raw, animal terror that had accompanied her out of the bedroom. 'And this business with the truck,' she said. 'Does that make you a thief or just some sort of lowlife grifter? Ripping off your old man?'

'Bit of both, probably,' Jeremy shrugged. 'But I'm not a *bad* thief. Honestly. I'm more of a Robin Hood than a Bernard Madoff or an Enron.'

'You're hardly a fucking saint, Jeremy,' Nikki snapped. 'And why did you bring us over here? You and Wes?'

'To make your sister better again. I swear.'

'Well, I'd love to believe that, Jeremy, I really would. Same as I'd love to believe that your friend Wes is also a doctor, and that Santa Claus is going to give my sister a free course of chemotherapy for Christmas.' Without taking her eyes off Jeremy, Nikki reached down and picked up the large leather holdall she'd abandoned on the floor a minute earlier. 'But you know what I found right next to your bed, Jez? In the drawer?'

Feeling his guilt and fear suddenly coalescing into cold terror, Jeremy found himself failing to meet Nikki's eye. 'No,' he said.

'Oh, I think you do, Jez.'

'Was it a gun?'

'Yes. It was a gun, Jeremy. A loaded gun. Danny's gun. *Danny's fucking gun.* Now what the fuck was *that* doing there?'

'I can explain...'

'Were you planning on shooting me, Jez? Is that what Danny wanted? Or were you waiting until you'd fucked me a few times first?'

'You're being ridiculous...'

233

'No, Jeremy. I'm being *real* fucking clear-headed.' Reaching behind her, Nikki struggled blindly with the catch on the front door. A moment later it opened, and she backed slowly into the doorway. 'Go home to Yorkshire, Jeremy,' she said. 'Go tonight. And don't try following me. Because if I ever see you or Wes again, I swear I'll fucking execute the two of you.'

And with that she was gone, slamming the door behind her so hard that the pictures rattled on the walls.

In the silent seconds that followed, when even Nikki's frantic footsteps were no longer audible in the corridor outside the flat, Jeremy stood in the hallway, paralysed by indecision. Then, as though waking from a hypnotist's trance, he suddenly found himself hurtling into the bedroom, scrabbling through the open drawers and cupboards. It was no good, though. His wallet had gone – and so had Danny's gun.

26

it can't be the prawns

It can't be the prawns, reflected Wes, gazing morosely at the mass grave of pink and red shells on the plate in front of him. *The prawns were outstanding. And I don't reckon it's the wine, either.* He picked up his glass and held it at eye level, lightly swirled the remaining half-inch of Rioja around the bowl for a moment, then tipped it into this mouth. It tasted just as good as the first mouthful had done two hours earlier. He glanced round at the nearby diners and, finding himself unobserved, reached across the table for Caitlyn's untouched glass. Sloshing half its contents into his own, Wes performed the same rigorous taste test – swirl, gulp, wince – and shook his head sadly. *Nope. Absolutely nothing wrong with the wine.* Finally Wes's eyes narrowed on the slice of Spanish omelette lying discarded beneath Caitlyn's napkin. *The egg*, he thought. *It's got to be the egg.* He reached unsteadily towards the suspect dish, pinioning himself against the table with his free hand, and swiftly hacked off a larger-than-intended chunk of omelette with his fork. A moment later it was melting in his mouth, washed down with the remainder of Caitlyn's Rioja. He sighed and allowed his head to loll over the back of his chair. *Nothing wrong with the prawns, or the wine, or the omelette. So why do I feel so fucking appalling?* He closed his eyes in resignation, judging that he still had a minute or two before Caitlyn returned from the loo. *Must be all the lying, I suppose.*

Lying was a bit like smoking, he'd recently come to think – not as easy to quit as you'd imagine. And while he'd started off as a social liar, he was now fully aware of his 'addict' status. *The cravings. The mood swings. The self-loathing.* That was the thing about lies, though. They tended to start off okay – plausible, well-intentioned little fibs – but recently they'd been revealing an alarming tendency to balloon into lethally uncontrollable whoppers. And even when he'd woven them together into tightly-knitted canopies of untruth – even when he'd hidden whole chapters of his life beneath them – there was no way he could have anticipated just how quickly or insistently they'd start to unravel.

'I'm so fucking sorry, Gabs,' he slurred, gently inclining his empty glass to one of the imaginary women sitting opposite him. 'I always liked you. Always. But getting married was just stupid. You should have known I was never going to fill your old man's boots. And with respect, my dear, you must have been out of your mind to ever think I could.'

Wes raised his glass once more to his lips, registering only mild surprise when he found it to be empty. Taking a deep breath, he now turned his attention to his other invisible companion, affectionately saluting her across the table. 'Cait,' he said. '*Cait, Cait, Cait.* What the fuck have I done to you, kid?' He averted his eyes from Caitlyn's unseeing gaze, ashamed even to address her ghost. 'I don't think I can do it,' he said. 'I know what I promised, but I don't think I can make you better again. And even if, by some fucking miracle, I could help you – well, it's still impossible, isn't it?' He nodded towards the mute spectre of his wife, then lowered his eyes. 'I can't leave her, Caitlyn. I want to, but I can't. Her old man owns the lot. The house, the car, everything. He made me sign things. Without her I'm nothing, kid. I've not even got the price of your plane ticket home.'

Attempting to collect his thoughts in spite of the wine he'd consumed, Wes found himself glancing warily around the dimly-lit restaurant. No one, fortunately, seemed to have noticed his mumbled soliloquy – or if they had, nobody had decided to pay it any particular attention. *London*, thought Wes gratefully, reaching for his untouched tumbler of mineral water. *So saturated with weirdoes that nobody notices you losing your mind. God bless it.*

Wes tipped the glass of mineral water into his numb mouth, refilled it from the bottle and emptied it again. He didn't feel any better, though. He'd necked a couple of co-codamol and a handful of Rennies half an hour earlier, but they hadn't helped much either – not that he'd thought they would. *Not when the diagnosis was a guilty conscience.* 'I think it's time for the lies to stop, isn't it?' he said, quietly addressing himself once more to Caitlyn's spectral self. 'All the hideous... *bullshit.*'

Wes glanced nervously around, aware that 'bullshit' had come out considerably louder than intended. A couple of nearby diners returned his gaze with mild annoyance before returning to their meals. 'It's all going to change, anyway,' Wes continued, now addressing his invisible companion under his breath. 'I love you, kid, and I'm going to tell you the truth. The truth about me. The truth about Jeremy. The truth about my non-existent career, and my complete failure to find someone who'll treat your cancer. You might not like me much when I've told you, but you need to know. I'm going to tell you everything. *Everything.* Soon as you come back from the loo.'

And then, through the dissipating haze of her ghostly

counterpart, Caitlyn was suddenly visible, weaving her way back towards the table. *Oh God*, thought Wes. *You're beautiful, aren't you?* He felt his pupils dilate as she approached, drinking in her image until she was once again sitting opposite him. When after some moments he still hadn't spoken, Caitlyn inclined her head to one side and reached across the table for his hand. 'You okay?' she said.

'Fine. Good,' said Wes. 'Why?'

'Nothing. You just looked a little freaked out, is all.'

Wes nodded. He *felt* pretty freaked out, truth be told – strangely light-headed and breathless. 'Bit drunk,' he finally conceded. 'Too much wine.'

'Happy drunk, though?'

'Uh-huh. Happy drunk.'

'Good,' she said, squeezing his hand and pushing the table's remaining plates aside. 'I think I've forgiven you for burning down my home, by the way.'

Wes nodded philosophically, trying hard not to overdo it. *Think sober.* 'Was it because I said you could have two lots of prawns?' he asked, his eyes panning over the cluster of tapas plates at the side of the table.

'Shrimp always helps. But it's mostly because I think I can see...' – Caitlyn dropped her eyes as she struggled to find the right words – '...I can see that you're seriously trying to help. And it means the whole world to me. And if having Dr Byron Wesley fighting my corner occasionally results in a trailer or two getting razed to the ground, then so be it.' She squeezed his hand again. 'So be it, Wes.'

'Cool,' said Wes, hoping that Caitlyn's next conversational gambit might not paint him in such an embarrassingly flattering light. 'No promises, but I'll try not to do it again.'

'Good.' Caitlyn allowed a magnanimous finger to stray lightly over Wes's knuckle. 'And since we're obviously in the mood for candid confessionals, I want to apologise for something,' she said.

'What? Why?'

'For an overdose of cynicism. For taking so long to trust you. I think it's because Nikki's the only person who's ever really looked out for me. The only person I've ever been able to rely on. And she's a... well, she can sometimes be...'

'...a bit of a loony?'

'A bit impulsive. Not a loony *per se*,' said Caitlyn reprovingly. 'Unless you define lunacy as unpredictable and erratic behaviour and a strong tendency to get involved in dangerous and self-destructive relationships and activities.'

'Like porn?'

'Like porn, and drugs, and criminal boyfriends, and occasional mindless acts of vengeance, yes.'

'I see.'

'Mm.' Caitlyn beckoned Wes closer with a tiny nod of the head. 'When I was a kid – before I developed my fascinating range of diseases and ailments – most boys only wanted to know me so they could get closer to Nikki.'

'Seriously?'

'You don't have to act surprised.'

'But I *am* surprised. You're gorgeous.'

'Liar,' said Caitlyn, but didn't remove her hand. 'Anyway, that's why my barriers tend to go up around the opposite sex.' She did the thing with Wes's knuckle again. 'Thanks to my deep-seated suspicion that all men are as deceitful as you.'

For some moments Wes gazed down at Caitlyn's hand, aware that the rest of the evening would be unlikely to offer him quite such a helpful cue to unburden himself of his catalogue of untruths. But when he glanced up at her face – when he registered her shy smile – Wes knew for certain that he couldn't do it. *Not just yet.* In fact, he realised, the only plan that made any sense would be to keep Caitlyn there in the restaurant – and the tiny, wonderful bubble of denial it represented – for as long as possible. *Forever, ideally.* Here in Navarro's, he was Dr Byron Wesley, the wealthy and respected gastroenterologist at the Chelsea and Westminster Hospital, not Wes the scheming parasite and coward. He stared at her hand again, wondering how he could prevent the evening coming to an end. Eventually he spoke. 'You don't fancy a pudding or something, do you?' he said.

'What?'

'As your friend and physician, I advise you to have a pudding.' Wes glanced around for a waitress. 'A dessert. In fact, I insist.'

'How about we share something – two spoons?'

'Could do. I think I might have another drink, too. A brandy perhaps.' Wes closed his eyes and held his breath. *Dutch courage – the only sort he'd ever known, but unlikely to make marshalling his thoughts any easier.* He opened his eyes again, suddenly resolute. 'Actually, there's something I ought to say,' he began. 'Something I need to tell you. Lots of somethings, really.' *Something about Jeremy. Something about who paid for the Mercedes. Something about lies and deception and the real possibility of getting you the treatment you need...*

'There's something I ought to say too,' said Caitlyn, her conspiratorial smile causing Wes to suffer a tiny flutter of nervous palpitations. 'But you first.'

'No. You. Please.'

'Well, mine's a bit awkward.'

Caitlyn reached across the table and took Wes's free hand, allowing his fingers a moment to seek out a comfortable equilibrium with hers. And when she looked up a second later, the only sound Wes could hear was his heartbeat pounding against his eardrums, and the only sensation he could feel was Caitlyn's pulse racing beneath his fingertips. He took a deep breath and held it, marvelling at the rhythms of their heartbeats slipping gently in and out of synch, suddenly knowing exactly what it would be like to sleep with her – and knowing, just as clearly, that it'd be something he'd be happy doing for the rest of his life. 'You were saying?'

'Well, I just wanted to say how... happy you've made me.'

'Me?'

'Yes. You. Before I met you, I didn't think I had anything to live for.'

'And now?'

'Now I do, yes.'

'Oh. I see. Great.' Breaking free of Caitlyn's fingers, Wes's hand blindly groped the table for something to drink. Finding nothing, it retreated to the table edge where it lingered pensively, toying fretfully with a discarded napkin. For some moments, Wes fought to quell the look of guilty panic he felt certain was creeping over his face, trying not to think about the words Jeremy had said in the darkness of the speeding Charger after the ill-fated barbecue. *All girls can read minds, kid. All of them.* It didn't seem as though Caitlyn could read *his* mind, though. If she could, she'd have known how very little faith she should have invested in his medical expertise; how very little hope he had of finding someone to treat her illness; how he'd lied and deceived her at every opportunity. Glancing up at Caitlyn's still-smiling eyes, Wes found himself pushing back his chair. 'I'm just going to the bathroom,' he said. 'Back in a tick.'

Steadying himself against one of the sinks, Wes appraised his sorry-looking reflection in the mirror. Then, on impulse, he ran a handful of cold water and splashed it over his face. Mopping the water from his chin, and shaking the worst of it from his shirt, he reappraised himself in the mirror. *Wetter, but no wiser.* He sighed and made his way back into the restaurant. With his head hung low, however, he was almost back in his seat before he realised that Caitlyn was no longer sitting at the table.

Suddenly, he found his head twisting towards a commotion at the restaurant door. There, swiftly sidestepping his way past a pair of waiters, was a familiar figure. 'Jeremy?' said Wes, steadying himself against the table. 'What are you doing here?'

'Where's Caitlyn?' gasped Jeremy, lurching towards him.

'In the loo, probably. I guess she is, anyway. Why? What's up?'

'Nikki knows everything.'

'What?'

'*Nikki knows everything.* About me not being a proper doctor. About Lisa. About the flat. She probably thinks you're a fake, too. And she seems to think we're friends of Danny.'

'Why would she think that?'

Jeremy glanced around, aware for the first time of the rapt audience of diners and restaurant staff, then leaned close to Wes. 'She found his gun in my bedside drawer.'

'*Shit*,' said Wes, suddenly horribly sober. 'And where's Nikki now?'

'I don't know. She ran off. She was in a bit of a state.'

'And you've no idea where she's gone?'

'Well, I thought she'd probably come here. To tell her sister.' Jeremy peered over towards the dark recesses of the restaurant, correctly guessing the location of the toilets. 'Are you sure Caitlyn's in the khazi, mate?'

'No. I'm not sure at all.'

For a moment the two men looked at each other. Then, clearly having reached a decision, Jeremy strode purposefully across the room and into the ladies' toilet. Five seconds later, with restaurant staff already converging on the doorway, he emerged. 'Caitlyn's not there,' he announced, his voice quavering with ill-concealed anxiety. 'Nikki must have got here before me.'

27

a reformed character

Despite being on the other side of the room when the
phone rang – and not having slept all night – it took
Wes no more than three seconds to reach the receiver.
'Hello? Cait?' he gasped, hooking the phone under his
chin and perching on the edge of Lisa's executive
recliner. A moment later, dashing in from the balcony
with a smouldering Rothmans stub clenched between
his teeth, Jeremy was at his side. 'Cait? Cait?' Wes
pressed, trying to keep the note of exhausted hysteria
out of his voice. 'Is that you, kid?'

After what seemed like an eternity, Caitlyn's tiny voice
echoed in his ear. 'Uh-huh. It's me.'

'Thank God for that,' said Wes, turning to Jeremy and
covering the mouthpiece. '*It's her.*'

'Is she okay?' hissed Jeremy, retrieving two more
cigarettes from the packet, lighting them and passing one to
Wes. 'Where is she?'

'Where are you, Cait?' Wes urged, fighting a rising
sensation of panic when she didn't reply. 'Are you still there,

kid? Cait? Cait?'

'I'm here,' said Caitlyn, clearly struggling to keep her cool. 'Why didn't you tell me?'

'Tell you what?'

A moment later, Wes found himself recoiling at the unexpected venom of Caitlyn's reply. '*Don't take me for a fucking idiot, Wes, or I'll put this phone down and you'll never hear from me again,*' she cried, before regaining something of her former composure. 'Why didn't you tell me Jeremy wasn't a doctor?'

Carrying the phone out on to the balcony, Wes found himself temporarily bereft of words. *Where were Caitlyn and Nikki? Somewhere out there beyond the grey Docklands mist?* 'Because we didn't think you'd come over to London if you knew the truth,' he eventually said.

'Then you were probably right,' said Caitlyn. 'Is he there? Your buddy?'

'Uh-huh.'

'Put him on.'

Turning back to the open doorway, Wes beckoned Jeremy over. 'Caitlyn wants to talk to you,' he whispered. '*Don't fuck it up.*'

Squirming beneath Wes's withering gaze, Jeremy took the receiver. 'Hey, kid,' he said.

'Hello Jeremy. So. My sister tells me that you're not a doctor at all.'

Jeremy winced. Doctor Sykes had been a role he'd occupied for so long, it was hard to admit the extent of his deception. 'It's more of an interest in anatomy,' he eventually conceded.

'But not in any professional capacity?'

'I'm not what you'd call a fully qualified physician, no.'

'So what are you?' said Caitlyn, her manner growing terse. 'A nurse?'

'An enthusiastic amateur?'

'When you first examined my sister's ass, you said your

name was Dr Sykes.'

'Mm.'

'But it isn't?'

'Not technically.'

'What do you mean, 'not technically'?'

Trying to avoid Wes's accusing stare, Jeremy quietly sucked the chilly morning air over his front teeth. 'The 'Dr' bit is a sort of... an *honorific* title,' he said. 'We have a lot them in Britain. Lord this, Lady that. The Duke of whatnot. You know.'

'And who gave you this title?'

'It was self-conferred, actually. I'm thinking of dropping it, now you come to mention it. People often find it misleading.'

For some moments Caitlyn was silent, and when she spoke again, her tone was on the chillier side of icy. 'What do you do for a living, Jeremy?'

'A spot of furniture restoring.'

'And what's Wes? Is he a furniture restorer too?'

'Ah, well, Wes *is*, in actual fact, a doctor. The *bona fide* article.'

'Put him back on.'

A moment later, Wes once again found himself talking to Caitlyn. 'Jeremy says you're a doctor,' she said.

'I *am* a doctor.' *An unemployed one. One whose connection with the world of cutting-edge medical practice pales in comparison with his knowledge of pubs, racehorses and widescreen television.* 'A proper doctor.'

'Nikki doesn't think so. Nikki thinks you're a fucking liar.'

Resisting the urge to sigh, Wes turned his back on Jeremy's now-contrite face and wedged the phone closer beneath his chin. 'What do you think?' he said gently. 'You've known me for months, Cait. All that time we were talking on-line.'

'I think you're a doctor,' Caitlyn said. 'Albeit a doctor

who also happens to be a fucking liar. Nikki also seems to think that Jeremy is good friends with Danny.'

'Well, he isn't. He just nicked his gun, that's all. For security. And because he's a certifiable mentalist with all the common sense of a brain-damaged orang-utan.'

'A fact he might have mentioned to my sister before he tried to fuck her.'

Covering the mouthpiece again, Wes turned on his shamefaced friend. 'Did you try to shag Nikki?' he whispered.

'*No way*. I'm a reformed character,' insisted Jeremy, cowering beneath Wes's withering stare. 'Admittedly, I did *almost* give her one, just to be sociable. But it doesn't count if it's a courtesy thing. And it would've been *firmly* in opposition to my will and better judgement.'

'*You haven't got any fucking judgement*,' whispered Wes fiercely, uncovering the mouthpiece. 'Where did you spend the night, Cait? Where are you now?'

'Why should I tell you?'

Covering his eyes with his free hand, Wes leant his elbows on the balcony railing and lowered his voice. 'Because despite the fact that I've been a bloody idiot, I love you. And I still want to help you,' he said. 'Do you believe me? Do you?'

'I think so. Although Nikki seems to think you're pond scum.'

'Is she there?'

'She's gone out.'

'Look, where are you, kid?' pressed Wes. 'You wouldn't have phoned if you didn't want to tell us.'

'We spent the night in some hotel. I'm still in the room now. It's called the Rathbone. It's only a few streets away from the restaurant where we ate. Do you know it?'

'We'll find it. Stay there, we're coming over.'

At the other end of the line, it was almost possible to

hear Caitlyn's frigid hostility fracturing in the tone of her voice. 'Come quickly, Wes,' she said. 'I just don't know what to do.'

Despite being drenched to the skin from the squalling London rain, Wes had enfolded Caitlyn in his arms the moment the hotel room door had opened – and twenty minutes later, he'd shown scant interest in letting her go. Initially Jeremy had been quietly impressed by the way his friend had managed to make three cups of undrinkable coffee – and take Caitlyn's blood pressure – while still cradling the distraught lass. After a while, though, he'd started feeling slightly superfluous to requirements and had installed himself under the extractor fan in the bathroom so he could chain-smoke in contemplative solitude. Propped silently against the foot of the bed, each lost in their own thoughts, Caitlyn and Wes watched as stray wisps of smoke drifted out of the bathroom. 'So Nikki said *nothing* about where she was going?' Wes eventually said. 'Which bit of town – nothing like that?'

Caitlyn shook her head sadly, just as she had when Wes asked the question for the first time, some ten minutes earlier. 'She just said she was going to get some money, enough for our flights. She told me to wait here until she came back, that she might be gone a few days, and that I should order food from room service when I needed to eat.'

'But who does she know in London?'

'No one.'

'No one at all?'

'Just you guys.'

'So how's she going to pay for two flights back to the US? I mean, she can't work. She's got no visa. She can't borrow money from a bank.' Wes glanced sidelong at Caitlyn. 'She wouldn't steal it, would she?'

Caitlyn stared at her feet in silence. Then, in a voice only just discernible over the hum of the bathroom's extractor fan, Jeremy spoke. 'Porn,' he said.

Wes frowned. 'What?'

'Porn. *Porn*,' said Jeremy. 'Isn't it obvious?'

'Isn't *what* obvious?'

'Porn,' he sighed, trying to keep the exasperation from his voice. 'She'll do porn. To get some quick money.'

'No she wouldn't,' said Wes, more out of loyalty to Caitlyn than because he really believed it. 'She said she was out of that business. She said she hated it.'

'She also said that being… *intimate* with people… was the only thing she was ever any good at,' countered Jeremy. 'And let's be honest, she's probably not thinking straight. She's vulnerable. God knows what she'd do to make a quick buck.'

'You can't just arrive somewhere and start making porn. How would you know where to go?'

Jeremy shrugged. 'How do junkies know where to go when they need a fix?' he said. 'It's instinct, isn't it?'

'Well, no, not really. You'd still have to find out who was *making* the porn. How would you do that, in an unfamiliar country?'

Jeremy's head emerged around the bathroom door, his face sombre. 'I think I might have the answer to that,' he said.

28

the ladies can do whatever they want these days

'I really don't see what your problem is,' Jeremy declared, weaving in and out of Oxford Street's mid-morning window-shoppers. 'It's really straightforward. Assuming they're not downloading it to their iPads, people still buy porn from sex shops, right? And sex shops buy *their* porn DVD's and so on from distributors. Now – for anything home-grown, anything UK-based – well, the distributors are going to being on pretty matey terms with the producers, right? I mean, these lads aren't unreachable. They're not Howard Hughes. They're not even Nerys Hughes. The distributor will probably *be* the producer, half the time – some sleazy chancer in a dirty mac with a camcorder and a bedsit in Neasden. So all we need to do is make some contacts at the retail end of operations, persuade them to make a few discreet enquiries on our behalf, and find out who's filming what in London at the moment. Then, hey presto – *cometh the porn, cometh the Nikki.*'

'You're out of your mind,' said Wes, wincing at Jeremy's choice of words and drawing to a halt at his friend's side. A moment later, Caitlyn had caught up too.

'I think we should do it,' she said.

Ignoring the smug eyebrow that Jeremy had raised in his direction, Wes put his arm around Ciatlyn's shoulder and shook his head. 'No, Cait. It's insane. All Jeremy's plans are insane. And you should be heading back to the hotel.'

'I've already said I'm coming with you.'

'Please go back, Cait,' Wes implored her. 'You haven't slept a wink.'

'Nor have you.'

'You're not well.'

'I'm well enough,' insisted Caitlyn, bobbing nervously from foot to foot. 'And anyway, Nikki's my sister. It's me who should be looking out for her.'

'Good lass,' said Jeremy approvingly. 'Right. I reckon we should split up. I'll do the shops down the Charing Cross Road and round Chinatown. You two start at Old Compton Street and work your way back north. Phone if you make any progress, or meet me at the little hut in Soho Square in two hours if you don't. Cool?'

'Cool,' said Caitlyn, hooking her arm through Wes's. 'Which way's Old Compton Street?'

'Wait, wait,' said Wes, seizing Jeremy's sleeve. 'We can't just trot into sex shops and ask them who's making all the local porn. I mean – how do you casually broach that kind of subject?'

Jeremy considered it for a second. 'Tell them you've got an implausibly large winkie and you want to give it a break in showbiz,' he said. 'Ask them whose nose you have to waggle it under. That should get you chatting to someone in the know.'

'And if that doesn't work?'

Jeremy shrugged. 'Threaten them, or something? You're a big enough lad. Chuck your weight around a bit.'

'But I'm an abject coward. A creature of thought, not deed.'

It was true, Jeremy reflected. Wes was, and always had been, a shameless softie – a floppy-haired, over-tailored fop. 'In that case,' he said, now addressing Caitlyn, 'you're in charge. Just use Wes for directions. You'll have to rely on your feminine wiles for finding out where Nikki is.'

'Okay. Cool,' said Caitlyn, tugging hard at Wes's arm and managing to pull him a yard or two along the pavement. 'We'll get her back, no problem.'

If Jeremy had learned one thing during the preceding hour, it was that illuminating and informative conversation was bloody tricky to come by in Soho's wide array of adult emporia. Helpful chit-chat of any variety was pretty thin on the ground, actually – whether it was from brazen slap-and-tickle dildo merchants or the subterranean grottos of side street bookshops, nothing but the vaguest impression of a hidden industry could be coaxed out from behind its beaded curtains and blacked-out windows.

It didn't help that he hadn't slept, he reflected, taking a final ravenous drag on his Rothmans and flicking the glowing butt into the damp gutter. For a moment he held his breath, allowing the nicotine to work its reviving magic on his fatigue-addled brain, before releasing a mighty cloud of pestilent smoke into the overcast London morning. Then he turned on his heel and strode through the shadowy doorway and into the cramped, strip-lit shop beyond.

This one was more depressing than most, he observed. The majority of the establishments he'd visited that morning had boasted at least a handful of shuffling, sideways-glancing punters, but this place – tucked between a decrepit-looking peep show and the walk-up entrance to a 'MODELS STUDIO' – was unoccupied except for its proprietor, an overweight bloke of indeterminate years squeezed behind an old-fashioned cash register. *At least that'll make it easier to have a chinwag,* thought Jeremy, sidling between the racks of luridly-jacketed DVD's towards the counter.

'Hello,' he said, carefully positioning himself so that his not-insubstantial shadow fell squarely across the open centerfold in front of the proprietor. 'I wonder if you could help me?'

When, after some moments, no response was forthcoming, he gently extended a hand and closed the magazine. Only then did the shopkeeper's deeply recessed eyes rise to meet Jeremy's broad smile. 'I'd heard this stuff made you go blind,' continued Jeremy cheerfully, 'but I didn't realise it made you deaf too.'

'What do you want?' the man eventually grunted.

'Well,' said Jeremy, leaning conspiratorially forward, 'I'm seeking the benefit of your professional expertise, actually.'

'All our stock's on the shelves. If you can't see it, we haven't got it.'

'You misunderstand,' said Jeremy, waving away the shopkeeper's agitated expression. 'Let me explain. I've got a young American friend who's recently gone missing, and I've reason to believe that she might be looking to make a bit of quick money in the field of adult entertainment.' He nodded in the direction of the groaning shelves behind him. 'Videos and suchlike.'

'Uh-huh.'

'And I'd like the opportunity to talk things over with her before she does anything she might subsequently regret.'

'I see.'

'And I wondered whether you might do me the small favour of phoning around any industry contacts you may have, to find out whether she's approached them in search of employment.'

'Right.'

In the silence that followed, Jeremy found himself willing the shopkeeper's hand to reach out and pick up the phone. When, after some moments, it had failed to do so, he tried notching his smile up a further millimetre or two. 'Do you think that's the sort of thing you'd be able to do for me?' he said.

The shopkeeper appeared to consider the matter deeply. Eventually he spoke. 'No.'

'There'd be the price of a pint in it for you. The price of some peanuts, too, if I manage to track her down. And I'd recommend your shop to all my pornographically-inclined friends – of whom, I have several.'

'I said no.'

'Why not?'

The shopkeeper sucked his breath over his teeth. 'Well, the way I see it – and this is just my personal opinion, mind – is that it's all about the little lady's own free choice, isn't it? How she wants to earn a crust, and all that.'

Jeremy nodded, but while the smile remained on his lips, the genial note had disappeared from his voice when he next spoke. 'I see.'

'It's like... *feminism*, innit? The ladies can do whatever they want these days.'

'I understand that,' said Jeremy. 'But I don't think my friend really wants to do this. It's purely an issue of an adverse economic situation as far as she's concerned.'

The shopkeeper shrugged and cast a lugubrious eye around the room. 'Who lives for their work, these days?'

'She's also in a very fragile emotional state. Lots of recent trauma.'

Finally the shopkeeper smiled. 'Look, mate,' he said, beckoning Jeremy closer. 'If there wasn't a ready supply of fucked-up, frightened little slags out there, I'd be out of a job, wouldn't I?' He leaned back in his chair and picked up his magazine from the counter. 'If you love somebody, set them free,' he said, flicking through the pages in search of the centerfold spread he'd been deprived of a couple of minutes earlier. 'Sting said that, didn't he?'

If the shopkeeper had chosen that moment to glance up at Jeremy's face, he might have noticed a subtle transformation playing over its features. Regular patrons of Whitby's Fat Ox pub, upon witnessing the same transformation – a barely perceptible hardening of the eyes, a silent stiffening of the muscles near the base of the neck – might have used this opportunity to quietly vacate Jeremy's immediate vicinity, or remove themselves to positions of safety well away from the premises. 'I really, really *hate* Sting,' he said.

'Yeah?'

'Aye,' said Jeremy, seizing the front of the shopkeeper's shirt in a bear-like grip. 'Particularly his lack of melodic invention in the post-Police years, coupled with an increasingly anodyne lyrical agenda.' His eyes narrowed on the shopkeeper's now-quivering face. 'And I'm not your biggest fan, either. And while I've recently been applying my girlfriend's policy of non-violence to the issue of conflict resolution, I get the very strong impression that she'd let me make an exception in your case.' He raised his free hand to head height, gratified to register the dawning of a very healthy terror in the shopkeeper's eyes. Jeremy flexed his fingers menacingly and pulled his captive a couple of inches closer. 'Do you get my drift?'

'I think so,' he gasped.

'So you've changed your mind about helping me out?'

'Definitely.'

'Good lad,' said Jeremy, scooping up the telephone from the counter. He lifted the receiver and pressed it firmly against the side of the shopkeeper's head. 'Then let's get dialling, shall we?'

29

a blue suzuki alto

It wasn't until he was halfway across Soho Square that Jeremy heard his mobile ringing in his jacket pocket. Such had been his need to clear his head, to vent the adrenaline he'd built up while holding his pornographic research assistant in a twenty-minute headlock, he'd decided to cover the distance between Greek Street and the Tube station at a sprint. Now, slowing to an unsteady jog amidst the handful of Londoners who'd decided to brave the wet Square during their lunch break, he groped in his pocket for his phone, peering intently at the screen before deciding whether to answer. 'Ah, Wes,' he gasped, fighting for oxygen as he dropped to face his own knees. 'I was going to call you, kid.'

'*Where the hell have you been?*' demanded Wes, his voice piping insistently from the ancient handset. 'I've phoned you five bloody times in the last ten minutes.'

'Chill, Wes. I've got news about Nikki. At least I think I have.' Jeremy gulped down a couple of lungfuls of air, righted himself and made off at a brisk trot between the clusters of scurrying Londoners. 'I think I've found out where she is.'

For a moment Wes was silent. Then, clearly having decided to temporarily postpone his own revelation, he steadied his voice and took a deep breath of his own. 'Where is she, mate?'

'Place called the Dollis Valley estate. It's up in Barnet. I had a friendly chat with a bloke in one of the sex shops I visited. Very obliging chap. He called a mate of his who does websites. Anyway, this mate of his was heading up to Barnet to get some stills from a video they're shooting there. Apparently an American-sounding lass had called one of the numbers they put in the backs of porno mags this morning. Said she wanted to get into the business. Said she'd do anything if the price was right.' Jeremy's eyes flicked left and right as he skidded to a halt at the edge of the kerb. Then, ignoring the approach of a speeding taxi, he skipped lightly across the road and continued his way up to Oxford Street. 'This lass was calling herself Candy, but I reckon it's Nikki. I'm heading up there now on the Tube.' He swapped the phone to his other hand, groping in an inside pocket for his Oyster card. 'Sounds like a rough place, mate. Could be the kind of set-up where there might be a spot of fisticuffs, if you fancy it.'

'I can't.'

'No?'

'No. There's been... something's... it's just... something's happened, mate. To Caitlyn.'

Jeremy yanked up his jacket collar, cocooning the phone tightly against his ear. 'What?' he said.

'Caitlyn... well, she collapsed again. Like she did in Santa Ana. She hit her head on the edge of a pavement.'

Jeremy swallowed hard. 'She's not – you know – is she?'

'No. She'll be okay. But they've rushed her to hospital. The Chelsea and Westminster. It's a good place – really modern. It's where Gabi works. It's where I told Caitlyn *I* worked, too, actually.'

'Right. I see,' said Jeremy, struggling to find appropriate words. 'Bloody hell, kid. I hope she's all right.'

'She'll be fine,' Wes replied, with more hope than conviction. 'I'm in a taxi, now, heading over there.'

Jeremy's stomach lurched, retching against nothing as he pocketed his phone. 'Fuck,' he murmured. '*Fuck, fuck, fuck.*'

Jeremy was not a bloke to scare easily. He said as much to himself as he strode briskly through the Dollis Valley estate. *I'm not a bloke to scare easily. I'm not a bloke to scare easily.* It didn't help though. Whichever way you looked at it, the Dollis Valley estate was a pretty bloody intimidating place.

Stopping beside a couple of burnt-out wheelie bins to fire up a fresh Rothmans, Jeremy cast a wary eye around him. If things turned a bit nasty, he reflected, the nearby buildings' bland concrete façades would offer nothing in the way of sheltering cover, bolt-holes or escape routes, while even the low-rise parade of shops and takeaways at the estate's entrance were boarded up or sealed behind drawn steel shutters. He pulled his coat closer around him, peering through the blue miasma of cigarette smoke at the flat numbers next to the communal doorway. In all probability, Nikki was up there. What else awaited him beyond the dank stairwell, though? *Bruised ribs? A broken nose? Worse?* Whatever it might be, Jeremy knew without a shadow of doubt that he was heading up there the moment he'd extinguished his cigarette – and if the cost of getting Nikki out unmolested involved dishing out a few bruised ribs and broken noses of his own, then so be it.

Jeremy took another hungry drag on his Rothmans, noting with silent apprehension that less than an inch of its length remained unsmoked. It would be tempting, despite the estate's almost comic-book grimness, to while away another ten minutes and a further cigarette with a bracing, head-clearing trot around its perimeter road. But he couldn't leave Nikki up there any longer. After all, while she might be savvy to the hazards of adult filmmaking in sun-kissed California, it was doubtful whether her antennae would be quite so well attuned to the social niceties of a zero-budget porn shoot on a rain-sodden north London housing estate.

Taking a few steps back over the cracked asphalt, Jeremy peered up at the rows of blank, unseeing windows above. *Which flat was Nikki in?* None seemed to be exuding any tangible erotic aura – unless you were particularly turned on by the smell of fried onions or the skittering beats of distorted dubstep seeping over an upper-storey balcony. He took a final drag on his cigarette, flicking the glowing butt into a puddle where it fizzed into mute oblivion. Then, flexing his fingers, first into starfish and then into fists, he crossed back to the stairwell and opened the door.

I'm a sizeable lad, he thought, willing himself against his fear and fatigue to keep climbing the stairs. *Not a bloke to scare easily. Not afraid of getting hands-on if the circumstances demand it.* He smiled guiltily at the naivety of his own mental pep-talk. When he'd lived at home in Whitby, it had suited him to believe that small towns were every bit as scary as big ones – just as unpredictable, just as liberally peppered with loonies and bullies and thugs – but here, reaching the summit of the concrete stairwell and glancing at the address he'd scribbled on to his cigarette packet, he was prepared to concede that he might have been wrong. *Horribly wrong.*

For a second, Jeremy's fingers strayed to his nose as he made his way along the drizzle-strafed walkway. *I've got such a lovely nose,* he reflected. *It's survived being twatted with a foot-long rubber cock. It'd be a shame to get it pulped today.* He sighed, drawing to a halt at a shabby-looking doormat and fixing his gaze on an unseen point beyond the door. Then he knocked.

In the long moments that followed, Jeremy tried to quell

an insistent sensation of rising nausea. Thinking about Nikki – or, more specifically, the sorry state he might find her in – had been having an unsettling effect on his stomach since the moment he'd stepped off the Tube at High Barnet, some twenty minutes earlier. When at last the door opened, however, the sight of a slight, rather bookish figure in the doorway – roundly bespectacled behind a mess of brown curls – at least provided a momentary distraction from the about-to-chunder feeling he'd been vigorously suppressing. Jeremy frowned in confusion, casting half an eye downward at the address on his Rothmans packet. 'You don't look like you're planning on giving me a slap,' he eventually announced, finding some indefinable comfort in voicing this most obvious observation aloud.

'I'm not,' replied the man.

'And you weren't – say – thinking about breaking my nose with a big rubber cock?'

'No.'

'Good,' said Jeremy cautiously, peering past the mass of curly hair down the dark corridor beyond. 'Well, I've come to see Nikki.'

'Nikki?'

'Candy, then. American lass. Texan. Short with blonde hair.' Jeremy's hands waved ineffectually as his exhausted brain struggled to find further words to describe his quarry. 'She's – you know – *an actress.*'

Finally recognition dawned. 'Oh, right. Cool. Candy's in the sitting room with Shaun and the boys. You'd better come through.'

Standing aside, the curly-headed bloke ushered Jeremy into the hall and towards the glass-panelled door at its far end. Now that he was away from the noises of the walkway, a number of murmuring voices and moving bodies could clearly be discerned within. Mentally bracing himself for the worst, Jeremy seized the door handle and stepped into the room beyond.

Immediately all eyes in the room fell upon him – including, from a low seat next to a filthy drop-leaf dining table, Nikki's. Momentarily ignoring all the room's other occupants, Jeremy was pleased to see a hint of relief and something like gratitude mixed in with the glare of accusation on Nikki's speechless face. 'Hello everyone,' he said as brightly as he dared.

For a moment, nobody spoke – although it was clear who was in charge from the way all eyes now swivelled in the direction of a heavily-built, shaven-headed man in the centre of the room. Naked from the waist up and dressed only in a pair of black sweatpants, he took a step towards Jeremy. 'Who the fuck's this, Mikey?' he said.

'Not actually sure, Shaun,' replied the curly-headed man who'd let Jeremy in – who had now, he noticed, retreated sheepishly behind a cheap-looking camcorder and tripod. 'He said he wanted to see Candy. I thought he was expected.'

'Well he's not,' said Shaun, advancing another step in Jeremy's direction. 'And he can't see Candy, because she's working. So I suggest he just fucks off before he gets himself into trouble.'

In a different context, Jeremy knew, Shaun's last utterance would've probably triggered a minor retaliation – a friendly knee in the bollocks, perhaps, or a couple of corrective slaps round the chops. But the cramped room into which he'd just stepped, fashioned into a crude film set with an improvised assortment of lights, sound equipment and props, was too heavily populated to even consider it. From behind a boom microphone, a pock-marked face regarded him balefully, while the three sizeable middle-aged blokes clustered by the kitchen door turned to face him with the sort of malevolent curiosity he'd only previously associated with hardcore pub brawl aficionados. Even Nikki's expression of passing relief, Jeremy noticed, had now been replaced by a look of savage contempt. 'Actually, I'd really like a quick chat with young Candy, here,' he said, trying to catch Nikki's eye over Shaun's shoulder. 'There's something we need to talk about, and it won't wait.'

'It fucking will,' said Shaun, now closing the gap between himself and Jeremy, and seizing his arm.

Jeremy's knees locked rigid as he took the strain against Shaun's weight, resisting his spirited attempts to shove him backwards through the open doorway. From his position of heaving deadlock, he was unsure whether or not Nikki had even registered what he'd been saying. Then she raised her head and met his eye. 'I thought I told you to go home to Yorkshire, Jez,' she said quietly.

'Aye, you did,' Jeremy grunted, now feeling another set of muscular hands attach themselves to his shoulders.

'And I told you what I'd do if I ever saw you again. I meant what I said.'

'I know you did, kid. And I'm really sorry about the, erm… *misunderstanding* we had. But there's something you need to know.' Jeremy flailed out with his free arm as another pair of hands sought purchase on his jacket. 'It's about Cait.'

'What about her?'

'She's been taken ill while she was out, looking for you.'

'Caitlyn's fine.'

'*Caitlyn's in hospital.*'

Perhaps it was the strained urgency of Jeremy's voice, but for a split second a flicker of something approaching doubt flitted over Nikki's face. Then her features hardened again. 'You're a fucking liar, Jeremy – as we established beyond reasonable doubt the last time we spoke.'

'I'm telling the truth this time, kid. Wes is at the hospital with her.' Swiftly elbowing one of his assailants in the diaphragm, Jeremy reached into his pocket with his free hand and pulled out his mobile. He tapped the speed-dial button and tossed the handset to Nikki, at the very moment his feet were kicked out from under him. 'Just talk to him. *Please.*'

In under thirty seconds, Nikki was ready to leave. '*For God's sake, let him stand up,*' she yelled, pulling hands away from Jeremy's motionless body and elbowing men twice her size out of the way. 'Get away from him *right now.*'

Slowly, as if resurfacing from a hypnotist's trance, the cluster of embarrassed and bewildered-looking heavies began edging away from Jeremy's prone, foetal form. A few jabbed ribs later, and only Shaun's hands remained attached to his victim. 'Let him alone, Shaun,' hissed Nikki, shouldering her holdall and tugging ineffectually at his wrist. 'You've made your point. Now we're leaving.'

Shaun's eyes narrowed on Nikki's. 'You're not off anywhere,' he said. 'You've got a job to do, and you're not going anywhere 'til you've done it.'

Unhanding the groaning Jeremy and allowing him to struggle to his knees, Shaun turned to address Mikey, who had remained behind his tripod for the duration of the fight. 'My little girls'll be back from school by three, and we haven't shot a single scene yet.' He beckoned to one of his friends. 'Get rid of this joker. And you' – he turned to Nikki – 'get your clothes off. I want to go for a take in two minutes.'

'No. We're leaving,' said Nikki, calmly resolute. 'You'll just have to make your little movie without me.'

'I don't think so.'

'I do.' Reaching down and hooking one of Jeremy's arms over the back of her neck, Nikki nodded towards the glowering heavies. 'Why not fuck one of your buddies instead? Make a gay porno.' She braced herself against Jeremy's weight and lifted. 'Branch out, Shaun. Experiment. Unleash your darkest fantasies.'

'You're not going anywhere until we've shot the scene.'

Shaun extended a hand and gently pushed the door shut. 'I'm not fucking joking.'

'*And I'm not your fucking hooker,*' said Nikki. In one swift motion, she reached into her holdall and produced Danny's pistol. At arm's length, its snub muzzle hovered an inch in front of Shaun's cranium. Nikki smiled as she deftly cocked the weapon. '*Am I?*' she whispered.

For a second no one spoke. Indeed, as Jeremy's view of the room began to reform into solid shapes and recognisable colours, he could have been forgiven for thinking that he'd regained consciousness in the middle of some nightmarish parlour game. He gently rubbed his throbbing temple, letting his arm slip from Nikki's shoulder as she turned to face the room's other occupants. 'Does anyone here have a car?' she said.

'I have a car.'

Nikki swivelled around to the curly-headed man behind the video camera. 'Give Jeremy the keys,' she said. 'What sort of car is it, sweetheart?'

'A blue Suzuki Alto.'

Nikki turned to Jeremy. 'Do you know what one of those looks like?'

'Uh-huh,' he grunted, struggling to visualise anything but the shooting stars still circling his head. 'They're blue.'

'Jeremy promises to look after it. Don't you, Jeremy?'

Jeremy nodded mutely. Then, as an afterthought, he turned to the cameraman. 'I might be a bit sick in it, though,' he said.

Beckoning Shaun away from the door with a fractious twitch of her pistol hand, Nikki passed the holdall to Jeremy and began slowly backing out of the room. 'If you promise not to report your car missing, Jeremy promises not to get you any speeding tickets. And if you *do* report it missing, you know I'll come and find you, don't you?' She waggled the gun playfully at the mute cameraman, now smiling with a sweetness that Jeremy couldn't help feeling he recognised. 'And – very reluctantly – I *would* have to execute you.'

'That sounds reasonable.'

'Good. Write down your cell phone number and give it to Jeremy. I'll let you know where to pick up your car when we're through using it.'

30

you're bloody sulking, aren't you?

'You can't shoot people in England,' Jeremy shouted, dropping the Suzuki into third and wedging his Greek army boot against the threadbare carpet. The tyres wailed in protest as the tiny car slewed suicidally into the centre lane of the North Circular. When the fanfare of horns had finally died down, he turned to face Nikki again. 'Even *threatening* to shoot people is considered pretty poor form, actually.'

Ignoring the double flash of the speed camera – the second in ten minutes – he jabbed fretfully at the cigarette lighter. A moment later, it sprang back with a tiny click and Jeremy lifted it to the tip of the Rothmans that had been dangling from his bottom lip since shortly after Finchley. A comforting haze of blue smoke filled the Suzuki's minuscule cabin. 'You're just grumpy because I dropped Danny's pistol down that drain, aren't you?' he said, turning accusingly on his mute passenger. 'You're bloody sulking, aren't you?'

For some moments, Nikki regarded him in baleful

silence. Then she shook her head. 'Do you know how many lethal toxins there are in every cigarette you smoke?' she said.

Jeremy eyes narrowed as he inhaled another lungful of lethal toxins. Even against the backdrop of his aching ribs and pounding headache, they tasted divine. He leaned over and gave Nikki's knee a quick, companionable squeeze. 'See if you can find any Thin Lizzy or Lynyrd Skynyrd on the radio, and I'll open a window,' he said.

31

still *virgo intacta*, relatively speaking

Two minutes earlier, Wes would have probably thought he didn't possess the physical capacity to withstand any more anxiety. Simply running the gamut of the Accident & Emergency and X-Ray departments of his wife's hospital had been a stomach-churning experience, of course – with or without Caitlyn's concussion preying on his mind. But when she'd been trolleyed to a fourth-floor room a mere *hundred yards* from Gabi's office, he'd felt his tension level ratcheting skywards towards the 'complete mental meltdown' zone. Now, though – seeing an all-too-familiar face bobbing towards him through the thick fug of fear and exhaustion that hung before his eyes – well, things look set to get even worse.

'*Dewhurst! Dewhurst!*' hollered the face. 'Hey, Wes, hang on. Hold the lift, will you?'

Feigning deafness – pointlessly, given that three seconds' horrified eye contact had already taken place –

Wes found his free hand jabbing viciously at the button for the fourth floor. It was too late, though. With only milliseconds to spare, Dr Sujita Ram wedged the tip of her shoe between the closing lift doors and they slid noiselessly apart.

'Bugger me, Dewhurst,' she panted gamely, installing herself at Wes's elbow. 'Didn't you see me? *I'm big enough!*'

'I didn't, actually,' said Wes, smiling wanly. 'Sorry, Sujita. How've you been?'

Grinning broadly, Sujita shrugged and emitted the sort of drawn-out, noncommittal groan that's most often associated with pre-war central heating systems. 'Yourself?' she finally asked. 'Still job-hunting?'

'Christ, yes,' said Wes, alarmed to find his own voice beginning to resemble Sujita's ludicrous Roedean whinny. 'I'd no idea you worked here, actually,' he lied, his eyes now following his free hand as it described an airy parabola in front of him.

'*I don't!*' squealed Sujita. '*Not in the lift, anyway!* No, Dewhurst, I'm over in Paediatrics. Have been for a couple of months, Tuesdays and Thursdays. Very rewarding, Dewhurst. *Very.*'

'Great.'

'I see heaps of Gabi, of course.'

'Do you?'

'Oh yes. She took me out for lunch today. To Aubergine. Excellent nosebag.'

'Uh-huh?'

'Oh yes. Are you popping up to see her?'

Wes swallowed a yawn, praying that Sujita would be insensitive enough not to notice. 'Gabi doesn't know I'm here, actually,' he eventually said.

For a moment, Sujita seemed uncharacteristically bereft of words. Then she turned and regarded Wes with a strange intensity. 'Doesn't she? Really?' she said.

'No. I'm going to surprise her,' Wes lied, lamely holding

up the two bottles of Pepsi and the copy of the *NME* that Caitlyn had requested from the hospital shop. 'Give her a little treat.'

'So – you're spoiling her,' said Sujita, apparently without irony, now fixing her gaze resolutely on the lift's ceiling. 'That's sweet, Dewhurst. Really romantic. But maybe you should phone her first. Just to make sure she's not, you know... in the middle of something. *You forget how busy hospital life can be!* she bellowed mirthlessly, gently squeezing Wes's arm and stepping towards the opening doors.

'Right. Right, I'll do that,' said Wes, hoping he'd regain control over his voice once Sujita had left the lift. 'Good to see you.'

'And good to see *you*, Dewhurst. *Do* take care of yourself, won't you?'

'Jez says he's on his way,' said Wes, pocketing his iPhone and making his way over to the window, hoping that the low winter sunshine might impart some energy to his sleep-deprived brain. 'He's picked up Nikki. She's fine. Bit shaken up, but still *virgo intacta*, relatively speaking. One of the guys at the shoot lent them his car. Said they could keep it as long as they needed it.'

Drowsily pulling the blankets up beneath her chin, Caitlyn regarded him fondly. 'English people are nice,' she whispered, reaching for Wes's hand and pulling him towards her bedside. 'Even English porn people. You're nice too. Thanks for staying with me.'

Wes shrugged and took her hand, eyeing the narrow strip of vacant bed at Caitlyn's side. 'I've always thought English people were barking mad, actually. Budge up a bit.'

A moment later he'd installed himself on the precarious ledge of mattress and pillow next to the Caitlyn-shaped sausage in the centre of the bed. 'I'd say you were all endearingly eccentric,' she said, allowing her fingers to mesh with Wes's. 'Quirky.'

'No. Definitely mad,' said Wes, stifling a yawn and closing his eyes. 'I met someone from medical school in the lift. A friend of – well, a friend of a friend. Mad as a bag of snakes, now. Howling. I think she might've been at the Ritalin. They all do it in Paediatrics.'

'There you go, see? Endearingly eccentric.'

'Mad. Mentally unstable in-breds, most of us,' he muttered. 'Particularly the medical profession.'

'You're not mentally unstable.'

'Yes, but I'm hardly a member of the medical profession, am I?' he grunted, nuzzling closer. 'Not that I'd vouch for my own sanity anyway. Not these days.'

If it hadn't been for Caitlyn's soft voice in his ear, and her fingers gently tightening around his own, Wes would have undoubtedly drifted away on the soft hum of the room's air conditioning. 'What do you mean – you're hardly a member of the medical profession?' she said.

'What?'

'You just said you weren't really a member of the medical profession.'

In a fraction of a second, Wes's eyes were wide open in the hospital room's half-light, his mind racing. 'Did I?'

'Yes you did. What did you mean?'

'Nothing really,' said Wes, thankful beyond words that his back was turned to Caitlyn. His eyes flicked frantically around the room, searching for excuses. 'Just that I'm between jobs at the moment.'

'I thought you worked here,' said Nikki, the artificial lightness of her voice exposing rather than concealing her anxiety. 'Here in this hospital.'

'Well, my wife Gabi – she works here,' said Wes, wincing. 'I was going to tell you last night in the restaurant. Just before Nikki abducted you. I'm really sorry. Are you angry?'

'Well, it's a bit of a revelation,' said Caitlyn, turning on her side and embracing Wes spoon-wise through the blankets. 'But no, I'm not angry.'

'Aren't you?'

'No. Honestly. But there's something else I need to know.' She pulled Wes closer towards her small body, pressing her face so deeply into the bunched sheets that her words were only just audible over the air conditioning. 'Something about my cancer.'

Wes sought a levity in his voice that he hardly felt. 'What about it?' he said.

'Are we any closer to finding someone who can treat it?'

'Actual treatment?' began Wes, feeling the first of Caitlyn's hot, silent tears in the soft hair behind his ear. 'Not as such. But I'm trying so fucking hard, kid, I promise. I just haven't found the right person yet. The right drugs and equipment.'

For nearly a minute, Wes felt Caitlyn's laboured breath warming the small damp patch at the nape of his neck. 'And is that going to change?' she eventually whispered, her voice cracking. 'Be honest.'

'I don't know.'

'*Be honest.*'

Wes swallowed hard, now contending with the onset of his own tears. 'Perhaps not,' he finally said, screwing his eyes shut and pressing his face into the corner of Caitlyn's pillow. 'You hate me now, don't you?'

'I don't hate you. Quite the opposite. And anyway, I think I always knew how it'd turn out. Even back in Santa Ana.' Caitlyn's arm snaked around Wes's stomach as she seized him in a short, fierce hug. Then she turned and rolled over on to her other side. 'So it really doesn't matter about the treatment, Wes. Honestly.'

'It *does* matter. It's the only thing that matters.'

'No it doesn't. Seriously, it doesn't.' Caitlyn cleared her throat, now sounding eerily calm at the other side of the hospital bed. 'When I said you'd made me happy, last night in the restaurant, it wasn't because you were going to magically cure me,' she said. 'It was because you cared enough to bother trying. That's why I felt – well, the way I feel about you. You tried everything, Wes. So it doesn't matter that it hasn't worked. It doesn't change anything.'

'But I'm not the person you thought I was. I haven't got a job. I haven't even got my own home. I'm a fraud. A nobody.'

'No you're not. And anyway, all that money crap is – just… crap. You've got a good heart, Wes.'

Now Wes turned over too, extending an arm around Caitlyn's waist. 'It's not just crap, though, is it?' he said softly. 'If I had any money I'd pay for your treatment privately. But I haven't got anything. Everything belongs to Gabi's family and her dad fucking loathes me.' He gently kissed the bump on top of Caitlyn's head and rolled off the bed, crossing to the window. Outside, the lights were beginning to come on in the nearby offices. 'There's no way he'd lend me the money. I'm a no-collateral zero as far as Old Man Wynstanley's concerned. The only thing I've got that he wants is his daughter.'

And then, with his words still hanging in the air before him, Wes suddenly knew the answer. He stared out into the gathering darkness, each streetlight now reduced to an out-of-focus smudge on his unbelieving retina. *Could it really be so simple?* Wes played the scenario over in his mind again, adjusting the likely parameters. It'd be a high-stakes gamble, certainly – but not an impossibility. 'No, not an impossibility at all,' he said out loud, now groping blindly for his jacket. 'Not if we're careful. Not if we play our cards right.'

'Wes?' said Caitlyn, her head rising from the pillow in confusion. 'What's going on?'

'I've got to pop out for a bit,' said Wes, as though suddenly remembering Caitlyn's presence in the room. 'There's someone I need to see. Try to sleep. Or read the *NME* or something.'

'Where are you going?'

'Out. Just for a while. I'll be back before you know it.' He leaned down, allowing his lips to fleetingly brush Caitlyn's before reconsidering his actions and subjecting her unresisting mouth to an urgent flurry of kisses. 'I'm going to sort everything out, Cait,' he said, making for the door. 'Tell Nikki and Jeremy I'll be back soon.'

'West London Executive Cars?' said Wes, tucking his mobile beneath his chin. 'Uh-huh. Yes, I need a minicab. From the Chelsea & Westminster hospital to Harley Street. Soon as possible. And as fast as possible.' Wes skidded to a halt at the entrance to the lifts, raising his eyes to the floor indicator above. Glancing at his watch, he took to his feet again, pushing open the door to the nearby stairwell and skipping lightly down the steps. 'Actually, you don't happen to know if Abiola's in the area, do you?'

32

she keeps talking about me
planting my seed in her belly

'With respect, Dr Wesley…'

'Yes?'

'…and with all due regard for your position as a world-renowned physician…'

'Yes?'

'…and a gentleman…'

'Yes, what?'

'…I think you must have taken leave of your senses. You English people are mad – quite mad.'

In the shadowy cavern of Abiola's cab, unseen to the exasperated Nigerian, Wes smiled. 'I have it on good authority that we're endearingly eccentric,' he said. 'Is this the place?'

Lifting his forehead from the steering wheel, Abiola peered upwards at the glowering edifice beyond the spiked iron railings. In the dusky twilight, its double doors and limestone portico looked particularly uninviting. He tapped his fingernail against the windscreen in the approximate direction of the brass plaque on the wall. 'The Wynstanley Centre,' he said quietly. 'There's still a light on upstairs.'

'Right. Cool. Excellent,' said Wes, with far more apparent conviction than he actually felt. 'I'm going in, then.'

For a second, perhaps assuming that his passenger might be bluffing, Abiola watched as Wes groped for the door handle in the dark. Then, hearing the low metallic moan of the hinges opening, he seized Wes's coat sleeve and dragged him forcefully back into the passenger seat. 'I *beg* you, Dr Wesley – *don't do it.*'

'I've got to, Abiola. I've no choice.'

'No. *No.* You *still* have options. *Options, Dr Wesley!*'

'Not as far as I'm concerned.'

'Yes, yes, you do. You are young. Virile. Your manhood is sufficient for more than one woman,' said Abiola, now gently kneading the steering wheel with the balls of his thumbs. 'You have a nice package. A *very* nice package – a blessing, not a curse.'

'But I only *want* one woman.'

Staring sidelong at his passenger, Abiola made a noise between his teeth that presumably meant something unspeakably damning in Nigeria. 'I have a wife at home in Lagos,' he eventually volunteered. 'But I also have a girlfriend on the Streatham High Road. Very young. Very sexy. It is a very nice package.'

'So?'

'So I think I could cut you a better deal.'

'You do?'

'Take me with you. I will be your lawyer.'

'Do you have legal experience?'

'I was a solicitor in Nigeria,' declared Abiola proudly. 'I could get you the Mercedes.'

'I don't want it.'

'But she is an S-series. Less than a year old,' Abiola

implored him. 'I have seen the way you look at her. The way your eye caresses her.'

'I want to give it back.'

'As your solicitor – *as your minicab driver* – I would *not* recommend it. Women come, women go. *But a Mercedes...*' He raised his hands and eyes heavenward. 'You once told me how she makes you feel, when you drive her to the Majestic Wine Warehouse on the King's Road.'

'Yes.'

'She makes you feel like a lord. *A lord*, Dr Wesley.'

'I know. But I'm not a lord, am I?'

'*You haven't slept for thirty-six hours!*'

'I know what I feel.'

'But you are not *thinking* properly, Dr Wesley! You smell unusual. You look like shit.' Abiola reached into the glove compartment and took out a crumpled paper bag. From the bag, he withdrew a small Tupperware box and emptied a couple of tiny white pills into his hand. 'Take these. Please. Before you go in. All minicab drivers use them.'

'What are they?'

Abiola frowned as though considering the question for the very first time. 'I do not know,' he eventually declared. 'But they make the colours brighter when you are driving at night, and you never fall asleep behind the wheel.'

For a moment Wes inspected the two anonymous-looking pills, picking one up and holding it up to the flickering vanity light. Then he smiled. 'Okay. Thanks,' he said, popping both on his tongue and unscrewing the lid of the thermos that Abiola had given him fifteen minutes earlier. A moment later they were gone, washed down by a mouthful of the minicab driver's soup. It was warm and more-ish and tasted faintly of ginger. 'And thanks for the legal advice.'

Abiola grunted.

'And the soup.'

Abiola grunted.

'And the deodorant.'

Abiola grunted.

'And for letting me smoke in your cab.'

Abiola grunted.

'And for stopping at that cash point.'

'*Please*, Dr Wesley,' said Abiola sadly. 'Please do not thank me for these things. You have already paid for them.' He turned and gazed morosely out of the window. 'I do not normally charge a hundred and fifty pounds to go from the Fulham Road to Harley Street.'

'Oh. I see.'

'You are a very frustrating passenger, Dr Wesley.'

'Sorry.'

'But for some reason – some reason I do not fully understand and frightens me slightly – I like you.' Abiola closed his eyes for a second, shook his head, then reached deep into an inside pocket. A moment later he produced the wad of notes that Wesley had given him five minutes earlier, and pressed it back upon its former owner. 'Take it. *Take it.* You are going to need it more than I am, my friend.' He smiled ruefully as he leaned over to open the passenger door. 'Good luck, Dr Wesley!'

It's true what he said about the colours, thought Wes, letting the heavy front door swing shut behind him. *But I wish he'd mentioned the bloody orchestra too.* He held his breath and closed his eyes, but it didn't make much difference. There, just audible above the train-track *staccato* of his heartbeat, effervescing through the airless stratosphere beyond true hearing, were violins – a distant cacophony of violins, seemingly tuning up for a gonzo remake of *Psycho*. Wes opened his eyes and cast a wry glance heavenward. *Thanks for the pills, Abiola. Thanks a billion.*

Trying hard to quell the seismic tremors below his beltline, Wes slipped through the inner doors to the brightly lit Reception. While he'd been waiting for his minicab to arrive at the Chelsea and Westminster – when his pulse was still racing from his first euphoric flash of bedside genius – he'd toyed with a dozen or more schemes for scaling Wynstanley's outer defences. *I've come for an amputation*, he'd considered yelling, skipping madly past the clinic's boggle-eyed receptionist. *An emergency Gabi-ectomy!* But now he was actually here, creeping across the deserted expanse of waiting room and into the hallway beyond, the quiet insanity of his plan was beginning to dawn upon him. *Maybe I've swum out too far this time*, he reflected, rounding the foot of a broad marble staircase. *Out of my depth. Losing my grip. My judgement's fucked. I can't even feel my eyeballs any more. Why can't I feel my eyeballs? Oh God.*

Catching his breath against the cool stone banister, Wes sought to reassure himself. *People don't need to feel their eyeballs*, he reasoned, *as long as they can see. And Wynstanley might be a Freudian train wreck with an unresolved God complex, but at least I've got something the old bastard wants.* Then, fixing his eyes once more on the top of the staircase, Wes began his climb. The violins were getting louder now – in fact, they seemed to be the only sound in the building that wasn't emanating from his own body. *Only a loony would want to go up there*, thought Wes, hoping that steadying his breathing might have the same effect on his mind. *But I don't think I can go back now.*

It was bizarre, he reflected, arriving at the summit of the stairs, that this was the only time he'd ever set foot in his father-in-law's fêted clinic. *Now, at the end of everything.* Somehow, though, through the migraine hiss of delirium and bathtub amphetamine, it almost made sense. Here, in the glacial opulence of the Wynstanley Centre – amidst its marble and alabaster and crystal – Wes felt like a foreign body, a social contamination. *I can finally see why he hates me*, he thought, taking another deep breath and holding it as he gently pushed open the door at the end of the landing. *And Abiola was right*, he reluctantly admitted. *I do smell a bit funky.*

Tiptoeing into the wood-panelled room beyond the door, Wes now discovered the source of the violins – a stereo system so blandly expensive that only three unlabelled buttons were visible on its brushed aluminium façade, perched at the end of a leather-topped desk wide enough to host a cup final. He peered round the room, taking in the plush burgundy carpets, the mahogany filing cabinets, the high antique screens, the low leather couch. *So this is it*, he thought. *The sanctum sanctorum.* Then, without quite knowing why, Wes found himself rounding the desk – undoubtedly Wynstanley's – and dropping into the ancient chesterfield armchair behind it, finding his eye drawn immediately to the single silver picture frame in front of him. *A sun-blanched snapshot of Gabi, sixteen or seventeen, running away from the camera, laughing at something unseen, smudged copper curls caught in a slow-motion blur across her cheek.*

Wes blinked. He'd first met Gabi only a year or so later; had been intoxicated from the moment he'd laid eyes on her. And now, gazing at her photograph, he could remember why. *Girls like Gabi were a different species.* They simply hadn't *made* them like Gabi, back home in Whitby – confident and brilliant and blindly ambitious. *They didn't tend to make them quite as brittle or neurotic, either*, he reflected. *Lovely but unlovable.* 'Oh, Wynstanley, Wynstanley,' he breathed, reaching for the stereo and finally silencing the violins. 'What am I going to do?'

He looked up, suddenly conscious of movement in the corner of the room. A second later, one of the wooden panels swung back to reveal a diminutive figure standing in the shadows of a concealed antechamber. 'You can get out of my fucking chair, for a start,' it said softly.

If it hadn't been for the way Wynstanley's chin had come to rest on the tips of his thumbs, Wes might have assumed that he'd actually fallen asleep. Even if he wasn't, though, it was still a blessing not to have to look into the elderly surgeon's eyes. Here, in the dimmed light of the consulting room, Abiola's pills had started playing disturbing tricks on his vision – and while he could cope with the frenzied swarms of fireflies around the light fittings, the molten clots of lava in the pits of Wynstanley's eyes had proved harder to deal with.

I was mad to come here, Wes reflected, struggling to marshal his thoughts. *It's too big a gamble for one toss of the coin.* For the second time in as many minutes, he found himself wiping his palms on his trousers – almost as though, when the time came, he'd have to place his stake on the table by hand. He smiled wryly, in spite of his parched lips and churning stomach. *Maybe I've already played my hand*, he thought, skimming through the events of the last ten minutes in his mind's eye. *Maybe I'm already bankrupt. Maybe I just don't know it yet.*

For a second, staring at Wynstanley's motionless eyelids, Wes was almost seized by the deranged impulse to just *leave* – to silently push his chair back from the desk and make for the still-open door. In his chemically-elevated state of mind, however, it was the work of a moment to predict the grim outcome of such a decision – a series of tumbling images, all of them of Caitlyn, spooling on an obscene fast-forward into nothingness. He closed his eyes and shook his head, trying to dislodge all traces of the poisonous thought – and when he looked up again, Wynstanley was once again staring directly at him. 'You realise,' said Wynstanley slowly, 'that in the event of a divorce – thanks to the prenuptial agreement you rather rashly signed – you *would* forego any claim to the marital assets.'

'So my solicitor informs me.'

'You'd lose the house, the car, credit cards.'

'Uh-huh.'

'Everything.'

'Yes.'

Leaning back in his chair, Wynstanley regarded Wes

with quiet loathing. 'You'd be a homeless, jobless bum. A piece of human flotsam. A nobody.'

Wes considered this for a few seconds. There was nothing in what Wynstanley had just said that he felt able to disagree with – and anyway, disagreeing with Wynstanley had hardly been part of the grand strategy. *The grand strategy he'd spent a whole fifteen seconds thinking about at Caitlyn's bedside. Stupid, stupid, stupid.* 'I'd be free,' he eventually volunteered.

'*You'd be worthless,*' spat Wynstanley. 'It's hardly the same thing. I only thank Christ that Gabrielle's kicking you out before you've had time to pollute the gene pool.'

For some moments, Wes's drug-addled brain struggled to process what it had just heard. Even for someone as blunt as Wynstanley, the words still echoing in his ears had seemed unnecessarily crass. He leaned forwards in his seat. '*What?*'

'I thank the Lord,' began the old man, enunciating each word as though addressing an idiot, 'that you never had *children* with my *daughter.* You do know where children come from, don't you? You're supposed to be a bloody doctor.' But when he shook his head contemptuously – when he glanced impatiently at his watch – Wes thought he saw the faintest hint of something else in his eyes.

What was it, though? Something he'd seen there before. *But where? When?* Wes cast his mind back. *The evening of the wedding rehearsal, when Jeremy had rolled up roaring drunk on Galliano? The weekend they'd driven up to Berkhamsted to show Gabi's parents her engagement ring?* Yes – both those times. And then – without warning – Wes knew exactly what the look in Wynstanley's eyes had been. *Fear.* Wynstanley's pantomime version of it, anyway. His own eyes narrowed as the elderly physician pushed back his chair and walked over to the window; he smiled behind his back. *You've just dealt me another card*, he thought. *Quite a good one.*

'I knew it when I first saw you,' continued Wynstanley, rounding once again on Wes. 'You couldn't believe your luck when Gabrielle gave you a second glance. But I knew you'd take what you could and be on your way.'

'Uh-huh.'

'I saw you for the opportunist you were.'

'Did you?'

'No staying power. No character. No substance.'

Wes considered this for a moment, weighing Wynstanley's words in his mind. Then he nodded. 'I think you might be right,' he said.

Wynstanley's eyes narrowed on Wes. 'What?'

'I think you're right.' Wes leaned back in his seat, smiling as blandly as he dared. 'I've always had itchy feet. Never been one for getting tied down.' He glanced out of the window. 'But you're completely wrong about Gabi.'

'I don't think I am.'

'You are, you know,' Wes sighed, trying to suppress the chemical head-rush that now threatened to sweep aside his little remaining self-control. 'It's not Gabi who wants the divorce. And she's been nagging me about having children since the day we got back from honeymoon.'

'*Rubbish*. She's got her career to think about.'

'And she's got a house husband. Free childcare for as many kids as she wants.'

'Gabrielle doesn't want *your children*,' scoffed Wynstanley, though now not trying to disguise the uncertainty in his voice.

'Oh, but she does. Aye, she's changed, these last few months. All she seems to talk about is starting a family. Babies – always babies. She keeps talking about me planting my seed in her belly. She can get quite wistful about it, at times.'

'But you don't want that, do you?' said Wynstanley, a palpable note of pleading in his tone. 'You want to be free. You said so.'

Wes stretched his legs out beneath the desk, affecting an appearance of studied nonchalance. 'Do I *want* to plant *my* seed in *your* daughter's belly?' he mused, as though considering the matter for the first time. 'We could make a wonderful child together. And it'd be a privilege for a bloke like me to bring a new life into the world. To fill it with my values. To shape its outlook. You must have found that with Gabi. But it's so hard to know what the best thing to do is, isn't it? That's why I've come to visit my father-in-law. For advice. It's like Joe Strummer said – *should I stay, or should I go?*

Wynstanley's hand closed on Wes's shoulder, his breath now coming in shallow gasps. 'Are you looking for a pay-off for divorcing my daughter?'

'No.'

'You can't have one.'

'I don't want your money,' said Wes, gently brushing off his father-in-law's hand. 'Honestly, Claude.'

'Then what *do* you want, Wesley?' Wynstanley hissed. And then there was that look again. The one Wes had seen before. *Fear.*

33

a tactical withdrawal

Wes had phoned Gabi, of course, the moment he stepped out of the clinic – but her mobile had gone straight through to voicemail, as it often did these days. *If that's Byron*, it'd said, *I'm working late at the hospital. Grab yourself a takeaway. Leave me half in the fridge. Don't wait up.* And so he'd meandered through London's glistening streets, past the Marble Arch and then down through Hyde Park until he eventually arrived at the Chelsea and Westminster. There, he tried calling Gabi's mobile just once more, hunched amid the mute fellowship of smokers in the bus shelter, before stepping into the hospital's brightly-lit atrium and scurrying over to the lifts.

It's pointless flagellating yourself over it, he tried reasoning, pressing the button for the fourth floor. *You're hardly the type. And the whole marriage was built on a fantasy anyway.* But whichever way he pictured the evening's events – however he edited the finale in his mind's eye – there was an unsettling hint of… *caddishness* in the way he'd behaved. He glanced down at his hand, reminded once again of the moment it had been clasped by Wynstanley's. It had been more than just an agreement they'd settled on, Wes couldn't help feeling – it had been… *a pact.* And while Wes had no evidence that Wynstanley had ever possessed horns, there'd been an undeniable whiff of sulphur in his father-in-law's cigar smoke as they'd sealed the deal. *Maybe guilt just… goes away,* he considered, stepping out of the lift and peering along the dimly-lit corridor. *I guess I'll have plenty of time to find out.* In any case, he didn't want its undiluted taste still lingering in his mouth when he went to give Caitlyn the news. *No, no, no.*

It was a good job that Gabi would be alone in her office, anyway – that was for certain. It seemed unlikely that she'd beg him to reconsider his decision, of course – and it was unclear whether she possessed the emotional range for full-blown hysteria – but she'd certainly inherited her mother's taste for histrionics, and wasn't above a little barbed invective or the odd well-aimed vodka bottle. They were the sort of things that had made her exciting in the early years, Wes supposed – her sharp corners and prickly wit. *Not necessarily the best ingredients for a happy marriage,* he reflected, peering at the unfamiliar names on the office doors. *But excellent assets for making it through your first divorce.* Not that Gabi would be likely to see it that way. *And if she ever found out about the conversation he'd had with her father…*

Wes shivered, his eye finally alighting on an all-too-familiar nameplate. On impulse, his hand reached for the doorknob, but stopped half an inch short of taking it, as though seized by an unseen power. *My old friend – cowardice,* thought Wes, nervously flexing his fingers in the half-light. *Nice timing, buddy.* It was no use prevaricating, though. From the corridor, he could clearly detect the sounds of movement inside Gabi's office, and the subdued light of her desk lamp filtering through the frosted glass panel above the door. Any moment now, she was sure to become aware of the invisible stranger standing outside her room and…

'*Fuck it*,' whispered Wes. '*Fuck, fuck, fuck, fuck, fuck.*' Then he took a deep breath, rapped twice on the door… and entered.

For a second nobody spoke or moved. Indeed, all that Wes was initially capable of registering was Gabi's horrified face, caught in open-mouthed freeze frame behind the desk. Then she spoke. '*Jesus*, Wes,' she gasped. 'What the fuck are you doing here?'

'Gabi,' Wes began, already losing track of his prepared speech as the room's peripheral details began filtering into his vision. 'There's something we need to – something we should…' For a moment, he was lost for words. Then his brow furrowed in surprise. 'Whose trousers are those?' he said.

'What?'

Wes stared at the discarded pair of pinstripe trousers on the edge of Gabi's desk, then at his wife's mortified face. 'The trousers,' he said. 'These trousers. On your desk. Whose are they?'

'They're mine, actually.'

Wes wheeled round. There, standing behind the door, was – *oh, God, no*. 'Oh. Hello, Giles.'

'Hello, Dewhurst,' drawled Giles Crozier, casually reaching for his trousers and pulling them on. 'Long fucky time, no fucky see.'

It's not often you get the chance to do a creditable double-take, thought Wes, manfully resisting the urge to do one. Feeling nothing more than a frown forming on his forehead, he turned first to Gabrielle, who averted her eyes, then to Giles. 'How long have you been sleeping with my wife?' he said.

'On and off – oh, about three years, I'd say. More, these last six months. Infidelity's got a bit more tang to it when you're married, hasn't it, Gabs?'

Wes turned once again to Gabrielle, now resolutely staring at her feet.

'We found we shared a taste for discipline at medical school, actually,' continued Giles blandly, reaching across the desk – the middle of which, Wes now noticed, had obviously been hastily cleared of obstructions – and picking up an all-too-familiar fish slice. Its silver blade glinted dully in the light from the desk lamp. 'You almost ruined this, by the way. Fried eggs, indeed.'

Fried eggs. Fried eggs. For one stunned moment, Wes's mind struggled to process the reference. And then, in an instant, he could almost smell the scorched fat, visualise the smashed smoke alarm, hear Jeremy's voice in his head. *Twat the cheeky git*, it said. *Punch his lights out.* Suddenly remembering himself, Wes turned to Gabi. '*Why*, kid?' he said. 'Why him?'

Gabrielle shrugged hopelessly and turned away. 'I've always liked a bit of a bastard,' she said.

'There's not much separating a bastard and a wanker, Gabs. I've learned that, recently.'

'Oh, that *is* profound,' sighed Giles, 'But I quite understand. You're in shock. It was just dreadful luck that you had to find out about' – he waggled the fish slice playfully under Wes's nose – 'everything this way. Bloody awkward for all parties concerned. Incidentally, your little problem – the American bint with the fucked glands – any joy on that front?'

'Yes. Yes, actually.' Wes fought the urge to glance towards the door, aware once again of the sweet agony of Caitlyn's proximity. He smiled, somehow warmed by the thought of her. 'I've got her into a top private clinic. She's going to be well taken care of. I sorted it out this evening.'

'Oh, good show, Dewhurst. Good show.'

Wes gently tapped Gabrielle on the shoulder. 'I saw your dad tonight, too, actually. He's in good form. Fighting fit.' He turned back to Giles. 'He doesn't want to become a granddad yet, though, Giles, so I hope you're taking precautions.'

'Oh, I don't think there's any risk of… *issue*. Not with Gabrielle's particular preferences.'

Still numb from fatigue and shock, Wes nodded, finding himself reaching for the door handle as if on autopilot. And then, without quite realising that he'd given his permission, he felt his fingers clenching, found himself turning on his heel and – as much to his own surprise as anyone else's – plunging his fist into Giles's nose. Shaking the pain from his throbbing hand, he leaned low over the prone physician. 'Just so you know, that wasn't for shagging my wife,' he said. '*It was for being a world-class tosser.*'

Two minutes later, Wes found himself grappling with an altogether more formidable opponent. '*What?*' he said, trying to pull Jeremy away from Caitlyn's doorway. 'What do you mean, she's *gone?* You don't mean…'

'God, no. Chill, Wes, chill. I just mean Caitlyn's gone. Elsewhere. She's moved. About nine o'clock tonight.' Jeremy dusted himself down where Wes had seized his jacket, ushering his friend a few yards down the corridor. He smiled wanly at the two young nurses whose enquiring frowns had been drawn to their commotion. Having registered their disapproval, and evidently deciding that the two men looked harmless, they moved on. 'Caitlyn's gone to another hospital, Wes,' continued Jeremy, whispering now. 'Well, a clinic, they said.'

'Who said?'

'The two lads who came to collect her. What's Gabi's dad's name?'

'Claude Wynstanley.'

'Aye, he was one of them. I remembered him from the wedding. Friendly old bird.' He shook his head wearily at Wes's incredulous expression. 'No, seriously, he was. Really nice. I think he took a bit of a shine to Caitlyn, actually. American accent and all that.'

'And when are they letting her out?'

'Tomorrow afternoon. They're just doing some initial tests to start with. Gabi's dad – that Claude bloke – said you had to give him a buzz in the morning. Tell him where you want them to bring her when they're done.' Jeremy gently punched Wes's shoulder, eventually registering Wes's pained expression through his fug of exhaustion. 'She's always welcome back at Lisa's flat, you know. 'Til Lisa gets home, anyway,' he added, hoping that the note of uncertainty in his voice wouldn't make his offer sound any less sincere.

Wes shook his head, slowly at first but then more decisively. Finding Caitlyn missing from her hospital room had been a blow he couldn't have anticipated; *and the prospect of being parted from her again...* 'No. That won't work. I need to be nearer to her than that.' *Adjacent. Conjoined. Inseparable.* 'I need to be with her. Like you and Lisa.'

'You only live in Putney, mate,' Jeremy sighed, now experiencing his own sharp pang of longing at the sound of Lisa's name. 'Just the other end of the District Line.'

'I don't live anywhere now. As of five hours ago, I'm homeless. I'm divorcing Gabi.'

For some moments Jeremy was speechless, staring at his friend with an expression that the exhausted young doctor had never seen before. Then, suddenly, he realised what it was. *Respect.* The tall Yorkshireman reached for his cheek with an affectionate thumb-grip. 'This isn't another gay phase, is it?' he said.

Wes shook his head. 'Don't think so. But it's the only reason Gabi's dad's agreed to treat Caitlyn.'

Behind the shadows that surrounded them, the look in Jeremy's eyes was now impossible to read. 'Right,' he eventually murmured. 'I see. Still, you'll be in Putney for a while, won't you? I mean, you can't divorce someone *immediately.* You've still got squatters' rights. I mean, it's still your kippers in the fridge, isn't it? Still your pubes in the plughole.'

'Maybe,' said Wes gently. 'But I've no house keys any more. Your mate Claude made me hand them over.'

'And what about..?'

'Aye, aye, the Merc too. He took my credit cards, everything.'

'*Shit*,' groaned Jeremy, shaking his head. 'Where are you going to live, mate?'

'I don't know. I might have to go home to my mum's.'

'Back to Whitby?'

Wes shrugged. 'She's always kept my bedroom free. Caitlyn could have it. I could kip on the sofa.'

Jeremy considered this for a few moments, then nodded emphatically. 'Well, Whitby could be just what young Cait needs. Sea air. Bracing walks up by the abbey. A restorative whisky and pep in the Fat Ox, every now and then. And Yorkshire *is* the Texas of England, mate. Plus, your mum would love her. *Love* her.'

'Do you reckon?'

'Oh, aye. No doubt about it. Ring her after breakfast. Ask her to give your duvet cover a nice hot dip in the twin-tub. Get all your nasty teenage stains out.'

Wes smiled, nodding quietly to himself in the dark corridor. A tactical withdrawal to Whitby was the only option his exhausted brain could contemplate, and it wasn't such a bad one at that. It had been too long since he'd last seen his mum. *Far too long.* 'So,' he yawned. 'What now? Are you – are *we* – off back to the flat?'

Jeremy shook his head, draped a baboon-like arm over Wes's shoulders and began steering him back towards Caitlyn's room. 'Too knackered to even think about it, kid. I'm stopping here. Nikki's asleep in Cait's bed and I'm not going to shift her now. Not after the day she's had, poor lass.' He leaned close to his friend, lowering his voice. 'That film they were shooting up in Barnet – they wanted her to do some *very* unhygienic things. It all made your uncle Jezzer *very* unhappy.' Jeremy gently pushed open the door.

There, curled up at one side of the bed and snoring gently, was Nikki. 'I thought we might just crawl in with her. I don't reckon matron'll kick us out before morning.'

'A threesome? With Nikki?' whispered Wes. 'Is that wise, mate?'

'For the purposes of sleep only, kid. I'm fit to drop. I've been awake for... a very, very long time.' Jeremy allowed his heavy eyes to rest for a moment on the soft silhouette of Nikki's sleeping form beneath the blanket. Even to his stunned brain, she was beautiful – small, perfectly formed, almost implausibly sexy. But she wasn't Lisa, and she never would be. 'You sneak in next to her, kid. I'll get in after you. I'll reckon we'll just squeeze in if we all lie on our sides.'

'You want me to... *spoon* you?' whispered Wes, easing off his shoes and inching his way backwards over the bed. Without fully surfacing from sleep, Nikki's hand unfolded itself from its position beneath her chin, and snaked around his chest. 'Are you sure about this?'

'Aye, aye. But no nibbling my lugs in the night, you bloody perv.'

Wes sighed, drowsily shaking his head against the pillow as Jeremy's weight descended on the mattress in front of him. 'Come here, then, you big lunk,' he grunted.

Fifteen seconds later, they were both sound asleep.

34

not long enough

No one could accuse Mr Jeremy Sykes, Whitby's ex-Shagfinder General, of being a prude. Anyone who'd witnessed his unlikely sleeping arrangement from the previous evening would attest to it. But when it came to watching other people snogging – particularly when he didn't have anyone to snog himself – he simply didn't know where to look. And so he drove his hands even deeper into his jacket pockets, half-turning his back on the writhing tangle of limbs that had formerly been Wes and Caitlyn, and peered diplomatically at the station clock.

Quarter to three.

'Bugger knows where she's got to,' he declared loudly, hoping that either Wes or Caitlyn might finally acknowledge his presence. It didn't seem very likely. For the past five minutes, they didn't seem to have heard a word he'd said – or the distorted station announcements – responding only to the fierce, urgent motions of each others' mouths and hands. 'Nikki knows what time the train goes,' he continued, 'and she promised she'd be back.' *And besides which, she's got your mobile,* he thought, glancing over his shoulder at Wes. *One of the very few material possessions you still actually own, Dr Love Pants.*

He sighed – loud enough to be heard over the squealing brakes of an incoming train at the adjacent platform – and glanced sidelong at Caitlyn. 'You're not allowed to do that 'kissing' thing in Whitby, you know. Not in public. It's all right in London, because people round here – well, they're pretty liberal-minded, aren't they? They've not got as many twitching net curtains as they have up north.'

Momentarily breaking free of Caitlyn's lips, Wes turned to Jeremy and smiled. 'Shut up, mate,' he grunted companionably, returning his attention to the intense, dark-eyed face in front of him.

Shaking his head sadly, Jeremy took a couple of steps along the platform, cast a quick eye around to check whether he was being observed, and removed a cigarette from behind his ear. 'You're probably okay with the snogging until around York. You're best backing off with the tongues after Doncaster, mind. And by the time you get to Middlesbrough, you might be safest sticking to hand-holding,' he said. He gazed through the blue haze of illicit cigarette smoke that now engulfed his head, along the tracks and out beyond the station canopy, suddenly feeling an odd yearning to board the waiting train himself. *It'll be bloody lonely in London without Lisa or Wes. I'll only have Lenny Jones to keep me sane.* 'Aye, they can be highly religious, some of them Smoggies,' he continued at length. 'A bit like the Amish, only with less facial hair and flatter hats.'

'Is he kidding?'

Jeremy turned round, winked companionably at Caitlyn and shrugged noncommittally from within his smoke cloud.

'I don't know,' said Wes. 'He's spent more time in Middlesbrough than me. He used to knock around with a pair of twins up there – Sally and Justine. They sounded quite liberated.'

'Aye, they were, kid,' Jeremy nodded modestly. 'By yours truly.'

At that moment, all three of them turned round, their attention now taken by the approach of Nikki, weaving towards them along the crowded platform, a tiny sliver of crimson amid the trudging ranks of brown- and grey-clad Londoners. She skipped to a halt in front of Wes and passed him his mobile. 'Thanks a million,' she said, catching her breath. 'You're a life-saver.' Then she turned to her sister, seizing her in an unyielding embrace. 'I'll be getting a cell of my own real soon,' she declared, pressing her face tightly against Caitlyn's. 'I'll call you every single day. And I'll be there whenever you come down to London for treatment. And I'll be coming up to Yorkshire at least once a month, I swear.'

'Thanks, Nik,' murmured Caitlyn, smiling through her tears. 'I'll miss you.'

And then the announcement came over the tannoy that the two-fifty East Coast mainline service to Edinburgh Waverley was ready to depart, and that all passengers should take their seats, and that was it – a last, urgent flurry of hugs and handshakes and promises. 'Be careful, now, Cait,' advised Jeremy, handing the last of the luggage up the steps to the carriage. 'I don't know what young Byron, here, has told you, but there's no guest bedroom at the old Wesley place…'

'Bye bye, Jeremy…'

'…and I'm not sure the lad's intentions are strictly honourable…'

'…take good care of my little sister…'

'…he was nibbling my ear all night, you know.'

'Liar!'

'…and you're hardly a well woman. Don't let him keep you up all night, pandering to his unwholesome urges. And make sure he sleeps on the sofa, for God's sake.'

Caitlyn grinned at Jeremy as the automatic doors began

to close. 'I think we'll manage just fine in the single bed,' she said. Then the doors heaved shut with a low mechanical sigh, and the train began to move away from the platform.

For almost two minutes – until the final glimpse of the departing train had disappeared beyond the monochrome haze of warehouses and tower blocks, in fact – Jeremy and Nikki said nothing. And when their eyes finally met – perhaps more shyly than either of them might have anticipated – both of them couldn't help feeling that a spell they never knew existed had somehow been broken.

Jeremy was the first to speak. 'Will you be coming back to the flat, then?' he said, finding his words sounding oddly stilted. 'Because if you are – and it's absolutely fine if you want to – well, I just wanted to say that perhaps it's best if we forgot about the whole 'bath' business.'

'Right, sure,' said Nikki, turning and beginning to make her way slowly back down the platform.

'Much as I'm sure we'd both have a really, really nice time if we picked up where we left off,' continued Jeremy. 'But the thing – the really critical thing – is that I love my girlfriend, Lisa. The one who's in Shanghai. I miss her like hell. And I don't think I really want to have a bath with anyone but her.'

'Oh. Okay. Cool.'

'Yeah?'

'Yeah, definitely.' Nikki turned to Jeremy then looked away, her attention seemingly caught by the light swing of her own hands by her sides. 'And actually, Jez, I wanted to thank you for letting me stay–'

'You've been no bother at all, kid.'

'–but I don't think I'll need your spare room any more.'

Nikki carried on walking for a few steps before she realised that Jeremy had stopped some distance up the platform. 'No?' he said.

She shook her head.

'How come?'

'You remember the guy whose car we borrowed yesterday?'

'Hairy feller. Little round glasses.'

'Uh-huh. Well, he's called Michael. I just called him to let him know where you abandoned his car. Turns out he works in TV.'

'He works in porn, kid,' said Jeremy gently.

'No, no, he doesn't. He was doing some undercover research for a show he's making about the UK's... adult... industry. My industry. My former industry, anyway.'

'Get away.'

'Seriously. Anyway, he said he liked the way I handled myself in front of Shaun. He wants me to be a consultant on his show – maybe even present it. He said I could stay with him until he'd got my visa sorted. He wants me to meet him at his office. Have you heard of a network called Channel 4?'

'Uh-huh.'

'That's where I'm going now.'

For a moment, Jeremy struggled to understand the way Nikki's revelation had made him feel, fighting to put a name to the sensation. Eventually, only one would do. *Bereft.* He glanced along the now-vacant platform, vaguely wondering whether anyone else might like to take the opportunity to abandon him. Then he forced a smile to his lips – probably not his most convincing smile, admittedly – and gave Nikki a tiny bow. 'Well that's bloody good news. Good for you, kid. That's really amazing. Do you want me to come with you, to this guy's office? Just for security – to size him up?'

'Yeah. I'd like that.' Caught off-guard by Jeremy's vulnerability, Nikki performed her own half-curtsey, smiled, and offered him her hand. 'That'd be real kind. A girl feels a whole lot more confident heading into a business meeting with six-and-a-half foot of Yorkshireman by her side.'

And if Jeremy's mobile had not chosen that very

moment to ring – if Jeremy hadn't rooted it out of his inside pocket and untangled it from a broken pair of sunglasses – that's how the new, entirely platonic phase of their friendship would have begun. But what Jeremy saw on the tiny cracked screen stopped him in his tracks. 'I've got to take this,' he murmured, suddenly oblivious to Nikki's still-outstretched hand – oblivious, even, to its now anxious-looking owner. 'I won't be a minute, kid.'

It wasn't until Jeremy had shot across the station forecourt and into the grey drizzle of the Euston Road that he realised Nikki was no longer with him. *Little legs*, he thought, wheeling around and peering into the milling mass of humanity before him. *Little legs and daft heels.* A moment later Nikki was by his side. 'What the hell was *that* about?' she demanded.

For a second, Jeremy pointed mutely at his phone, catching his breath. 'That was Lisa,' he eventually gasped. 'Lisa, my girlfriend. She's back from Shanghai. She's heading for the flat.'

'Oh. Great,' said Nikki, before her face suddenly clouded. 'Oh shit. Where exactly is she? At Heathrow?'

Jeremy shook his head frantically. 'In a taxi. Just coming off the Hammersmith Flyover. Look, kid – you'll have to go to your meeting by yourself. I'm really sorry.'

'It's cool. No problem.' Nikki's face looked up at Jeremy's, her brow furrowing with concern for what she saw there. 'How far away is the Hammersmith Flyover, Jez? How long have you got?'

Jeremy swallowed hard, his eyes closing as he performed the required calculations. When they opened again, they were filled with something approaching terror. '*Not long enough*,' he said.

35

all girls can read minds: 2

The honeymoon period – the euphoric morsel of time when Jeremy *actually believed himself to have beaten Lisa to the flat* – lasted approximately ten seconds. And for most of that time, he did little more practical than slump insensibly against the hall bookshelf, dragging oxygen into his nicotine-ravaged lungs and trying not to pass out.

Not that he could be blamed. The previous half hour, quietly having kittens in the back of a black cab – then hurtling on foot through the damp east London streets when his fare money had run out – had been among the most stressful of his life. It had been at least a fortnight or so, for a start, since he'd given any serious consideration to whether Lisa, during her sabbatical in Shanghai, had finally forgiven him for his own unannounced jaunt to Barcelona. And it had been longer still since he'd weighed up the odds of a long-term reconciliation following Lisa's return to London – whether she reappeared bearing the gentle bulge of mid-term pregnancy or not.

Attempting to calmly evaluate the situation in a seething

Friday afternoon tailback on Commercial Street, trying to weigh up the implications of Lisa's hurried phone call, her agonisingly inscrutable voice... well, it was impossible, really. But all that paled into insignificance when he considered the fact that since leaving for Shanghai, he'd had two illicit lodgers kipping in her spare room – two sisters he'd illegally imported into the country, one of them an ex-porn actress with whom he'd almost – *almost* – done the wicked deed... He'd jammed a cigarette between his lips as he jumped out of the taxi, emptying all his remaining money into the driver's outstretched hand and pounding off along the damp pavement. Jeremy had always admired Lisa for her open-mindedness, for the fact that she'd learned to live with his ex-Shagfinder status – but there were undoubtedly limits. And finding even *one pair* of carelessly discarded knickers could easily push her beyond them. *An unfamiliar bra. Lipstick on a wineglass. A stranger's toothbrush...*

Jeremy's vision cleared as he greedily gulped down air, his mind's eye now telescoping out into the silent flat – along the hall passage, through the sitting room and into the bathroom. *That was where he'd start Operation Clean Conscience – minesweeping the bathroom for telltale feminine odds and ends.* After all, it'd be the first place Lisa would need to go when she got home. Then he'd scour the guest room, the sitting room, the kitchen, the bedroom, the balcony, himself... He inclined his nose in the direction of his armpit and sniffed. *Oh God.* Yes – *definitely* himself. Taking unsteadily to his feet, he lurched off along the corridor and flung aside the sitting room door. And there – standing by the window, gazing out across the brooding Docklands skyline – was Lisa. *Lisa.*

For some moments neither of them spoke. Then Lisa half turned round, seemingly caught in limbo between the world beyond the window and the familiar cocoon of the flat. For a second, Jeremy wondered whether she might be about to cry, and when speech eventually came, her words snagged audibly on something in her throat. 'Hi,' she said. 'I'm back.'

'Hi,' said Jeremy, unsurprised to find his own voice also cracking. 'How was your flight?'

'Good. Fine.' Lisa shrugged. 'Long.'

'And how was Shanghai?'

'Strangely similar to Birmingham. Bigger. Further away. More Chinese restaurants.'

'Right. Cool.' Jeremy nodded, suddenly finding himself without a means of escaping the island of small talk he found himself stranded upon. 'Well, it's great to have you back, kid,' he finally blustered, realising immediately how presumptuous his words sounded. 'You know – good to see you,' he added, somewhat lamely. 'You look well.'

'You look...' – Lisa's eyes broke away from Jeremy's for the first time since he'd burst through the door, sweeping over his face and body like a searchlight. Momentarily relieved of her unblinking gaze, Jeremy swallowed hard and breathed deeply, snatching his own illicit glimpses of Lisa's legs, her tightly constrained breasts, the soft veil of her hair. He was still drinking her in when her eyes returned to his. 'Actually, you look bloody awful,' she concluded.

'Aye. Aye, well – I've been pining, you know.'

'Have you?'

'I have, as it happens. Bitterly. How've you been?'

'Bit upset, actually. But physically fine.' She bit her lip and looked away again, an artificial lightness now entering her voice. 'I wasn't pregnant, by the way. As it turned out.'

'Ah.' Jeremy nodded, finally locating the emptiness he'd been aware of since they first started talking – the space inside that felt very much like a tiny, unexpected bereavement. He blinked hard and tried forcing a little smile to his lips, noticing a moment later that Lisa was having just as much difficulty doing so as he was.

'It's probably just as well, really, since you seem to have bought me some new clothes,' Lisa eventually said, nodding towards the spare room.

The spare room. Jeremy's heart leapt to his throat as he desperately sought to recall what had been left there by Caitlyn and Nikki. He hadn't really paid much attention to the spoils of Nikki's shopping sprees, but he'd remembered leaving some of the more luridly coloured bags at the foot of the bed when he'd shoved the girls' essentials into a rucksack on the morning of Caitlyn's phone call. 'Erm, yes,' he said. 'Yes I have.'

'Some of which are quite – erm, *sexy*.'

'I suppose they are.'

'I hope you kept the receipts.'

'Er, no. Why?'

'Just because I'm not pregnant, it doesn't mean I can start wearing size 8 dresses. I haven't been a size 8 since I was seventeen years old. Although it's nice that you still think I'm a waif.'

'I think you're lovely.'

'Thank you.' Lisa leaned down and picked up one of Nikki's interior design books. 'So. You *feng-shui*'d the flat, too, then,' she smiled.

'Rigorously,' Jeremy lied.

'And very, very badly.'

'Really?'

'Uh-huh. Very badly indeed,' Lisa said. She disappeared momentarily inside the kitchen and dropped the book into the bin. Emerging, she quietly advanced upon Jeremy until her feet were only inches from his own. 'But thank you for making the effort,' she whispered, stretching upon on tiptoes to kiss him airily on the lips and cheek. 'You must've missed me.'

'More than I can say, kid,' replied Jeremy, trying not to get too distracted from the question he'd spent the previous two minutes bracing himself to say. 'Have you decided, then?'

'Decided what?'

'Whether you want to be with me?'

'Yes,' whispered Lisa, now turning her attention to Jeremy's throat.

'Yes you've decided, or yes you want to be with me?'

'Both,' she said, breaking away just far enough to catch Jeremy's eye. 'I thought you might have guessed by the whole 'kissing' thing.'

'I just wanted to make sure, that's all,' said Jeremy. Then, suddenly recalling an agreement he seemed to remember having made – maybe in a former life, maybe even with his former self – he found himself gently pulling free from Lisa's hands. He regarded her with seriousness, afraid of what he now felt compelled to divulge. 'Actually, there are a couple of things I need to tell you about,' he said. 'Stuff that happened while you were away.'

'Uh-huh?'

'I got into a bit of grief with the police,' Jeremy began. 'Nowt serious this time. Just something about Dad's van being stolen. And I went to California with Wes and pretended to be a doctor and saved a porn star from a life of sexual degradation. Then I helped save her sister from dying of cancer.'

Lisa appeared to process this for a moment. Then she smiled, returning her attention to the base of Jeremy's throat. 'I'd have expected nothing less,' she said.

'I didn't do anything bad, though. I swear.'

'I believe you.'

'Do you?'

'All girls can read minds,' she whispered, gently running her lips around his collar line. 'Didn't you know?'

'I've suspected it for a while, now.'

'Let's go to bed.'

'Okay,' breathed Jeremy. And then, just as Lisa's fingers entwined around his own, he found himself suddenly stiffening. 'Actually, I haven't got any of those rubbery things,' he winced, a note of quiet desperation in his voice.

'The lack of which caused all our problems in the first place–'

'Doesn't matter,' said Lisa, silencing him with a kiss. 'We'll manage without. I don't mind if you don't.'

Without another word, she led him through the bedroom door and flicked out the light. And suddenly, in the darkness of her arms, he realised that it didn't matter. Lisa was the girl he loved, the one he wanted to be with forever – and nothing else really mattered at all.

36

a hairy igloo

'Was that nice?'

Caitlyn looked across at Wes. For a moment she didn't speak. Then she kissed his cheek. 'It was very nice,' she said, gently burrowing back beneath the bedclothes. 'If you were listening carefully, you could tell by the noises I was making.'

'Oh. Right,' said Wes. 'Of course. The noises.' He smiled, revelling in the notion that Caitlyn should choose to provide feedback on his sexual performance via breathless whimpers of joy – as opposed to, say, the series of barked orders that Gabi had usually employed. Wes kissed the top of her head, just as impressed with her burrowing technique as with the new repertoire of sound effects she'd just unveiled. *Gabi never did much post-coital burrowing,* he reflected. *It was all about power showers and laundering the duvet cover, with Gabi.*

Suddenly Wes found himself frowning. Thinking about Gabi – however fleetingly or unflatteringly – seemed like a tiny betrayal of Caitlyn's trust. But, he consoled himself, he'd been doing it less and less over the last few days. There'd been less pining for his widescreen TV, too – and virtually no pangs for the Merc at all. He kissed the top of Caitlyn's head again, gazing out of the window at the wheeling seagulls above the harbour. Somehow his life in London, the life he'd waited so long to begin, now seemed almost like a film he'd once seen and not particularly enjoyed. *The Phantom Menace, perhaps. Or Billy Elliott.* But he was a different person, then, Wes reasoned. *I wasn't nearly as good at sex, for a start*, he reflected, his eye straying to the Durex box on top of his Rupert The Bear annuals. Would he remain a Love God when he'd worked his way through the condoms he'd borrowed from Jeremy, and moved on to ordinary, shop-bought contraceptives? *It'll be fun finding out*, he thought. *Lots of fun.* Wes nudged Caitlyn gently beneath the covers. 'Fancy a brew?' he said.

Caitlyn nodded, sitting up and pulling her knees up to her chest. From the far end of the bed, propped up on pillows, she had an unimpeded view over the harbour – a constantly changing panorama of colour and movement she felt certain she'd never tire of. Throughout the previous night, she'd insisted that Wes should keep the curtains wide open – even as the rain lashed the window and the thunder shook the panes in their sashes – and she'd been content to let him hold her until the first glimmer of morning, watching lightning split the horizon and freeze-framing the surging waves in ghostly monochrome.

Now the sky over the distant limestone crag was a piercing blue, with just enough wind in the air to flick the crest of each sea swell into a miniature white horse. Caitlyn shivered, perversely pleased by the tiny house's half-hearted attempt at central heating and its ancient, un-bled radiators. A week ago, Wes's mum – with whom Caitlyn had discovered an instant rapport over a vast casserole of beef and onions – had said the room would warm up once it was occupied again, but Caitlyn wasn't sure and didn't particularly care. The Wesleys, it seemed, had long ago perfected a method of insulation that simply involved throwing more and more layers on the bed until – around the time it started resembling a hairy igloo – it eventually began to retain heat.

She closed her eyes and listened as Wes rattled around in the kitchen below. She smiled to herself, hugging her knees tighter. Her treatment with Dr Wynstanley – or Claude, as he'd insisted on being called – had only just begun, but moving to Whitby had somehow made it feel like she'd already turned a corner with her life. *Life*. Caitlyn breathed in the cold Yorkshire air, savouring its marine tang inside her lungs. Then she skipped lightly out of bed, ignoring the room's chill, and opened the wardrobe. Inside were the t-shirts that Wes claimed to have abandoned when he moved to London, aged eighteen. *Not my favourites*, he'd warned her. She found one with Morrissey's face on it and slipped it over the Arctic Monkeys t-shirt she was already wearing. Then she leapt back beneath the covers.

'Are you out of bed?' Wes called up the stairs. 'As your doctor, I insist you stay warm.' A moment later, he was pushing the door aside with his foot and edging into the room, bearing a tray piled high with toast and tea things.

'What's that?' said Caitlyn, inclining her head towards the tray.

'Tea cosy,' he said. 'Keeps the tea – well, erm, cosy. Obviously.'

'Obviously.'

Wes picked up a piece of warm buttered toast and dangled it in front of Caitlyn's nose until she took a bite. He'd been doing this kind of thing – usually citing 'doctor's orders' or a recent NHS directive – a lot, the last couple of days. Ever since his paperwork from York had arrived, in fact – the paperwork confirming his place on the GP training course. 'So. What do you fancy doing today?' he said, a fresh cascade of toast crumbs landing on his lap.

Caitlyn shrugged and put her mug on the tiny bedside table. Tea – at least, tea the way the Wesleys made it – was something she hadn't got used to yet. Pushing herself down from her perch on the piled-up pillows, she slid back into the bedding, pressing herself against Wes's body, still chilly from its epic trek across the kitchen's stone tiles. 'I don't know,' she said, finding Wes's feet and rubbing her own against them. 'You've got the local knowledge. What happens in Whitby?'

Wes frowned. It had been a while since he'd had to take on the role of tourist information officer. 'Locally? Well – there's a sort of goth-fest thing. They have bands and so on. Smaller than SXSW, but still fun.'

'Cool.'

'Ah, yes. Except that the next one's in April.'

'Well, we'll put it in the diary, then.'

Wes closed his eyes, momentarily distracted from his breakfast. After all, putting things in the diary appeared to be an activity that required a good deal of kissing. 'Then there's the Dracula Experience,' he eventually said. 'Except it's only open at weekends, this time of year.'

'Shame.'

'There's the North York Moors railway.'

'Which is..?'

'A railway. An old one. With steam trains and so on.'

Caitlyn nodded. 'Sounds like a day out.'

'Well it *would* be, yes. Only they don't run a full timetable in winter.'

'Understandable.'

'Of course, you haven't visited Whitby unless you've had fish and chips from the Magpie caff.'

'Fish and chips. Britain's most significant contribution to world cuisine. Sounds good.'

Wes frowned, pulling the bedclothes over his head. 'But not especially cheap, unfortunately.'

'Another time, then.'

For some moments, Wes was silent as he rummaged beneath the blankets. 'You can go fossil-hunting,' he eventually volunteered. 'That's free.'

Caitlyn raised the bedclothes a couple of inches and peered into the darkness. 'Is that what you're looking for now?' she said. 'Fossils?'

'No,' said Wes, his voice now barely audible. 'It's just that you've got my Morrissey t-shirt on. I wanted to wear it today. I was trying to get it back.'

Caitlyn sighed companionably, raising her arms above her head so that Wes could complete his task. 'You've got your Arctic Monkeys t-shirt back as well, now,' she observed.

'I know.'

'So, Dr Wesley. What are we going to do today?'

'I'm not sure,' admitted Wes, once again retreating beneath the blankets. 'To be honest, things might be a bit tight, cash-wise, until I've started my GP training.'

'Uh-huh.'

'And that's not for another six weeks.'

For a moment, Caitlyn considered attempting to pull the sheets over her own head, to continue the conversation face to face. One hungry breath later, she realised that they were communicating perfectly well just as they were. 'Right,' she gasped.

'So we might be forced to stay in for a while,' continued Wes after a few moments. 'Maybe make our own entertainment.'

Caitlyn closed her eyes. Outside the window, she could hear the breaking waves of the incoming tide on the quayside; almost taste the salt spray on her lips. She smiled, reaching down to stroke Wes's hair. 'Then I think we'll be fine,' she whispered. 'Just fine.'

Jeremy Sykes *will return*
in **'Apeman'** *and* **'The Oik'**

Read about Jeremy's earlier
adventures in 'Single To Morden',
available in paperback and
digital formats.

www.spikeevans.com

SPIKE EVANS

Spike Evans was brought up in Yorkshire.
He lives with his wife, Jo, with whom he devotes an
inordinate quantity of time pandering
to the whims of their cat, Fred.

SINGLE TO MORDEN by Spike Evans

Available Now

How do you solve a problem like Sarah?

Especially when she's buggered off down to London
and neglected to leave a forwarding address?
All Tim Howden knows is that the love of his life is
living 'somewhere near the Northern Line', and vows
to spend a day at each of its stations until he finds her.

Part romantic comedy, part urban travelogue and part
treatise on The Vital Importance Of Minding The
Gap, *Single To Morden* is every Londoner's ideal
commuting companion. Anyone who's ever visited
London, lived in London or had an erotic dream about
Boris Johnson will empathise with the culture shock of
a small-town boy forced to confront the gritty (and, all
too often, sticky) realities of metropolitan life.

Rush hour will never be the same again...

APEMAN by Spike Evans

Available in 2016.

Lenny Jones (actor, gadabout) is on the verge of losing it all – his home, his self-respect, the thirty-year-old Audi that was supposed to get him to Hollywood.

Unwilling to swallow his pride by returning to mum, Lenny bites the bullet and signs on as an Alternative Provider of Education – an 'Apeman' – delivering education to north London's out-of-school 'unteachables'.

Just as he's acclimatising to his new career, however, opportunity comes knocking in the form of a major film role. But Lenny Jones soon discovers that kids – even if they're not, strictly speaking, your own – are more of a commitment than he could ever have anticipated…

Printed in Great Britain
by Amazon.co.uk, Ltd.,
Marston Gate.